The Cartel Deluxe Edition, Part 2:

Books 4 and 5

The Cartel Deluxe Edition, Part 2:

Books 4 and 5

Ashley & JaQuavis

www.urbanbooks.net

Urban Books, LLC
300 Farmingdale Road, NY-Route 109
Farmingdale, NY 11735

The Cartel Deluxe Edition, Part 2: Books 4 and 5
Copyright © 2019 Ashley & JaQuavis

ISBN 13: 978-1-60162-089-7
ISBN 10: 1-60162-089-6

First Trade Paperback Printing February 2019
Printed in the United States of America

10 9 8 7 6 5 4 3 2 1

This is a work of fiction. Any references or similarities to actual events, real people, living or dead, or to real locales are intended to give the novel a sense of reality. Any similarity in other names, characters, places, and incidents is entirely coincidental.

Distributed by Kensington Publishing Corp.
Submit Orders to:
Customer Service
400 Hahn Road
Westminster, MD 21157-4627
Phone: 1-800-733-3000
Fax: 1-800-659-2436

The Cartel Deluxe Edition, Part 2:

Books 4 and 5

by

Ashley & JaQuavis

The Cartel 4

Chapter 1

"The sleeping beast had finally awoken."
—Unknown

Mecca heard the sound of a gun being cocked behind him and he wasn't even startled. He didn't even turn around, for that matter. He just took a deep breath and placed his hands together in a praying form.

"Our father, which art in heaven, hallowed be thy name . . ." Mecca said as tears slid down his face. He already knew who was behind him, and it came as no surprise to him. Carter began to recite the prayer along with his brother, as he pointed the gun to the back of Mecca's head.

Mecca had always known that Carter would eventually seek revenge for Miamor's death. He had loved her way too much to not come after him. Mecca's only dilemma had been to figure out when and where Carter would take his life. Mecca was a seasoned street veteran and the one thing that he knew for sure was that "the eyes don't lie," and on that day, Carter could not hide the hatred he had inside.

Carter knew that if he let Mecca live, Mecca would possibly turn on him one day, just as he did to Monroe. He also felt obligated to avenge Miamor's death, so killing Mecca was inevitable.

Mecca also knew the game. Mecca realized that if he was in Carter's shoes, he would have done the same, so he wasn't mad at Carter for what he was about to do. Once the prayer was over, Mecca stood unflinchingly with his heart pounding through his chest. There was no malice in his heart, only regret, but he knew that his oldest brother was about to deliver his retribution.

"I love you, Carter," Mecca said as he straightened up his tie and prepared for his death.

"I love you too," Carter replied sincerely as he wrapped his finger around the trigger. "I always will, bro."

Boom!

It seemed like he had heard that boom from a year ago. Slowly his senses began to be restored after a long slumber. It seemed as if he looked through Mecca's eyes just before he died. All he could see was the face of Mecca Diamond as his eyes were closed shut.

His ability to smell was the first sense that came back to him. The fresh scent from the ocean was like heaven as he took a deep inhale through his nostrils and the moist air journeyed into his lungs. Second, the sounds of the waves traveled through the air and to his ears as the waves crashed onto the shore. A light, steady beep echoed through the room from the heart monitor that sat at his bedside. The cool breeze blew through the window and caused goose bumps to form on his arm.

He took a deep breath and slowly opened his eyes. At first the sunrays were too much for his sensitive pupils, so he quickly closed them back shut. After a few seconds, he built up enough courage and tried again. He opened his eyes and his blurred vision slowly began to focus as he looked toward the open window. The beautiful ocean was in clear sight and just above it there were the blue skies; it mesmerized him.

He had been in a coma for five years and had finally come back to life. He swallowed his spit and his mouth was drier than he had ever remembered. He was thirsty. He was thirsty for water, but he also was thirsty for knowledge. He didn't understand how he had gotten there. The last thing he remembered was looking down the barrel of a gun . . . pointed by his own blood brother. He remembered hearing a shot and then everything went black. The sleeping beast had finally awoken. Monroe "Money" Diamond was alive.

Money looked around and the setting was so unfamiliar. He had no idea where he was, and his mind began to race rapidly. He had an IV hooked into his arm and patches were on his bare chest to monitor his heartbeat. Although he was under care, he noticed he wasn't in a hospital. He was in a plush, spacious bedroom that looked to be some sort of luxurious beach house, and the back French doors that led to the beach were open.

He had no idea where he was, and panic began to set in. Money felt his heart begin to speed up, and along with that the heart monitor began to beat louder and more rapidly, signaling the homecare nurse, who was in the other room. Money quickly sat up, causing him to become dizzy. He lost his balance and fell onto the floor. He tried to pick himself up, but that's when he realized how weak his limbs were.

Two Dominican nurses rushed into the room, and they were in shock as they looked at the frail, bearded man that lay on the floor. They had taken care of him while he was in a coma for years, but never had they met him personally.

The two ladies began to frantically converse in Spanish. Money picked up the accent and immediately knew that he was in the Dominican Republic. As a child, his mother would speak that language when she got angry, so he caught on quickly.

They just stared at him in shock as they placed their hands over their mouths. Monroe, being fearless and refusing to be defeated, tried to get to his feet again. Almost instantly, he crumbled to the ground, not being able to get his legs under him. The nurses rushed over to him, one of them grabbing him by each arm. He aggressively snatched away and grimaced.

"I . . . I got it," he said faintly as he clenched his jaws so tightly that veins began to pop out in his forehead. One of the nurses ordered the other one to go call Estes and notify him that his grandson had awoken.

He gathered himself and tried to get up again. This time he used the bed as a crutch as he climbed to his feet, gritting his teeth as it took all of his might and willpower. He slowly got to his feet and stood up straight and poked his chest out. He refused to be defeated, and the nurses watched as he breathed heavily. He was obviously in pain.

"Where am I?" he asked as he looked at the nurses.

Just as he finished the sentence, the nurse who had left the room returned with a phone in hand. She walked up to Money and gave it to him. He reached for the phone as he leaned on the bed to help him stay upright. He then slowly raised the phone to his ear. He just listened as he waited to hear who was on the other side of the phone.

"Monroe Diamond. Is it true?" Estes asked as he listened to Monroe breathing on the phone. It was silence in the air, and Estes wanted nothing more than to hear the sound of his favorite grandchild's voice.

"Speak to me!' Estes yelled through the phone in an attempt to confirm the news. Monroe's mouth felt like sandpaper, and he cleared his throat so that he would be clear.

"I am here, Papa. I am here," Monroe confirmed.

"I am on my way!" Estes said calmly. Estes knew that he had a tough task ahead. He had to let Monroe know that things weren't as he had left them. Taryn, his mother, had been murdered, his sister had been through hell, and his twin brother had met his fate in Brazil. "Get some rest and I'll be there immediately," Estes ordered.

"Wait, Papa. Where am I? Why am I here?" Monroe asked, trying to fill in the blanks.

"You are in the Dominican Republic at one of my private estates. You used to go there as a young boy every summer with me. Do you remember?" Estes asked.

Monroe looked around, and slowly the memories began to resurface. "Yes, Papa, I remember. But why am I all the way out here? How long have I been out?" Monroe questioned.

"Five years," said Estes.

"Wha . . . What?" Monroe said as he sat down on the bed in confusion.

"It has been five years since you slipped into the coma. A lot has changed since then. I will talk to you as soon as I get there," Estes said as his voice began to crack. He knew that telling Monroe the news would be one of the hardest things he ever had to do.

"Five years?' Monroe said almost in a whisper as he was mentally thrown into the abyss.

"Yes . . ."

Estes was on the first jet to the Dominican Republic to break the news to his grandson that he was the last male of the bloodline alive. He would tell Monroe the whole story, excluding nothing of what had happened.

***

Young Carter woke up in cold sweats as the thundering and lightning caused chaos in the sky. He sat up from his bed, breathing deeply as he wiped the sweat from his forehead. His bare chest was drenched as sweat beads covered his whole body. He slowly got out of bed and walked over to the bathroom that was connected to his room. He turned on the water and bent down to splash water in his face.

The nightmares had haunted him every day since he murdered Mecca. He always wished that he could take the murder back, but when he thought deep about it, he knew that he had to do it. Mecca's character was flawed, and he eventually hurt the people who were close to him. Young Carter knew he did what he had to do.

He looked into the mirror and into his own eyes. Unlike many, he could see his soul. He was content with the person he was. The last year had been a peaceful one for him. He fell all the way back from the streets and let Zyir take over. He only came into the picture when it was time to meet with their supplier.

Carter knew that he wouldn't be able to go back to sleep, so he slipped on a T-shirt and walked into his living room. He clicked on SportsCenter and walked over to his mini bar to pour a glass of cognac. He needed to take the edge off and get his mind off the murder.

The loud roars of the thunder were like a soundtrack to a horror film, and the rain began to pour down like cats and dogs. As he poured himself a glass, he felt a chill go up his spine. Things weren't right.

Just as he put the glass to his lips, he heard his doorbell ring. He instantly focused his attention on the door and frowned up. *Nobody knows about this place but Zyir,* he thought as he walked to his room and grabbed his gun off the dresser. He tucked it in the small of his back and headed to his door. He unlocked his door, and when he saw who stood on the other side, he dropped his glass. He was seeing a ghost—he had to be, because he was looking at a person he thought was dead a long time ago. *Oh my God,* he thought as he looked into the eyes of . . .

Chapter 2

"If you can't forgive me just kill me, Carter, because I can't live without you."

—Miamor

Miamor stood before him, hair soaked as the heavens cried tears of retribution upon her. Her wet skin glistened under the glowing porch light, while her body shook from the chill that settled into her bones. Hers was a face that Carter hadn't seen in four years, but he had committed it to memory in his feeble attempts to hold on to the love that they had once shared.

Young Carter's knees weakened as his heart matched the rhythm of the lightning bolts that struck the black sky. Pain pierced his chest as heartbreak seared through his body. It was as if Cupid himself was pulling the arrow out of his heart, ripping him to pieces with every tug. His eyes widened in shock as he let go of the glass of cognac he had been sipping. It shattered in a million pieces at his feet, resembling the current state of his broken heart.

There was so much history between them, and as his mind recalled their past, a myriad of emotions passed through him. Rage, hurt, and betrayal caused a lump to form in his throat as they stared silently at one another.

A pistol rested on his hip, but he didn't even think to reach for it. Had she been any other person, he would have put a bullet between her eyes, but this one woman was the exception to his street rules. Miamor had always been his weakness.

Silence surrounded them. There was so much that needed to be said, but Carter couldn't find his voice. Lost in her eyes, he saw a woman who had been through hell and back just to stand at his door. She was thinner than he remembered, and scars covered her neck and wrote imperfections onto her beautiful face.

The world seemed to move in slow motion, and Carter couldn't help but to think that he was dreaming. His mind had played this trick on him many times before. In his sleep he had held her, kissed her, made love to her, but when he awoke each morning, the loneliness of his existence always crept in. Her absence was always present. He didn't believe his eyes, despite the fact that this time he was seeing the truth.

Miamor stood, terrified as she waited for Carter to react. Butterflies fluttered in her stomach and her chest heaved up, then down, in anticipation. Her soul was bleeding out, and tears began to flow down her cheeks in turmoil. The hatred she saw in his eyes dissolved into hurt, then confusion, but behind it all she still saw love. She knew that there was a possibility that Carter would murder her where she stood, but seeing him again was worth the risk. The feeling of completion that he gave her when she was in his presence was enough to put it all on the line. She had tried staying away, but in the end living without him was not living at all.

"Please say something," she whispered as she lowered her head to her chest. For the first time she was ashamed of herself. She was so full of regret that she couldn't stomach it. Carter was always so statuesque and strong, but her reemergence had sucked the air out of his lungs. He was vulnerable, and seeing him so hurt sent a dagger through her heart.

Carter was a man of strict composure, but the melody of her voice caused him to lose it all. Tears clouded his eyes.

"This isn't real. You're dead," he whispered as he walked out onto his porch and into the heavy rain. He stepped so closely to her that there was no room between them.

Miamor's breath caught in her throat. She was afraid to breathe, afraid to move, afraid of what he was going to do to her. Certainly there was vengeance and betrayal on his heart, but she hoped that the sight of her sparked the love that they used to share. All she needed was a tiny spark to ignite a flame so great that he couldn't deny her return.

He brought his hand to her chin, lifting it so that she had to face him. His index finger traced the outline of her face as he took her in. Miamor felt the steel of his pistol pressing into her stomach, and she didn't move as she watched him weigh his options in his head—to kill her or to love her.

Carter knew that there was only one true choice. No woman could ever do for him what Miamor did for him. He had entertained plenty of playthings during her absence, but the connection that they shared was one that was only gifted by God once in a lifetime.

"Miamor," he whispered as a single tear escaped him.

His voice was like a gunshot releasing her from a racing block, giving her permission to move. She reached up to wipe his tear away.

"I'm sorry, Carter," she said.

Carter cleared his throat and took a step back from her as he grabbed her hands and removed them from his face. He moved to the side and extended his hand in welcome.

"Come inside," he said.

His voice was low, sad, and revealed a hint of disdain, but she was ready to face him. She was ready to be with him, if he would have her. She didn't need to stand before God to be judged. Reuniting with Carter Jones was her judgment day. She only hoped that he didn't send her to the executioner. She took a deep breath and walked into his home.

"There's so much I need to say to you . . ." she began. Before she could finish her sentence she felt the cold kiss of the gun as Carter entered behind her and pointed it to her skull.

Her body tensed and she closed her eyes. If she had to go, this would be the way to do it—at the hands of the man she loved. The perfect end to an imperfect existence. It was almost too poetic. "I never meant to hurt you, Carter," she said. Her voice was so full of sorrow that her words caused Carter's pulse to quicken and his jaw to clench. "I don't deserve your forgiveness. I knew that it could come to this if I came back, but I had to see you. I had to see you see me. Even after you pull that trigger, just know that I will always love you. I always have, and if I could do things over again, I would do them differently."

She waited for words, for bullets, for any type of response from him, but Carter was silent. "Carter, say something," she pleaded as she began to cry. "Tell me you love me. Say that you hate me. Just say something because the silence is torture."

Carter had never been a novice when it came to his pistol. When he drew his gun he always popped off, but Miamor was tugging at his heartstrings. He had lived for too long thinking that she was dead. He had grieved over her. Now that she had miraculously reappeared in his life, could he really be the one to make her extinct? His heart said no, but his mind said maybe. Still no part of him was able to say yes.

His hand shook, and Miamor could feel the uncertainty in his aim. She raised her hands in defense.

"I killed Mecc . . ." Carter couldn't even finish his sentence as he closed his eyes, finally allowing his pain to release in the form of flowing tears.

"I know," she whispered. "You killed Mecca for me, and I'm sorry I put you in that position, Carter. If you hadn't done what you did, I would have spent the rest of my life running from him."

Emotions ran high as Miamor spoke and Carter's conscience weighed heavily on him. "He was my brother."

"A brother that murdered *my* sister!" she contested with emotion, her voice raising an octave in defense. The loss of Anisa was still very real to her, and Carter was picking at the scab.

She closed her eyes and composed herself, taking a deep breath. She had no right to ever raise her voice, not with Carter. He was a victim of her betrayal. She lowered her voice to just above a whisper as she continued. "That's what started it all. What was I supposed to do, Carter? I kill. That's all I've ever known." She raised her hands and looked at them; although they were clean, in her mind they were covered in blood. "I've taken more lives than I can count. It's who I am, and your brother took my sister from me. So I did what I do best, but then you happened. *We* happened."

Carter smirked sarcastically and said, "Big coincidence."

"It was, Carter," Miamor replied, breathless because her heart was beating so intensely. "I didn't mark you. Meeting you was the best thing that has ever happened to me and it was not planned. You weren't on my shit list. What we had was the realest thing I have ever known. I'm in love with you, Carter, and I need you to save me from myself," Miamor sobbed.

Carter's grip loosened around his gun as she melted his resolve for vengeance. His eyes were focused on the nape of her neck where delicate tendrils of curls lay perfectly against her skin. Anger surged through him like an electrical current, but he couldn't will himself to pull the trigger.

He lowered his gun and wrapped his arms tightly around her waist, burying his face in the crease of her neck. It was at that moment that her legs gave out as she wept. Carter lowered her to the ground and kissed the back of her neck while her sobs of regret filled the room. They both were being smacked with the reality of the mistakes that they had made.

"If you can't forgive me just kill me, Carter, because I can't live without you. I've tried and it's too hard," Miamor cried.

Carter tossed the gun out of arm's reach and held her tightly. She leaned back against his chest and allowed herself to become weak as he rocked her slightly. They sat in the middle of his extravagant foyer, clinging to each other desperately, because neither of them knew how long this moment would last. There was so much deception between them that love could transform into hate within the blink of an eye, and when it did, Miamor would have no one to blame but herself.

She felt him lift her from the floor and she buried her face in his chest as he carried her up the stairs. When they reached one of the rooms, he stopped and placed her on her feet.

"Look at me," he said, his voice steely and despondent, yet commanding.

Miamor could barely look Carter in the eyes, but upon hearing his request she lifted her head.

"Take a shower and meet me downstairs. We have a lot to talk about," he said.

Miamor nodded her head and then retreated inside the room as he walked away from the door.

Carter's head was so clouded that he didn't know if the choice he was making was right or wrong. He wasn't a man of indecision, but when it came to Miamor he was stuck.

He wanted her in the worst way, but with a ruthless history like the one she possessed, how could he ever trust that he wouldn't fall into her crosshairs? Love hadn't stopped her from betraying him before. He couldn't trust her, but it didn't stop him from wanting her by his side all the same.

Tears stung the lids of Miamor's eyes as she stood under the steaming hot water with her head hung low. She wept, biting her bottom lip to stop her cries from being audible. Her chest heaved and her mind spun. The slightest sound caused her to jump as she pulled back the shower curtain in paranoia. She half expected for her brains to be blown out while she washed her body. A seasoned killer, Miamor knew that the most convenient place to murder someone was in a bathtub. That way all the blood and evidence could be easily washed down the drain. To her surprise no Grim Reaper stood waiting to deliver her fate.

Miamor quickly stepped out of the shower and wrapped herself in a towel. Wiping the condensation from the mirror she stared at herself. Miamor silently condemned the woman who stared back at her. She didn't deserve Carter's forgiveness. Anything less than a bullet to the head would be generous of him.

Her sixth sense told her to run, but her heart kept her still. Miamor was tired of running in the opposite direction of the love of her life. She wanted to run toward Carter—more importantly, beside him.

She wiped the tears from her red and swollen eyes, then exited the bathroom.

Warm colors decorated the large master bedroom. This was home to Carter, and she had never thought she would be welcomed into his life again. Just being in his proximity made her feel lightheaded, grateful, and terrified all at the same time. She quickly dressed, throwing on one of Carter's button-up shirts, then hesitantly made her way down the stairs to meet her fate.

Carter stood in the dining room staring into the flickering fireplace as the amber flames danced and crackled before his eyes. Although his back was to the entryway he immediately felt Miamor's presence when she entered the room. He sucked in a breath and held it for a brief second before releasing it along with the tension that burdened his shoulders. Turning toward her he stared, coldly, in confusion. Carter had been through a lot, had seen a lot, had lived a lot, and no one had ever affected him the way that she had. Her disappearance from his life had cut him deeply, but her reemergence was like salt to a bleeding wound. It burned.

"Carter," she said with a hint of desperation in her tone, and in an instant he was across the room, standing in front of her. His hand wrapped around her fragile neck, and his body weight pushed her against the wall. His powerful presence humbled her, and standing before him she felt small, like a chastised child who was awaiting punishment for a bad deed.

Miamor breathed erratically. He could snap her neck easily, take her life in a split second and get his revenge for the things that she had done. Somehow she knew he wouldn't, or rather, he couldn't.

"Carter," she repeated. She had thought of him often over the years, but had never dared to speak his name. The syllables felt odd falling from her lips. He had been a memory for so long, someone she was supposed to let go of and forget, but he was such a prevalent force in her life that she couldn't. His face haunted her dreams every night.

He caressed the side of her cheek. He was weak and vulnerable to this one woman. The street code that he lived by wasn't complex enough to analyze his current predicament. To love a woman like Miamor was dangerous, but to not love her was torture. The hate dissolved from his stare, and against his better judgment he kissed her. His full lips covered hers as their tongues did a slow, seductive tango. Carter pulled her lips into his mouth roughly, passionately, pouring his wanting into her as their bodies pressed together.

She could feel how much he missed her and she creamed her panties thinking of the way he used to slow stroke her. Miamor's heart was stuck on Carter, and there had not been another man for her after him. His shoes were too large to fill, and as his hands gripped her face she knew why. They were designed for one another. Carter couldn't kill her if he wanted to.

His hands moved south from her neck to her collarbone, discovering her breasts, and eventually finding the wetness that flowed between her thighs. His fingertips awakened her nerve endings, causing her nipples to harden and her thighs to clench together in anticipation. He groaned as his own erection swelled. He roughly lifted her off her feet and she wrapped her legs around his waist. She reached down, her fingers fumbling as she pulled at his belt and unbuckled his designer slacks. They moved with intensity; with the passion of star-crossed lovers who had been deprived of one another. Four years was a long time to be disconnected from the one you craved. Carter had an insatiable hunger that only Miamor could fulfill.

Miamor gasped and her mouth fell open in pleasure as his thickness parted her southern lips. He filled her up and made her breathless as he discovered the deep valleys of her womanhood. Miamor's brows dipped in pleasure as Carter handled her roughly, taking out his frustrations as he hit the back of her pussy. His rhythm was slow, but powerful as he fucked her deep, long- stroking her into a frenzy as she creamed around him.

"Carter," she gasped.

His mixed emotions caused him to handle her differently. He wasn't as gentle as she remembered. He was punishing her love box, and Miamor loved it as she arched her back and brought her hips forward to match his stroke. Her shoulders balanced on the wall as Carter ripped open her shirt, revealing her perky breasts. Her nipples were hard, rippled, and Carter palmed one breast, rolling her nipple gently between his thumb and index finger.

Miamor's head fell back and her eyes followed suit as they rolled in the back of her head. Ripples of ecstasy flowed through her body as Carter sexed her into an orgasm. It quaked her body from head to toe as she held him tightly.

He buried his face in the groove of her neck, planting gentle kisses on her delicate skin as he felt the blood surge to the head of his dick. She felt his nut building. The strong veins that ran through his shaft pulsated inside of her, and Miamor clenched down on him, as she wound her body slowly, grinding her sex into him. Miamor had beaten Carter to the finish line, but she was determined to make him catch up.

Carter gripped the back of her hair and pulled her neck back slightly, taking complete control over her. Their sweaty bodies grinded harder. Faster. Harder. Miamor exploded again. She squirted all over him, and her wetness caused Carter to release. He came so far in her belly that she screamed his name and clawed at his back before finally letting the wave of ecstasy wash up on the shore.

Spent, Miamor rested against the wall as Carter leaned into her, breathing erratically, heavy as their foreheads met. He cupped her face with one hand and her knees went weak as she stared into his pained eyes.

"Forgive me," she whispered, their lips only inches apart.

Carter shook his head from side to side, closing his eyes as he memorialized Mecca in his mind. Could he possibly pardon her?

"Look at me," she said, her voice small and distressed. He did as she asked. "Forgive me, Carter." She could see the inner battle that he was fighting in his mind. To trust her or not, that was his dilemma.

He cleared his throat and stood upright as he sniffed and flicked his nose quickly, gathering himself. He adjusted his clothing and shot her a look that was filled with disappointment. He walked over to the fully stocked bar and poured himself a glass of expensive cognac. He wasn't a drinking man, and he usually gave himself strict limits. He indulged in nothing that had the ability to affect his reasoning, besides Miamor. She was his only vice, the addiction that he couldn't quite kick. But tonight he needed something to take the edge off.

He shook his head and stared at Miamor from where he stood. He scoffed slightly, thinking of everything that she had done, all the lies that she had told him. Holding his glass in his hand, he extended his pinky finger and pointed at her mockingly.

Miamor stood still as she let him go through his emotions. She was afraid to speak, because she knew that nothing she said could make things right between them. Carter brought the glass to his mouth and in one swig he downed the rest of the Louis and then tossed the crystal glass against the wall nonchalantly as he walked out of the room. Miamor flinched when it shattered into a thousand pieces against the wall. She didn't call for him. She simply stood there devastated as she thought, *He'll never look at me the way he used to.*

Defeated, she walked over to the shattered glass and began to pick up the pieces, wishing that her life were just as easy to clean up. Overwhelmed, she collapsed against the wall and cried out tears of regret. Part of her wished that she had never met Carter Jones. Then she wouldn't be so lost and stuck in such a dark place. Whoever said that it was better to have loved and lost obviously didn't know her story. To lose a love like Carter's hurt tremendously and would surely fill her days with regret as long as she lived. No one understood her plight. The game had her loyalty and she was in it to win it, but since the moment she saw Carter across a crowded casino, he seized her heart.

Suddenly, Carter reentered the room. "I want to hear it from you. I want to hear it from your lips what happened and everything that you've done. You've got to show me who you are, Miamor, because right now I have no clue," he said. He pulled out one of the dining room chairs and motioned for her to come to him. "Sit down. Tell me your story."

Miamor and Carter stayed up all night as he listened to the candid tale that was her life. She left nothing out, admitting to it all, even the death of Taryn, as she spilled her guts to him. She watched as shock, anger, and sadness filled his eyes. Certain parts enraged him while others made him sympathetic. He grilled her, asking questions that he had pondered on for years, and she answered him honestly.

It took hours for her to tell it all, but only seconds for him to decide that he loved her despite it. No one would understand the connection he had to her, but he was the boss so no one needed to. He answered to no one, and as he heard her hidden truths he realized that he couldn't pass judgment. The same way that she had taken life, he had taken life, Mecca had taken life, and his father had taken life. It was a part of the lifestyle they led. They all had their burdens to bear and their own crosses to carry. Killing his brother would weigh down his heart for the rest of his days, but he couldn't let Miamor disappear from his reach once again. The first time had crippled him. The second time would kill him. His only resolution was to forgive.

As the sun rose above the clouds, Carter reached across the table and grabbed Miamor's hand. She was emotional, frenzied, and weak as she trembled from his touch. Her red eyes met his.

"You hate me?" she asked.

"No," he replied simply. He stared into her soul and concluded that she was his. Jaded past, faults, and all, she belonged to Carter. "Can you be loyal to me?" he asked.

"I want to be loyal to you, Carter. I can be," she replied as she lowered her gaze.

"Look at me, Mia. I want you to understand what I'm asking you because should you misstep again the consequence will be severe. There will be no more room for forgiveness."

She lifted her head and witnessed a glint of the devil that hibernated inside of him.

"Yes, I can be loyal to you," she said.

He leaned in and kissed her forehead. "Then welcome home."

Chapter 3

*"You're in Miami, bitch, and mi familia
quisiera matar tu . . . lentamente."*
—Breeze

"Look at what you did to me!" Breeze screamed as she
stood over Illiana, the woman who had almost taken her life.
Her shirt was open and a long scar ran from her sternum to
her navel. It bubbled gruesomely and its red hue stood out
against her bright skin. It was the only imperfection on the
perfectly pampered Diamond princess. It was her war wound,
a reminder that she had been involved in one of the worst
street beefs that Miami had ever seen.

"It suits you. I just wish I had cut a little deeper; then you
wouldn't be standing here right now," Illiana replied slickly
as she spit at Breeze's feet. Breeze looked down at the now
ruined Giuseppe pumps. Breeze hauled off and slapped Illiana,
causing her head to snap violently to the right. The two goons
who held Illiana in place didn't flinch as they stopped Illiana
from lunging at Breeze, restraining her by the arms.

"My family is going to kill you," Illiana said with a sneer as
she jerked against the two goons who held her in place.

Breeze smiled mockingly and replied, "No, dear, I think you
have that the wrong way around. Let me put this in a way
you can understand. This isn't Mexico. You're in Miami, bitch,
and *mi familia quisiera matar tu . . . lentamente.*"

The threat of a slow death at the hands of The Cartel
was enough to instill fear into Illiana's cold heart. Her face
drained of all color as she blinked away tears. Zyir stepped up
and placed a hand on the small of Breeze's back. "It's time to
go. You don't need to see what's about to occur," Zyir said. He
kissed the back of Breeze's neck and she turned to face him.

"Make it hurt," Breeze said. She put her Burberry glasses on her face and then walked out of the warehouse with a model's precision.

Illiana's eyes followed Breeze and her temper flared. The click-clack of Breeze's stilettos taunted her. "You bitch! You fucking bitch!" she shouted.

Zyir nodded his head to the goons as he rolled up his sleeves patiently, his face tense and focused for the upcoming task at hand. "Hoist her from the rafters, and find me a steel pipe." The goons dragged her away kicking and screaming. "And cover the floor in plastic. It's going to get messy!" Illiana had almost taken everything from Zyir, and now he was going to turn her into a human piñata. He had goons to put in this type of work, but this was a death sentence that he wanted to personally deliver.

The humid, salty air blew through Breeze's short hair as she whipped through the Miami streets. Little Breeze Diamond had done a lot of growing and was no longer the naïve little girl her father had once shielded from the streets. Unlike most, she had seen the other side. She knew what it felt like to die. The doctors had narrowly saved her after being stabbed up by Illiana. She had coded five times before they finally put her in a medically induced coma. She had sat at a table with her dead loved ones, but it hadn't been her time to take her seat yet. God gave her another chance at life; consequently Breeze just wanted to live. She knew that she would never be able to do that as long as Illiana breathed. The world wasn't large enough for the both of them, so when Zyir asked her what she wanted him to do about it, Breeze put in the order of extermination. *She fucked with the wrong one,* Breeze thought.

Breeze had been through too much to remain the same. Her eyes had witnessed death in too many ways and it had changed her. It made her realize the lifestyle that her father, brothers, and even her mother had led was more dangerous. They weren't living the lifestyles of the rich and famous; they were living the life of American gangsters, and she had learned the hard way to move accordingly.

Breeze's fingers lightly touched the still painful scar. It was tender to touch and it brought tears to her eyes. She was so grateful to be alive. To have had a second chance to love a man like Zyir for a lifetime humbled her. He was her everything. Nothing could ever tear her away from that man, not even an envious, conniving force like Illiana. *You lose, bitch,* Breeze thought. She pulled into the driveway of her oceanfront double villa and placed her car in park. Her head spun as she thought of all that her family had been through. Thinking of the pieces of her life that she had lost, her chest became heavy. The Diamond family had once been so close, so strong, but outside forces had come in and annihilated them. *Rest in love,* she thought. She gripped her steering wheel and lowered her head as she began to cry.

The Cartel was in transition, and Zyir was the new head of state. Breeze had just been crowned the new queen, and it excited and frightened her simultaneously. The last thing she wanted was to be someone else's target in another war, and as Zyir's wife she was vulnerable. She hoped that he would keep her protected and untouchable to the street's ills.

A knock at the window alarmed her, and she quickly wiped her eyes as she turned to see Leena holding her nephew, Monroe II, in her arms. Breeze exited her car and gave Leena a smile and quickly scooped the baby from her.

"Are you okay?" Leena asked.

Breeze nodded and replied, "Yes, I'm fine. Are you two headed out?" Breeze asked.

"Just to grab lunch. You wanna join us? It looks like you could use a sangria or two or three," Leena said with a charmingly beautiful smile.

Leena had become a part of the family. She held the only connection left to Monroe. She had borne his son and that immediately endeared her to The Cartel. She was kept and protected as if her last name were Diamond as well. Breeze even welcomed Leena into her home so that she wouldn't miss a beat of her nephew's life. The women had grown closer than close. Leena helped Breeze balance out the testosterone-heavy Cartel. She was like the sister Breeze never had.

The sound of her cell phone ringing caused her to pause. "I'll get the baby set up in the car while you take your call," Leena said.

Breeze looked down at the screen and didn't recognize the number. She immediately sent it to voicemail, but when the number called back her curiosity was piqued.

"Who is this?" she asked, knowing that only a select few had her number.

"It's your grandfather."

Breeze's breath caught in her throat at the sound of Estes's voice. She missed him dearly, but had mixed emotions toward him because of his refusal to supply Zyir and Carter. He had been the connect who kept The Cartel strong while her father reigned, but things had gone stale after her father's death. Her grandfather refused to supply The Cartel with Young Carter and Zyir as its leaders, and consequently his relationship with Breeze hadn't been the same since.

"Hello, Estes," she replied.

"I need to meet with you immediately. Come to my estate tomorrow evening at eight o'clock. It is imperative, Breeze. Do not be late."

Breeze stood there dumbfounded by the unexpected call as she heard the dial tone blare in her ear. His instructions were clear and he gave away no clues as to what she should expect. One thing for sure was that when Estes called there was usually a storm brewing. Breeze just hoped that her family could withstand whatever blow he was about to deliver.

Chapter 4

"He is dead to the world, not us."

—Estes

As Young Carter looked around the roundtable, he saw his family. Although his body was there physically, his mind was a thousand miles away. Visions of his Miamor clouded his thoughts. Her scent, her face, and the thoughts of all the deception she had been a part of. He looked around the table and saw all of the family that he had left, which were Zyir and-Breeze. The sound of the French doors opening interrupted his thoughts. All eyes shot to the entryway, and the tension in the room was so thick that it could have been cut with a knife. As the remaining members of the Diamond family sat at the table, no one said a word. They all were clueless and wondering what was the cause for the meeting called by Estes.

Estes, with a walking cane in his right hand, slowly walked toward the table and took a seat at the head of it. Everyone's attention was on Estes as he pulled out a cigar and lit it, taking his time as he usually did. He slowly puffed on the Cuban until it was well lit and blew out a cloud of smoke.

"I want to thank everyone for coming this evening. I called this meeting to make an announcement. I made a very important decision a couple of years back," Estes said as he took his time with his words, enunciating every syllable. "I made a decision to keep a secret from the family and, looking around the table, I believe I made the right call," he stated.

The room was so quiet you could have heard a pin drop. Everyone was wondering what Estes was about to say. However, the anticipation would not last long. Just as the last word slipped out of Estes's mouth, in came Monroe "Money" Carter. He hadn't missed a beat. He walked in in a three-piece Armani suit with a model's posture. His face was clean shaven, just as he always kept it, displaying his strong jawbone and smooth skin.

Everyone's heart dropped as they saw the familiar face appear. Breeze let a small gasp escape as she put her hand over her lips. It was as if she had seen a ghost. She actually thought she was seeing a ghost, seeing that she had buried her brother years ago. It was too unreal to her.

Money walked directly to Breeze and she stood up. Money was slightly taller than she, and he looked down at his sister. They stared directly into each other's eyes, both not knowing what to say. What could a person say after going through what they had been through? Before Money slipped into a coma, his whole family was alive and well. Fast-forward years later . . . everyone was gone.

"Monroe," Breeze whispered as she gently cupped the right side of his face. "Oh, my God. It's really you," she said as she shook her head in disbelief. Her brother, twin of Mecca, was there in flesh. Monroe was back.

It seemed like Money had an instant flashback when he saw his sister's eyes. The horrible night that put him in the coma resurfaced to his memory when he saw his baby sister.

Five Years Prior

Money drove Mecca's Lamborghini down the highway toward Leena's home. Money hated driving Mecca's cars. In his eyes they were way too flashy and drew too much attention. Money glanced over at Leena while she cried quietly, wishing she had never come out that night. Money wanted so badly to be with Leena, but he couldn't betray his brother in that way. He gently ran his hand over her cheek and wiped her teary eyes, trying to comfort her.

"Mecca doesn't mean any harm. He does love you; he just has a fucked-up temper, nah mean?"

"He sure has a fucked-up way of showing me he loves me," Leena said as tears streamed down her face and she kissed Money's hand as he rubbed her cheek.

Money thought Leena was crying because of what Mecca had just done to her, but that was the furthest thing from her mind at that point. The tears were coming from the thought of her knowing that she and Money could never be. Leena placed her hand on her stomach as she melted in Money's hand. She had found out that morning that she was three weeks pregnant with Money's child. She knew it was Money's because she hadn't been intimate with Mecca in months. He had been too busy to satisfy her lately. She decided to have an abortion and take her secret to her grave, but the pressure was too much to handle by herself; she had to tell Money.

"Money, I'm pregnant," Leena said almost in a whisper.

"What?" Money asked as he swerved in traffic, not believing what he had just heard.

"I said I'm pregnant, Money! It's your baby."

"What are you talking about? How do you know it's mine? It ain't mine. I strapped up every time!" Money expressed with skepticism in his voice.

"I know it's yours because you are the only person I have been with. Mecca and I haven't done anything in months. I know it's yours! Remember that night . . . after those niggas tried to rob Mecca?" Leena asked, referring to the last time they had made love without using protection.

Money kicked himself inside, knowing the time she was talking about. He was so caught up in the moment he slid up in her raw, and now he was paying the consequences of his actions.

"Fuck!" Money yelled as he hit the steering wheel out of frustration. The guilt began to set in as Money thought about how he had betrayed his best friend and twin brother.

"I love you, Leena," Mecca whispered just before he lowered his face to his table to inhale the line of cocaine. As soon as Breeze dropped him off, his conscience began eating at him. He felt bad for putting his hands on the only woman he had ever truly loved. His long hair was wild and unbraided, which made him look like a madman as he used his nose as a suction vacuum for his preferred drug.

Mecca threw his head back and held it up to prevent his nose from running. Mecca was high out of his mind. He had snorted five grams of coke within twenty minutes, and the effects of the drugs were kicking in. He grabbed the bottle of Rémy Martin and took a large swallow of it. Mecca distantly heard a Tupac song pump out of his home stereo and recognized the tune. He stood up, almost stumbling, and went over to turn the music up. "'All I need in this world of sin is me and my girlfriend . . . Down to ride to the very end, just me and my girlfriend.'" Mecca held the bottle of Rémy in his grasp and drunkenly rapped along, thinking about his love, Leena. He couldn't take it anymore. He had to go over to Leena and make things right. His conscience was getting the best of him. Although he treated Leena bad at times, he really was in love with her and she was the only woman he had truly ever loved. Mecca staggered over to the keys to his Benz and snatched them off the counter. He was about to confess his love for Leena.

"Leena, I love you, baby. I'm sorry," he said as he stumbled out the door and into his Benz. He was about to go see his woman.

"I don't know what to do, Money. I'm in love with a man I can't have," Leena said as tears streamed from her eyes. She sat on her sofa across from Money expressing how she felt about him. Their brief love affair turned into an undeniable desire to be with one another.

Money was speechless as he looked into Leena's eyes and realized the feeling was mutual. He began to slowly shake his head, knowing that what they had done was wrong. His father taught him that family always comes first and loyalty is the single most important thing a man can have for his family. Money's father's teachings were embedded in his brain as his heart and mind played tug of war. On one hand he knew that betraying his brother was wrong, but on the flipside, not taking responsibility for what he had created would eat at him. His father also told him that abortion is wrong and a real man takes care of his family by any means necessary. Money was lost.

"Leena, this ain't right. This ain't right," he mumbled as he buried his face in his palms. All Money could think about was his twin brother. Money had no other choice but to force an abortion upon Leena. He wasn't willing to let a woman come between him and his sibling.

That's my flesh and blood, my brother . . . Blood in, blood out. I can't let her have that baby, Money thought as he looked at Leena crying her eyes out. What he felt for Leena was more than just a sexual attraction; he reluctantly loved her.

Money sat next to her so that he could console her. He ran his fingers through her hair and gently put his finger under her chin and made her look at him in the eyes.

"Leena, we are going to get through this . . . together. We can't have this baby, though. It is wrong," Money said as he returned the deep stare at Leena.

"I never wanted it to be like this," Leena added, heartbroken.

"Everything is going to be okay. But this between us has to stop," Money replied as he gently kissed Leena on the lips. Money's lips were magic to Leena. Just by his touch, he drove Leena wild. She felt her friend in between her legs begin to thump, and before she knew it her hands were in his pants looking for his rod. She gently began to stroke it, to make it grow. Money promised himself this would be the last time he would have sex with his forbidden love.

"'All I need in this world of sin . . .'" Mecca sang drunkenly as he approached Leena's house. He was going to apologize to his woman and make things right.

When he pulled up he noticed his Lamborghini parked in her driveway. "Money still here?" he asked himself as he pulled two houses down from Leena's house. He threw the car in park, grabbed the half empty bottle of Rémy, and hopped out. Mecca staggered to Leena's house and noticed that the front light was on. He walked in front of the house, and what he saw through the front glass made his heart drop.

Mecca dropped the Rémy bottle, causing it to shatter into pieces on the sidewalk. He saw his twin brother passionately kissing his woman and sadness overcame him. He watched as Money pulled out one of Leena's big brown breasts and began to suck on it.

Mecca was in complete shock as he watched Leena straddle his brother. His eyes bugged out as he saw his brother rub on Leena's behind with one hand while removing her thong with the other. "What the . . ." Mecca stammered as he looked in disbelief. He walked closer to the front glass and witnessed the treachery happening.

Money and Leena were so into one another that they didn't notice Mecca staring at them through the large front glass. Leena's moans could be heard from the outside as she rode Monroe with more passion than she had ever given to Mecca.

Mecca's sadness instantly turned into rage as he reached for his gun and headed for the front door. Seconds later, bullets from Mecca's .40-cal pistol were ripping through the front door wood. Leena scrambled to the corner of the room out of fear. She didn't know what was going on. Money grabbed his pistol from his waist and pointed it at the door out of instinct. He saw Mecca bursting through the front door with tears in his eyes.

"Mecca!" Leena yelled as she saw the look in his eyes. She knew that their secret was out of the bag. She had gotten caught with Money red-handed.

"I can't believe you, bitch!" Mecca screamed as he pointed his gun at Leena.

Money put away his gun and tried to calm down his brother. "Mecca, put the gun down! It's not what it looked like," Money tried to explain.

"It's not what it looked like? Nigga, fuck you!" Mecca said as he pointed his gun at his brother. Mecca's heart was broken. The two people he thought he could trust were the very ones deceiving him. Mecca pulled the hammer back on his gun and aimed it at his brother's head. Money put both of his hands up and tried to reason with his brother. Money knew his brother very well, and when he looked in Mecca's eyes, it was obvious that he was high as a kite.

"Bro, listen! Put the mu'fuckin' gun down. You high! Now stop before you do something you gon' regret," Money pleaded.

"The only thing I regret is fuckin' with this stankin' ho!" Mecca yelled as he pointed his gun back at Leena. The thought of her being intimate with his brother sent him over the edge. "I hate you!" Mecca screamed as he put both of his hands on his head. His tears began to fall freely with no shame. "I loved you," Mecca whispered just before he pointed the gun at Leena and let off two rounds. He watched as the bullets ripped through her chest and she fought for air.

"Noooo!" Money yelled as he rushed over to Leena and cradled her in his arms. "Breathe, Leena, breathe!" he instructed her as blood oozed out of her mouth. Leena fought for her dear life as she gripped Money's hands and looked into his eyes. "Breathe, Leena!" Money screamed as he tried to keep her from slipping away. "Call an ambulance!" he yelled as he looked back at his brother. Mecca was pacing the room with both of his hands on his head.

"Oh my God. What have I done?" he whispered as he frantically continued to pace the room. He looked over at his brother and Leena and what he saw and heard broke his heart. Before she lost consciousness, Leena looked Money in the eyes and whispered, "I love you, Monroe Carter."

A single tear slid down Money's face and he felt Leena's grip suddenly loosen and he knew that she was gone.

A tear fell from Mecca's eye also, but it wasn't one of sorrow, but a tear of rage. He just witnessed the woman he loved tell his brother that she loved him. "Her last words were that she loved you . . . not me," he whispered as he slowly raised his gun and pointed at Money. Money ran his hand over Leena's eyelids to close them and then he gently kissed her forehead before he turned his attention on his brother.

"Mecca, put . . . the gun . . . down," Money instructed as he put his hands in front of him.

"You always thought you were better than me, nigga! You could have had any woman you wanted, but you had to take mines. Now look at you! Look what you made me do. Look! Papa and Ma always favored you over me," Mecca cried as the tears fell freely down his face and his hand began to shake. He remembered what his parents used to say when he would get in trouble, and he began to mimic them. "You need to be more like Monroe . . . Monroe wouldn't act like that."

Mecca's voice was shaky, and Money knew his brother was unstable. As all of his emotions boiled over, Mecca looked Money in the eyes and let off a single shot that entered the left side of his chest where his heart resided. Monroe heard the gunshot, but didn't believe his own flesh and blood had shot him. As the burning sensation in Money's chest settled in, Money fell to the ground and his life slowly slipped away. High out of his mind, Mecca watched as his brother lay in a puddle of his own blood . . . dying.

Estes and Taryn looked at Monroe through the clear glass and watched as he struggled for his life. They had registered him under John Doe to be cautious. They were in the middle of a war and didn't want to take any chance. Estes held his daughter Taryn in his arms as she wept like a baby. To see her son on the hospital bed with tubes stuck down his mouth was very frightening.

"I already lost my husband to this war with the Haitians. I can't lose my son, Papa. Please, Lord!" she pleaded as she crumbled in his arms.

Estes hated being so powerless and wished he could change the situation, but it was in God's hands at that point. Estes wanted revenge on the Haitians badly, but at his old age he understood that he wasn't built for war.

They watched as the doctor observed him closely and exited the room. As he entered the hallway, he headed straight to Estes and Taryn.

"I have good news and bad news for you guys," the older Caucasian man said as he used his index finger to balance his glasses on the bridge of his nose. Estes took a deep breath and took a step forward. While one hand was still over Taryn's shoulder, he prepared himself for whatever the doctor would say.

"The good news is that he is going to make it," the doctor said, cutting straight to the point.

"Thank God," Taryn whispered as she put her hand on her chest in relief.

The doctor closed his eyes as if what he was about to say hurt him to say it. "However, he has slipped into a coma," he said.

"What? A coma?" Taryn asked as she felt her knees get weak and almost give out on her.

"How long?" Estes asked.

"That's something we don't know. It could be a couple hours, years, or . . . never. It all depends," the doctor said. Estes turned to his daughter and hugged her tightly.

"I can't do this anymore, Papa. I cannot lose my son," she stated as she cried inconsolably.

Estes's mind began to race. He knew that it was only the beginning of the bloodshed and heartache. He knew that the Haitians were coming for blood and would not stop until one side was completely gone. With Big Carter gone, he knew the odds were not in their favor. He, at that moment, made a decision for the sake of his bloodline.

"Monroe is dead," he said as he grabbed Taryn by both of her shoulders and looked into her eyes.

"What?" Taryn asked confused. She looked over at Monroe through the glass and saw that he was still breathing and she didn't understand what Estes was talking about.

"He is dead to the world, not us. I have to make a decision for the family and our bloodline. This has gone too far and it is only going to get worse. The Haitians *will not* stop until everyone in this family is destroyed. Monroe can't defend himself, so I have to do it for him."

Taryn looked into her father's eyes and saw him tearing up. She had never once in her life witnessed that from her father. A man who possessed so much power and so much strength had finally let his emotion seep out. Taryn knew that her father knew what was best for the family. With that being stated, she would keep Monroe's status a secret until he came to. Unfortunately, that would be the last night she would ever see her son. She died at the hands of an enemy before Money's resurrection.

Present Day

"I thought you were dead," Breeze continued as a single tear slid down her face. She felt her knees tremble and she could not believe what she saw.

"I was in a coma for five years. I'm here, Breeze. I'm not going anywhere," he whispered as he fought back tears. He clenched his jaws, displaying the muscles in his jaws. He then grabbed Breeze and hugged her tightly.

He looked over at Leena, who had an expressionless face. Once his secret lover, she was now the mother of his child—a child he had no idea he had up until the previous night when Estes told him everything.

He released Breeze and headed over to Young Carter. Carter stood up and couldn't believe what he was seeing. Monroe embraced his only brother and hugged him tightly.

"I can't believe this," Carter said as he embraced Monroe.

"I can't either, bro," Monroe said. They unlocked their embrace and Carter immediately began to look into a man who resembled Mecca so closely. It was like he was seeing two ghosts in one person.

"How? I thought you were dead. I went to your funeral," Carter asked, trying to make sense of the situation.

"He wasn't dead while in that casket. You would be surprised of the things people overlook while in a church. Like, is the body still breathing while in a casket? People assume that everything in a church is the truth. This made the deception fairly easy," Estes interjected. The explanation began to unravel and everyone in the room was astonished.

"We have to move forward. Enough about the past," Monroe said as he straightened up his tie and had a look of braveness on his face. He showed no emotion at all and his backbone was as straight as an arrow. He was wearing the last name of Diamond with pride just as his father had taught him.

"A lot of things have changed while you were away," Breeze said as she dropped her head, thinking about the death of her mother and brother Mecca. "I have something to tell you," Breeze continued with water in her eyes. A tear was on the verge of dropping as she took a deep breath and closed her eyes.

"Breeze, I already know everything. Papa already told me everything there is to know. However, I have to stay strong for the family; just like Father taught me," Monroe said without a flinch. He had mourned in solitude and promised himself to stay strong for Breeze and carry on The Cartel legacy with a straight back just as his father did.

Young Carter listened closely as he watched his brother display courage and strength. Monroe just dismissed the fact that his twin brother and mother had been murdered, and he was ready to jump back into the family business. Young Carter began to grow butterflies in his stomach, realizing that he would one day have to tell Monroe that he was responsible for Mecca's death. Nevertheless, now wasn't the time, and he was glad to have his brother back.

"Welcome back, bro. Welcome back," Carter said as he looked into the eyes of his only blood brother left. Monroe returned the gesture with a nod and charismatic wink. Monroe was back.

Chapter 5

"It's amazing how many peer into a
casket but never check to see if the
person inside is breathing."

—Monroe

Monroe's hands gripped the steering wheel of Carter's BMW
745 as he made his way across town. Life seemed surreal now
that he was home and reunited with his fractured family. The
streets had most definitely changed, and Monroe was slowly
realizing that taking over his family's empire wouldn't be as
simple as he had anticipated. His entitlement to his father's
empire was being ignored, and Monroe knew that it would be
a battle to regain his position within his own family. He would
have to go get his spot, but in the meantime he would have to
make some power moves independently.

He had some old business to attend to. His life had been
left hanging in the air, but now that he was back it was time
to settle his affairs. It was apparent that life had moved on
without him and that he had missed a lot in the time that
he was gone. What should have been handed down to him
was placed in Zyir's lap, and Money felt slighted. Zyir wasn't
blood. He had no right to the kingdom that his father had
built from the ground up. Money wasn't into beef, but he fully
intended on taking over The Cartel. It was his destiny to head
the infamous dynasty, and no matter who stood in the way he
would take his place as king of Miami. It was only a matter of
time.

Jamison Wildes was the most respected accountant in all
of Miami. Money man to the stars, he was known for keeping
everyone out of the crosshairs of the IRS. From kingpins to
ball players and entertainers, his clientele were the elite of

South Beach. If you were in the seven-figure gentleman's club, then you were smart enough to be a client of Jamison Wildes.

Money had been groomed for business ever since he was a young boy. He had a knack for the money flip, and his father had made sure he taught Monroe the value of a dollar. Niggas hadn't shortened his name to Money for nothing. He was about his paper, and there was a large sum left unclaimed when he had disappeared that he had to retrieve. He walked into the high-rise building and took the elevator to the top floor where the penthouse office suite sat overlooking the ocean. Jamison's company occupied the entire floor, making up an impressive modern space.

When Money entered, his presence easily overpowered the room. The Italian designer suit was tailored to his medium build perfectly, and he adjusted his slim tie as he stepped toward the receptionist.

The young woman's eyes dissected him as he approached. His handsome face and penetrating stare had her dumbfounded as she struggled to find the words to greet him.

"Umm . . . hi . . . um, do you have an appointment?" she asked.

Monroe shot the girl a charming smile and thumbed the bridge of his nose arrogantly as he said, "No, but let Jamison know that Monroe Diamond is here to see him."

The girl picked up her phone and paged Jamison's line, delivering Money's message. She frowned in confusion and put her hand over the receiver.

"I'm sorry, what's your name again? There seems to be some kind of confusion," she said.

"Tell Jamison there's no confusion. My name is Monroe Diamond," he answered.

The girl removed her hand and said, "He says he's Monroe Diamond." Moments later she hung up the phone, giving him an uncomfortable smile and reported, "He'll be right with you."

A flustered Jamison emerged from the back. "Vanessa, there has to be a mistake. Monroe Diamond is—"

"Very much alive and well," Monroe finished as he stood to his feet and extended his hand to his accountant. Jamison's eyes widened in shock and his face turned pale. "What's wrong, old friend? You look as if you've seen a ghost."

Jamison finally accepted Monroe's hand and shook it firmly. "Monroe. Forgive me, I thought . . ."

"Let's step into your office," Monroe said, taking control of the situation. "Vanessa, clear Jamison's schedule for the rest of the day. We have some business to discuss."

Monroe entered Jamison's office and walked behind the desk to take in the beautiful ocean view. Shades of turquoise and blue filled his vision as he admired the scene. "I see business is good," Monroe commented.

"I thought you were dead. I came to the funeral. How?" Jamison stammered as he watched Monroe take a seat behind his desk. Jamison sat in the visitor's chair completely thrown by the ghost of yesterday's past that had just reentered his life.

"The funeral was an illusion to trick the enemy and keep me safe. It's amazing how many peer into a casket but never check to see if the person inside is breathing," Monroe stated. "I'm not here to talk about that. I'm here for my money." He leaned in and folded his hands across the Brazilian wood desk.

"The money is unavailable," Jamison said timidly.

"Unavailable? My five million dollars that I put in your hands is unavailable?" Monroe asked. His voice was so cold that it froze Jamison in his seat. He dared not to blink or move. He could see the anger burning in Monroe's eyes.

"I . . . I . . . thought you were dead. The money was just sitting there . . ."

"Sitting there?" Monroe questioned. "So instead of taking my money to my grieving mother you did what with it?"

"I . . . I invested . . ."

Money's eyes turned dark. "You invested my dough?"

"There is a new pharmaceutical company that has created a new drug. It's not FDA approved yet, but it's only a matter of time before it happens. The money is tied up in its stock. When the FDA approval comes through I could turn five million dollars into fifty overnight," Jamison explained nervously.

Monroe was slightly irritated that Jamison had tied up his money without his permission, but he had to admit that it was a move that he would have made himself if given the opportunity. If things went according to plan the flip on Jamison's investment would be crazy. The potential gain didn't help his current financial state, however. Monroe wasn't for playing the little nigga in Carter's camp. He didn't need anyone trying to son him with handouts. He needed cash now.

"Open the account to your business," Monroe instructed.

"Excuse me?" Jamison asked. "Monroe, I don't think my company's earnings has anything to do—"

Monroe leaned back and opened his suit jacket, giving Jamison a slight glimpse of the 9 mm he had holstered underneath. Jamison began to sweat as his body temperature rose.

"You can bring me into your business, or I can focus on how you've mishandled mine," Monroe said calmly.

Jamison stood and rubbed his goatee as he walked around to the computer. He opened up his personal files, and Monroe was pleased to see that business was flourishing. Jamison was bringing in more than three million per year and had a business line of credit worth seven figures.

"Until I have that fifty million in my hands, you've got a new business partner and the split is sixty-forty," Monroe said. "Is that a problem for you?"

Jamison shook his head. Monroe stood and checked the Presidential on his wrist. "I've got to go. I'm glad we could work this out peacefully. I'll expect my name to be added on all the accounts by morning, and clear this office. It's mine now. Let this be a lesson to you, Jamison. The next time you won't touch what doesn't belong to you."

Monroe exited, and Jamison breathed a sigh of relief, letting out a slight whimper. He knew that things could have ended very badly for him. Sacrificing a piece of his business was a minor punishment in the grand scheme of things.

Standing at the site where her loved ones were buried caused Breeze to tremble as tears glided down her cheeks. She stood in the land of the dead. The cemetery always seemed so cold. Even if the sun was out, a coldness always overcame Breeze when she visited the resting place of her loved ones. As she stood in front of her parents' tombstones, a cold chill ran up her spine. She was so grateful for her life and so very happy to be reunited with Monroe. Her father, her mother, and Mecca lay side by side, resting eternally. She wished that she had come from a normal family, with a blue-collar pops and a hardworking housewife. Being the child of the first family in the streets had its perks, but the downside was much worse. The violence that came with the title made Breeze yearn for regularity. "I miss you all," she said.

Breeze turned around when she heard a car door close and smiled warmly when she saw her brother's face. He approached her, and Breeze reached up to touch his face. "I can't believe you're back," she said. "I love you so much, Money. I'm so sorry you had to come back to nothing. Things got really bad after Papa died."

"How did Carter let this happen?" Monroe asked.

"The war with the Haitians crippled us, Money. There wasn't much any of us could do," Breeze whispered. Ma'tee's face flashed in her mind and sent a shiver down her spine. She quickly shook the bad memory from her thoughts as she continued. "I come here sometimes just to talk to them. I feel like they can hear me. I almost died and I saw them. I saw you too. We were sitting at a table, all of us: me, you, Papa, Mama, Mecca. . . . We were happy. We were in . . ."

"Paradise," Money finished. He knew exactly what she had seen, because he had seen it too. He was sure that there was life after death and that his family was waiting for him on the other side.

Breeze looked at him and nodded as emotion overtook her. She sniffled as she wiped her tears. "Yeah. They're in paradise. They're watching over us, Money," Breeze said. "There is so much hurt in our past, now I want to bring you some joy. I want to introduce you to your future."

"You're talking in circles, Breeze," Monroe said as he kissed her forehead.

"It'll all make sense soon. There's something you need to know."

***

Leena fidgeted nervously in the mirror as her son played at her feet. Butterflies danced in her stomach. She had so many questions that she wanted to ask, but her brain didn't work at the moment. A ball of tension and nerves, she tried to calm herself, but there was no use. She was about to see the man she loved, the twin who had stolen her heart from the very first time she met him. Their situation had always been messy. She was Mecca's girl, but now things had changed. Mecca was gone and Leena bore Monroe's son. A son he didn't even know existed. *What if he doesn't want me?* she asked herself. She gripped the edge of the vanity and lowered her head. *God, please let him want me . . . let him want us.*

A knock at the door forced her to gain her composure, and she inhaled deeply than exhaled slowly. "Come in," she said.

Zyir cracked open the door, and her son jumped up to run to him. Zyir's exterior was so serious and focused, but when he interacted with Baby Monroe he always softened. Leena was grateful for men like Zyir and Carter. They had been the only male figures her son had known, and they took their roles in his life very seriously. "They're here," Zyir announced.

Leena nodded and ran her hands over her dress then made her way to the door. She grabbed her son from Zyir, and he gave her a reassuring nod as she walked by, headed to meet her long-lost love.

She saw him before he ever knew he had an audience. He stood just as powerful as she remembered, with his shoulders squared, hands tucked into his designer slacks as he waited patiently in the foyer. By the time he noticed her, tears were flowing down her face.

"Leena," he whispered as she descended the steps. His heart fluttered from her presence, but even in his brother's death he still felt guilt from the fact that she used to belong to Mecca.

"Hello, Money," she said. His eyes drifted to the little boy she held in her arms. She adjusted her son so that Monroe could see his face. "I'd like you to meet your son."

Breeze and Zyir stood off to the side, holding on to each other as they watched Monroe's hard persona break down.

"My son?" he repeated. His brow creased as he examined the child. He immediately knew her words were true. He was

staring at a mini version of himself. The little boy was the
spitting image of his father, and Monroe ran his hand down
his face, overwhelmed. He truly was being given a second
chance at life. Yes, he had lost so much, but with the birth
of one little person he felt restored. A son was more than he
deserved.

He took the little boy into his arms and held on to him
tightly as he fought the emotion that was threatening to spill
out of him. He couldn't imagine how hard her life had been in
the time he had been gone. She had buried him and had still
chosen to keep his seed knowing that he would never be able
to help raise him. His love and appreciation for her doubled in
that moment. She was a good woman, a woman he deserved.
He pulled Leena close and whispered in her ear, "Thank you."

"I can't believe that you're here. I prayed for God to bring
you back to me so many times," Leena whispered.

"I haven't always done right by you, Leena, and for that
I'm sorry," he said. Monroe could see years of insecurity and
hurt in Leena as she stared into his eyes. He had put those
things on her heart by forcing her to keep their relationship
a secret. In an attempt to spare his brother's feelings he had
destroyed hers, and yet she still kept his child when she could
have easily gotten rid of any memory of him. When the world
had put him to rest, Leena kept him alive by giving him the
greatest gift . . . a son to continue his name.

"My son," Monroe whispered in awe as he kissed his mini
replica on the cheek. He was in a state of disbelief, but his
heart had never felt so full. He wondered if his own father
had felt the same way when he had first laid eyes on his own
children.

"Pack your things. I'll be back to get you and my son tonight,"
Monroe said.

"I feel like when you walk out that door you'll disappear
again," Leena said as she lowered her head and gasped in
emotional turmoil. She knew that there was no guarantee
that Monroe would end up with her, but she needed him to
take charge in her son's life. A boy needed his father, and she
would fight for the chance for her son to know his.

"There is nothing on this earth that can stop me from coming back for you. I just have to make a few arrangements. I'll be back before you can even miss me, ma," Monroe assured.

Leena nodded and then took her baby from him before ascending the steps.

Monroe gathered himself and then turned toward Breeze and Zyir. "Thank you, Breeze, for keeping her close and taking care of my son when I couldn't," Monroe said.

"Of course, Money. She is a part of this family now," Breeze replied.

"We wouldn't have had it any other way," Zyir spoke up.

Monroe turned toward Zyir, and his face soured in contempt. He gave Zyir a cold stare but didn't acknowledge him with words. The tension placed an uncomfortable aura over the room, and Monroe scoffed and sucked his teeth in irritation as he walked past Zyir and out of the house.

His distaste for Zyir was evident, and had he been any other nigga, Zyir would have bodied him for the disrespect. Zyir tightened his jaw, reminding himself that Monroe was his brother by law. He would have to use patience when dealing with Monroe.

"He's been through a lot, Zyir," Breeze said as she rubbed her husband's face. "Give him some time to come around. Our father didn't like outsiders, and to him you're a new face."

Zyir could see the concern on his wife's face, and he kissed her lips tenderly. "Don't worry yourself, baby girl. We're all on the same team," he said. The words were true, but he knew that Monroe didn't see it as such and treachery from within was not an option. Zyir would cut the cancer out before he ever let it spread. He just hoped that it didn't come to that. He made a mental note to place a phone call to Carter, to see if he could bring his newly revived brother into the fold.

The smell of new leather permeated Monroe's senses as he pushed his brand new Maserati off of the lot. He spared no expense when it came to the whips he pushed. He enjoyed the feel of the engine as it leapt underneath the hood while he pressed his feet on the brake, gunning the gas simultaneously.

The car leapt as if it were a pit bull on a leash as Monroe floored his new toy.

He checked his rearview mirror and saw that Carter followed him in the brand new Mercedes GL he had copped for Leena as well. Monroe was determined to establish a new life, an affluent life for his family, and Leena was a permanent part of his world now. A car and a home were the least he could provide for her. With the help of Carter's realtor, Francesca, Monroe had found a steal on a property in a posh, secluded neighborhood of Coral Gables and a condo in Aventura. He could never have too much real estate. He would put Leena up in the large estate and use the condo whenever he needed to be closer to the action of the city.

He pulled into his new home, opening the security gate, and drove down the long driveway until he was finally in front of the massive mansion. Carter pulled up behind him and got out of the car, approaching Money as he looked around.

"Leena's going to love this, Money. I'm proud of you, bro. This was a good choice for your family. It's damn near perfect," Carter said as he admired the lush greenery and elaborate fountain that sat in the center of the circular driveway.

"I've got to pipe it out with security. Cameras, motion sensors, a guard at the front gate, the whole nine. I'm not sparing any expense on Leena and Monroe Jr.'s safety," Monroe said. He was jumping headfirst back into the streets, which meant his family would be a constant target. He was aware that they were his only vulnerability. A smart man would remain single and bear no children. A hustler with nothing to lose was the only one who could win in a concrete jungle.

"I've got a guy who can help you out. I'll have him give you a call," Carter offered.

The men circled the property to check out all of the exterior features of the home. "My father made sure that I grew up in a house like this. Grand, magnificent, and most of all safe. I had no worries as a child. I want the same for my son."

"This is the first step and despite what you may think, you don't have to protect him alone," Carter replied. "Your family is my family and is Zyir's family. He has uncles who love and care about him. So in the event that something happens to you, your family will always be protected."

"No offense, Carter, but Zyir is your man. I don't know him like that," Monroe said. "I don't extend the same amount of confidence in him as you do."

Carter stopped walking. "I want to make sure that you and Zyir iron out whatever differences you have. He is my brother, Monroe, as are you, and that means you two are linked by a common thread. You just have to get used to there being someone new inside of your circle. Don't worry. Zyir has passed my tests of loyalty time and time again. He will pass yours too, I'm sure," Carter replied. Monroe didn't respond as he drifted deep into his thoughts. Carter patted his brother's back and said, "Trust me, Money."

Monroe nodded and slapped hands with Carter, embracing him before they went their separate ways.

"Where are we going?" Leena asked as she sat shotgun next to Monroe.

"Just sit back and enjoy the ride, Lee," Monroe responded as he steered the car with one hand and held her hand with the other.

Leena admired Monroe, watching him as he nodded his head to Jay-Z's classic anthem, "Can I Live."

They drove forty-five minutes out of the city until they pulled up to her soon-to-be residence. Monroe entered a code into the keypad and the gate opened, allowing them access.

"Whose house is this?" Leena asked as they pulled up to the front entrance.

Monroe got out of the car as Leena looked around and watched him walk around the car to her door. He opened it and held out his hand. Reluctantly, she took it.

"This is your house, a place where you and my son can always call home," Monroe said.

Leena's hand shot to her mouth, covering it in shock. "This is not my home. This house is mine?" she shrieked in disbelief as her eyes scanned the massive gift.

Monroe removed a key chain and held it up for her. "It's yours, Leena, and so is that."

He pointed the key to the Benz that sat in front of the attached garage, and Leena couldn't contain her happiness. She actually laughed because a smile wasn't enough to express how much joy she felt. For so long she had depended on others to take care of her. First Estes, then Breeze and Zyir. She was always dependent on someone else, and she never had a place to call home. Now Monroe was offering her something that was hers, something that she could decorate, something that she ruled. He had given her a kingdom of her own to do with what she pleased.

"So what does this mean for us?" she asked.

"It means that I want to take care of the ones that I care for. Things have always been complicated between us. You understand more than anyone else the sense of loyalty that I had for Mecca. Death doesn't erase that. I still feel like loving you is wrong," Monroe admitted.

Leena lowered her head and shook her head at the statement. Just like that Monroe had taken her into her past. Her past of being torn between two brothers, loving them both but wanting one more. They had been like night and day.

"Just because it's not right doesn't make it wrong, Money. I loved both you and Mecca. I was in love with you and your brother too. Mecca and I had a thing. We tried to make it work after you died. He helped me with Monroe. He was there when I needed him, and I loved him because he understood that I loved you too. He accepted the fact that I was, am, will always be torn between two great men. When I look at our son, I see you both.

Mecca was high the night that he caught us. He wasn't in his right state of mind, Money. He would have never sent bullets flying our way if he had been. He loved me, yes, and I loved Mecca. He will always have a place in my heart, but nothing can ever compare to the way I felt when I was with you. I can tell you that love has no rules, Monroe. It isn't so black and white," Leena said.

Monroe nodded his head. "It's gray," he responded as he kissed her lips.

Leena pulled away and peered up at him. "I won't love you, Mecca, or anyone else in secret, Money. I've been down that road and I won't do it again. I love you and I want *you*. I want you to live here with me and to raise our son *with* me."

Monroe stepped back from her and put his hands in his pockets. "You don't know what you want, Leena. You say you had this do-over with Mecca . . . that you loved him and he accepted your faults. Well, let me ask you, Lee. If Mecca was still alive, which one of us would you choose?" he asked.

Leena's chest heaved as her stomach knotted. There was the fated question. Which brother did she love more? This was the showdown that had been postponed for years. They were airing out all of their issues—issues that had put tension between them since day one. Tears filled her eyes but she didn't let one fall.

"I've always chosen you. You just never had the courage to choose me back. You wanted me to be a private affair. You had me in the streets strutting on Mecca's arm, but you were the one in between my legs at night! Do you know how that made me feel, Money? I felt like a plaything, like your whore," Leena shot back.

Monroe looked at her in exasperation. "You were never my whore, Leena. You were the classiest chick I'd ever met. The only one fiery enough to handle my hotheaded brother, but the only one beautiful enough both inside and out to intrigue me. Mecca needed you more than I did. That's why I never wanted you to leave him. You made my brother better! You made him happy! He just didn't know how to show you, but he always told me! My whore? Nah, you weren't my whore, Leena. You were the love of my life, ma," Monroe said.

"But I never felt that you would truly choose me over Mecca. The two of you together weren't perfect, but on the off day when you were, the entire city saw how you both shined. On those days, jealousy ate me up inside. You were his bitch, Leena. You never would have chosen me. You asked me to tell Mecca about us, but you were asking for something that you didn't really want. If you wanted it then you would have stopped fucking with Mecca on your own. You chose him."

"I wanted you!" Leena snapped, feeling angry, overwhelmed, and vulnerable all at once.

"Then prove it," Monroe said, his voice calming.

He pulled a black satin box out of his pocket and got down on one knee.

Leena's eyes widened in surprise as her tears now made a trail down her cheeks.

"Marry me," he said.

Leena was speechless as she got on her knees in front of him and clasped his wrists as she looked at the flawless, princess-cut diamond and platinum ring.

"Really?" she asked in disbelief.

"You would make me a very happy man, ma," Monroe replied with a charming crooked smile.

Leena nodded her head as she smiled happily. "Yes. Monroe Diamond, I will marry you."

Chapter 6

"You need to leave Miami. Disappear.
If you don't, the next time we cross paths
I will cut your fucking head off."
—A ghost from her past . . . Mecca Diamond

Miamor closed her eyes and retreated inside of herself as her body endured the brutal beating Fabian put on her. Physically she was present, but her mind was a million miles away. Detached from the reality that loomed over her, Miamor no longer felt the pain. Each blow was absorbed into a woman who was mentally and emotionally drained.

This had been her entire life. Death. Destruction. She was a terrorist and out of all her years on this earth, she had never known true happiness. A killer by nature, she had been so focused on revenge, on efficiency, on the money, that she had never truly lived. Miamor was well acquainted with death and the ills of the world, but she knew nothing about life.

Fueled by her thirst for revenge, she had hunted Mecca relentlessly, but as she sat looking into his eyes, she couldn't help but wonder if it was all worth it. In this final moment it all felt so pointless. In a normal life he was supposed to be the brother of her future husband. They were supposed to be connected by a man they both loved dearly, but her existence was far from normal. Her world was not so black and white, but instead a shade of gray where nothing made sense to her but green and red . . . money and blood.

Miamor's head hung low as her chin hit her chest. Visions of Young Carter filled her mind as her soul slipped slowly away. Her heart ached of sorrow as she remembered his smile, his confidence, his energy. She recalled how it felt to fall head over heels for his undeniable charm. It was his face that kept her mind strong as her body began to fail her.

Miamor knew that if she let Mecca into her head then she conceded defeat. He could beat her until no breath flowed through her body, but he would never conquer her mentally; she wouldn't allow it.

Her cunning wit was what separated her from the average chick. She had always been able to outthink those around her. Prideful and ruthless, Miamor couldn't be conquered, but Mecca was determined to make her break. With every vicious blow that Fabian dealt, she forced herself to take it. Her body was painted in red as if Basquiat himself had used her as his canvas. Blood flowed from her wounds like water as the irony of her impending death haunted her.

Mecca stood in the background watching intensely as Miamor was tortured slowly. The average man would have given into the pain by now, but Mecca could see in Miamor's eyes that she would not give up her life easily. She didn't want a quick death. She wanted to feel until she couldn't feel anymore.

For the first time ever, Miamor was realizing how valuable life was. She was saddened that her value had been wasted. The way that she had led her life would not earn her a spot in paradise. Her eternity would be spent in hell, and it was a fate that she feared.

A tiny voice inside of her told her to beg, plead, and bargain for her life, but the killer she had become wouldn't allow it. She was overdosed on pride and refused to ruin the hood legacy that she had built by dying on her knees. She had lived by a code that only a murderer could understand. When the streets recounted her story, she wanted them to speak the truth. She was ruthless and calculating, even when staring into the eyes of the Grim Reaper. No one, not even Mecca Diamond, had been able to break her. Miamor was the greatest to ever do it, and she refused to let Mecca take away her power.

"You fucking heartless bitch," Fabian seethed through gritted teeth as he pulled her head back. She felt the cold kiss of the gun as it met the back of her skull, and tears involuntarily welled in her eyes. Fabian's finger danced on the trigger. There weren't many people who could kill

*without remorse. It was a specialty that Miamor and Mecca
had perfected.*

*"Put the bitch down and get it over with. I'm bored with
this shit," Mecca stated, his voice sending chills of hatred up
and down Miamor's spine. "Fuck you waiting for, nigga?"*

*Fabian looked up at Mecca, the unsteady grip on his pistol
giving away his uncertainty as his hand shook slightly.*

*"You still scared of this bitch? She's tied up and you the one
with the gun, but she still got you shook? Pull the fucking
trigger!" Mecca ordered, shaking his head in disgust.*

*Fabian stood, his lean torso shaking as his bottom lip
trembled in uncertainty. "I . . . I . . . can't," he admitted.*

BOOM!

*Without warning, Mecca sent a bullet through Miamor's
shoulder.*

"Aghh!"

*"Fuck you mean you can't?" Mecca barked at Fabian. "See,
it's simple."*

BOOM!

*With precision he sent another shot in Miamor's direction,
this time hitting her midsection.*

*"Aghh!" she howled through gritted teeth as she balled her
fists tightly. The bullet ripped through her organs, making it
feel as though she were on fire.*

*Fabian backpedaled until his heel hit the bottom step of
the basement. He was in over his head. Fabian dabbled in
the streets every now and then, but he wasn't major. He
had never led the lifestyle that Mecca had and knew nothing
about this heartless side of the game. Revenge had sounded
so sweet, but when it came down to it, Fabian couldn't put in
the work. As Miamor gasped for air, Fabian shook his head
back and forth. Jailhouse blues filled his soul as he became
overwhelmed by the possible consequences of his actions.
Suddenly, he wanted no part of this murderous plot.*

*Mecca turned toward Fabian and before he even realized
it, Fabian was hightailing it up the steps.*

*Mecca smirked as he saw Fabian run out of the basement.
"Pussy-ass nigga," Mecca scoffed, making a mental note to
handle Fabian later. Mecca didn't leave loose ends. Fabian*

was a liability, and it was imperative that he was removed from the equation. Mecca was leaving zero witnesses, but first Mecca was going to enjoy his final round with Miamor.

"Now that there are no cowards in the room, the real fun can begin," he taunted.

Mecca grabbed the metal chain off the floor and circled Miamor. The chain scratched the floor like nails on a chalkboard, causing the hairs on the back of her neck to stand. Mecca examined Miamor as she struggled to lift her head. Her eyes followed him back and forth as he paced the concrete floor. He stopped and knelt directly in front of her, waiting to see the fear creep into her eyes. But when he stared at her all he saw was acceptance and regret.

He wrapped the thick chain around her neck. His heart beat furiously inside of his chest as he thought of avenging the death of his mother. He had waited so long for this moment that it made his dick hard.

Miamor was like a rare specimen. The Cartel had warred with a thousand armies before her, but somehow she had been able to dismantle their entire operation. One woman had annihilated his entire family. The empire that the Diamond family had built was standing on its last leg. She had destroyed the infamous Miami Cartel. Mecca hated her existence yet envied her efficiency all at the same time. She was thorough and conniving, professional and about her paper. No mark had ever been too big to hit. If the money was right, then she had no problem making it rain bullets. No questions asked. She was the Grim Reaper.

Mecca lived by the gun and knew that one day he would die by it as well. As he looked at Miamor he realized that she lived by the same creed. If he had been half as calculating as Miamor, his family would not be lined up in metal coffins under the dirt.

Since the death of his father, Mecca and Miamor had played a deadly game of cat and mouse. There was no prey among them; they were both predators. With no sheep to slaughter they had gone at each other's throats and it all culminated in this one moment. He pitied the fool who looked at Miamor and underestimated her. Her pretty face had hidden *the ugliest of intentions, and it was only by God's grace that Mecca hadn't ended up on the other side of her gun.*

They stared at one another silently and for a brief moment they came to a mutual understanding.

"Just do it," she whispered as tears finally came to her. "If anybody had to do it, it may as well be you. You're just like me."

Her words connected with Mecca, digging a hole straight to his heart as he nodded his head. Miamor was tired of fighting him, tired of feeling guilty for being the way that she was. She was ready for this to end.

"Tell Carter I'm sorry," she whispered, barely audible.

Mecca pulled the ends of the chain, cutting off Miamor's oxygen supply instantly. He pulled so hard that the metal pierced her skin, causing it to become raw as her eyes bulged in distress. Mecca gritted his teeth as he stared at her while choking her to death. The light in her eyes began to dwindle and the sounds around her became muffled as a natural reaction to fight overcame her. Her body jerked violently as her lungs begged for air. The tighter he pulled, the more her body rebelled, but she was helplessly bound to the chair. All she could do was die.

"Aghh!" Mecca roared as he pulled tighter and tighter on the chain. You're just like me. *Her words replayed in his head, taunting him and reminding him of the evil that lived inside of them both. Mecca stared into her face with anger, with resentment, but when he saw his own face staring back at him he froze. Sympathy poured into his heart as his chest became heavy.*

She's right, he thought as he backpedaled and put distance between them. *Taken aback by the naked truth, he realized that as much as he hated Miamor, he couldn't condemn her. He was not without sin.*

Her lungs felt like they were on fire as she coughed uncontrollably and sucked in as much air as she could.

Mecca felt as if he were going insane. For so long he had dreamt of this very day. He had never hesitated to make an example out of a mu'fucka, but with Miamor it was different. Killing her would be like killing himself. They were the same.

They both had blood on their hands, and their hate for one another kept them teetering on the edge of insanity.

"Just do it," she said with no more fight left in her voice.

A moment of clarity passed over Mecca as he turned away from her and placed his hands on his head in distress. Something bigger then Mecca's conscience was coming into play. The universe was intervening. It wasn't in God's plans for Miamor to die. Not by Mecca's doing.

"I can't," he whispered as he lowered his hands to his side and allowed the chain to fall to the ground.

Miamor was barely conscious as she craned her head to the side and replied, "What?" The blood that fell into her line of sight clouded her vision, and she was so close to giving up that she knew she couldn't have heard Mecca correctly.

"I am you," Mecca whispered with sorrow as his own tears came to his eyes. He quickly pinched the bridge of his nose and shook the emotion away. Mecca was evolving right before Miamor's eyes, and she was so close to death that she was missing the sight. "I should fucking kill you. You deserve to die," Mecca stated, larcenous venom lacing his tone. "But something in me won't allow me to. You need to leave town and stay the fuck away from my family."

Miamor's eyes opened and closed weakly as silent tears flooded down her face.

"Don't contact Carter. Don't even enter the city limits. You need to leave Miami. Disappear. If you don't, the next time we cross paths I will cut your fucking head off," Mecca raged.

Miamor wept as his words pierced her ears. She had never felt more connected to anyone in her life. Mecca was her adversary, but today he chose to be her savior. If he could put his prideful vengeance aside and leave her with air in her lungs, then he deserved to see her break.

Miamor lifted her head, her neck bobbling loosely as she felt every broken bone in her body. "I . . . I'm sorry," she whispered.

Mecca stared at her in hatred while forcing himself to remain composed. "Disappear," he stated with finality. "Leave and never look back."

He was instructing her to do the very thing that he had wished he could do. He was pardoning her and forcing her to start over. All she had to do was pick a place and act as though a girl named Miamor had never existed. Mecca turned and walked up the steps with an agonizing ache in his heart, but a lighter soul. His mind was telling him to put a hollow tip through Miamor's chest, but his spirit was teaching him the hard lesson of forgiveness. He never looked back as he left Miamor. He was afraid that his rage might change his mind if he ever saw her face again.

Miamor waited until she was sure that Mecca had gone before she lost all composure. The cry that erupted from her battered body reflected years of pain. No one knew the things that she had suppressed, but deep inside she knew that Mecca understood. He did her no favors. She was still bound and beaten near extinction, but he had left her with a tiny chance to survive. He owed her nothing, so that tiny act was a gift. It was ironically the kindest thing that anyone had ever done for her.

Miamor grunted in excruciating pain as she used her body weight to tip the chair on its side. She wasn't ready to meet her Maker, and the only thing stopping her from surviving was the rope that bound her. She pulled with all of her might, but the beating she had endured had robbed her of her strength. She was too weak to break free, and as she twisted her wrists, the friction burned into her skin.

"Aghh!" she screamed out in frustration before finally giving up. The room spun around her as she lapsed in and out of consciousness. "God forgive me," were the last words to escape her crusted lips before everything faded to black.

Miamor's eyes opened slowly and her heartbeat rapidly increased as she awakened from her four-day slumber. She was on full alert as her senses kicked into full gear. Her eyes darted around the foreign room, disoriented and confused. The sterile smell invaded her nose, making her ill instantly. It was so dark that all she could see was the fluorescent light that shined in the hallway, outlining the door to her room.

Her pain was so great that it was immeasurable. Bruised and battered, Miamor was beyond repair. What she needed most was time for her body and mind to recuperate from the trauma she had endured.

How did I get here? *she thought as she lay deathly still.* I have to get out of here. If Mecca finds me . . .

The steady tone of the heart monitor and busy sounds of medical staff scurrying about outside of her room gave away her location. She was in a hospital, but she had no idea how she had gotten there. He told me to leave town. If he gets wind that I survived and that I'm here, he'll come finish the job.

Panicked, her body temperature began to rise and her pulse raced as fear caused her adrenaline to soar. Mecca had instilled a permanent terror in her heart. She had never been afraid of anyone, until now. Not even God had taught her a lesson so tough. Mecca had given her the craving to live, and in order to do that she had to get out of Miami . . . fast.

Her panic caused the machines around her to sound off and she cursed herself silently. Miamor knew that the police would undoubtedly have questions for her that she wasn't prepared to answer.

She closed her eyes just as the handle on the door twisted open. Playing possum, she listened to the commotion around her.

"What's going on with our Jane Doe?" the doctor asked.

"Blood pressure is up, heart rate is elevated," a nurse responded. Miamor lay still as they checked her vitals. With her eyes closed and ears open she listened carefully.

"She is lucky that those kids found her when they did. Another day and she might not have made it," the nurse said with sympathy in her voice. "I can't imagine why someone would hurt a young woman this way. With her injuries, I'm surprised she is even alive."

The doctor, focused on his job, merely grunted a reply. He had seen much worse in his ten years on the job. He wasn't emotionally attached to the patients like the young, novice nurse. "Monitor her closely," he finally said as he jotted notes on Miamor's chart. "As soon as she wakes up, inform me and call this detective." The doctor handed the nurse a card. "He would like to speak with her immediately. They're running her prints now to see if they can gather some information on her."

Miamor's internal alarm sounded off. She was in trouble. If those fingerprints came back, her juvenile records would pop up, giving them her government name. She had committed so many murders over the years that there was no telling how many times she had slipped up. In her mind, she had been so careful, so untouchable when she hit her marks, but all it took was one mistake . . . one partial fingerprint to lead the police directly to her. Every doorknob she had ever touched was now threatening her anonymity. Had she been careful, every time, all the time? Miamor couldn't be so sure. Miamor tortured herself as she scrolled through her mental Rolodex, recalling every nigga she had ever hit, but the possibilities were endless. If those fingerprints came back, her freedom was in jeopardy.

She waited until the nurse and doctor left the room before she shot up out of her bed. I've got to get out of here, now!

She reached over and shut off the machines, then ripped the IV out of the front of her hand, wincing as blood tricked down her wrist.

"Hmm!" she grunted while using all of her might to meander out of the bed and stand to her feet. They instantly gave out underneath her, and she fell hard to the cold tile floor. Miamor gripped the side of the bed, struggling to pull herself to her feet as she kept her eyes trained on the door. What should have been an easy task took all of her effort as perspiration gathered on her forehead. She steadied herself, panting hard as she willed her knees not to buckle. Her legs trembled like leaves in the wind and threatened to give out at any moment. Miamor had never been so weak in her life. The painkillers they had filled her with numbed the pain, but did nothing to erase her fatigue.

Miamor's fear was greater than anything she had ever felt. Her back was against a wall, and Mecca had taken all of the fight out of her. She struggled over to the door, using the bedrails as support as she slowly made her way across *the room. Her body urged her to quit, but desperation fueled her shaky limbs.*

By the time she made it to the door, she felt as if she had run a marathon. The thin fabric of the hospital gown clung to her sweaty body, and her eyes were wide in alert. Nothing had ever taken so much energy or effort to accomplish.

The walls of the hospital were the equivalent to death row. She was just waiting around to die . . . waiting for Mecca to get wind of her whereabouts and come finish the job as he had promised. The light in the hallway blinded her as she put her bare feet on the cold tile. Miamor felt the room spin, and she closed her eyes as she leaned against the wall to keep herself upright. Her deep breaths calmed the world around her, and when she opened her eyes a few stray tears slid down her cheeks.

Overwhelmed, she took a step, avoiding eye contact with everyone around her as she crept along the wall. Nurses and doctors hurriedly bypassed her, too busy to notice that she was out of place. Miamor slid into the first supply closet she found. She rummaged through it silently, taking everything she could possibly need. When she found a pair of nurses' scrubs folded on the shelf, she immediately changed into them, knowing that they would help her blend in with the other workers.

Miamor tossed the hospital gown and stuffed gauze, alcohol pads, and a scalpel into her pockets before exiting again. This time, no one noticed her and she fit right in as she made her way slowly to the elevators on her floor. If anyone had looked down, her shoeless feet would have given her away.

She slid into the elevators and sighed in relief as they shut behind her. Miamor's body was threatening to shut down, but she knew that if she lost her strength, she was dead.

DING.

The elevator doors opened in the lobby and when Miamor saw the entrance to the hospital, her heart fluttered. She was so close to freedom that she could taste it. Miamor walked out into the lobby, but when she saw three uniformed police officers enter the building, she halted. She turned instantly and crept into the stairwell, heading down.

"Fuck! Fuck! Fuck!" she whispered as she half ran, half stumbled down the flight of steps. She burst into the basement, but stopped in shock when she saw the dead bodies lying on cold metal slabs. Footsteps behind her resounded as she heard someone descending the steps. There was nowhere to run. Like a fly trapped in a spider's web, Miamor was stuck, and in her current state she was too weak to fight.

Miamor rushed over to the wall and fear pulsed through her. The steel wall housed metal drawers where bodies could be stored. Miamor pulled open a drawer, finding a stiff, cold body lying on a slab. She quickly closed it and moved to the next drawer. Another body. She looked back at the door, hearing a man's voice as it drew near. She rushed to the next drawer. She breathed a sigh of relief when she saw that it was empty. She climbed on top of the metal slab and shuddered when she thought of how many lifeless souls had lain there before her. Her stomach turned and she felt as if she would throw up. Doing the unthinkable, she slid the drawer closed.

The instant drop in temperature caused her to shiver. Her chest heaved as if she had just run a marathon, and her mind played tricks on her as she imagined the bodies around her. It was so cold that her teeth chattered, and she covered her mouth, blowing into her hands to create some warmth.

The space that she was in was so tight that she could barely move. Claustrophobia set in as Miamor began to feel trapped. She had always been so composed, so strategic, but at this moment she was feeling emotional, irrational, and the death that surrounded her sent chills down her spine. Miamor wasn't used to being so vulnerable, and if she didn't get out of there she would crack.

She listened as the coroner worked, listening to music and humming carefree while she froze inside her hiding spot. She didn't know how long she would make it without giving herself away. Suddenly the entire refrigerator illuminated and Miamor gasped as one of the metal slabs slid out. Miamor looked left, then right, and her eyes widened in horror as she realized how many dead bodies surrounded her. Some of them hadn't even been processed yet.

Open gunshot wounds and lifeless eyes were all around. Her hands trembled as she cupped her mouth and she quickly snapped her eyes closed. It felt like she was lying in her own coffin, and if she didn't calm herself she would explode. Her anxiety built as tears of frustration overwhelmed her.

Stay quiet . . . just stay quiet, *she urged herself.*

The clang of the drawer closing caused her heart to drop into her stomach. This had to be punishment for the murder count she had racked up. Now death was outnumbering her, and she felt as if she was going to lose it.

Miamor was tortured for four hours as she waited for the coroner's shift to end. When she finally heard the coroner leave for the night, her limbs were so frozen that her body was numb. Miamor pushed her feet against the wall in front of her, causing the drawer to burst open. Her blue lips trembled and her teeth chattered as she climbed down.

Miamor stumbled toward the counter and leaned against it for support as she shivered uncontrollably. Her entire body tensed when she heard the door to the morgue clatter open. Like a deer in headlights she turned around. A middle-aged woman in a white lab coat stared back at her, stunned.

"Hey! What are you doing down here? This area is—"

Miamor doubled over and groaned in pain, clenching her abdomen, interrupting the woman's line of questioning.

"Oh goodness! Are you okay?" the woman asked as she crossed the room to come to Miamor's aid. It was the biggest mistake she could have made. Miamor slid the ten-inch scalpel from the pocket of her stolen scrubs and using all of her strength, she arose and wrapped her arm around the woman's neck.

"If you move or scream, I'll slit your throat from ear to ear. You got me?" she asked.

The woman was scared shitless and nodded her head in compliance.

"Now, who else are you expecting to come down here?" Miamor asked. The woman was paralyzed in horror, and Miamor pricked her skin with the blade, causing a small trail of blood to begin to flow.

"Please don't hurt me," the woman pleaded.

"Then answer my question," Miamor said. She was so weak that the woman could have easily overpowered her, but she kept her voice steady, deadly, and strong, hoping that the woman didn't test her.

"No one. I'm the third shift coroner. I work alone," she replied. "Are you going to kill me?"

"If you do what I say, you'll be fine," Miamor said truthfully.

Miamor's mind spun as Mecca's threats clouded her judgment. He'd told her to disappear. Miamor knew that she had no choice but to run—run and never look back. The only problem was the two bad bitches she was leaving behind. Aries and Robyn would never stop looking for her. As long as they thought she was alive, then their loyalty would keep them searching for her. *I've got to die,* she thought.

"Sit on your hands in the corner," she ordered. The woman did as she was told as Miamor walked over to the wall of the dead. She began pulling out the drawers, one by one, until she came across one that suited her—a black girl who was too young to be lying lifeless before her. The tag on her toe read JANE DOE.

Damn, *Miamor thought.*

"I need her hands," Miamor choked out. Not even she believed what she was about to do. Mecca was pushing her to the brink of insanity. Her fear and desperation forced her to take drastic measures.

"What?" the woman responded.

"I need you to cut off her fucking hands," Miamor snapped, this time more stern.

The woman rose to her feet and meandered toward the surgical saw. She just wanted to leave the situation alive. Avoiding eye contact with Miamor she did as she was instructed, shaking the entire time. After she was done, she put them in a plastic zip bag and handed them to Miamor.

"Please, I've done what you've asked. I have a family . . ."

Miamor walked over to grab the woman's leather briefcase. She emptied its contents onto the floor until she found the woman's wallet and keys. She grabbed her driver's license and read the woman's address aloud.

"Fifty-four seventy-one Brookgate Court, Miami, Florida."

The woman's eyes bulged.

"You have no idea who I am or what I look like. You were too fearful to look me in the face. You don't know anything. You can't remember anything. Those are the answers to your questions when the police ask. You understand?" she asked.

The woman nodded.

Miamor pulled out an empty drawer.

"Get in," she said.

The woman's eyes widened, horrified as she began to cry. But she didn't protest as she climbed on top of the slab. Miamor removed the woman's shoes and then closed the drawer.

Miamor fell backward, letting her back rest against the wall as she breathed erratically and closed her eyes. Yes, she was a killer, but she was on some other shit at the moment. Not even she had the stomach for what she was doing. She grabbed the woman's bag and stuffed the hands inside, then stuffed her feet into the coroner's shoes.

She knew she couldn't rest. She had to keep it moving. By now, the entire hospital knew that she was missing. Surely they would be looking for her. Miamor urged her legs to work as she stumbled from counter to counter, knocking over instruments and paperwork as she crossed the room. Finally she made it to the door and slowly ascended the steps. When she finally made it to the top, she was winded and sweating profusely, the scrubs clinging to her wet body. Nothing had ever been so hard to accomplish in her life, and her injuries screamed for her to stop, but she was like a shark. The minute she stopped moving she would die. The EXIT sign that hung above the door was so close yet torturously still so far away.

Everything in her wanted to call for help, needed Young Carter to use his position and power to get her out of this mess, but she couldn't. Calling him would be signing her own death certificate, because with Carter came Mecca. The blood bond they shared made her obsolete.

Miamor half walked, half stumbled as she headed to the door. Her head was down, but her eyes stayed up, scanning the room. No one noticed her as she slipped through the double doors and out into the dark night. As soon as her feet hit concrete she ran, falling repeatedly because she was barely able to stand up.

Miamor willed herself to run faster, but the more steps she took the more hopeless her escape became. She hit the ground, her feet unable to withstand much more. She scooted her back against a parked car and gripped the scalpel in her pocket. She fished inside the bag until she located the woman's keys then hit the alarm button.

HONK! HONK! HONK!

Flashing lights and a loud car horn sounded off as Miamor looked around until she located the car. A brand-new silver CLK called her name as she brought herself to her feet and rushed to the car. Miamor started the ignition and pulled off into the night as tears finally ran down her face. She sobbed so hard that she could barely see while making her escape.

Miamor stumbled inside of her apartment and quickly rushed to her safe. She pulled out the money that she had saved up. $250,000 to be exact. She then removed two 9 mm pistols. She stuffed the cash and one of the weapons into a duffel bag, putting the other gun into one of her handbags for easy access. Miamor showered quickly and threw on more comfortable clothes before grabbing her bag and kissing her life good-bye.

Miamor wiped down the stolen car, then got into her own as she put her new life together in her head. She checked into a seedy motel and gave into the pain and exhaustion that crippled her.

Miamor jumped out of her sleep and grabbed the gun from underneath her pillow all in one action, pointing it straight ahead of her. She breathed heavily as she looked around, paranoid as the drapes blew from the small breeze that came through the open window. "I have to get out of here," she said. The sleep had done nothing to heal her ailing body, but it had given her enough time to clear her mind. She grabbed her car keys and headed out to her last stop.

***

The sound of bells opening announced her presence as Miamor entered the tattoo shop. Tattoo art drawings covered the walls, and she looked around impressed, knowing that she had found the perfect man for the job. The hum of the tattoo gun resounded loudly in the shop as Miamor made her way toward the back.

"Hello!" she called out.

The buzz of the tattoo gun ceased and a white boy with spiked hair and a fully art-covered torso appeared out of the back.

"What can I do for you?" he asked.

"How much for a tattoo?" she inquired.

"Depends on what you get. You got anything in mind?" he asked.

"Two words. No color. Just black. Small font," she replied.

"That'd be about seventy-five dollars," he said.

Miamor nodded to the back where she saw a young girl lying on her stomach, waiting for him to return. "If you clear the shop, I'll pay $7500," she offered.

The tattoo artist chuckled slightly and began to turn away from her. "What kinda bullshit you on, sweetheart?" he said dismissively. She pulled out a knot of money and tossed it to him, instantly piquing his interest. He thumbed through the bills, finding all Benjamin Franklin faces staring back at him. "Give me five minutes."

Miamor smirked and waited until the shop was empty before she proceeded.

"So what you want tattooed?" he asked.

Miamor pulled out the clear bag and tossed it to him. "These."

The man jumped back, letting the hands hit the floor as he knocked all of the tattoo guns on the floor. "Holy shit!" he cursed. "Where'd you get those from? Are you insane?"

Miamor calmly sat down. "Lower your voice. Rule number one: don't ask me any questions. Rule number two: you've got an hour to get it done," she said. "Now are you in or out? Because if not, I'll be taking my $7500 to the next mu'fucka."

The man weighed his options in his head: his morality or the wad of money he gripped in his hand. As tightly as he was holding it, he knew that he wasn't passing up the opportunity. He'd have to do a hundred tattoos to make that kind of dough.

"I'll do it."

He picked up the bag with his thumb and index finger, feeling his stomach turn. "This is some freaky shit," the tattoo artist stammered as he wiped the sweat from his forehead.

"Stop bitching and just do it," Miamor stated. "I need you to emulate this perfectly. Same font and everything." Miamor held out her own wrists to show the white boy her own artwork: MURDER MAMAS

The tattoo artist went to work, copying the tattoo perfectly, and when he was done he sat back in admiration.

"Think it's a perfect match," he said.

Miamor looked and nodded in approval. The man turned to bag the hands.

BOOM!

Miamor sent a bullet through the back of his skull. She hated to do it, but he didn't seem like the type to keep quiet, and she couldn't risk anyone knowing she was alive.

She grabbed the hands and put them in the prepackaged box then dropped them at the nearest shipping store on her route out of town. The next day Aries and Robyn would receive "her hands" on the doorstep of their Los Angeles home. Once they did, there would be no one else to come looking for her. She would be dead to the world, dead to her old life, and she could heed Mecca's warning to forget that a girl named Miamor ever existed. It was time for her to start a new life.

Chapter 7

"I've never murked anybody
that didn't deserve it."

—Miamor

Miamor jumped out of her sleep, panting and gasping for air. She covered her racing heart with her hand and closed her eyes until her pulse slowed. The nightmares of her past stopped her from moving forward. Every night she dreamt of how she had escaped Mecca's clutches, but it seemed as though he still had her mind imprisoned in fear. She arose from the bed and wrapped her body in the sheets as she left the room in search of Carter. Miamor was being given a second chance at life. All she had to do was let go of the past, but it was easier said than done.

The sound of a crackling fire drew her toward Carter's study. She stepped inside and was immediately taken aback by the beautiful room. His home was so massive that she had not yet explored it all. In fact, their reunion had been contained to the bedroom. They couldn't get enough of one another, and this was the first time she had taken notice of her new surroundings. The walls consisted of bookshelves that went from the floor to the top of the twenty-five-foot ceilings, the lighting was low, and the mahogany furniture was antique. A king's throne sat behind his desk, and it was so fitting because Carter truly was royalty. A leather sofa sat off to the right, directly in front of the glowing fire that Carter stared right into.

"It's late. What are you doing up?" he asked. His back was toward her and he never looked her way, but he felt her presence as soon as she entered the room.

"I can't sleep," Miamor replied as she shifted uncomfortably. She didn't know if she should sit or stand, stay or leave. Things between her and Carter were still quite tense. They were getting reacquainted all over again, and this time she held no secrets. He knew all of her, and she was sure that there were parts of her that he didn't approve of.

"Join the club, ma," Carter stated. "I haven't gotten a wink since you came back. It's hard to rest around someone like you." Carter never fully let his guard down around Miamor. The trust in their relationship was fragile and in need of repair. He knew that rebuilding their foundation would take time.

His words knocked the wind out of her as she realized that he thought the worst of her. "I would never hurt you, Carter. I've never murked anybody that didn't deserve it. I'm not a monster, and the niggas I've come at always saw it coming," she said, slightly offended. "Maybe I shouldn't have come here," she said, speaking more to herself than at him.

She shook her head, feeling foolish for ever believing that he could accept her past.

"Miamor." Carter's voice echoed against the walls and halted her steps. "Come over here, ma."

Her feet moved obediently. This man was the only person on earth who could make her do anything. It was as if he had her under a spell. She wanted to follow his lead. Wherever he may take her, she wanted to be the woman behind him. She would obey any rule just to keep him. A born leader, Miamor had always been hard to tame, but with Carter she found herself wanting to submit. She needed him to have faith in her—faith that she could change.

She walked over to the couch that he sat on and kneeled in front of him as she raised her eyes to match his intense gaze.

Carter cupped her face in his hands. "I apologize, ma. I want you here. There's just a lot going on right now. My brother Monroe is back," Carter said.

Miamor's eyes widened in shock. She had seen Monroe's body lying cold and stiff in a casket years ago. "From the dead?" she gasped.

Carter smirked and let out a chuckle. "Seems that way, yes. It's a long story, but now that he's returned things will be complicated. I have a lot on my mind, but I don't mean to take it out on you."

"And what about us? Your family will never accept me. They won't forgive me for the things I've done," Miamor said.

"The only person's acceptance that you need to worry about is mine. Nobody else matters. No harm will come your way, no old scores will be settled. You get a pass because of me. Niggas ain't got to like it, but they will respect it. For now no one even needs to know that you're here. I have to think of a way to introduce you back into their lives without causing more conflict. Until then I need you to lay low, be unseen. You think you can handle that?"

Miamor nodded her head and replied, "Yes." Everything about Carter was intoxicating to Miamor. The way that he stuck up for her warmed her heart. She stood to her feet and dropped the sheet that covered her naked body. The amber hue from the fireplace provided the only light in the room and outlined the silhouette of her body.

His hands found her hips and he pulled her closer to him. His mouth was perfectly aligned with her womanhood, and he didn't hesitate to explore it. His warm, thick tongue opened her southern lips as he licked her gently. Circling her clit while French kissing her lips, he feasted on Miamor's sweet honey pot.

"Ohh," she moaned as she massaged the back of his head while falling victim to his head game. Her legs weakened as Carter took her love button between his teeth. Gently he bit down and Miamor lost her mind. "What are you doing to me?" she asked as she began to quiver in ecstasy. Carter inserted one finger, then two, then three inside of her. Miamor's body was so responsive to his touch that she rode his hand, squeezing her vaginal muscles around his fingers as he tickled her insides and palmed her clit. Carter curved his fingers, hitting her G-spot.

"Wait. Ooh no, wait, Carter," she whispered. The pressure was building inside of her and she felt as if she would pee on herself. It felt so good that she didn't want to stop it. Her pussy lips were so swollen that it looked as if he had beat it up, and her clit throbbed for attention.

"Put your mouth on me, baby," she whispered. Carter's fingers worked her over as he simultaneously kissed her clit, and that was all she wrote. Miamor screamed as her love came down. Warmth came over her as her head fell back in sheer bliss.

Carter licked her gently as he looked up at her with sincere eyes. He was hypnotizing her with his slow rhythm, and she felt obliged to return the favor. She pushed his forehead back, depriving herself of his vicious head game, and he sat back on the leather couch. At lightning speed she had his manhood in her hands, stroking his length and tracing the veins that throbbed in his shaft.

Carter's dick was perfectly thick and long, but most importantly he knew how to use it. He pulled her down onto his lap and filled her walls. Miamor worked her hips and relaxed her muscles, allowing him total access to her body.

His body was so tense and she rode him into relaxation. She felt the stress leaving him with every move she put on him. His fingers dug into her hips as he lifted then lowered her onto his girth. Their rhythm was slow, sensual, and he pulled her taut nipple into his mouth. Bolts of electric pleasure shot up her spine, and Miamor picked up her pace, grinding into him with passion.

He palmed her voluptuous behind, spreading her cheeks in an effort to go deeper. He flipped her over, wanting to take control as he rocked into her. Carter was knocking the bottom out of her pussy, pushing her to the threshold between pleasure and pain. He slow-stroked her, exploring parts of her body that she didn't even know existed.

Her nails staked her claim as she clawed at his back. She opened her eyes as she took in all of him. Every muscle in his toned physique flexed as he handled her body. His brown complexion glistened in sweat as his face contorted in pleasure. Carter Jones was a work of art. The man was a masterpiece. He kissed her lips, and the feeling of his tongue dancing in her mouth, the taste of her sweet mouth took him over the edge. His lovemaking quickened and he went deeper, and deeper, and deeper.

"Ohh shit, ma," he bellowed, his voice a masculine grunt.

"Cum inside me, Carter," she whispered as tears came to her eyes.

He stopped briefly, panting, as he looked in her eyes.

She nodded her head. "Put a baby in me, Carter," she confirmed. Carter placed his forehead against hers and looked her in the eyes as he pumped inside of her until he spilled his seed inside of her womb.

"I love you, ma," Carter said. "I don't want to, but I do. A lesser man would never admit that to you, but I don't want there to be any indiscretions between us. Our home has to be strong. I have too much to lose to allow anarchy into my world."

"I will love you until our end, Carter," Miamor replied before falling asleep in his arms.

Chapter 8

"We just trying to get money
and stay off the radar."
—Young Carter

Money definitely was not going to waste any time. He wanted to get acclimated to the new regime quickly. Monroe longed to take over the streets of Miami once again. He wanted to take back the throne and then retire at the top like his father was supposed to do. Also, to cope with his losses he would have to stay busy. He wanted to get into the swing of things and build the empire that had fallen during his extended slumber. Therefore, Carter set up a meeting with the head soldiers of their crew, along with Zyir, to meet and reintroduce Monroe to the streets and the "new look" Cartel.

The rendezvous was at an empty warehouse that Zyir had been leasing. It was where they kept the coke and guns hidden. The steel doors and concrete floors gave the place a cold feel. Steel gates separated portions of the facility, and the only sound was the loud buzzing from the light. A single card table sat square in the middle of the floor, with a single beam of light shining directly down on it.

The mechanical door rose and in came Carter's black Range Rover, followed by a black tinted SUV driven by Zyir. Zyir had his soldiers with him, and they were about six deep. All of them were under twenty-one, but all of them were also live wires and would do anything at Zyir's command. They were all excited and also nervous about meeting the notorious Monroe "Money" Diamond. They all grew up admiring him and when he "died" it only made his legacy grow. While Mecca had the streets in fear when he was alive, Monroe had the love. He had swagger, a gentle kindness, and the muscle that made for a great gangster. But those days were gone, and they would soon find out that Monroe wasn't the same as he once was.

Everyone got out of the cars and gathered around the table, waiting for Money to arrive. Zyir and Carter slapped hands, and Carter nodded at the young soldiers as they formed a circle.

"Where is ya man?" Zyir asked as he checked his watch, referring to Money.

"I told him ten. He should be pulling up any minute now," Carter said as he glanced at his wrist and checked his watch.

"Well, he's late," Zyir said, not really liking the idea of adding someone to their crew. However, out of respect for Young Carter he would not raise any sand.

"I've been here. I'm never late, homeboy," Money said as he stepped out of the shadows, startling all of them. They all reached for their guns and froze when they realized it was Money. He walked over to the table and joined the men. He and Carter embraced, and Monroe looked around the table and was disgusted. Back in his day, young niggas couldn't even be in his presence. They hadn't lived enough or experienced enough in life to be at a table with a boss in his eyes, so he immediately was turned off by the situation. His body language told it all as he mugged each of the youngsters as Carter began to talk.

"I want to introduce you to the crew. This is Bo, Fly Boogie, and Damon. And of course you know Zyir. This is who holds everything down," Carter stated. Fly Boogie, a skinny kid with a knack for fashion, was the first to speak.

"Yo, it's a pleasure to meet you, big homie. You're like a legend in Miami," he said as he extended his open hand to greet Money. Money looked down at Fly Boogie's hand with a blank expression on his face. He then looked at Carter in disbelief and chuckled.

"Let's get this meeting started," Money said as he totally ignored Fly Boogie as if he wasn't even there.

Zyir looked at Carter and shook his head discreetly. Zyir didn't like the fact that Money dismissed his man, but he opted to stay quiet.

"Okay, this is how it is. We have a sweet connect in Brazil on the coke. He goes by the name of Buttons. We get it catered to us for an extra twenty percent. He brings it over to the port of Miami and we get it fresh off of the boat. We run through about one hundred joints a month," Carter said as he began to slowly walk around the table as he explained the workings of their business.

"I take care of the distribution, and once it gets off the boat, I take it straight to the streets. We have about twenty trap houses around the city, and we work out of them. We have friends down at the police department to keep us in the know on any investigations or random raids. It's pretty simple," Zyir explained as he rubbed his hands together while helping Carter explain.

"That's right. It is very simple. I was thinking you can play the back and let Zyir handle the day to day since we got a smooth operation going on. Maybe try to look for some sources to clean up the money so we can transition, feel me?" Carter said, now looking directly at Money.

"Play the back?" Monroe repeated as he looked at Carter as if he was crazy. He didn't like the sound of Carter's plan. He was ready to jump headfirst into the game and take over all that was lost. The "new" Cartel couldn't hold a candle to what Monroe had left behind. "You only have twenty houses in all of Miami? When did we downgrade to running trap houses, huh? My father started this thing of ours, and it wasn't meant to move fifty bricks a month. We did that in a day!"

"Calm down, homie. We—" Zyir said, trying to ease the building tension that was forming.

"And who the fuck are you?" Monroe asked, interrupting Zyir. He wasn't trying to talk to anyone except his brother. He was tired of beating around the bush. He was the boss and he wanted to make it known.

Immediately Zyir's goons put their hands on their waists, ready to bust. At that point they didn't care who Monroe was. He was disrespecting their boss and they were ready to get busy. All of their eyes were on Zyir, and if Zyir would have given the slightest indication for them to react, Money would have been Swiss cheese.

"Just give me the green light," Fly Boogie whispered to Zyir without moving his lips. Money smirked at Fly Boogie's comment and slid his hand to his waist where his gun rested.

"Everyone calm down!" Carter demanded as Zyir and Money stared at each other tensely, both of them clenching their jaws tightly. Carter continued, "Money, you have been gone a long time. I'm not trying to box you out. I just want you to ease into this. It's not how it was five years ago. Feds are on us, and with all the murders from the last war, it made us hot. We just trying to stay low, get money, and stay off the radar. It's a new day, bruh."

"You sound crazy right now. Instead of having ten cops on payroll, you should pay the chief of police. Everybody has a price! That means you only have to deal with one person rather than ten. Also, why aren't we wholesaling? Who runs trap houses? *We move weight!* Back in my day, little niggas like this couldn't even be in my presence. But now, you bringing them to the table?" Monroe ranted, pointing out every flaw he saw in Carter's system.

Carter, wanting to be diplomatic, kept his cool and knew that he had to take control before it got out of hand. "I need everyone to leave now. Money, let's talk," Carter said as he stepped to the side, giving Zyir and his crew a clear path to the truck they pulled up in. No one moved until Zyir nodded his head and then just like that, they headed to their cars. Zyir followed close behind and stopped just as he walked past Carter.

"You good?" Zyir asked, not knowing whether he should leave Carter alone with Money.

"Yeah, I'm good. I'll call you later," Carter confirmed and put one hand on Zyir's shoulder. Zyir shot a look at Money, and they exchanged menacing stares as he walked away. Carter tapped Monroe on the chest to try to break the tension between the two of them. "Let's talk."

"Seem like there is nothing to talk about. You have everything figured out I see," Monroe said sarcastically and released a small smirk. Carter shook his head at Monroe's answer and put his hands together as he thought about Monroe's viewpoint.

"Listen, I know what it seemed like, but it's the way it's going to be. Just give it a couple of weeks and feel everything out before you jump in," Carter said, trying to be as diplomatic as possible.

"Feel things out? I was moving weight when you were back in Michigan small timing. Remember that, my nigga! But you know what; I'm going to play the back. You right," Monroe said, easing off of his hostility. He knew at that moment that it was a line drawn in the sand, and he understood what side he stood on. He kicked himself for expressing his frustrations and knew that the old him would have never let anyone know what he was thinking. *I am a little rusty I see,* he thought as he looked at Carter, trying to read his mind.

Carter clenched his jaws at Monroe's remark, but didn't show any emotion. If that had been anyone else, Carter would have rocked him to sleep just off of GP. Nevertheless, the calculating boss just released a small smile and put his hand on Monroe's shoulder. "Listen, I meet the connect in a couple days. To show you that I'm not trying to box you out . . . I want to introduce you to him," Carter suggested.

"That's what I'm talking about. Let's get to the money," Money said calmly as he rubbed both of his hands together.

Carter noticed something strange about Monroe. His mannerisms weren't like he remembered. Everything about Monroe reminded Carter of Mecca. Carter chalked it up to guilt playing with his own mind, but he knew Monroe wasn't quite the same as he remembered. It was as if Mecca's soul had flown into Monroe.

Carter quickly shook off the notion and began to break down the logistics to his brother and caught him up on what was going on in the streets. In addition to breaking down the product and flooding the streets, they were heavy in whole-sale. The Cartel was getting all the money from the bottom up, and he hoped that Monroe could see that they had a good thing going. However, in the back of his mind Carter knew it could all go bad if Monroe ever found out that he killed Mecca. Only time would tell how it would unravel, but until then . . .

***

The private jet landed on the airstrip in Brazil. Inside were the pilot, Carter, Monroe, and Zyir. They were landing there to meet their coke connect, Buttons, a tall, fair-skinned Brazilian who specialized in the coke business. Carter had met him a year back while being there for Breeze's wedding.

As the plane doors lifted up Monroe's heart began to rapidly beat. It was something that only a hustler could relate to. The rush and allure of getting to the money was like an adrenaline rush for a street nigga, and Monroe's burning flame for the streets had been dormant for years. It had just been relit. He was ready to put his staple in the game. He was still very young and had the world ahead of him. He looked over at Zyir, who remained quiet the entire flight, and knew that he would eventually be a problem.

The Brazilian setup was beautiful. Gorgeous women with bronze skin were everywhere, and the land itself was stunning. The narrow streets and tall brick buildings had their own personality, and Monroe was amazed as he took in the sight. They all sat in the back of a Jeep that Buttons had sent for them as they maneuvered through the bumpy roads, on their way to Buttons' cocaine sanctum.

"Here it is," Carter said as they approached the massive brick warehouse. The place was surrounded by steel gates, and vicious pit bulls ran freely within them. Monroe looked at the top of the building and saw young gunmen with assault rifles and binoculars. None of the gunmen looked to be a day over eighteen, but all had menacing stares and an eagerness to prove to their boss that they were loyal and worthy to move up in the ranks.

"Buttons is a different type of nigga. Fair warning," Carter said as they approached the gate.

Two armed goons were standing at the gate. When they pulled in, the goons immediately began to look inside the car with AK-47s in their hands. Once they saw that the coast was clear, they waved the driver in. Just like that, they were granted access to the biggest drug distribution and manufacturing business in Brazil. Rio was mostly known for its beautiful women and sexual escapades, yet the black market there was just as lucrative and successful. Just as the sexual fantasies that attracted lusting men, the pure cocaine and cheap prices drove in the drug bosses.

As the Jeep made its way through the property, the men looked at the property and how well it was secured. Buttons had shooters literally everywhere on his property. Monroe instantly knew that they were dealing with a made guy.

They pulled up to the single building that was in the rear of the property. They pulled up to the steel garage door and the driver blew the horn twice. Seconds later the door rose and exposed the factory-like assembly line where the coke was being cut, measured, and packaged for distribution.

Buttons stood at the top tier that overlooked the whole operation. He stood six foot three inches and had the stature of a model. His long, curly hair was pulled back tightly into a ponytail as he slowly paced back and forth, overseeing his operation. He smoked a cigar and took his time as he deeply inhaled, letting the Cuban smoke dance on his lungs. Buttons was the kingpin of Rio and had a long history with the sale of cocaine. He had political connections and was literally untouchable inside of his country. He took a liking to Carter because of his business savvy and consistency.

Carter led the pack as they walked on to the floor and in between the long tables full of coke. Everyone seemed to be focused on their particular job and not on Carter and his crew. Buttons stopped pacing and looked down at Carter.

"Carter! Glad you could make it," he said with open arms and a smile. Buttons made his way down the stairs followed closely by a young Brazilian gunman.

"Buttons. Thanks for having us," Carter said as he walked toward Buttons and shook hands with him. Carter then turned around and looked at Zyir and Money. "Of course, you remember Zyir," Carter said. Buttons nodded his head at Zyir, acknowledging him. Carter turned to Monroe and nodded toward him. "This is my brother, Monroe."

"Monroe. How are you? I am Buttons," he said with a heavy accent.

"I'm good," Monroe said as he stepped forward and extended his hand to Buttons. Buttons shook his hand and was impressed with Monroe's demeanor and fearlessness. While

Zyir usually played the back, Monroe wanted to make his presence known; Buttons sensed this.

The rendezvous was about an hour, and Carter discussed a bigger shipment with Buttons, and Monroe listened closely and analyzed their business relationship. For what Carter was getting them for, Monroe used to get them for half that price when he was over The Cartel. Monroe's mind immediately began to churn, thinking about a master plan. He saw a lot of holes in their operations and wondered why Carter was copping from a Brazilian connect who was obviously taxing him. Little did Monroe know, Estes had retired from the drug game and didn't give his connections to Young Carter. Estes didn't believe in connecting people who weren't blood. So the connects ended when Mecca died. Monroe already began to make plans to return to see Buttons, but the next time Monroe would come alone. He would be coming to sell and not to buy cocaine.

As they wrapped up the meeting with handshakes, Monroe made sure he looked Button in the eyes and said, "I'll see you soon. Very soon." Carter didn't realize it, but he had just introduced Buttons to his competition.

Hours later they were back on the jet, and Carter looked over at Monroe, who seemed to be in deep thought, staring out of the window while resting his index finger on his temple.

"I just brought you to the table. I introduced you to the connect. Hopefully you understand now that I want you to play the back only temporarily," Carter said as he poured himself a glass of cognac, Louis XIII to be exact.

"No doubt. I understand now. Let's get it," Monroe said, but his eyes didn't match his words. He was thinking about how he was about to box both of them out and take over the streets once again. "I am the son of Carter Diamond. Miami is mine," he said as he sat back comfortably and closed his eyes with a small grin.

Zyir watched closely as he remained quiet. He was growing to dislike Monroe more and more by the minute.

Needless to say, when they returned to the States, Monroe turned right back around and headed back to Rio to see Buttons. As Monroe made his way through the airport, he called his grandfather, Estes.

"Papa, I need a favor," Monroe said as soon as he heard his grandfather's voice on the opposite side of the line.

"Anything for you," Estes said in his usual low and raspy voice. It seemed as if Monroe could hear the cigar smoke in his grandfather's lungs as he spoke.

"I need you to make a couple of calls on my behalf. I need my father's old connect. I need you to make that happen pronto," Monroe said as he made his way to his boarding gate.

"Enough said. I was wondering what was taking you so long. I will set up a sit down immediately," Estes said as if it was a cake walk.

"Yeah. It is about that time. I'm not liking what I am seeing. A lot has changed since I was away."

"I agree. I never extended the family's connections because I am a firm believer in keeping the family's name reputable. I couldn't trust those that weren't my blood to uphold that. You understand?" Estes said, dropping game on his only male bloodline.

"Understood. Let's make it happen. I will be back in town in a couple days. Prices are still the same?" he asked.

"Indeed. They never change for customers like us," Estes explained as he alluded to the coke prices that his connections offered. People like Estes had connections that never raised prices, no matter how the market was. At that level of drug dealing, bosses sold for the sport . . . not for the money.

Now that Monroe had convinced Estes to introduce him to his Miami connect, it was the beginning of Monroe's second era. Monroe figured since Carter wanted him to play the backseat, he would just rather take over the whole vehicle. It was Monroe's turn to take back the streets . . . his way. He was about to make Buttons an offer he could not refuse.

Chapter 9

"Let the games begin, gentlemen."

—Monroe

Zyir rode through the city, and in a matter of weeks the streets had dried up. It looked like a ghost town. From Opa-locka to Carol City, all the way to Little Havana, all of his operations were at a standstill and nobody was getting paid.

As he pulled up to Seventieth Street and Fifth Avenue he was more than livid. His most profitable blocks were turning no profit, and this alarmed him. He parked his black S-Class along the curb and checked his surroundings. The notorious hood was known worldwide for its ruthless stick-up kids, and Zyir made sure that he was acutely aware of everything moving around him. He pressed a button on his custom radio console, and a hidden compartment slid out. He grabbed the handgun that lay inside and tucked it in his waistline before exiting the vehicle.

He approached the small project building, and all eyes were on him. Zyir was the smallest nigga on the block, but he had the heart of a lion. Slim in stature, many men had learned the hard way by sizing him up at first glance. Zyir didn't pop his gums, he popped his guns, so anyone he had ever caught beef with usually didn't live to tell about it. He had made an example out of plenty since arriving in Miami, which was why as he approached he was shown nothing but respect. The littered streets were unusually quiet.

"What up, baby?" he greeted Fly Boogie, one of the young'uns who worked as a lookout. Fly Boogie leaned against the graffiti-tagged wall and was the perfect definition of a new school hustler. Fresh Adidas kicks laced his feet. He wore rock-washed skinny jeans that sagged slightly off his hips, and a white wife beater. His snap back hat, nerd glasses, and chain belt accessorized his outfit. At first glance he looked like a skater kid; one would never guess that he was a thorough shooter. His body count was official. He was never afraid of a gun battle, which was why he was the perfect lookout. He would peel a nigga cap back and ask questions later. No one was coming near Zyir's trap spot unless they were already authorized to be there. Fly Boogie made sure of it.

"Ain't shit up 'round here. We dry than a muuu'fucka," Fly Boogie said in his heavy Southern drawl.

Zyir frowned because that was the exact same response he had gotten from each of his spots. Shit had slowed up, and most of his lieutenants were out of product. This was unusual when each of his spots usually blew through five bricks each week, easy. "What happened to the shipment? Shit just came in yesterday? Why that work ain't ready yet?" Zyir questioned.

"Maannn, you gotta ask them niggas," Fly Boogie responded. "You know I'm just the lookout. As long as I don't see them red and blues or no niggas lurking then I'm good. I don't worry too much about that other shit, Zy. I play my position, you feel me?"

Zyir kept his hand near his hip as he hooked his fingers in his belt loop and nodded his head. "Yeah, I feel you, fam. Keep an eye on my whip. If the police roll by here, drive my shit around the block," he instructed as he pulled out a knot of money and peeled off a one hundred dollar bill for the young kid.

"No doubt," Fly Boogie responded as he shook his head and pushed Zyir's hand away. "I got you, fam. It's not necessary. I'm sitting here anyway. It's my job to patrol the block. Your car good, bro. Handle your business," he said.

Zyir liked the kid's style. Most thirsty niggas would have pocketed his money, but Fly Boogie was loyal. He felt honored for a dude of Zyir's stature to even talk to him, let alone trust him with his car.

Zyir tossed him his car key and ascended the steps that led to the second level of the raggedy apartment building. He operated out of every unit on the top floor. There were four in all. One was where the coke was cooked; in the second unit his young'uns stacked the dough; the third served as an artillery closet with every type of automatic weapon in that apartment; and the fourth was a parlay spot for his workers.

He knocked four times on the door in a distinct rhythm, and a small rectangular peephole slid to the side. He was allowed inside immediately upon recognition.

"Hey, Zy!" the ladies called out sweetly as he walked through the apartment, headed toward the back. Ten beautiful stallions stood in high heels and nothing more, cooking up hard for the fiends and bagging powder cocaine for the free base users. There was so much product cooking in the small space that Zyir could smell the distinctive scent in the air. He walked directly toward the back and entered the bedroom, which functioned as a small office.

"Zyir, what's good, baby?" Angel, his head lieutenant, greeted.

"You tell me," Zyir said. "From what I'm hearing nobody's making money. Where's the shipment? I pay you the most because I give you the most responsibility, fam. If you can't handle your position, it's a lot of hungry mu'fuckas under you who would love the opportunity to step up."

Zyir wasn't one to raise his voice, but just from his disposition Angel could tell that his boss wasn't pleased.

"I don't want to have to come all the way to your side of town only to find out that my money is short. Fuck is going on, fam?" Zyir asked.

"The shipment wasn't on deck, and we running off of last month's product. It's only a matter of time before this shit runs out. Plus niggas ain't fucking with us. Some new mu'fuckas set up shop out in Hialeah. They selling the shit for dirt cheap. Niggas is selling bricks for sixteen thousand dollars. That's them 1999 prices, you feel me? I sling these shits for that and we losing money. We can't compete with that. So anybody buying weight is going to these new niggas. We still got the lower level shit on lock, but like I said, we almost out, and if we don't re-up we gon' lose our footing in the streets real quick," Angel explained.

"I'll check on the shipment. I just met with my man, so that should have been right on time. In the meantime run the competition off the blocks. We can't compete with their prices, but they can't compete with our muscle. They can stay, but they got to pay a tax. This real estate belongs to The Cartel, so the niggas got to pay rent if they want to hustle this way. Be diplomatic, and if they buck, then we put our murder game down. I hope it doesn't come to that. In war nobody makes money," Zyir stated. He slapped hands with his man and then made his exit.

Fly Boogie threw up a salute and tossed Zyir his keys as Zyir walked by. Zyir sped off and immediately called Carter. Business with Buttons had always gone according to plan. Their dealings with him were so consistent that there was never room for error. This missed shipment was no mistake, and Zyir couldn't put his finger on it, but something fishy was in the air. He pulled out the burnout phone that he used to contact Buttons. He dialed his number from memory, knowing that the information was too sensitive to ever record.

"The number you have reached is not in service," the operator announced.

Yeah, something is most definitely up, Zyir thought. They had been doing square business with Buttons for too long for things to change now. Zyir immediately thought of their recent trip to Rio. The only factor that had changed in the situation was Monroe. He didn't know exactly what had gone down, but Zyir's hustler's intuition told him that Monroe had fucked up the game for everybody.

Carter sat on the wooden park bench tossing crumbs to the birds as he sat in deep contemplation. His life had come full circle, and it seemed as though all the people he had thought were lost to the game had come back to him. His family felt more complete.

Carter had handed over leadership to Zyir for good reason. The streets had sucked the life out of him. After killing Mecca, Carter knew that the game had pushed him too far and that it was time to step down. He was confident in his successor, but now that Monroe was back it created confusion. Jealousy was in the air, and Carter knew that he would have to play mediator between his blood brother and his brother by circumstance.

"Look at you, big homie, out here in the open. I know retirement don't got you slipping like that. If I wanted to get you—"

"You couldn't," Carter finished as he stood and turned
around to greet Zyir, who had approached him from behind.
He pointed his finger fifty yards ahead of him and then off to
both sides, showing Zyir that he was never left unprotected.
Three of his shooters patrolled the perimeter of the park, eyes
on Carter at all times.

Carter moved like a boss. He knew the position that he
had in the streets. He was like a trophy to thirsty young
wolves. The reputation one could get from taking him out
was enough to make him a target. The only thing that kept
him secure was the respect he had earned over the years.
Many niggas had the courage to take the shot, but very few
had the courage to miss. Hitting Carter was easier said than
done, and should someone try and fail, the repercussions
were deadly.

Zyir smirked and shook his head. "I should have known,"
he said. The two men began to stroll through the park as Zyir
filled Carter in on the situation. "I think we've got a problem
with Buttons."

Carter stopped abruptly and turned toward Zyir attentively.

"The shipment didn't come in. I just left from the trap and
shit is Sahara dry," Zyir stated.

"Did you call Buttons?" Carter asked.

"Line is disconnected. It's like he cut all ties with us after
the meeting with Money. I know that's your bro and all, but
I'm allergic to snakes, if you get my drift," Zyir said seriously.
"We've been doing square business for years, and now when
Money come into the picture the shit turns sour?" Zyir looked
at Carter skeptically. "That sound right to you?"

Out of the corner of his eye he saw Monroe's car pull up.
"Speak of the fucking devil," he mumbled as the aura turned
thick.

"I've got it. Money's official. Buttons and anybody else
that got a problem with him better get comfortable with his
presence real quick. We've got to keep our circle strong, Zyir.
All we've got is the family," Carter said seriously.

Zyir held his tongue. He had serious doubts about Monroe, but he was aware that it was a sensitive subject so he treaded lightly. Monroe approached and slapped hands with Carter.

"What it's laying like, bro?" he asked.

Carter noticed that Monroe never acknowledged Zyir. He glanced at his two brothers, one adopted through life's tests of loyalty and the other blood born. He would have to fix this divide for sure, but decided not to force it. Time would cause the two men to respect each other, or so he thought.

"I'm sending Zy back down to meet with Buttons. We out of product and suddenly he's unreachable," Carter explained.

Money nodded and smirked, knowing that he was the reason why all communication had ceased. As long as Zyir was the leader of The Cartel then the entire Cartel wouldn't eat. Monroe would make sure of it. A position of power like that had to be earned, and Zyir was handed the crown by default. Monroe would burn the entire kingdom to the ground before he allowed Zyir to rule. He definitely didn't want Carter finding out he had undermined him, however.

"You want me to fly over there and make sure everything's smooth?" he asked.

Carter shook his head. "I don't think that's wise. Zyir's more familiar with Buttons. He'll be more comfortable with him. We are easing you back into the swing of things, Money. Trust me, more responsibility will be delegated to you in due time."

Delegated to me? I'm a boss; a nigga ain't delegating shit to me. He want to send his mans to Rio, I'ma make sure he don't come back, Monroe thought angrily. He showed no signs of displeasure outwardly.

"Whatever you say. You're the boss," Monroe stated.

Carter turned to Zyir. "You'll leave in the morning."

Monroe sat in his car, watching as Zyir and Carter pulled off. His distaste for Zyir was growing by the day. Monroe had been away from his family for too long, and he couldn't help but feel as though he had been replaced. Monroe picked up his cell and placed a call.

"*Hola*, Monroe," Buttons answered.

"*Hola*, Buttons. I just called to give you a heads-up. Carter is sending Zyir down to Rio with his goons. He's upset that he's been cut off. They will be there tomorrow. It's in your best interest to annihilate anyone associated with The Cartel if they show up on your doorstep. They are coming to kill you. Make no mistake about it," Monroe said. He knew that if he put Buttons on the defensive, there would be no way Zyir would come back alive.

"I will prepare for their arrival," Buttons said, his voice menacingly cold.

Monroe ended the call and then checked his rearview before pulling away from the park. "Let the games begin, gentlemen."

Carter entered his home and for the first time since he purchased the place it felt lived in. His world had been so cold and lonely that he never appreciated the things that he had attained. The aroma of food filled the air and reminded him that he had neglected to eat. He walked into the kitchen and found Miamor over the stove. He smiled when he saw that she wore nothing but a bra and thong. Her long, shapely legs, juicy behind, and slim waist instantly sent sparks to his loins. The stilettos that graced her French-manicured feet caused him to smile. He stood back and watched her work. She clearly knew her way around a kitchen. He had missed her in his life, and her return made his entire existence complete. He walked up behind her and wrapped his arms around her waist, burying his head in the creases of her shoulder as he inhaled deeply, loving her scent.

"I could have gotten you. You didn't even know I was behind you," Carter whispered as he kissed her neck. Miamor's head fell to the side as she enjoyed the feel of his lips against her skin.

"Hmm. That feels good," she whispered. She turned toward him and kissed his lips, deeply and sensuously. "A nigga will never catch me slipping, Carter Jones. Take a look under that kitchen towel." Miamor slipped out of his embrace and walked over to the cabinet, grabbing two wine glasses.

Carter lifted the towel and saw a small-caliber pistol lying underneath it. He chuckled and thought, *Damn.*

He found her incredibly sexy. The fact that she was so thorough impressed him. He was getting to know this new side of her, and now that there were no secrets between them, he respected it. She was feminine and incredibly sexy, but the little bit of street she had in her drove him wild. She made up the perfect recipe of a woman.

"Now come have a seat and let me feed my man," she said.

"What's for dinner?" he asked as he sat down in the chair that she had pulled out for him. She was treating him like a king.

"Steak and seafood," she replied.

"And for dessert?" he quipped.

"Me," she answered.

Miamor straddled Carter. The only thing that stopped her wet pussy from soaking the crotch of his pants was the tiny fabric of her thong. The sexual chemistry that was between them was supercharged. That was the one part of their relationship that they had always gotten right.

"Or we can have dessert first," she whispered. Carter stood, lifting her as he swept everything off of the table. Dishes and silverware went flying to the floor as he laid her down on top of the expensive marble.

He removed his manhood, and in one Casanova movement he slid her thong to the side. Her wetness warmed him as he slipped inside of her. With one arm wrapped around her arched waist and the other braced against the table he controlled the pace. He stroked her slowly, powerfully, as their bodies move rhythmically.

"I love you," Miamor whispered as he kissed her neck.

His dick penetrated depths of her that she didn't even know existed. Carter's sex game was official. An unselfish lover, he always pleased her first. His touch was gentle, but he moved with authority, making commands of her without ever speaking any words.

His girth made her blossom bloom, and with every dip of his hips she matched his intensity. She grinded upward, throwing her love at him as their bodies became one. Miamor knew that she had the best pussy around. Very few had sampled it, but the ones who had were easily put under her spell. Miamor had that "make a nigga fall in love" pussy. It was inevitable to become trapped in her world, but with Carter Jones she fell just as hard. Like a magnet, she was drawn to him and not Mecca, not life, not death, could pull them apart. It was serendipitous for them to spend eternity loving each other.

Miamor closed her eyes and enjoyed the ride as she felt her orgasm build. She saw blinding white as she came, and the pulsating tool inside her along with the look of fulfillment on Carter's face told her that he had gotten his too.

He pulled out of her and grabbed her hand. "Join me in the shower, ma. I've had a long day. I just want to be around you."

"What about the food?" she asked.

"I'll have the staff wrap everything up. We'll order a pizza or something," Carter said.

It was his simplicity that endeared him to her. He could take her around the world and back. His money was long and his reach wide, but he didn't stunt to impress her. Time with her was enough to make him happy. Whether in a cardboard box or within the massive walls of his five-star mansion, they were satisfied with just the presence of one another.

Miamor followed him to the master bedroom and sat on the edge of the travertine-tiled bathtub as Carter ran the water. Vanilla bubbles and bath salts scented the room, and she lowered herself into the warm water. Carter pulled her close, her back against his chest as they both relaxed.

"I appreciate you cooking for me. In fact, I love that, but right now no one knows you're here. You have to stay low. My family doesn't know that you've returned, and until I figure out how to handle things you have to stay inside. No more grocery runs," Carter said.

"You're right. It won't happen again," she answered. It wasn't what she wanted to say, but she was learning to bite her tongue. She was afraid that if she made one little mistake or displeased Carter in any way, he would dispel her from his life. He knew her well, however, and could tell that she wanted to say more.

"Why do you do that? You didn't used to hold anything back from me," he said.

"I'm just trying to be what you want, Carter," Miamor said. In that moment she felt small, like she was dimming her light in order to help Carter shine, something she thought she would never do for any man.

"I want a woman that speaks her mind, Miamor. Don't tiptoe around me. Respect me, be honest with me, and I will respect you and be honest with you. That's all I want from you. Now what's on your mind?" he said.

"How long do you expect for me to hide? I don't want to feel like a prisoner here," Miamor replied honestly.

"Just give me a little bit of time. I'm dealing with a lot right now," Carter admitted.

She turned around so that she could face him. His face was etched with stress.

"What's wrong?" she asked.

"Monroe and Zyir aren't on the best of terms. They aren't feeling each other. It's hard to choose one brother over another. I've got Zyir meeting with our connect tomorrow, but by selecting him to go I can tell Monroe feels slighted."

"Why don't you just make the trip yourself? That way you're not choosing sides," Miamor suggested.

Carter didn't respond, but he definitely heard what she said. It seemed to be the most diplomatic solution to his problem.

He rose from the water.

"Hey, where are you going?" she asked. "I thought we would go for round two."

Carter leaned over and kissed her lips. "Not tonight. I've got to pack and so do you. Since I can't guarantee that you'll stay put while I'm gone, you'll have to come with me. Tomorrow we're flying to Rio."

Chapter 10

"When in Rome."

—Miamor

The ocean waves washed ashore as Miamor walked through the soft white sand, leaving indents of her feet as she went. She couldn't believe that the beach was so empty. The entire coastline was clear; there wasn't a person in sight. It felt like she had the entire ocean to herself. She lifted her head to the sky and closed her eyes as the sun kissed her cheeks. Rio de Janeiro was a beautiful place, and she hoped that they found time to explore the city. She understood that they were in town so that Carter could handle his business, but certainly they could find time to play before they left. Rio was the sexiest city in the world, and Miamor wanted to fuck her man on the beach, under the stars.

She looked back and saw Carter motioning for her from the second-story balcony. She turned around and headed back to the luxury villa. She entered and found him standing in white linen shorts, a white linen shirt, and a crisp wife beater underneath. He was dapper, and Miamor smiled at how lucky she was. Carter could have any woman in the world. He could certainly have any of the sexy vixens in Rio, but he wanted her.

"I plan to meet Buttons in the morning," Carter said.

"Why not tonight?" she asked.

"Because tonight is ours," he replied. "There's no way you would ever let me live it down if I flew you in and out of Rio without letting you explore your way around."

She laughed and kissed his lips because she loved that he knew her so well.

"Well, we're in Rio and tonight I want to dance," she exclaimed.

"I don't dance, ma." Carter chuckled. "And since when do you dance, gangster?" he asked mockingly, never figuring Miamor to be the type to indulge in Latin dance.

"When in Rome, right?" she asked with a laugh.

Carter and Miamor rode through the city streets presidential style as their driver escorted them to the hottest nightclub in Rio. The streets were definitely alive as the attractive people came out to play. They could see the line to the club from a block away as it looped around the building. The club was more like a hole in the wall, but it was the place to be on a Saturday night. Carter looked out the window and frowned. "You sure this is the place?" he asked the driver.

"Sí, sí," the driver replied.

"It looks like a fucking dive," he said.

"Lighten up, Carter Jones. Tonight we welcome the unexpected," she whispered.

Carter put his pistol in his waist and Miamor put a small .22 in her clutch before exiting the car. They walked straight up to the entrance, and Carter tipped the bouncer generously to be let directly into the club.

As soon as they stepped inside, Carter realized why it was so popular. The vibe was sensual, seductive, and the dance floor was packed full of people dancing to Latin music. The club glowed red, casting an illuminating hue all over the room. Everyone in the club seemed to be the most beautiful people either of them had ever seen. Carter found his eye wandering as they made their way through the crowd. The thick shapes of the Rio women enticed Carter, and the fact that they were scantily dressed left nothing to his imagination.

Miamor laughed and said, "See, I told you that you would have a good time."

They found a table and a waitress brought them a round of drinks. "*Hola, Americanos,*" she greeted with a smile.

Every waitress in the place served in boy shorts and bra, but the one who served them made the uniformed look seem erotic. Her breasts popped out of the bra, sitting perky and high, and her flat stomach was flawless. Her wide hips were accompanied by a beautiful behind.

"My name is Lucy and I'll be serving you tonight. This first round of tequila is on the house. Let me know if I can get you anything else," she said. Her accent was exotic and her dark hair gave her a mysterious look.

"You need to loosen up!" Miamor shouted over the music. "Drink up!"

Carter and Miamor hit a shot of tequila, and then Carter ordered cognac as Miamor indulged in her cocktail.

"You want to try it?" she asked, nodding at the dance floor.

"Nah, ma, you know my movements don't change much. I don't do the two-stepping thing. Go ahead though. I'll enjoy the view," he said as he leaned into her ear.

As Lucy placed their third round of drinks on the table, she smiled and asked, "You guys aren't going to dance?"

Carter shook his head.

"You have to, *papi!* Do you know how many American men run away down here just to visit this very club?" Lucy exclaimed as she stood with her hand on her hip.

"I'll pass, ma," he said with a smile.

"I guess that's easy for you to do with a girlfriend like this," Lucy said as she winked at Miamor. "How about you? You no dance?"

Miamor shrugged and Lucy shook her head. "Oh no! *Mamacita,* you are too pretty to be a wall flower," she said.

Lucy grabbed Miamor's hand and pulled her to her feet. "Can I borrow her?" Lucy asked. "Please, *papi!* I promise I will bring her back in one piece."

Carter waved his hand and sat in the cut as he watched Miamor be pulled onto the dance floor with Lucy as her partner.

"What do I do?" Miamor asked.

"You let me seduce you, *mami.* Just relax and have a good time. The little pill I put in your drinks will have you rolling in no time," Lucy whispered in her ear.

Miamor's mind numbed as Lucy circled her like a predator. Her nipples hardened, and Lucy pulled her close. Her breath caught in her throat as Lucy's hands roamed all over Miamor's body, leaving a tingle every place that she touched.

"You're a very pretty girl. He is lucky to have you," Lucy whispered in her ear as she planted a wet kiss on her neck.

Miamor's mind spun and everything felt good. Her entire body tingled, ached, begged to be touched. She had never popped Ecstasy before, but now that it had been slipped to her, she enjoyed the ride. "Did you give him some?" Miamor asked as she glanced over at her man.

"I did, *mami,* and I usually don't partake in the club's activities, but as soon as you two sat down in my section I knew that I wanted to suck the sweetness out of your pussy while you suck on his black dick," Lucy whispered.

Miamor's eyes popped open, and it was then that she realized that she had even closed them. Lucy's words made her panties wet, and she moaned helplessly. She had never been so horny in her life.

"I bet his dick is big, eh?" Lucy asked. "Tell me it's big, *mami.*"

"It's big." Miamor panted as Lucy grinded on her to the slow beat of the music. Her hands were planted on Miamor's hips as she aligned their pussies, grinding and winding slowly.

"I want to suck that black dick. Can I suck his dick, mama?" the Latina asked.

Under normal circumstances Miamor would have cut the girl's tongue out of her mouth, but Miamor was in the moment. The overwhelming desire that she felt made her consider sharing Carter with the voluptuous South American vixen. It was every man's fantasy to bring another woman into his bed with wifey, and Miamor smirked as she thought, *That just might happen tonight.*

Carter leaned back in the booth and felt his dick jump as he watched Miamor dance with Lucy. Undoubtedly they were the two most beautiful women in the club, and the steamy session they were having on the dance floor had Carter on brick. He ordered a cigar, and a pure Cuban was brought out for him. He clipped the end and held it up to the flame that a waitress held for him. All the while his eyes never left the show Miamor was putting on for him.

Their eyes locked, and Carter exhaled a mouthful of smoke. He nodded for her to return to the table, and Miamor obliged, bringing Lucy back with her.

"That was quite a performance, ma," Carter said as he licked his lips. The way he did it told Miamor that he wanted to lick another set of lips as well, and she smiled.

"Why don't we head back," she said.

Carter stood to his feet and Miamor added, "All three of us."

Momentarily thrown off kilter, Carter paused. He didn't know if this was a trick or if he had heard her wrong.

"When in Rome, right?" she asked again with a mischievous smile. Carter loved the spontaneity of it all. He would have never asked her for a threesome, but he for damn sure wasn't going to turn one down at her suggestion.

Carter grabbed Miamor's hand, and Miamor grabbed Lucy's hand as they left the club and entered their awaiting car.

"Back to the villa," Carter instructed as he rolled up the window that separated them from the curious eyes of the driver.

As soon as their privacy was official, Miamor lowered her head into Carter's lap, releasing his already hard penis.

"Oooh, *papi!*" Lucy moaned as she admired his size. Carter sat back in the seat as Miamor pushed Lucy's head down onto Carter's dick. Carter gasped as Lucy's mouth took him in.

"Oh shit," he whispered as she went to work.

Miamor kissed his lips and whispered in his ear, "This is going to be the best night of your life."

He gripped the back of her head, intensifying their kiss as he clenched his ass and fucked Lucy's mouth at the same time. Her head game was out of this world as she topped him off, licking and sucking his dick.

"Scoot down, *papi*," she whispered as she pulled him off the edge of the seat. There was something about the way she called him *papi* that made Carter want to cum in her mouth, and when he felt her tongue dip in his ass he moaned out loud.

"You like that, baby?" Miamor whispered. Miamor lowered her head and went south on her man as she sucked his dick while Lucy licked his ass. Carter felt as if he would explode at any moment. He placed his hand on the back of Miamor's head and sucked his teeth.

"Psss, damn, ma. Suck that shit," he groaned. Carter had hit a lot of women in his day, but he had never had a session this good. He had no idea that it was the E taking him to new heights.

The nut that built up inside of him finally erupted, and Miamor locked eyes with him as she swallowed every drop. She and Lucy arose as the car stopped moving.

"Let's take this inside. I'm not done with you yet," Miamor said. He had never seen her so uninhibited, and he liked it.

The threesome adjusted their clothing and then rushed into the villa. The women couldn't keep their hands off of Carter as they fumbled to get him out of his clothes. Carter kissed Miamor passionately and pulled back suddenly. "You got any condoms?"

Miamor shook her head because they didn't use them with one another, but she wasn't so high as to let another bitch sample her dick without protection.

"I have them," Lucy whispered as she removed a Magnum from her purse. She ripped it open and slid it onto Carter's dick. It was hard, as if the first nut had never even happened. The softness of her hands made him close his eyes as Lucy began to stroke his dick gently.

Carter turned Miamor around and pulled his hardness away from Lucy. He slid into Miamor from behind, standing in the middle of the room, and gripped her hips so that she had nowhere to run.

Lucy loved the sight and couldn't feel left out for long. She got on her knees in front of Miamor and parted the petals of her delicate flower.

"Oh my goodness!" Miamor yelled in pleasure when she felt Lucy's mouth on her clit. The dick Carter was serving from behind and the ecstasy that Lucy provided in front threw Miamor into a frenzy. Her body shook, having earthquakes of pleasure as the pair pleased her. She scared herself because she loved this threesome so much she knew that she would definitely try it again, and next time it wouldn't be only for Carter.

Lucy folded her lips over her teeth and bit down on Miamor's clit, feasting on the juicy piece of flesh until Miamor could no longer take it.

"Eat it! Please, keep going, Lucy. Oh shit, Carter! Oh, Carter!" Miamor screamed.

"Cum for me, ma . . . let her taste it," Carter whispered. His deep baritone in her ear pushed Miamor off the cliff, and she enjoyed the free fall as she dove into a sea of orgasms. Her eyes rolled in the back of her head, and Lucy backed up as Carter bent Miamor over onto the arm of the couch.

He stroked her deep and at a rapid pace until finally he exploded.

The threesome fucked all over the villa, going round after round. Miamor fucked Carter, Carter fucked Lucy, Lucy fucked Miamor, and every other combination possible. They all lowered their inhibitions for the sake of animalistic desires. They simply wanted to please and be pleased for the night. Finally exhaustion plagued them, and Lucy fell asleep in the couple's bed as Miamor and Carter lay in each other's arms.

"Did we really just do that?" Miamor asked with a laugh.

Carter nodded as he turned toward her and brushed the hair from her face. "Do you regret it?" he asked.

Miamor shook her head. "No, as long as you enjoyed it as much as I did, then I don't regret any of it. You're my man and my king. Every king deserves to have a concubine every once in a while." Miamor winked at him and reached up to kiss his lips. "I'll do anything for you, Carter. For forgiving me and taking me back into your life, I will do all that I can to make you happy."

"You don't have to do anything, Miamor. This was good, but this isn't you, ma. Don't get me wrong—I enjoyed it. I more than enjoyed it, but you don't have to do anything extra. Just by ringing my doorbell on a rainy night you made the rest of my life a happy one. Now get some sleep," Carter said. He kissed her forehead and closed his eyes, positive that at the moment there wasn't a man on earth in a better position than he.

Chapter 11

"I guess he wasn't the good twin after all."
—Miamor

Carter leaned over and kissed Miamor's forehead and then took one last look at the lovely Lucy as they both slept peacefully, legs intertwined sexily with each other. Carter shook his head as he recalled the steamy sex session from the previous night. He tapped Lucy's thigh, stirring her from her slumber.

"Hmm . . . Morning, *papi*," she whispered as she reluctantly rolled over to face him.

Down boy, he thought as his dick jumped from the way she addressed him. He smirked and she crawled on all fours. "You like it when I call you *papi?*" she asked seductively.

"Time to get dressed, ma. Playtime's over," he said. "And be careful not to wake her." He motioned toward Miamor as Lucy nodded in compliance.

He walked out of the bedroom, giving Lucy some privacy. He walked to the spare bedroom and opened the closet. It looked like a military arsenal inside. He removed two handguns and put them into his shoulder holsters. He placed one in his waistline. He didn't anticipate a problem with Buttons. They had done business amicably for too long for anything to go wrong, but he never went anywhere without his strap. It was just another accessory for him.

He wrote a note for Miamor and placed it on the kitchen counter.

"Hmm-hmm."

Lucy cleared her throat behind him and he turned around to face her. He pulled his Armani leather wallet out of his pocket and removed a card.

"Last night was good, *papi*. Anytime you and your girlfriend are in Rio, please look me up. I'd love to see both of you again," she whispered as she stood close to him, so close that he smelled the peppermint on her breath.

Carter handed her the card. "You call that number and my man will take care of you. Five thousand dollars for the night."

Lucy's eyes widened in surprise. "I'm not a hooker."

"I never implied that, sweetheart, but those tips you're getting at the club can't possibly take you very far. Accept the money on behalf of me and my lady. For the good time you showed us last night," he replied.

"Wow, *papi*," she replied. "That girl in there really is lucky. I hope she knows."

"Nah, I'm the lucky one," Carter answered. He extended his arm for her to walk out in front of him, and they headed for the door.

His driver was standing attentively out front. "My driver will take you anywhere you need to go," Carter said.

Lucy smiled and bid farewell to Carter as he watched her get into the car. He waited until it pulled away before he signaled for one of the local cabbies who sat along the street.

Carter's mind immediately shifted to business as he entered the shabby vehicle. He gave directions to Buttons' home as he sat low while the speed of the cab caused the streets to fly by in a blur.

As the cab drew closer to Buttons' private estate, the cab driver spoke up. "I didn't even know this road existed until a few weeks ago, and now this is the second time I've come here. You Americans must know something we don't," he said.

Carter frowned as he sat up in his seat. No one knew of Buttons' whereabouts except for The Cartel. This spot practically didn't exist, so the fact that the cabbie had been there before alarmed Carter.

"You say you've been here before? Recently?" he asked.

Carter could see Buttons' home in the near distance as the cab hobbled down the extremely bumpy, underdeveloped road.

"Yeah, another American came here a while back. A bigshot from Miami. He tipped me a pretty penny. Isn't that what you Americans say?"

Carter reached in his holster and removed a pistol as he cocked it, suddenly feeling as though he had eyes on him. He looked around him, feeling threatened.

"Yo, my man. Do you remember the man's name that you drove out here?" Carter asked.

"Oh *sí*, senor! He was the money man! Money was his name," the cab driver stated.

As soon as the words filled the air, bullets filled the car. The rear windshield shattered as bullets flew, causing glass to rain down over him.

"Fuck!" Carter yelled out as he ducked in the back seat. "Drive!"

The cab driver didn't move as Carter pointed his gun out of the back of the car and fired.

BANG! BANG! BANG!

A van of three gunmen had pulled up behind him. His 9 mms were no match for the rapid blasts of the AK-47s of Buttons' goons. He was a sitting duck.

He turned to encourage the driver to go, but quickly discovered that the man was slumped over the steering wheel. Carter busted back, using his marksman aim, but the way the car was being Swiss cheesed, he knew that it wouldn't be long before one of the bullets would deliver his end.

Sweat covered his brow as he threw his gun in frustration after emptying the clip.

TAT! TAT! TAT! TAT! TAT! TAT!

He removed another pistol and let it spit as he pushed open the back door of the cab. As soon as he crawled out, a biting burn penetrated his left shoulder.

"Agh!" he shouted as the blast sent him flying backward, flooring him. He lay perfectly still as blood flooded from the wound in his shoulder. He bit his inner jaw as pain seared through him, but he lay still.

The firing stopped as the men spoke in Spanish. One of them approached, and Carter heard the footsteps crunching against the dirt as they drew near. His finger was already wrapped around the trigger of his gun as he lay with his eyes closed.

The other two goons stayed back as their comrade went to check Carter's status. The goon stood over him, seeing the blood that now covered Carter's entire shirt. Carter held his breath, not wanting to give away the fact that he was alive.

"He's dead!" the goon called out.

Carter prayed that Buttons' men weren't as thorough as his own. Zyir or any of his other goons would have put a bullet in his head just for good measure, just to make sure that the job was done. Luckily for him, this did not happen.

"Let's get out of here!" he heard one of them call out as the goon standing over him rushed back to the escape van. Carter waited until he heard the van pull away before he rolled over onto his side.

Groaning and in extreme pain, he heaved as he leaned against the cab. He was soaked in his own blood and feared the worst. He struggled to his feet and then pulled open the driver's door.

"Arghh!" he roared as the pain in his shoulder vibrated throughout his entire body. He pulled the driver out and left his dead body in the dirt as he got into the bullet-riddled car, skirting off at full speed as he raced back to Miamor.

Miamor slowly came out of the sex- and drug-induced fog as she opened her eyes. The bed was empty and the room bright as the sun blared through the open windows. She could smell the salty ocean coming in with the breeze and she sat up, groggily, as she meandered to her feet.

"Carter!" she called as she walked out of the bedroom. She half expected to find him sexing Lucy on the living room balcony. *I'd kill him,* she thought with a laugh, shaking her head because she knew that her jealousy over her man would rear its ugly head sooner or later. She found the entire villa empty and then went into the kitchen. Her mouth was extremely dry and as she opened the refrigerator she finally noticed the note that Carter had left. It was placed underneath a 45 mm pistol. She smiled as she moved the gun and picked up the letter.

Gone to handle business. Be back shortly. I love you.

–C

Miamor crumbled the note in her hand and poured herself a glass of orange juice before retreating to the bathroom. Suddenly she felt hot and her mouth watered as vomit tickled the back of her throat. She lunged for the toilet and buried her head inside as she keeled over, her insides erupting. *What the fuck is wrong with me? What did Lucy give me last night?* she thought as her stomach clenched and she vomited again. Miamor breathed heavily as she closed her eyes and stood.

She leaned over the sink to rinse out her mouth, then headed for the shower. She turned on the water and tested it, placing her hands underneath the stream before she stepped inside. The rain showerhead was soothing as she closed her eyes and enjoyed the tiny beads of water that massaged her entire body as they fell upon her.

Her body felt alive after last night's rendezvous, and she shook her head as she opened her mouth, inviting the water to rinse away her sins. When Miamor opened her eyes, a shadow danced on the door of the bathroom, followed by a creak of the hardwood floor. She swiped her hand across her face and looked again, but nothing was there except for the blowing sheer curtain that covered the window.

Miamor's heart thumped rapidly inside of her chest. She had lived years of this paranoia, watching over her shoulder, thinking everyone was out to get her. She saw ghosts when no one was there, but in her years of being in the game she learned one thing: to always follow her gut.

Miamor slid out of the back of the shower curtain but left the water running as she hid behind the door. She knew that it couldn't be Carter. He knew her checkered past. He would have announced himself before sneaking up on her.

She winced when she thought about the gun that she had left lying on the kitchen counter. She would have to do this the hard way. She picked up the porcelain cover to the toilet and waited behind the door. She felt foolish after a minute passed and nothing happened.

Am I tripping? she thought.

When she heard the door creak open, she knew that she was on point. A masked man entered the bathroom quietly, moving with the stealth of a clumsy-ass giant. If he thought he would catch her slipping, he had another think coming. Compared to her murder game, this goon was an amateur, or at least he moved like one.

Miamor knew that he had an advantage over her because he was armed and twice her size. She waited, and just as he reached for the shower curtain she charged him. She lifted the heavy top over her head.

"Agh!" she yelled from her gut as she brought it crashing down over his head. She lifted her foot and kicked him in his back, sending his him flying into the bathtub. He fell clumsily inside as the gun fell from his hand. Miamor had no time to reach for it as the man fumbled out of the tub. She saw his hand wrap around the gun, and she closed the shower curtain, blocking his view as she darted for the window.

BANG! BANG! BANG!

She dove headfirst out of the window as the glass tore through her skin and she fell fifteen feet to the sandy beach below. She hit the ground hard, knocking the wind from her lungs. She staggered to her feet as she looked around, her vision slightly blurry from hitting her head.

Shaking the stars from her eyes, she gripped the side of the house as she ran up the back stairs that led directly to the kitchen. She raced to the gun that lay on the counter and gritted her teeth as she saw red. She cocked the pistol, and just as she stepped toward the bathroom, the goon came stumbling out. She aimed.

BOOM! BOOM!

She hit him with two shots—one in the head and one in the heart. He dropped to his knees then landed face first into the hardwood floor.

"Bitch-ass nigga," she mumbled as she stepped over his dead body and went into the bedroom. She quickly threw on her clothes from the night before. She moved as fast as she could until Carter's voice boomed through the villa.

"Miamor!" he yelled.

She rushed out to him. "Carter!" she gasped when she saw that he was bloody. She covered the room in a flash as he gripped his shoulder in agony.

"I'm fine!" he shouted urgently. "We've got to get out of here now. Grab the passports. Get a gun and let's go."

Miamor took instruction well and didn't freeze under pressure. She sprang into action, gathering their belongings and two handguns. She also grabbed anything that looked as if it could help her stop Carter's bleeding before they exited the villa. Carter's driver opened the door in alarm.

"To the airstrip as quickly as possible," Carter instructed.

Zyir sat at the kitchen table as he watched Breeze cook.

"I love the way you move, ma," he said as she turned toward him. He smiled, causing her to blush.

"Oh yeah?" she asked as she sashayed over to her husband. "I love that you love it," she responded. He opened his legs and pulled Breeze into his space as she bent to kiss his lips. His hands slid up her dress.

DING! DONG!

The doorbell rang and he groaned, knowing that whoever had visited had interrupted their flow.

"You expecting anyone?"

Breeze shook her head and removed her apron as she went toward the front entrance. "It's probably Leena. I haven't heard from her much since she moved out, but some of her stuff is still here. Maybe she's coming to pick it up," Breeze said.

"Tell Leena to call first next time!" Zyir said with a wink.

Breeze chuckled as she pulled open the door.

"Money!" she exclaimed. She opened her arms for a hug. "Hey! What's up?"

Money smiled at the sight of Breeze. He truly loved and worshipped the ground that his sister walked on. Ever since they were children he had always protected her. Now she stood, the image of beauty in front of his face. She reminded him so much of their mother that it was uncanny.

He had gotten the call from Buttons that the execution was a success, so he was coming over to be with his sister. He knew that she would take the news hard when the phone call of Zyir's death came in. He expected it at any moment.

"You gonna leave me out here on your doorstep?" he asked playfully, holding out his hands as he looked around.

"No, of course not. Come in. Me and Zy were just about to sit down to eat. You want to stay for dinner?" she asked.

"Zy?" Monroe questioned, confused. "I thought Zyir was in Rio."

Zyir suddenly walked into the room. "Change of plans. Carter went in my place," Zyir stated.

Monroe's face drained of all color as his eyes widened in alarm.

"Why didn't anyone tell me?" he asked.

Zyir frowned and noticed that Monroe appeared worried. "Why would anyone need to tell you?" he asked.

"I've got to get out of here. I forgot I've got a late meeting," Monroe stammered as he backed out of the house.

"A meeting? At nine o'clock at night?" Zyir grilled.

Monroe shifted uncomfortably in his stance, feeling transparent as if Zyir could see the guilt resting on his shoulders. "You a'ight?" Zyir asked as he stepped to Monroe suspiciously, placing one hand on Monroe's shoulder.

Monroe shrugged Zyir's hand off and stared him in the eyes. Breeze watched the tense moment in confusion. Neither Zyir nor Monroe broke the hard stare.

"Zyir," Breeze called his name. "Monroe!" Breeze shouted once she saw that there was an obvious beef between the two men she loved. "What is going on? What are you two not telling me? What is wrong?" she demanded as she looked back and forth between them.

Zyir stepped back, allowing his wife to separate him from Monroe. "Nothing's wrong, baby girl. Right, Monroe? Everything's good in our camp? No snake niggas calling plays or no shit like that? Monroe Diamond." His voice was accusatory and his glare no nonsense as he stood his ground, his hands folded in front of him as he emphasized each word with a head nod in Monroe's direction.

The way Zyir stared at him made Monroe's temper flare and his conscience as well. He was eager to get out of the house and make a call to Buttons. He had unknowingly given the green light for Carter, his flesh and blood, to be murdered.

"Everything's good, Breeze," Monroe said. He leaned in and kissed his sister's cheek and then walked off, obviously stressed.

Breeze stood back and folded her arms as she cocked her neck to the side. "What was that?" she asked.

"Leave it alone," Zyir snapped as he stormed off, retreating to his study.

Carter was silent as Miamor nursed his wound as best she could. They were thirty thousand feet in the air and she was far from a doctor, but she managed to slow down his bleeding.

"Does it hurt?" she asked sympathetically.

"I'll be fine, ma. Don't worry yourself. I just need to get back to Miami as soon as possible," Carter said as his thoughts drifted to his disloyal brother.

"Who did this?" Miamor asked.

"Monroe," Carter replied.

Miamor saw Mecca's face flash before her eyes. "I guess he wasn't the good twin after all," she whispered. She kissed his cheek and took her seat as Carter grunted an inaudible response.

After taking Mecca's life, he knew that taking Monroe's was not something that he wanted to do.

"It's time to settle all scores," Carter said as he grabbed Miamor's hand. "Yours as well. I'm calling a meeting and we are going to settle this once and for all. I'm tired of the treachery tearing this family apart."

"So you're going to forgive him?" Miamor asked.

"Didn't I forgive you?" he responded.

Chapter 12

"Today we are each other's judge,
jury, and executioner."

—Carter

Miamor sat at the table terrified as the eyes of the Diamond family burned holes through her. Never in her life had she felt so persecuted. It was if she had a scarlet letter burnt into her forehead. The family was divided, and she knew that she was a big part of the turmoil, if not the cause itself. She felt naked, like a deer in hunting season, as she sat next to Carter. A 9 mm would have put her mind at ease, but she had promised Carter that she would give up that lifestyle. She had to play the role of wifey and as such, she had to allow him to be her protector. Old habits died hard, however, and Miamor's trigger finger twitched against the table as she kept a stone face while staring straight ahead.

Carter placed his hand on her thigh beneath the table and gave it a gentle squeeze, reassuring her that she was safe. As long as she was sitting next to him, no one dared to harm her, but it didn't put her mind at ease. Considering that Monroe had sent goons at Carter in Rio, it let her know that he wouldn't even blink at the thought of killing her. She inhaled deeply as Carter stood. His arm was bandaged and in a sling; his anger was etched in a grimace on his handsome face.

"Our empire is in jeopardy. We've faced a lot of adversaries over the years—the Haitians, the drug cartel out of Mexico—and we're still here. We're still standing, but we won't be for long if we don't air out our grievances. There is nothing worse than a snake in the grass. Deceit within our own organization is the only thing that will make The Cartel fall. We each have our own sins that we have committed over the years. The game doesn't allow you to make it this far without having some regrets. Those secrets are our greatest threat. We have to keep The Cartel strong or the little niggas lurking and preying will tear us apart. If there is one crack, one weak link, the entire team will fall," Carter said as he walked around the table, addressing his loved ones.

"I have built a power circle. Everyone at this table is family. I trust each one of you with my life. So in turn, you should trust each other with your lives. There can be no treachery among us, so today we are going to air everything out. We're going to lay all of our sins on the table. Today we are each other's judge, jury, and executioner," Carter spoke seriously.

Silver platters lay in front of each person and were covered with a silver top. It appeared as though the table was set for a feast, and Carter nodded his head toward the display. "Lift the tops," he instructed.

Miamor lifted the top that lay in front of her, and her breath caught in her throat when she saw the pistol lying in front of her. Instinctively she reached on top of the table and checked the clip. It was full. Carter smirked, somewhat attracted as he watched her put one in the head and click off the safety before placing it back on the table.

"What is this, Carter? What's going on?" Breeze asked as she looked around the table in confusion.

"Breeze, in order to trust one another, we have to admit the things that we've done. Let the person without sin cast the first stone," Carter said.

"Or bullet," Zyir added as he stood to his feet. "I'm thorough. Admission of our sins, right?" he asked rhetorically. "I'll go first. This has been on my chest for a long time." He looked down at Breeze and she smiled at him reassuringly, confident that no matter what came out of his mouth she would still love him. Zyir was like the sun to Breeze. Her world revolved around him. She gave him a wink, and Zyir turned to his captive audience and spoke. "The day that Breeze was kidnapped was my fault. I got caught slipping. Carter told me to look after her, and instead of protecting her I . . . entertained her. We entertained each other. I was distracted and we were about to have sex when she was taken."

Monroe's jaw clenched as he stared at Zyir and watched his beautiful sister stand up by her man's side. The sight made his stomach turn. Their father would have rolled over in his grave if he knew Breeze was dating a man like Zyir. Big Carter always wanted the best for his children, and Zyir wasn't it.

"I don't blame him for what happened to me, so for any of you to would be wrong. We were young. We moved sloppy, but I'm here and I'm breathing and Ma'tee is dead," Breeze said, defending Zyir with conviction. "Those are skeletons that I buried a long time ago. That experience made me stronger. Nobody was to blame except for Ma'tee and the bitches that helped him take me . . ."

"And me," Miamor spoke up. Her voice shook as she stood to her feet. Her eyes filled with tears as she looked around the room. Her bottom lip quivered as she reached for the gun. "What I'm about to tell you will not be easy to swallow, and I've never let bullets fly my way without busting back, so you can either take what I'm about to say peacefully or this can get very ugly."

She looked unsurely at Carter, and he nodded his head for her to continue. The more she exposed her true self, the more infatuated with her he became. She was a gangster. Her only fault was that she had been commissioned by his enemy to take down his family. That he could forgive, because now she was by his side and the way she moved he knew that if needed she would be an asset. He hoped she never had to come off the bench, but if she had to, she could and would. That alone endeared her to Carter. As his eyes scanned the room, he realized that he would let no judgment come her way. If he could look past her flaws, everyone else would have to as well.

She looked at Breeze sincerely and took a deep breath. "The women who helped snatch you the night you were kidnapped were my friends. We were a part of a group called The Murder Mamas. Ma'tee paid us to kill the leaders of The Cartel," she said.

As soon as the words left her mouth, she had two weapons aimed directly at her. Zyir and Monroe both held their positions, standing, arms extended, guns ready to pop off in her direction.

Miamor had anticipated their anger, and her own gun was pointed back at them, going back and forth between Monroe and Zyir.

"Let her finish," Breeze said as she stood to her feet, pressing her hands firmly against the table as she stared across at Miamor. "I want to know why!"

Miamor swallowed the lump in her throat as she continued. "Because he paid us to. I wasn't there that night, but I did know that they were determined to get to The Cartel. By that time I had already fallen in love with your brother. I told them I was out, but they took it upon themselves to still work with Ma'tee."

"You've got this bitch around us like she's family after what she did?" Zyir asked as he looked at Carter.

"Lower your pistols," Carter said.

"Let her finish. That's not all, is it? There's more to the fucking story, right, ma?" Monroe asked. "You were hired to take out our family, ruin The Cartel. I've heard about The Murder Mamas, so I know that you didn't fail. So who else did you get at? Which one of my family members is in a shallow grave because of you?" Monroe grilled.

"It's more complicated than that. I didn't just point and shoot your family. Your brother Mecca. We tried to set him up. He sniffed us out and killed my sister in a hotel. After that it became personal. I got caught up in a game with him. I wanted him dead. I hated him for taking her away from me. So I gunned for his head, but I never got the opportunity to catch him until I saw him at the memorial that was thrown for Breeze when you all thought she was dead. I was a guest of Carter's, and he slipped me a drink that I gave to your mother. Mecca tried to poison me, but ended up watching his own mother drink what was intended for me," she admitted. Tears of regret flowed down her face. "Your mother was the only innocent life I have ever taken."

Breeze picked up her gun as Monroe pulled back the hammer of his.

"Lower your pistols," Carter said, trying to intervene.

"We can't just shoot her," Leena said as she stood to her feet, holding her son in her arms. "Monroe, our son is here!" she protested as she looked around the room in distress. "Carter, stop this. Do something!"

Carter came off his hip with a chrome .45 automatic. "I said lower your fucking guns," Carter shouted angrily. "If

you judge her, you judge yourselves. You judge me! Hold up
a mirror and think about the things that you've done. What
betrayal have you brought to the table? What about Leena,
Money? Huh? You fucked Mecca's bitch. He was your brother
and he loved her! He loved her so much that he shot you
over her! That entire situation started a war between us and
Ma'tee! A war that almost crippled us! And what about that
play you just put down in Rio?"

Carter's tone lowered as he stared intently at Monroe. He
saw a glint of recognition in Monroe's eyes, and that was all
it took to confirm that Monroe had plotted against his own
team. He stepped so close to Monroe that he was whispering
in his ear. What he was about to say no one else in the room
needed to hear. "Fuck was you thinking?" he grilled through
clenched teeth, unable to contain his anger. He kept it moving,
but both men knew that it was a conversation that they would
have soon.

"Zy! What about you? You want to add up bodies? Huh? I
know what your murder count look like, fam! Even I'm not
without guilt. I killed our brother. I shot Mecca while he was
praying at an altar for forgiveness."

Carter's emotion was written all over his tortured face as
he advocated for Miamor, and upon his confession Monroe
broke down as well. He turned his gun on Carter, forgetting
all about Miamor. Breeze and Zyir dropped their weapons.

"He was my brother!" Monroe shouted.

"And you were mine!" Carter yelled back. "I thought he
killed you! I thought he went against the family. If he could
draw on you and lie about it, I knew that he would eventually
betray me. I made a choice! In your honor, Monroe! I took
a life! For my brother! The same way she took lives for her
sister! The same way you are ready to take my life for Mecca!
Forgiveness, brother," Carter said, heaving from the adrenaline that was racing through him. "That is what we are here
for. This is the only family we have left. Let's solidify it. Let's
expand."

Miamor stood, holding her belly as she thought of the child
that grew inside of her. She was carrying Carter's seed, and as
long as it had a small part of him, she knew that it would be
special. Carter was the greatest man she had ever met, and as
she looked at him she felt pride in being his woman.

As Miamor admired Carter, Breeze studied her. She saw the undeniable connection that Miamor had with her brother. There was a glow about her that Breeze recognized.

"You're pregnant," Breeze whispered, her own tears building in her eyes.

Miamor's neck snapped to the right to look at Breeze, and Carter looked down at Miamor in shock. Miamor had not even told him yet and somehow Breeze knew. Miamor nodded her head as the gun she now held at her side slipped from her fingers and clattered loudly as it hit the floor. "I am," she admitted emotionally as she held up her hands. "And now I'm defenseless. No gun, no weapons, no motives. You can kill me now if you want, but I want you to know that I am so sorry for the role I played in harming your family. I can't take it back, but it is one of my life's biggest regrets. I love your brother, Breeze. I love him with every part of me and I want this baby . . . this life with him. I hurt you and your family, but I would want nothing more than to be a part of it now."

Breeze stared Miamor in the eyes and wished that they had met under different circumstances. "I'm sorry for the things that Mecca did to hurt you. I can still see the loss in your eyes. I know how that feels. We all know how that feels. You are carrying my bloodline inside of you. No one at this table will do harm to you, Miamor. It's time to let bygones be bygones," Breeze said. She took her seat at the table and slid her gun to the center of the table, out of arm's reach.

"There's been enough loss in this family," Zyir said.

"You don't speak on this family," Monroe stated harshly.

"I am this family, homeboy," Zyir shot back. "I'm the family that took care of wifey and your seed while you were gone. So whether you like it or not, I'm here. I was here when you couldn't be."

Zyir took his seat and slid his gun to the center as well. Leena followed suit, pushing the weapon in front of her away in disgust. She was in over her head. She had never been more than arm candy for one of the Diamond men. She didn't know anything about this side of their lives. She just wanted to restore normalcy and peace into their lives, and if it meant accepting Miamor, she was all for it.

"Forgiveness, Monroe," Carter stated. He put his gun on the table and walked toward his brother, hands up, until he was directly in front of Monroe. He was so close that Money's gun was pressed into his chest, directly over his heart. He felt Money's hand begin to tremble. "If you sit down at this table, then we let go of the past and work toward building our future. If not, then pull the trigger now and let it be known where you stand."

Monroe lowered his head in turmoil. The entire room was an emotional mess. Everyone except Zyir was a wreck. He kept his composure, his hand near his hip where his extra pistol rested. He anticipated Monroe's every move. If his finger moved an inch, Zyir was prepared to pop off. There was no way he was letting a nigga take Carter's life, brother or not.

Monroe's resolve melted as Carter wrapped his hand around Monroe's gun and removed it from his hand. Carter grabbed the back of Money's neck and pulled him in close as they both bowed their heads in silence.

"I love you, brother, and I'm sorry. Extend me your forgiveness, Money," Carter whispered in his ear. The way Carter spoke to him reminded Monroe so much of his father, taking him to an emotional place.

Monroe nodded his head and wiped his face with his hand while composing himself. "Forgiveness," he repeated. Carter could see the reluctance written all over Monroe.

Miamor breathed a sigh of relief as Carter returned to her side and everyone took their seats. A knock at the door sounded off, and Carter summoned in his chef.

"Now we break bread together as family," Carter said as his kitchen staff brought in a feast fit for a king. Wine was poured around the table, and Carter raised his glass.

"To The Cartel," he toasted.

Although tension still filled the room, everyone knew that this brought them one step closer to unity. They all raised their glasses in salute. "To The Cartel!"

Chapter 13

"Light that mu'fucka up."
                                        – Monroe Diamond

Monroe sat through the dinner and was reserved as his thoughts worked overtime. He wasn't feeling the direction that The Cartel was being taken in. There was no honor among thieves. Carter had stolen Mecca's life and Zyir had stolen Monroe's identity. He wasn't feeling either of them too much at the moment. Carter would forever get a pass because he was family, but Zyir . . .

The only reason Monroe even conceded to the notion of forgiveness was because he was outnumbered at a table full of armed individuals. He had no wins in that circumstance. He wanted no part of any empire as long as Zyir was its leader. So he ate and drank, but rarely spoke as he readied his own troops for battle.

The clock struck midnight, and Leena leaned into him. "It's late. The baby is tired," she said.

He nodded toward the door. "You go ahead and let the driver take you home. I'll be there shortly. There are a few things I need to run by Carter and I don't want you waiting around," Monroe instructed. "My driver can drop you at your house, too, Breeze. I figure me, Carter, and Zyir have a lot to discuss."

Breeze turned to Zyir for confirmation. He nodded. "I guess that is good night then." Leena gathered her son's things as Breeze approached Miamor. "I want to sit down and talk with you whenever you have time for me," Breeze said.

Miamor nodded and Breeze gave her hand a gentle squeeze before walking out of the house. Leena followed suit.

Miamor kissed Carter's cheek and whispered in his ear, "I'll start clearing the table. I know we have a lot to talk about.

I'm sorry I didn't tell you about the baby. You handle your business and we can talk as soon as everyone leaves."

She stood and removed his plate from in front of him.

"Let's take this to the sitting room," Carter said as he stood and led the way. The three men entered the room and an awkward silence fell among them.

"Now that we have all pulled down our skirts, can we get back to getting this money?" Zyir asked.

"I'm thinking along those same lines, but one thing has to change in order for me to be onboard with this," Monroe said.

"What's that?" Carter responded.

"Zyir is no longer head of my father's empire. Clearly his ties aren't strong enough to hold us down," Monroe said, speaking as if Zyir wasn't even in the room.

"I realize that you don't like me, Monroe, but don't speak about me like I'm a little-ass boy. I see through you, Money," Zyir said with a sarcastic chuckle. "You're like one of those little rich kids who thinks they're entitled to everything. You didn't even earn the spot you're begging for. You weren't in the thick of the war. You were off hiding somewhere, healing somewhere while we were here taking the shit to the streets. So miss me with the family speech. You hide behind that Diamond name like it's supposed to mean something to me. Miami has belonged to me for the past four years."

"Now isn't the time for change, Money," Carter said.

"There is never a good time for change," Monroe answered, his jaw tight. "We're blood. You and I both know that we should keep the power inside the family. It's how Papa would have wanted it."

"Look at this shit, Carter," Zyir scoffed as he shook his head disgracefully. "I can't get money with this nigga. You may let shit slide with him, but I'm not going to wait until the nigga put a bullet in me before I cut him off."

"Li'l nigga, I'll cut you off. You married into the power. Breeze is your only connection to this here. You don't got a bid in this circle," Monroe roared. He turned to Carter. "Your man either steps out of my father's seat or I'll make him. Ain't no compromising."

"Monroe, this is the snake shit that is putting holes in our ship. Think about what you're saying. Think about how you're moving. You thought I wouldn't find out that you were the one froze our connect with Buttons?" Carter asked. "I'm asking you, Monroe, to come on board. We need you, and there is a role to be played by each of us, equally important."

"As long as he's in then I'm out," Monroe said truthfully. "And you're without a connect. Meanwhile I'm plugged with Estes."

Carter knew that with Monroe's connection to his grandfather he couldn't be stopped. He was getting the bricks straight off the boat for next to nothing.

"The nigga's a snake, Carter. Fuck him. We don't need him," Zyir spat.

Monroe shook his head. He really didn't want to lose another brother. "You should have let this nigga go to Rio and it would have been taken care of. He would be a memory right now," Monroe finished.

Zyir shifted his stance and frowned. "What the fuck you say?" He approached Monroe.

Carter stepped out of the way, knowing that there was no point in standing between the two men. This confrontation had been brewing ever since Monroe's return. Carter leaned against the arm of his leather couch as he wiped his face with his hands, exasperated, as Zyir addressed Monroe.

"Fuck you say?" Zyir asked. Before he knew it his gun was out and he had Monroe yoked up with a pistol to his head.

"You might as well pull the trigger now because either way I'm going to put you in a grave for the disrespect," Monroe threatened as no fear passed through his eyes.

Carter shook his head. It was the first time in his life that he didn't know what to do. Usually he was calculating and sure in his ability to solve a problem, but in this situation he came up clueless. He watched his two brothers draw a line in the sand. It was at a point of no return. Guns had been drawn, threats had been made, truth had been revealed. Finally Carter spoke.

"This is my home, Zyir," he said.

"Another time and place then," Zyir sneered as he pushed Monroe away and backed down, keeping his gun in his hand, however. "Pussy-ass nigga."

Monroe chuckled as he adjusted his collar. "I tried to give you a chance on the strength of Carter, but you refuse to step down. Either you standing with me or against me, and anybody standing next to you can get it too," Monroe stated harshly. He looked at Carter. "You love my enemy, you become my enemy. So make your choice, brother. It's me or your man."

Carter was silent, but it was all the answer that Monroe needed. He wanted no indecisive players on his team.

"Then watch me burn The Cartel to the ground," Monroe said, his voice so full of hatred that it sent chills down Carter's spine. Monroe stormed out of the house and headed toward the cars that were lined up in front of Carter's home. He had already anticipated this feud, and his young wolves were just waiting for the orders. They sat curbside outside of Carter's mansion, guns loaded, eager to follow Monroe's lead. Monroe climbed into the first car and pulled out his phone to place a call.

"Light that mu'fucka up," he ordered.

He nodded his head for his goon to drive off and then listened as the carful of goons behind him unloaded their automatic assault rifles on Carter's mansion.

Bullets broke through every window as glass shattered everywhere and Zyir and Carter hit the floor.

"Get down!" Zyir yelled as he went to the window to try to bust back. He watched as Monroe's goons got into their cars and pulled off recklessly. He looked back at Carter bewildered.

"Miamor," he whispered. "Miamor!" Carter stood to his feet and ran toward the dining room. He sighed in relief as he saw her rising from the floor.

"Are you hit?" he asked as he patted her entire body, fearing the worst.

"I'm okay," she replied.

Zyir came into the room.

"I knew that he didn't mean it. I could see it in his eyes," Miamor said. "Money doesn't want to forgive, Carter. He wants war."

"Then that's what the nigga gon' get," Zyir interrupted.

Carter nodded his head, but his heart broke inside. He was caught in the middle of two men he would lay down his life for. He wished they could become one large circle of power, but Monroe couldn't see past his own ego trip. His jealousy had caused him to cross those who loved him. Carter knew what he had to do.

"Take care of him, but keep Breeze out of it," Carter replied.

"With pleasure," Zyir replied.

Chapter 14

"You are a part of our family now, Miamor.
There are no more secrets."

—Carter

Miamor waited for hours for Carter to come to bed, but he never showed. Minutes turned to hours and her eyes grew heavy. She thought of going to him, but knew that if he wanted her company he would have sought it. So she gave him space, giving him time to think as she hugged a pillow to her lonely body. She stared at the red numbers on the clock.

3:45 A.M.

She wished that he would talk to her, that he would confide in her. Carter undoubtedly had a lot on his mind, but so did she. She wanted to comfort him and in return to have his comfort.

She closed her eyes, giving into the exhaustion just as he walked into the room. The silhouette of her body could be seen from the doorway, and her light snores told him that she was asleep. He had brought her into his life thinking that they could settle down, when in actuality things were out of control. He crawled into bed beside her. The weight of him caused the bed to shift slightly, announcing his presence. Miamor turned to face him.

"Hey, stranger," she said.

"So you're having my baby, huh?" he asked.

"I am," she whispered. She touched his face and ran her thumb across his bushy eyebrows, taming them. She wondered what a child between the two of them would look like. "Is that a good thing?" she asked.

"That's the best thing, ma," he replied. "You are the only thing in my life that makes sense right now. How long have you known?"

"I suspected it in Rio. I was nauseated the morning after our big night. When we came back home I took a test. Needless to say it was positive," Miamor replied.

"You'll have the best of everything. The best doctors, the best insurance, the best care. I'll have Breeze help you with the arrangements," Carter said.

"I don't know if that's a good idea, Carter," Miamor replied hesitantly. After all the admissions of guilt Miamor just knew that Breeze would resent her.

"You are a part of our family now, Miamor. There are no more secrets. It will take time to heal all of our wounds, but this baby will bond the two of you. I know my sister. She has a very forgiving soul. She will do all that she can to help you bring her nephew into the world," Carter promised.

"Nephew, huh? How do you know it's not a girl?" she asked with a smirk.

"I make boys, ma . . . kings," he answered with a charming wink as he rolled on top of her. He kissed her passionately and slowly made his way south. He put her to sleep with an earth-shattering orgasm as the sun rose into the sky.

The atmosphere was unusually tense between Zyir and Breeze. He hadn't spoken a word to her since he returned from Carter's. She lay with her back against the headboard as she watched him put on his clothes. "Zy," she said, breaking the silence. "What happened after I left last night?"

He didn't look her way as he grabbed his presidential Rolex off the dresser and slid it onto his wrist.

"I know something happened. What are you keeping from me?" she asked.

"Nothing, B, nothing happened," Zyir replied.

She heard the stress in his tone and knew that he was lying, but she didn't press the issue. When he was ready to talk to her about it he would. Zyir was her best friend, and there wasn't much that he kept from her. So she knew that once it became needed for her to know, then she would. Until then she dropped it. She rose from the bed; her silk Donna Karan pajamas hugged her slim frame.

"Well, whatever is bothering you, I hope it gets better," she said as she kissed his lips.

"I'm gonna go prepare breakfast," she said as she exited their bedroom.

Zyir sighed, his heart heavy as he sat on the edge of the bed. Beefing with Monroe was a lose/lose for him. If he murdered him, then he would break Breeze's heart, and if he let him live, then Monroe's jealousy would eventually be Zyir's downfall. He knew what had to be done; he just hated that it had come to this. There was enough money for everybody to eat, but Monroe wanted fame—or rather, infamy. He wanted to be the boss in an organization where one was not needed. So instead of getting to the money, they were embarking on war. A war between brothers—one that no matter who was left standing, everybody would lose.

Breeze sat in the middle of the crowded restaurant waiting patiently for Miamor to arrive. Accepting the woman who had torn her family apart was not an easy thing to do, but off the strength of Carter she was willing to try. The apparent bond that Miamor and Carter shared was deep, and Breeze knew that forgiving Miamor was the only option as long as she held the key to her brother's heart.

She sipped a mimosa as she looked around Breezes. She had owned the restaurant for years, and it was the only business that she made sure to maintain after her father's demise. He had purchased it for her, and Breeze felt like it was the only piece of him that she had left. It had survived through two wars, and Breeze smiled as she watched the busy patrons fraternizing around her establishment.

She smiled slightly as her mind drifted to better days, when adversaries and disloyalty didn't exist in her world. Now her world was corrupted. She sat toward the doors in public places to see who was coming and going. She felt wary at traffic lights when sandwiched between two cars. She carried a small handgun in the bottom of her handbag just in case she should need it. Breeze no longer lived under the veil of safety that her kingpin father had provided for her. She lived in a constant state of awareness at the fact that she now played her mother's role. She was the kingpin's wife.

She wondered if Taryn had ever felt so overwhelmed by her position. Her mother made life look so glamorous and effortless when she was alive. Breeze had no idea how her mother had pulled it off, but she hoped to learn to wear her crown just as gracefully.

Miamor walked through the door and Breeze's back stiffened. She scanned her enemy from head to toe. Breeze quickly saw Carter's money dripping off of Miamor. Not many women could rival Breeze's fashion sense, but Miamor proved to be a contender with the most expensive pair of Jimmy Choo heels from the upcoming fall collection gracing her feet. The Chanel bandage dress she wore showed every curve of her body, and Breeze gave the nod of approval in her head. Miamor was wearing Carter's money well, that was for sure. She watched Miamor scan the crowd and take a deep breath as she finally spotted her. She tried to approach, but was halted by two large bodyguards who sat discreetly at the table beside Breeze's. She was taking no chances. Breeze had done her research on Carter's new girlfriend, and after having experienced so much destruction at her hands, she decided to move accordingly. Breeze sat as her bodyguard intercepted Miamor.

"Check her," Breeze said.

The bodyguards patted Miamor down and took a look inside her bag before allowing her access to Breeze.

"Have a seat," Breeze said as she motioned for the chair across from her.

Miamor rolled her eyes at Breeze's security measures then took her place at the table.

"I have to admit that I was surprised when I got your phone call," Miamor said.

"You're pregnant with my brother's child. I love Carter and I don't want to lose him. So we may as well get better acquainted," Breeze answered.

Her tone was chillier than Miamor appreciated. Usually Miamor took attitude from no one, but she knew that Breeze had earned the right to be displeased with her. She gave her a pass knowing that it was in her best interest to repair her relationship with the youngest member of the Diamond clan.

Miamor could teach Breeze a thing or two. If Miamor wanted to touch Breeze, the big bodyguards could have done nothing to stop her. Her girls would have had the scope on him before he could even check her Birkin.

Miamor motioned for one of the bodyguards to approach her. He leaned down toward her.

"You need to patrol the perimeter of the restaurant. Secure the inside before Breeze arrives and then put one at both entrances. If someone wants to get at her, by the time they get this close it's too late. They shouldn't even make it through the door," Miamor schooled.

The men looked toward Breeze for confirmation. She peered curiously at Miamor and then nodded her approval.

"Tips you picked up in your line of work?" Breeze commented snidely.

Miamor sighed and folded her hands across the table as she looked Breeze square in the eyes.

"I'm not in that life anymore, Breeze. I know you have a lot to hate me for, but I truly hope that we can be civil. I'm not perfect and I have a lot of skeletons in my closet. What I've done to you isn't half of the bad things that I've done, but targeting you and your family is my biggest regret. I love Carter, Breeze, and he loves you. I want us to get to a point where we can call ourselves acquaintances," Miamor said, hoping to establish an understanding with Breeze. She would love for things to be all rainbows and flowers with Breeze, but she wasn't naïve. Breeze would need time to get over all of Miamor's past transgressions.

Breeze was silent for a moment as she tapped the bottom of her champagne flute with her blue manicured nail. Miamor couldn't read her, and she smiled at the fact that Breeze Diamond had grown up. She wasn't as green as she had been upon the very first meeting. Life had caused her to transform from a girl into a beautiful young woman, with limitless power in her hands.

"Have you chosen a doctor yet?" Breeze asked out of the blue.

Miamor shook her head. "Carter suggested that I ask you to help with that," Miamor said.

"You'll meet with our family doctor. I'll make the arrangements for you," Breeze offered. "I can't help but be excited about your pregnancy. This family needs some new blood in it. Maybe a child can restore the purity in our lives."

Breeze beckoned for the waitress and then said, "And just so you know, I forgive you. We don't have to discuss anything that has happened in the past ever again. As long as you make Carter happy, then I'm happy. Treat him well."

Miamor nodded. She was grateful for Breeze's kind heart. There was no way that Miamor could have done the same if the shoe was on the other foot. "I will. And thank you."

"It's nothing," Breeze responded. A huge smile spread across her lips. "Now let's talk baby names."

Chapter 15

"It was like Mecca's ghost
flew into that nigga."

—Fly Boogie

Monroe took to the streets the way a duck took to water, and he made no apologies for his brute way of ruling. He had already set up shop in all of The Cartel's most profitable territories, but instead of sharing blocks, he was taking them over. Monroe pulled up to Zyir's most profitable trap and exited the car with his goon squad in tow. Fly Boogie stood up and saluted Monroe.

"What's good, boy?" he greeted.

Monroe was stone faced as he removed his gun from his waistline and popped Fly Boogie without remorse. The young kid folded like a lawn chair as the hot lead fired from Monroe's gun filled his belly. Monroe was on some terminating shit. Anyone who rocked with Zyir was a threat and on his list to be laid down.

He ascended the steps and knocked on the door in the rhythm that allowed him entry. His goons stood on the sides of the door, out of the view of anyone who looked out of the peephole. When they saw that it was Monroe, he was given access and welcomed inside, but when they saw the niggas with burners who came in after him they quickly regretted the decision.

Gunfire erupted, and a complete massacre occurred as Monroe stood and watched his team put in work. They were so thorough they only delivered head shots. No vest in the world could protect against a hollow to the dome, and that's what he trained his mob to deliver. All five men in the trap were executed, and the cook-up queens were tied up ass naked. Monroe smoked a cigar, enjoying the feel of the smoke in his lungs as he paced up and down the line of women. They squirmed and cried as they tried to free themselves from their constraints. As he paced, he poured gasoline from the can in his hand. The stench of the liquid filled the room as he doused the women.

"This is the price you pay when you work for Zyir," Monroe stated. He handed the gas can off to one of his goons and then pulled the cigar from his mouth. He looked at it as he blew a cloud of smoke from his mouth, and then he flicked the cigar onto the line of women. Flames instantly erupted and howls of immeasurable pain sounded out in the apartment.

"Let's go," Monroe ordered. He noticed that his squad had bagged up the money and the product that they had found in the spot. Monroe stopped them. "It's not about the money. Leave that shit here."

He took one last look at the destruction that he had caused before he walked out, leaving a pile of ash where Zyir's number one money spot used to be.

"Yo' man Money is on some other shit," Fly Boogie stated as he lay in the hospital bed with a colonoscopy bag attached to his stomach. "The nigga might as well have killed me, bro! I can't get no pussy carrying around this fucking shit bag."

Zyir smirked at the young kid's sense of humor at a crucial time like this.

"The nigga burnt the shit to the ground like it was nothing. Had hoes screaming for they lives, ya feel me? I can still smell the bodies, fam. On some real shit, it was like Mecca's ghost flew into that nigga. The streets ain't seen a massacre like that since Mecca."

Zyir saw red as he listened to Fly Boogie tell his version of what had gone down. Monroe had taken their beef public by personally attacking The Cartel. Usually the one to strike first, Zyir kicked himself for hesitating. He had wanted to handle Monroe accordingly, seeing as how his demise would crush Breeze, but Money wasn't holding any punches. He was forcing Zyir's hand, and now they were on some gangster shit.

"You ready to put in some work? I need you on the team so I can see firsthand some of the stories I been hearing about you," Zyir said. "Your murder game proper?"

"No doubt, big homie, my shit's official. Only reason these niggas caught me slipping is because I thought my man was family. Won't happen again, I'll tell you that," Fly Boogie stated with venom lacing his tone.

"A'ight, rest up. You're gonna need it. And hold on to that for me," Zyir said as he slyly passed Fly Boogie a burner.

"Good looking, bro. I felt naked than a muuuu'fucka without my joint," Fly Boogie replied. "Holla at me though. Whatever you need done, I got it. I'm about that work."

Zyir nodded and then made his exit. The two goons he had posted outside the door followed him out as he headed to see Carter; all the while murder plots played in his head.

Chapter 16

"She's not to be underestimated."

—Monroe

"You niggas ready to make a name for yourselves, right?" Monroe asked as he sat at the table with three youngsters. He had recruited them from Opa-locka for a specific job and they all were hungry live wires. They were the type of goons who killed for nothing. They were looking for a come up, so when Monroe knocked on the door with an opportunity, they were ecstatic.

"No doubt. What we got to do?" the oldest of the young clique asked. Monroe smiled and rubbed his hands together, as he quickly scanned the nearly empty restaurant.

"I need a job done and I need it done right. I need a bitch kidnapped," Monroe said without blinking an eye.

"Kidnapped?" the kid asked as a smile formed on his face. "Shit's easy, son. We a'snatch that bitch up. Just point us to her. We will handle the rest, big homie," he said with confidence as the two other goons nodded in approval.

"Nah, li'l nigga. You are going about it all wrong. It's not an easy job. This isn't an ordinary chick. I mean . . . she move like a nigga. She is not to be underestimated, so I need this done right with no mishaps. You got me?"

"I got you. We just need the rundown on the bitch. You want us to slump her?" the goon asked as he began to lick his chops, eager to kill. He wanted to put in work so badly.

Monroe shook his head in frustration and folded his hands together, trying not to show his frustration. "Listen close. I want you to snatch her up. That's it! Understand?"

"Got it," the leader said.

"Meet me here tomorrow at the same time and I will give you all the info. I'm going to set up a spot that I want you to take her to. Once she's there, tie her up and wait for me. You do that and I got twenty-five stacks for you . . . apiece," Monroe stated.

"Apiece?" they all asked in unison, not believing what they had just heard. They would have done it for free, but to find out that they was about to get paid handsomely, it was a bonus.

"That's right. If you guys pull this off, I will put all of you on. No more small-time shit, li'l nigga. Welcome to the big leagues. You have the ticket to the money train right in front of you. What you gon' do?" Monroe asked as he sat back in his chair and looked at each one of them in the eyes.

"We gon' get that money," the leader said. Pandora's box had just been opened, and Monroe knew that there was no coming back on what he had just put in motion.

Miamor looked at the paper in her hands and smiled seeing her baby's ultrasound pictures. She couldn't wait to show Carter. The baby was getting so big, and the realization that she would finally be a mother hit her. This made her heart warm, and a smile spread across her face involuntarily. Just as the thought of Carter danced in her mind, her phone rang. She looked at the caller ID and saw that is was him calling.

"Hey, baby. I was just—"

"Look, Mia. Listen very closely to me. I need you to check into a room in South Beach. Do not go home," Carter said, cutting her off midsentence. Miamor could sense the urgency in his voice, something very rare with Carter. He seemed worried.

"Wait, wait. What's wrong, baby? Is everything okay?" Miamor asked as the smile that was just on her face turned into a confused frown.

"Everything is okay. I just need you to do that for me. As soon as you get there and check in, text me the room number. I will meet you there later tonight," Carter instructed.

"Carter, you are scaring me. Tell me what is going on," she demanded as she made her way over to her car.

"Just do what I said and I will explain it to you later tonight, okay?" he responded.

"Okay. Carter . . . I love you," Miamor said as she stopped walking for a brief second.

"I love you too," Carter said just before he hung up the phone. Miamor pushed the end button on her phone and headed directly to her car. She began to get a bad feeling in the pit of her stomach and she hated the feeling. She knew something was wrong. She had never heard Carter sound so anxious.

Miamor hurried to her car and started it, looking around apprehensively. She pulled out of the parking lot and fixed her rearview mirror. She was growing nervous and paranoid because of Carter's instructions. She maneuvered through the streets and headed toward South Beach. "I don't know what's going on, Carter, but—" Her thoughts were interrupted by a bum walking across the street and she hit her brakes abruptly, stopping just short of him. Her whole body tensed up, and she blew her horn to alert him. Just as Miamor made eye contact with the bum, a black truck pulled up next to Miamor's car with three youngsters inside. Miamor held her breath as she noticed the menacing looks on their faces and knew that something wasn't right. All three pairs of eyes were on her, and she felt her heart begin to pound hard. She noticed that their eyes looked past her, and she followed their eyes. Before she could react, a black van pulled up on the opposite side and a masked man jumped out and got into her car. He had a gun to her head and threw her car in park.

"Nooo!" she yelled as everything happened so fast. The bum pointed a gun at the young boys as his partner grabbed up Miamor and forced her into the van. The youngsters were defenseless as they had their hands in the air. The goon posing as a bum walked backward to the van and hopped in. The sound of screeching tires filled the air as they bent the corner and sped off.

A black pillowcase was put over Miamor's head as she cried for Carter, but he couldn't hear her. No one could.

Chapter 17

"You either let me walk out of here or
Carter will send his goons to get me . . ."
—Miamor

Miamor coughed uncontrollably as she struggled to catch her breath. She had no idea how long she had been out, but as she opened her eyes she was hit with a splitting headache. Her mouth fell open in distress, but no sound came out as she grimaced in pain. *Where am I?* she thought.

Surprisingly, she was left unbound, and she hesitantly stood to her feet. Miamor's eyes danced around the room to find something to defend herself with as her heart raced. The room was small but comfortable. A queen bed and a bureau were the only contents of the room, but with no window Miamor was unsure of what time of day it was. Had she been out for hours or days? How long had she been gone? Did Carter realize she was missing? Miamor was at a mental loss as she tried to assess her current unfortunate event.

A greasy bag of food sat on top of the dresser, and Miamor silently went over to it, emptying the contents. A burger and fries sat inside. She bypassed the food and opened the drawers, hoping to find anything that she could use to protect herself. A gun would have been nice, but Miamor wasn't picky. A pen, a wire hanger . . . she'd take anything at this point, but to her dismay all of the drawers were empty. She had been tossed into an empty room, and her imagination was getting the best of her. The longer she waited, the more worry filled her heart.

Miamor had never been afraid of anything in her life, but as she sat waiting for the unknown, she feared for the life of her unborn child. Maternal instinct caused her to think of the seed growing in her belly before thinking of herself. *Where the fuck am I?* she thought uneasily.

Her frustration grew until she couldn't contain herself. Fuck waiting for someone to come; she was going to make them come. Miamor walked over to the door and kicked it as hard as she could.

BAM! BAM! BAM!

Always one to confront her attackers, she wanted to see who she was up against. She wasn't about to cower and have the hours of the day tick by torturously slow. Someone had wanted her; now she was here, and she wanted to know the who's and why's behind the setup.

"I know you're out there! Who are you? If you think someone isn't looking for me at this very moment you got the game fucked up! Do you know who I am?" she screamed as she beat the door with her fists, causing a commotion.

Miamor had been a part of the streets long enough to know that whoever had taken her wanted something. Otherwise she would be dead already. Her first thought told her that Monroe was behind it. He had more than enough reason to want her extinct, but something about the situation just didn't feel right. The new sheets on the bed, the mediocre but accommodating setup, the meal—none of it was Monroe's style. *Money would have put me in a dirt hole by now,* Miamor thought. At the least he would have gagged and bound her. The freedom of movement and speech was a luxury in this situation, and it was one that Monroe would not have afforded her.

Miamor lifted her foot to kick the door once more, but momentum caused her to stumble forward slightly as the door opened.

A masked goon entered the room, enraged at her outbursts. She was loud, screaming at the top of her lungs. They were in the middle of nowhere, in the Florida Everglades to be exact, and there was no one around to hear her, but he'd be damned if he listened to her wails all night. "Bitch, get your ass over there and shut the fuck up before I cut your tongue from your fucking throat!" he ordered as he grabbed her roughly and threw her onto the bed.

It took everything in Miamor not to come out of her mouth crazy at the dude in front of her. Fire danced in her eyes as she stared him down maliciously. Her pride told her to pop off, but the flutters of her child kicking in her stomach won the battle of reason, making her play it cool.

"I'm sorry. Please, I just want to go home. What do you want? Is it money? I have money. I can get you—"

"Shut the fuck up!" the goon yelled. A hard slap to her face caused Miamor to see stars, and she curled on the bed in a fetal position as she held her injured jaw.

The goon stared lustfully at Miamor. Her breasts heaved under the thin fabric of the Chanel dress she wore and her ass could barely be contained, while her hips caused the hemline to rise. She held her face as she squirmed across the bed, putting her back against the wall.

"Where you going? Huh? You running? I bet you run from the dick just like that, don't you?" the goon asked as he hovered over Miamor, grabbing at her legs. Miamor kicked his hands away as she panicked. Carter's face flashed through her mind. She needed him now more than ever.

"No!" she screamed as her foot met with his mouth.

"Fuck! You bitch!" the goon shouted in pain. Her protests only made him angrier, and despite the strict instructions he had been given regarding the job, he decided that he would have a piece of Miamor. She was too enticing not to sample. Her gripped her thighs with both hands and pulled her forcefully toward him. His hands squeezed her skin so tightly that he left bruises where each one of his fingertips dug into her flesh.

"Don't do this, please. I'm pregnant," she whispered as he climbed on top of her and pulled out his dick. A crooked leer spread across his face, and he lowered himself, positioning for entry.

"Even better," he cracked. "That's the best pussy."

Miamor wanted to fight him, but he was three times bigger than her. The only thing she could think of was something happening to her child. If he hit her hard enough, in just the right spot, it could endanger her seed, and she had to protect that at all costs. She was in a delicate state, and her body stiffened at the foreign touch of another man.

He opened her legs with such force that it felt as if her pelvis cracked. Tears flooded her vision. In the past he would have had to kill her to take what he wanted, but things were so different. Now, she had something to live for. Now, she would sacrifice a piece of her soul in order to survive. She lay stiff like a cadaver and closed her eyes as the goon ripped her panties. Her chest heaved in distress and . . .

BOOM!

The gunshot rang in her ears, forcing her eyes open as the weight of the goon collapsed over her. His now limp body pushed the wind from her lungs, and she placed her hands on his dead chest and rolled him off of her.

Her body shook as his blood covered her dress and she looked up into the eyes of his killer. He was masked, but there was something familiar about him. The dark eyes that looked through the holes in the ski mask penetrated her. He saw through her.

She squinted curiously as she opened her mouth to speak. "What do you want from me?" she asked.

"I just want you, little mama. That's it and nothing more," the masked man responded.

Her eyes widened in surprise as she rushed to stand. Her mouth opened slightly in disbelief. *This can't be happening. This isn't real. He wouldn't do this to me,* she thought. The gun that now hung at his side, gripped loosely in his hand, did nothing to stop Miamor from crossing the room. She reached up to remove his mask, but a firm hand gripped her wrist to stop her. They stood there for a moment, Miamor looking through the eyes of a killer as she shook her head.

"It's not you," she whispered. "Is it?" she added unsurely. The goon released her hand and Miamor pulled off his mask.

"Murder . . ." The whisper could barely be heard as she backpedaled away from him.

"I missed you, li'l mama," he replied.

Mixed emotions filled her. He had taught her everything she knew and was the first man she had ever loved.

"Murder?" she repeated in confusion, unable to wrap her mind around what was happening. Suddenly it was all so overwhelming. Rage bubbled to the top, over everything else.

"Why would you do this to me?" she asked as she charged him, pushing him in the chest in frustration.

Murder took her assault as she released years of pent-up resentment. The question wasn't vague. It was deeper than just her kidnapping. When Murder had been sent away to prison, her entire world had changed.

"You've been out of my life for years! You just can't show up here! You can't just come back!" Her anger turned to sadness as the things she felt for him in the past came rushing back to her. He was the only person who had ever seen her softer side. He knew her before she was an infamous Murder Mama. He had groomed her.

Her resolve softened as she found comfort in his embrace, and she cried on his shoulder as his arms closed around her.

"It's all right," Murder whispered as he pulled her tightly to his chest, holding the back of her head securely, his fingers lost in her hair. "Let's get you cleaned up and let me take care of this nigga. After that we'll talk and I'll explain everything to you."

She pushed away from him, gathering her composure. "I don't want to hear an explanation, Murder. I want to go home," she said, her voice low. She couldn't look him in the eyes, because the sincerity she saw in them took her down memory lane. In the past her affection for him had been so strong that she couldn't deny him, but now things had changed. Now Carter had entered the picture, and her feelings for Murder dwindled when measured against her love for Carter.

"I am home, Miamor. I came all the way down here to bring you home. I took on the biggest drug organization just to get you back. When I thought you were dead, I hunted these niggas, Miamor. Somebody was going to pay for what I thought happened to you, but when you resurfaced, I had to have you. You crossed my mind every day while I was locked up. Your face kept me alive in there, and I'm not leaving Miami without you, li'l mama," he answered, his voice serious.

"So you kidnap me? You snatch me off the streets and put me in harm's way?" Miamor argued. His words tugged at her heart's strings, but angered her all the same.

"You were never in any danger," Murder said. "Just give me a minute to explain, Miamor. Get out of the bloody clothes and just come sit down and talk to me. This is me. You can't tell me that you're not happy to see me." Murder walked up on her and placed his hand beneath her chin. "You can't say you didn't miss me."

Miamor turned her head and attempted to walk around him, out of the room. He grabbed her arm and turned her back to him.

"You're not leaving. I'm sorry," he stated sternly.

Miamor scoffed in disbelief. "So you're going to force me to stay? You're keeping me here when I'm telling you I want to leave!"

Murder was visibly wounded by her words. "I'm asking you to give me a week. I know you, Miamor. The life you're living ain't you. You don't want to be wifey to a nigga like Carter. The nigga's pussy. All of this Cartel bullshit. You telling me that's the life you want? That ain't you. You're a loner. You're a recluse. The only family you love was the little one that we created. Me, you, and . . ."

"My sister," Miamor whispered as she closed her eyes and saw Anisa's face in her head.

"You laying up with the very niggas that took her life, Miamor! She in the dirt and you sitting on a throne with the mu'fuckas who murked her. That ain't you. You don't want that. I know you. That nigga Carter has got you brainwashed, li'l mama. Just give me a week to remind you of who you are," Murder bargained.

"I know who I am," Miamor replied. "I'm with Carter because I want to be. No brainwashing, no angles, I love him. Fuck a week. I'm not looking back to the past, Murder. You're the past, and I'm leaving all of that shit behind. Now you either let me walk out of here or Carter will send his goons to get me, but either way I'm leaving. He'll never stop looking for me, Murder, and you don't know what I know. His reach in the streets is long. He'll find me."

"It hasn't been that long, Miamor. You know how I get down. The nigga bring smoke to my doorstep and I'ma leave him leaking on it," Murder replied venomously. "Now go take a shower and clean yourself up. You try to run and I'll rip that baby right out of your stomach."

Miamor blinked away her tears. "And that's love? You came back here because you love me, right? Love don't do shit like that, Murder."

"I love every piece of you, but I hate every part of him, including . . ." His words trailed off as he pointed to her stomach.

Miamor knew him well enough to know that he wasn't lying. He didn't use scare tactics. If he said it, he meant it. *Carter, please come for me,* she thought. Miamor was superior to every nigga she had ever gone up against with the exception of Murder. He knew her too well for her to have the upper hand.

"How could you, Mia? You were my li'l mama," Murder asked. "Now you're pregnant with this nigga bastard kid."

Miamor broke down, hearing his heartbreak and feeling heartbreak of her own as she thought of her fate. It was possible that she wouldn't make it out of this one alive. She gave him no response besides the sobs that racked her.

"Get out of the bloody clothes. By the time you get out of the shower, I'll have dinner for you and I'll take care of this mess," he said, pointing to the goon's dead body. He kissed the top of her head, and she closed her eyes in despair as he exited the room.

Miamor was stuck between a rock and a hard place. She wanted to hate Murder, but she couldn't. She knew that he had been locked up for so long that she was all he remembered. His world had been on a standstill while hers had moved on. There was a time when she thought that she would never replace him, but upon meeting Carter, all of her doubts had gone out of the window. He was the greatest man she had ever known, and her loyalty was with him. Miamor just had to figure out how to get back to him in one piece.

By the time Miamor emerged from the bathroom, the dead body was gone and Murder stood outside the bathroom door, waiting patiently for her. He held a shopping bag for her.

"It's not designer like what you're used to, but it'll do," he said.

Miamor held the cotton towel tightly around her body and took the bag from Murder. Murder tugged at the towel that was tucked snugly under her armpits.

"Murder . . . don't," she said.

He snatched the towel anyway and pulled it away from her, revealing her naked body. "Relax, li'l mama. I never had to take it," Murder said.

His hands explored her body as he slowly ran his hands over her stomach. She was perfectly sculpted, but her once flawless body was marred with scars. They showed the struggles she had endured at the hands of Mecca Diamond. Her baby bump was subtle and barely there, but Murder knew her so well that he knew that she was pregnant without her having to tell him. He noticed the slight weight in her face and the thickness around her hips and breasts.

Miamor's breath caught in her throat as she waited for him to hurt her, to hit her in the stomach and hurt her unborn child. She was surprised when she felt how gently he touched her. His hands graced her like feathers, and she placed her hands over his.

"This is supposed to be us, li'l mama. This is supposed to be us . . . our baby," Murder said. Miamor removed his hand, squirming out of his grasp as she covered herself with the towel.

"Things have changed, Murder. I've changed. A part of me will always care about you, but I love Carter. Since you're not leaving me any choice, I'll stay a week, but I don't want to mislead you. I will not stay after that. If you try to make me, you will have to sleep with one eye open for as long as I'm here, because the first opportunity I get, I'll kill you," she said.

Murder pushed her against the wall, trapping her in his personal space as his hand went to her neck. Miamor tensed. "You couldn't kill me any quicker than I could kill you," Murder said. His hand moved from her neck to her cheek as he traced her jaw line. "I'd always hesitate, and we both know that in the murder game there is no room for second-guessing. Thank you for the week, though. By the end of it, you won't want to go home."

Chapter 18

"I want anybody affiliated with them to be in pieces in the Atlantic. Fish food."

—Carter

Carter paced back and forth with worry on his mind, but his heart was ablaze with anger. Zyir had assembled the entire Cartel at Carter's request. They all sat silently. No one dared to say a word as they waited uneasily for Carter to speak first. Everyone seated at the table knew that there were two people in Carter's life who were off-limits—Miamor and Breeze. Someone had disrespected him, and the veins bulging out of his neck indicated that someone's life was on an official countdown. He held his hands behind his back as his jaw tensed.

Zyir stood ominously in the background, rubbing his chin as he bowed his head while leaning against the wall. He was the leader of The Cartel. Unlike Monroe, Zyir wasn't threatened by a brotherhood of power. Zyir was the face that the streets saw. Carter had put him in the forefront of The Cartel, and he wore his crown with humility. If Carter wanted to step back into his seat, Zyir would step aside and support his decision. It was love and loyalty that kept Zyir and Carter on the same page. There was no competition between them because there were no weak links in their chain. They reigned over Miami as a team. Monroe wanted it all for himself, and in his attempts to overthrow The Cartel, he had crossed the line.

Carter had been feeling extreme guilt in his decision to press the button on Monroe, but now that Miamor had been snatched, Carter felt no remorse. All bets were off and nothing was off limits. If Monroe wanted to play hardball, then Carter would school him on the rules of the game.

Monroe had put down a play that couldn't be taken back, and now Carter was all in. This was different than the war with the Haitians. This was more serious than the beef with the Mexican cartels. This was blood against blood, and the aftermath of their war would be one that could level everything that The Cartel had built over the years.

Carter was strategic in the way he chose his words as he addressed the heads of his empire.

"Something has been taken from me. Someone dear to me has been touched. A line has been crossed. I've got a hundred racks for whoever can bring Monroe Diamond to me. I don't want him harmed, just delivered to me. I've got ten thousand dollars for any members of O.M.G. I want anybody affiliated with them to be in pieces in the Atlantic. Fish food," Carter stated, his voice even, like the calm before the storm.

Zyir could see the anger simmering in Carter's heart, and he recognized the thirsty look in the eyes of the hustlers who sat around the table. Carter had put a six-figure bounty out on the streets, and niggas were determined to make that cake.

Carter dismissed the room, and Zyir stayed back as the rest of the men exited the house. Tension was high, and Zyir didn't know what to say to reassure Carter. They had been through thick times before and had weathered the storm, but the current opposition was someone who occupied space inside Carter's heart. There was no easy answer, no easy out. Whatever he decided would destroy him, the same way that killing Mecca had. He was about to annihilate another brother on behalf of the woman he loved.

"She's pregnant, fam. She's carrying my kid and a nigga got her tied up somewhere," Carter stated in disbelief. If she hadn't been expecting, Carter would have more confidence that Miamor could hold things down. She wasn't the average victim, and vulnerability wasn't a characteristic that she showed often, but in her current state there was no way that she could defend herself. Carter had to get her back home. If something happened to her, Carter would never forgive himself. She was his woman. She was his responsibility, and the baby growing in her stomach meant everything to him. Carter felt as if his worst fear was coming true. He had promised

Miamor that he would take care of her if she laid down her gun, and now that she had, he had failed her.

"If something happens to her or my baby, I'm going to paint the fucking city red," Carter said as he walked over to the picture window that looked out over his beautifully landscaped estate.

"It won't. I'll put my ear to the streets. Somebody knows something. If I hear anything I'll hit you, fam," Zyir said. He gave Carter a reassuring pat on the back before making his exit.

Carter sat in his black Porsche Cayenne, maneuvering through the streets on black rims and hidden behind the black tint as he headed to Coral Gables. He knew where he could find Monroe. Just months ago it was he who had helped his younger brother pick out the secluded estate. He rode in silence, his heart clenched like an iron fist inside his chest, and his stomach felt hollow.

Since Miamor's return he had held out on her, not wanting to give her his all just in case she betrayed him again. Now he realized that no matter how hard he tried to keep his feelings for her at bay, she had him. Miamor captured his soul and his heart in her hands, and without her he felt empty. He would kill a nigga for her, including his brother. There was no exception when it came to her. Now that she was pregnant with his son, he would never allow anyone to bring harm to them.

As he drove, the city gradually disappeared and he turned right onto the uncharted road that led to Monroe's estate.

Since establishing O.M.G., Monroe lived like something out of the movies. A guard sat in the security booth outside the gated home, and three more patrolled the perimeter of the grounds. There were cameras everywhere, and two beautiful black Rottweiler pups made the plush estate seem more like a prison than a place one called home. Monroe had taken all of these measures to ensure that Carter could not touch him, but he had forgotten one thing. Carter was the one who had set him up with the security company in the first place. After a hefty $25,000 payment, Carter had easily purchased the code to Monroe's gate and the blind eye of the security guards on payroll. Carter nodded to the guard at the gate as he keyed in the access code.

The electronic black steel gate swung open and Carter guided his car inside. He pulled directly to the front of the home, parking his car in the circular driveway. Taking a deep breath, he pressed a button on his console and watched the hidden compartment slide out. It was a trick he had put Zyir up on and a necessity for every car that he owned.

He removed his Glock .40 handgun and kept it in his hand as he got out, approaching the door. Two ferocious dogs came running toward him, barking their threats. They were two beauties, a black man's stallion, but Carter didn't hesitate to lay them down. He shot them down at his feet, delivering one bullet each before stepping over their bodies and knocking on Monroe's door.

The butt of the gun caused his knocks to sound like thunder as he beat down the door. He didn't want his visit to be a surprise. He was there to confront Monroe head on and negotiate Miamor's release. He wasn't leaving without her, and he hoped for Monroe's sake that he made this simple, because Carter was prepared to make things difficult.

The door flew open, and Carter was surprised to see Leena standing on the other side of the door. She stood clinging to her silk robe, her hair slightly messy, as she looked at Carter in confusion. Clearly she hadn't been expecting anyone. Her presence had slipped his mind, but it definitely sweetened the pot.

"Carter!" she exclaimed in surprise.

"Where is Money?" he asked. His voice froze her instantly as her eyes shifted to the gun in his hand and her brow wrinkled in worry.

"He's not here," she replied. "Should I be afraid to let you in here right now, Carter? Your nephew is in here." She closed the door a bit and spoke to him through a small opening as she tried to keep him on the outside of her home. He had always been gracious to her. He was family, but the murderous look in his eyes and the fact that he stood at her door, gun in hand, caused her much distress.

Carter eased her inside the house, using his weight to push her aside, and then closed the door behind him. "I'm sorry, Leena. Money took something from me; now I have to take something from him."

"Leena!" Monroe screamed as he stormed into his home. He recognized Carter's car as soon as he pulled up, and the dead dogs out front prepared him for the worst. "Leena!"

"No need to yell, Money. She's still alive . . . for now," Carter said, his voice low and threatening as he watched Monroe enter the living room. Leena held her sleeping son in her arms as tears of fear fell down her cheeks while sitting in a chair at Carter's gunpoint.

"Money, please," she sobbed as Carter held the gun at point-blank range, preparing to blow her brains out.

"What are you doing? My fucking family, Carter! This is how you want to play it?" Money barked.

"Why not, little brother? This is how you're playing it. My girl and my seed are missing. She's carrying your nephew, Money. My son! This is out of character for me, but please don't doubt that I will take everything from you right now with just the pull of a trigger. You give me back my family and I'll leave your home without harming yours. Where is she?" Carter asked with murderous intent in his eyes. His heart galloped with adrenaline as his temper flared.

Carter wanted to put a hollow point between Monroe's eyes. For Monroe to have the audacity to snatch Miamor was a show of disrespect. Had he been any other nigga, Monroe would already be mourning the loss of his bitch and kid, but because they shared the same blood, Carter was throwing him a line of redemption. One chance was all Monroe had to right his wrong.

"Carter, I don't know what the fuck you're talking about. We're at odds, but I would never—"

"Never torch my stash houses, never shoot up my blocks? What are your limits, Money? Miamor is missing! You're the only nigga in the city that has the balls to come at me like that. You put in the call to them O.M.G. niggas and have her released now," Carter demanded.

"Carter, I swear to God, fam—"

"Money, I've been going easy on you because you're my brother, and you have obviously mistaken my kindness for weakness. You've got five seconds before you're planning a double funeral," Carter threatened.

Leena broke down as she cradled her son to her chest. His tiny hands clung to her as she closed her eyes and prayed over him. She cringed as the cold steel marked the kiss of death on the back of her skull. "I will put her brains on the floor!" Carter yelled.

"Carter!" Money yelled in distress as he watched his family squirm as his son awoke from the commotion and began to reach for him. Leena held on to their child tightly, however, as she was racked with heartbreak.

"Money, just tell him what he wants to know," Leena begged. "Please."

"Five," Carter began his countdown, eyes cold and his will unflinching.

"Don't. You don't want to do this," Money negotiated. His hands were extended as if he could calm Carter. He wanted to shoot him dead where he stood, but he would never make such a risky move as long as his love and child were in harm's way.

"Four," Carter continued.

"I don't have her, Carter," Money said.

"Three . . . Where is she, Money?" Carter demanded.

Money's eyes widened. "Carter!"

"Two!" Carter moved the gun from Leena to Monroe Jr.

"He's my son!" Money protested, anxiety causing his voice to raise an octave as his eyes grew as wide as saucers.

"One."

Monroe dropped to his knees and extended both hands in a desperate plea as tears blurred his vision. "I don't have her!" Money yelled. "It wasn't me! That wasn't my play! I didn't take Miamor! I admit I thought about it! I had my people in place, but someone else got there first!"

Carter fingered the trigger.

"No! Brother! I swear on everything it wasn't me. My little niggas were all set to go when somebody pulled up in black

SUVs and did the job for us," Monroe said, the words spilling out of his mouth as sweat shone on his forehead.

"Who?" Carter barked.

"I don't know! All I know is that it wasn't me! Now please let your nephew and Leena go!"

Carter heard the sincerity in his words and he withdrew his gun. He knew that Monroe would never gamble with the lives of those he loved, especially the son he was just getting to know. *He's not behind this,* Carter thought as a new confusion swept over him. He had no other enemies. Who would make such a bold move against him?

Carter stepped away from a sobbing Leena and walked up to Monroe, who now stood on his feet. They stood toe to toe as they stared each other in the eyes.

"If you're lying, Money . . ."

"I'm not," Monroe responded. "Now get the fuck out of my house."

Monroe rushed over to his family as Carter stormed out.

Carter sat with the newspaper in front of him, staring at the dead faces of Monroe's security guards and the owner of the security company that employed them. Carter knew that Monroe had executed them for not protecting his home. The moment Carter stepped foot on his soil, the guards' lives had been put on a countdown. Carter didn't flinch or feel a sliver of remorse. As long as Miamor was missing, he didn't care how many people lost their lives in his persistent search to find her.

His bell rang, and one of his goons stood, instinctively placing a hand near his waist. Carter checked one of several monitors that were positioned discreetly around his mansion.

"Let her in," he said as he recognized Leena's face.

He stood and awaited her presence as she was given access to his mansion. She was the vision of beauty standing before him. Her flower-printed Prada dress flowed serenely behind her as she walked toward him while her heels clicked the floor. She stood across the room, twiddling her hands in front of her with worry written all over her face.

"I'm sorry it didn't work, Carter. I tried to make it look as real as possible, but your bastard brother would rather hold his secrets than to tell the truth to save me and his son," Leena said, her eyes watering. Carter would never put her or his nephew in harm's way. The clip wasn't even in the gun the night before when he held her at gunpoint to get Money's cooperation. "In one sentence he says he loves us, but when faced with a chance to prove it . . ."

"He loves you, Leena," Carter interrupted. "He wasn't lying. He doesn't have Miamor," Carter said. "This I'm sure of."

His words silenced her, and she looked down unsurely. "How can you be so sure?"

"I know my brother," Carter answered solemnly.

Leena had been around Carter long enough to see that he was hurting. His spirit was broken, and she could see the emotions taking a toll on him.

"She will be all right," Leena said, only half believing her words.

"Will she?" Carter replied.

Leena reached up and hugged Carter, planting a sisterly kiss on his cheek. "I have to get back. I'm not even supposed to be here. I told Monroe that I wouldn't leave the house, and the baby is with the nanny. I wish this war between you and your brother would end. I miss my family."

Carter kissed her forehead but didn't respond as he turned and walked out of the room.

Chapter 19

"What's a ring without a wedding?"

—Leena

Leena walked softly on the plush carpet as she approached Monroe's office. His door was wide open, and she stood there watching him nervously as she wrung her fingers in front of her body. He was intent, focused, powerful, and the most beautiful specimen of a man she had ever seen. Her heart thumped and she was overwhelmed with admiration every time she stood before him. He looked down at the paperwork before him, but was always aware of those around him. He sensed her presence the moment she had crept up.

"Come in here, beautiful," he said as he looked up from his busy work and sat back in his plush leather executive chair.

Leena walked in and rounded his desk until she stood directly between his legs.

"What's on your mind?" he asked her.

"That's what I've been wondering about you," she replied.

"Don't mince words, Lee. Tell me what's wrong, baby," he said.

"I miss Breeze and Carter and Zyir. Money, they're our family and this beef, this war, it's eating me up. It's not supposed to be like this," Leena said as she touched Monroe's face gently, making sure that he was looking her in the eyes. She needed him to feel the sincerity in her words. "Monroe misses his uncles, baby. They're all he knows."

Money's jaw tensed, but his temper didn't flare. Leena was his everything. He wished that his comeback could have been one big family reunion. He remembered the days of peace and unity within the Diamond clan, but it seemed that those times had died right along with his father, Carter Diamond.

Maybe if Monroe had never gone away, then he could **accept** Zyir as family. He would have been around to see the **love and** loyalty that Zyir had proven time and time again. **But as it** stood, Monroe felt that Zyir was trying to take his **place.**

Monroe refused to feel like an outsider in his own **organi-** zation, so he had built his own. The Opa-locka Money **Gang** showed him all the loyalty that a king deserved. The **streets** were eating his product up and no one, not even Zyir **with all** of his Cartel affiliation, could compete. If you weren't **seated** at Monroe's table then you didn't eat. He wasn't **saving any** sea bass for niggas who didn't rock with O.M.G.

"I need you to be like a chameleon, Leena. You **have to be** able to adapt to your surroundings. There are no **guaran-** tees in this lifestyle, Lee. The only thing that I can **promise is** that I will love you. I will love you until my body hits **the dirt,** and I will provide for you. You will be safe and we'll **live life** as long as God and the law lets me. The faces that **surround** us may change, and I need you to get used to that. **Don't get** too attached to anyone, because at any moment disloyalty **can** make them replaceable." Money pointed to his chest **and then** pointed to hers. "This is our family. You, me, and our **son . . .** we're all we got, and that's all you need." He lifted **her left fin-** ger and admired the flawless stone that he had placed **on it.** "That's why I gave you this."

"What's a ring without a wedding?" she asked sadly. **"With** everything that's going on, when will we have time **to get** married?"

"We'll make time, Lee. We can do it whenever you **want. In** fact, planning a wedding will keep you occupied. We **can do it** tomorrow if you want," Monroe said with a charming **smile.**

Leena smiled. "I need a little more time than **that," she** answered wistfully as she began to daydream about **colors** and floral arrangements.

"There's my girl," Monroe said with a wink.

"How about a month. I can get with a wedding **planner** and it can be small and intimate. Maybe I can invite **Breeze?"** Leena said.

Monroe missed his sister, but in his attempt to **keep the** beef hidden from her, he had barely seen or reached **out. She** was a sensitive subject, and Leena could see the wheels in his head turning as he considered the possibility.

"How about two weeks?" he suggested as he kissed her nose.

Leena leaned back and wrinkled her brow. "What's the rush? What aren't you telling me?" she asked. It was unlike Monroe to jump so quickly into commitment, and she knew that there had to be an ulterior motive behind this sudden rush to matrimony.

"I want you to be my wife, Leena. I want you and my son to be secure. We're at war, and if something happens to me, I need to know that you're entitled to everything I have," Monroe said honestly. "It's important that I leave you with the world at your feet."

"Seems like we're planning your funeral, Money . . . not our wedding," she whispered. Leena rose from his lap and walked toward the door.

Monroe didn't want to hurt her feelings or diminish her excitement, but he didn't want to lie to her. She could have the romantic side of things. His love for her was very real, but he knew that with street fame came the possibility of death. He just wanted her to be prepared for it, and as his wife, she would be.

Dear Carter,

I'm writing you this letter to let you know that I'm safe. I staged an entire kidnapping to run away from you. It was all fake. I didn't know how to tell you that I wanted out, and the entire setup just went too far. I hear that you're looking for me, that you've killed trying to find me. I want you to stop. I chose to leave you, Carter. No one forced me to. I walked away. I was suffocating in your world, and I can't go through life pretending that I am someone I'm not. I'm never coming back to you. Having your child would have been the biggest mistake I've ever made. I got an abortion, Carter. We're too different, and at the end of the day you're my enemy and your people took my sister from me. I've disappeared before, but this time

I promise I won't return. Move on, because I have. We're
just not meant to be.

Miamor

The words on the paper knocked Carter off of his feet, and he
slowly sat down on his couch and lowered his head. *I trusted
you,* he thought as he felt his heart splitting painfully in half.
The earth felt as if it had stopped spinning. He loosened his
Gucci slim tie as if it would help him breathe, but he was still
stifled. He couldn't inhale. Miamor had just pulled the rug
from beneath him, and he was falling into an emotional black
hole. She had done it once before, and now he kicked himself
for even giving her a second chance. He had supplied her with
the hope to better herself, but instead she had slipped a noose
around his neck and sent him flying off of a chair.

"Magdalena!" he called as he stood to his feet.

"Yes, Mr. Jones," his housekeeper replied as she instantly
appeared in front of him. The middle-aged woman stood
before him in a maid's uniform, awaiting his request.

"Please box up all of Miamor's things. Place them in storage.
She won't be coming back," Carter instructed. The housekeeper frowned yet nodded in compliance.

"And the baby's things? Would you like for me to box his
belongings as well?" she asked.

It was at the mention of his seed that Carter's resolve weakened. His eyes burned, but he willed his devastation away as
he replied, "No, leave the nursery exactly as it is."

He knew that there was no more baby to plan for, but he
didn't have the strength to see the room return to a blank
canvas with white walls.

Magdalena looked at him with sympathy.

"I'm sorry, Mr. Jones," she said. She didn't know the full
story, but she could see the sadness hanging from Carter's
shoulders like coats from a rack.

"Me too," he replied. He looked at the picture of Miamor
that sat in a small frame on the mantle of his fireplace. He
thought of the things that he had done for her, the people he
had crossed for her, and wars that had started over her. It

seemed as if he was always the one sacrificing to make them work, and still she was disloyal. He pulled the picture down and tossed it into the fire. "Me too."

As the days passed Miamor grew resentful. She didn't want to be with Murder. She didn't need him in her life. His season had passed a long time ago, and he refused to accept the fact that she had moved on. His attempts at conversation were blocked by her obvious disdain for him, but he was patient. He looked at Miamor like a drug addict. She had become dependent on Carter, and he was determined to be her morphine. He was weaning her off. After the letter he had forged to him on her behalf, Carter would no longer be looking for her anyway. Little did Miamor know Murder had destroyed their bond with one little Dear John.

"You can't just keep me here," she said, her arms crossed as she sat across the room from him. "I'm pregnant. I need medical care. I need vitamins and checkups. I'm extremely high risk. I need to be home. Carter—"

Murder was on her in a flash, across the room, and flipping over the coffee table, clearing his path to get to her. "Don't mention the nigga name in my presence. You lucky I'm even letting you keep that fucking baby. I'm trying real hard to keep shit cool with you, Miamor. But you're pushing me! Shut the fuck up about that nigga. You're here until I say it's time to go. You're never going back to that nigga. When you stop being fucking stubborn you'll realize that's what's best for you."

"What happened to you in there? I don't even recognize you," Miamor said with tears in her eyes. "Since when do you treat me like this? Since when do you talk to me like this?"

"Since you started fucking the next nigga," Murder spat. "When you act like the old you, I'll become the old me."

Miamor shook her head, disgusted. It didn't matter what Murder did. He couldn't turn back the hands of time. She had outgrown him, plain and simple. "If I meant as much as you say I do, then you'd get me to a doctor. . . . You would let me go."

Chapter 20

"One to the heart. No head shots, no torture."

—Carter

"You're beautiful," Breeze said as she stood back and watched Leena try on the beautiful ivory wedding gown. It was Vera Wang, and although the popular wedding designer was booked clear through the next two seasons, Money had given her a bottomless budget to make his bride-to-be's dreams come true. Leena spun around and rushed to Breeze.

"You made it!" she squealed in joy as the two women embraced. "It's so good to see you!" Leena was genuinely elated to be around Breeze. The two women were more than close, and it had been too long since they last spoke.

"Of course I made it!" Breeze said. "You're getting married tomorrow, and I'm honored that you want me to be the first person to see the dress. It's amazing!"

Breeze noticed the sad look in Leena's eyes. "What's wrong? Why aren't you happy? This is what you want, right?"

Leena shook off her poor mood and masked it with an insincere smile. "Yes, I'm fine. Sorry. I guess I'm just nervous."

Breeze wasn't buying Leena's excuse, however. She frowned and turned to the saleswoman. "Could you excuse us for a moment?" Breeze asked. The woman exited the fitting room and Breeze grabbed Leena's hand. "This is not the face of a woman getting married tomorrow. Now spill."

"Things are complicated, Breeze. I love Money and he's good to me, but this isn't how I envisioned this day. It all feels a little rushed. You're not even in the wedding."

"Yeah, well, considering you decided this two weeks ago, I'd say that it is rushed," Breezed answered with a smile. "It doesn't matter, Leena. You are meant for Money and he is meant for you. As long as the two of you are happy, no one else matters. Besides, I'll be there. I wouldn't miss this day for the world."

"Does Zyir know you're here?" Leena asked.

"You asked me not to tell him so I didn't. He's been distant lately, focused on other things," Breeze said, more to herself than to Leena.

Leena knew that Breeze didn't know what was going on between Zyir and Monroe. As much as she wanted to tell her, it wasn't her place. Breeze was the baby of the family, and she had been through a lot. No one liked to add burdens to her delicate shoulders.

"But we're not talking about me, we're talking about you." Breeze turned Leena toward the mirror and stood behind her as they looked at the reflection. "Now where's the veil?" Breeze asked. She spotted it in a box on the floor and pulled it out, admiring it briefly before clipping it in Leena's hair.

They both gasped in amazement.

"Now that's the smile of a bride," Breeze said. "You're perfection."

They embraced and Breeze checked her Burberry wrist piece. "I've got to go, but I'll see you tomorrow. You're staying at Turnberry Isle tonight?" she asked.

"Yeah, Money put me in a suite there. The entire glam squad is coming in the morning," Leena said.

"I'll see you then, bright and early. I love you, Lee!" Breeze said as she headed for the door.

"Love you too! Don't be late!"

Breeze leaned back against Zyir's chest as he held the book they were reading in front of him. It was a ritual that they had started when they first met, and to this very day they still read to one another every night that they were together.

"Flip the page, B," Zyir said.

Breeze sighed and turned it to the next page, but Zyir could tell that she had stopped indulging in the juicy exploits of *Six and Free* long ago. He put down the book and she didn't even protest. She was too distracted to notice.

"You want to be with Leena right now, don't you?" he whispered.

Breeze turned toward him in shock. It was as if he had read her mind.

"This is the first lie you've ever told me, baby girl, and I must say you're not very good at it," Zyir said. "I've known about the wedding since you found out. You're very loud on the phone, ma. Where'd you learn to whisper, a helicopter?"

Breeze laughed and cut her eyes as she exclaimed, "Why didn't you say something? I've been trying to keep this a secret for two weeks!" Breeze exhaled, relieved that the secret was out. She hit him playfully with the book they had been reading. "I know you think that I'm naïve, but just because I follow your lead, Zyir, doesn't mean I'm blind to the things happening around me."

"Why aren't you invited to the wedding? Why isn't Carter? Why haven't I talked to Money since that dinner at Carter's house?" Breeze asked. "I have a feeling; I'm just hoping that it's wrong. I don't want to have to choose between the men in my life."

Zyir kissed the top of her head and inhaled her angelic scent. Her Cashmere Mist perfume, her signature scent, enveloped him.

"Things have been . . ." He paused to choose his words carefully. He didn't want Breeze to know too much. How could he tell her that the first chance he got he was going to blow her brother's head off his shoulders? Admitting such would be marital suicide. It would destroy their relationship forever.

"Things have been what?" Breeze asked.

"Tense," he finished. "We're all trying to figure out our place in The Cartel." Before she could ask any more questions he added, "But that shouldn't stop you from being with Leena and your nephew tonight. I'll call a car for you."

"Promise me that you'll work things out with Money," she said.

"I can promise to try," Zyir replied honestly. She turned and kissed his lips.

"I need you to try your hardest, Zyir. He's my brother." Her eyes told him that a storm would come if anything happened to Monroe; little did she know that Monroe had signed his own death certificate. He would fall, and soon Breeze would have to decide exactly where she stood. Zyir only hoped that their love would be strong enough to endure.

He sent her with a driver to Leena's suite and watched her drive away. As soon as the taillights could no longer be seen, he called Carter.

"Zyir, is everything smooth, fam? It's late," Carter answered, seeing Zyir's name on his caller ID.

"The nigga Money is getting married tomorrow. This is the first time I've been able to pinpoint this nigga's location. I'm not invited, but I'ma be there, nah mean?" Zyir said.

Carter was silent as he weighed the pros and cons in his head. "I don't know, Zy. Shit could get messy. Leena and my nephew will be there," Carter said. He was still trying to figure out a way to keep the peace and restore balance to the situation, but Monroe was making it very difficult.

"I sent Breeze to Leena's suite in Aventura. Li'l man is there with them. My driver will be on call in the morning to take them to the wedding, only I've already made sure that they never get there. By the time they realize something's wrong, the nigga Money will be leaking at the altar," Zyir stated.

A lump formed in Carter's throat, but he fought his conscience and said, "Make it quick, Zy. One to the heart. No head shots, no torture."

His voice was sad, and he felt nothing but regret as he gave the nod of approval.

"We got to get him before he gets us," Zyir said. "He sent bullets flying through your windows, fam. If the shoe was on the other foot and he had a clear shot, Money would pull the trigger."

"I know," Carter answered. "What kind of brotherhood is this?" he asked. He sighed and finished, "Take care of it. That solves our beef problem, but we still need a new connect. I'll hop on a flight in the A.M. to the West Coast. I've got a few connections out there that might be able to accommodate us."

"Sounds good, fam. I'll hit you after that thing is taken care of," Zyir said. Zyir hung up the phone and a crooked smile crossed his handsome, youthful face. Carter had just given him the green light, and it was all the permission he needed to make Monroe Diamond extinct.

Chapter 21

"I want shrimp and lobster, naked bitches and good pussy,
linen suits and ocean views."

—Polo

Carter looked out into the night sky from the window of his private jet. In deep contemplation, he couldn't help but to think of Miamor. He shook his head, tossing her from his train of thought, and focused on the task at hand. He sank deeper into the plush leather seats.

He was bound for sunny California—Los Angeles to be exact, where he hoped to link up with his father's old running partner, Polo. The streets were a perfect distraction from Miamor, and he was ready to jump back in headfirst.

Monroe only had the game locked because Carter had allowed him room to eat. With his shark Zyir on his tail, it was only a matter of time before Monroe was out of the picture. His reign would be short-lived indeed, but it was a choice that Monroe had made the moment he had turned against the family. Carter knew that Monroe's death was one that would tear his entire family apart, but also a death that was necessary. His heart could not be any more broken than it was so fuck it, he was sending the Grim Reaper to Monroe's door with no remorse.

The pilot prepared for landing, and Carter gazed out over the lights of the city. Polo wasn't expecting him. Carter never liked to let anyone know his next move; the unexpected was always the safest way to move. That way no one could see him coming. In fact, Polo thought he was living in seclusion, cut off from all of his Miami ties. Little did he know that Carter had always known where he was, down to the four numbers on his mailbox.

As the plane made its final descent over the city, Carter gathered himself. Polo would definitely know where to go to get the product that Carter needed, and he wanted to hit the ground running. This wasn't a parlay trip. It was all business all the time for Carter, and he wasn't leaving without a brand-new cocaine connect. He wouldn't complain if he could corner the heroin trade either. Prescription drugs even. Los Angeles was the land of opportunity, and Carter was going to take advantage of the things it had to offer.

A black Maybach waited at the end of the clear port upon Carter's arrival, and he wasted no time instructing the driver how to get to Polo's Santa Monica apartment. He wondered why someone who had hustled so large now lived so small, and he vowed to make smart money moves with his dough so that he wouldn't end up living mediocre after his own retirement.

As the driver pulled onto Polo's street, Carter sat up attentively as he surveyed the area. "Spin the block for me," Carter instructed the driver, who nodded in reply. His paranoia was what kept him free and living. Many niggas had gotten caught slipping by being too relaxed. Carter would rather be safe than sorry. "Park up front. Do not move the car under any circumstances," Carter said.

"Yes, sir," the driver responded. He got out of the car and opened Carter's door.

Carter emerged and buttoned his Ferragamo suit jacket before heading to the entrance. The building was nice, luxurious even, and sat across the street from the Santa Monica beach, but still Carter wondered why Polo wasn't put up in a Beverly Hills estate. Ownership was key in Carter's book. Why lease a unit when you can own the building?

He knocked at Polo's door. It had been half a decade since they had last seen one another. He hoped his father's right-hand man was well, and he was eager to check in on him. The door opened, and Carter stood face to face with Polo the God a.k.a Uncle Polo, the godfather to all of Carter Diamond's children, including Carter Jones. Recognition registered in his gaze, but the words that came out of his mouth didn't match.

"Who are you?" he asked.

Carter stepped back, thrown off guard as he frowned. "It's me, Carter," he replied in confusion. "You don't know who I am?"

Polo shooed him away from his door. "G'on, young'un. Ain't nothing for you at my door. It's a young lady live a few doors down. You got the wrong apartment number, son," he said.

Before Carter could get another word out, the door was slammed in his face. Carter stood there for a second, stunned and obviously lost. He turned around and walked hesitantly away from the door. He looked back at the closed door, wondering what the hell that was all about. *I'll come back tomorrow,* he thought, hoping that Polo hadn't gone crazy from baking in the hot L.A. sun.

Carter checked into one of the swankiest five-star hotels in West Hollywood, reserving the penthouse suite for his stay. After tipping the bellman to deliver his bags, he was escorted by the concierge to the fiftieth floor.

Italian marble graced the floor, and the expansive floor-to-ceiling windows made Carter feel as if he were the king of the city. All of L.A. was at his feet as he looked out over the nightlife. The concierge left him well appointed with his requested vintage bottle of wine and a steak dinner already prepared and waiting for him to enjoy. He tipped the man generously and then sat down at the large dining table to indulge in his dinner for one.

He looked at the vacant chair across from him and emptiness filled his chest. His thoughts drifted to Miamor. Her absence was suffocating Carter, and he had never felt more alone than he did in that moment. He should be courting her all over the city, wining and dining, shopping and sightseeing. Instead he was solo and missing life as it passed him by.

BUZZ!

The bell to the room rang, and Carter stood, knowing that it was his bags being delivered. He grabbed a twenty dollar bill out of his money clip and headed for the door. He pulled it open.

"Young Carter."

"Hello, Polo," Carter replied as he embraced him. "It's good to see you. I thought you had lost your wit for a minute there, old man. What was that all about?" Carter asked in confusion.

Polo pointed to the steak that could be smelled clear across the room. "Why don't you order another one of those three hundred dollar steak dinners and let me fill you in?"

The two men sat over dinner, and Polo cut into his steak. He savored the flavor and said, "Now that's a steak."

Carter chuckled. "How did you know where I was staying?"

"You're Carter Diamond's son. I picked the most expensive hotel in L.A.," Polo said. "But look, you can't just show up out here unannounced. I've got a lot going on out here—things that you don't want to get wrapped up in."

"Try me," Carter said, fishing for more details.

"What I'm about to tell you will probably make me look like a snake, but it's the only thing keeping me free. After I left Miami, I began cooperating with the Feds against Estes," Polo admitted.

Carter put down his knife and fork, and his eyes immediately went to the door.

"You don't have to worry about them, Carter. They didn't follow me here, but they are watching every single person that steps foot to my door. That's why when you showed up out of the blue I acted like I'd never seen you before," Polo explained. "The last thing you need are ties to me. That'll automatically put you under a federal scope."

Carter silently kicked himself for walking right into the middle of a federal investigation. He knew that the DEA was the most thorough crime fighter on the planet. They had a war against drugs that had taken down some of the greats in the game. Just by putting his face on their cameras he knew that they would be asking who he was and what he did. He had drawn attention to himself.

"Are you wired?" Carter asked sternly.

"What? No, never against you," Polo assured.

Carter pulled his pistol off of his hip and placed it on the table. "Then you won't have a problem standing and unbuttoning your shirt," Carter said.

Polo paused briefly, slightly offended that Carter wanted proof, but as a major player in the game, he understood. He stood and unbuttoned his shirt, revealing nothing but a slight gut and hairy chest.

Carter exhaled, relaxing slightly. "I have to take every precaution. I hope you understand," Carter said.

"I do, Carter," Polo responded.

"Now what the fuck would make you turn into a federal snitch, Polo?" Carter asked with contempt.

"The muthafucka Estes is a snake. He played the game dirty, young blood. The nigga left me in the middle of the fucking Atlantic in a boat the size of a bathtub. The fucking US Coast Guard pulled me from the water, and guess what they found taped underneath the fucking boat?" Polo paused and shook his head as he rubbed the top of it, clearly stressed from the recollection of events. "Five fucking kilos of cocaine. The nigga set me up. I was going away, and I don't know about you, but I don't want to spend my golden years behind steel and concrete beating my dick to naked photos. I want shrimp and lobster, naked bitches and good pussy, linen suits and ocean views. So I either had to take those years or turn on the nigga that set me up. Estes robbed me and your father for years, giving us bull-shit prices and bad coke. We still built an empire off of that shit, and it burned him up. Wetback, Dominican muthafucka tried to put me under the jail, so I turned on him. I'm the master at the double-cross," Polo said.

Carter rubbed his goatee and shook his head. "Damn." Carter didn't condone Polo's method of revenge, but it was his choice. They were grown men, and Polo had made his bed.

"Anybody associated with that scumbag is going down," Polo said.

Carter thought of Monroe. "Money is associated with Estes," he revealed.

"What? Monroe is dead," Polo shot back.

"Estes staged Monroe's death to protect him from the Haitians, Polo. He is very much alive, and he's doing business with Estes," Carter said as he stood to his feet. He began to pace the room.

"I had no idea," Polo said regretfully. "I'd never do anything to destroy The Cartel."

"He's not aligned with The Cartel anymore, Polo. I came here to get a connect from you so that I could take back the streets from Monroe. He wanted out. He wanted to do his own thing," Carter explained.

"And now you're at war with your brother over real estate in Miami," Polo summarized. "He is your brother, Carter, your younger brother. You are his keeper. Me and your daddy were like brothers, and I don't give a fuck what beef we had; I would never bring him harm. You take care of your brothers, Carter."

Guilt weighed down Carter's shoulders, because he had just given Zyir the okay to take care of Monroe.

"Money is out of control. He tried to have my young'un Zyir murked. He's murdering our men, burning our trap houses. . . ."

"He's your brother. Money and Zyir aren't fighting over money, drugs, turf. . . . They're fighting over you. They both want to be at your right. You've got to make them realize that they both are equally valuable to you. You're the oldest; you can dead the beef," Polo said, cutting off Carter. "Monroe and your friend Zyir will follow by your example. You have the power to remedy things, but whether you do or not, chances are the war will be over soon. I hate to say this, but Monroe is under scrutiny of the Feds. There is no way that he can make it out of this one, and unless you want to see him spend his life behind bars, you have to warn him."

"You should have warned us all, Polo," Carter answered.

Polo stood to his feet and placed his fedora hat back on his head.

"I'm sorry, Carter. I've still got some connections in South America and a few over in Asia. These are safe; nobody knows about these," he said as he wrote down contact information for Carter. "These connects make Estes's coke look like baby powder."

"Is this a setup?" Carter asked, disappointed that someone so thorough had turned informant.

"No, Carter, this is the real deal, baby boy," Polo replied. He looked at Carter with sympathetic eyes. "Take care of your brother. Get him out of the country as soon as possible. They have been building this case against Estes for four years. Money doesn't want to be anywhere near Estes when the other shoe drops."

Chapter 22

"The massacre reminded her
of her father's funeral."

—Unknown

Leena sat at the vanity mirror and Breeze stood directly behind her, admiring her beauty.

"You are beautiful," Breeze said as she looked at Leena, who was dolled up and looking glamorous. It was the day of Leena and Monroe's wedding. The sun shone beautifully and was the making of a fairytale day for Leena. Breeze stroke her hair and smiled at her, giving her approval.

"Are you ready for this big step?" Breeze asked as genuine joy was in her heart for her brother and his soon-to-be wife.

"Yes. I am," Leena said and smiled at Breeze. Just as the words came out of her mouth, they were interrupted. Little Monroe came running into the room with his tuxedo on, looking more like his father than ever. Breeze grabbed him up playfully and kissed him on the cheek.

"Where you think you going, li'l man?" she asked as she beamed from ear to ear. He playfully laughed, and she put him back down and began to fix his bowtie. "You look so handsome, Mr. Diamond," she added. When she looked at little Monroe, she not only saw the resemblance with big Monroe; she saw all of the three men she lost: her father, Mecca, and Monroe. The realization that her whole family had crumbled hit her. She felt the tears begin to build in her eyes, thinking about what the Diamond family had endured.

The sound of a car horn blew, and all of their attention immediately went to the window and snapped Breeze out of her sad thoughts.

Breeze looked out of the window and saw that the car service had arrived. "Okay, it's time to go," Breeze said as she looked at Leena. Leena took a nervous, deep breath and returned the smile.

"I'm ready," she said. With that, they left to head to the wedding.

A tall, well-built driver with a suit and shades waited by the car, the back door open for them. Breeze held the back of Leena's dress to prevent it from dragging on the ground, and Leena had little Monroe in her arms as they made their way to the car. They got into the SUV and headed to the site of the big wedding.

Monroe fixed his bowtie in the mirror as his goons stood around him. His black-on-black tuxedo was tailor fit, and it flawlessly hung on his shoulders. He looked sharp, resembling a black James Bond, but even more debonair.

Monroe looked around, and it hit him like a ton of bricks. He was around a whole bunch of niggas who were not family. He knew they were all there because they were working for him. None of them were there on the strength of love for him. It was his wedding day, and he was surrounded by shooters rather than his brothers.

"You ready, big homie?" one of the Opa-locka goons asked.

"Yeah, just ready to get this over with," he said as he checked his cufflinks. Just as he was doing so, Estes walked in. Monroe looked at his crew and gave them a nod, signaling them to leave the room. Almost instantly they filed out of the room, each of them greeting Estes on their way out, out of respect.

"Grandson, today is your big day," Estes said as he walked up to Monroe and straightened up his shirt and his bowtie perfectly.

"Yeah, I can't lie. I'm kind of nervous," Monroe said, being truthful with his grandfather.

Estes chuckled as he rested his hand on Monroe's shoulder to provide his support. "You know what? Years ago, your father said the same thing on the day that he married my daughter. Don't be nervous, son. You are doing the right thing by your family and stepping up to the plate as a man—an honorable man. I just wish your mother and father were here to see you today. They would have been so proud of you today," Estes lectured as he released a rare smile.

"I know that they would have," Monroe said as he returned the smile. "I love you, Grandfather," Monroe said. The two men embraced, and Monroe heard the music begin playing to serenade the few guests who attended the wedding. "I guess that's my cue," Monroe said as he looked back toward the door.

"Let's go," Estes said as he put his arm around Monroe.

They both headed to the front of the ceremony where the priest was waiting. Abruptly, Estes went to the back, having to take a leak before the ceremony started.

"Wait. Isn't the wedding that way?" Leena asked as she pointed at the southbound interstate sign.

"Yeah, you right," Breeze said as she looked out the window, noticing that they were going the wrong way. "Excuse me, sir. You are going the wrong way. We need to be going south," Breeze said as she yelled to the front.

It seemed as if the driver didn't hear her, because he didn't flinch or respond. He just acted as if she wasn't there.

"Excuse me!" Breeze said, and rang her voice a level higher. The response was just the same . . . nothing. At this point, they knew something was wrong.

"Pull this car over right now!' Breeze yelled as she looked on in disbelief.

The driver finally acknowledged Breeze and looked at her through the rearview mirror. "Look, ma'am, I can't do that," he said with a respectful tone.

"What the hell you mean, you can't?" Leena chimed in as she was trying to figure out what was going on.

"The man who hired me gave me specific instructions. He said drive as far from the wedding as possible. Take it up with him," the driver said, trying to get the women off of his back.

Zyir made the driving arrangements. He had a plan, and to execute it he needed Breeze out of harm's way.

"What? My wedding starts in thirty minutes! You need to turn your ass around and get me there!" Leena yelled as she began to burn from the inside out.

The driver was following orders, but with the two women in his ear nagging him, he knew that it was smart to take them where they requested. He turned around and headed to the wedding site. Little did they know, they were walking straight into a bullet-filled melee.

The wedding setup was beautiful and elegant. It was outside, and everything was draped in white. A live band serenaded the guests, and slow jazz filled the air as a crooner began to zat flawlessly.

Zyir's goons were scattered throughout the crowd, including Fly Boogie, who was trying to stay low key in the back row. He had a Tech tucked inside of his tuxedo jacket. His black shades did little to hide his identity, but at that point he didn't care. He was just ready to get the party started. On top of the people in the audience, Zyir had shooters pretending to be waiters.

Little did Monroe know, he had walked into a big booby trap. Monroe walked up to the front of the crowd and stood next to the preacher, who held a Bible in his left hand. The wedding was scheduled to start in five minutes. Everyone was just waiting on the bride to show up . . . but Zyir had a different plan for that particular day.

Zyir also sat in the back, hoping not to get noticed before he gave the signal for hell to break loose. He wanted Monroe and his crew dead. Zyir had just put a major chess move on Monroe, and with Carter's blessing it was about to go down.

Zyir looked across the room and nodded at Fly Boogie. That was all Fly Boogie needed to let the pandemonium begin. He stood up and whipped out the Tech that he had concealed. He instantly pointed to the whole front row and let it off, hitting four of Monroe's goons with one sweep, Fly Boogie was getting busy.

Just as planned, Zyir's other shooters pulled out their guns and began hitting anybody who didn't come in with them. The sounds of thundering blast and bullets whizzing filled the air, and the place went into a complete frenzy.

Monroe ducked down and immediately looked for Estes. However, it was pointless, because Zyir had locked him in the restroom, not wanting to bring any more pain to Breeze's heart. He opted not to kill the grandfather, but everyone else was fair game. He came there on that day for blood, and he was not taking any shorts.

Zyir immediately began to let off shots at Monroe, trying to take his head off. Monroe, never slipping, reached and grabbed the small-caliber gun from the inside pocket of his tux and began to bust back as he took cover.

The massacre had begun as the bodies began to drop and bleed. Zyir's crew and Monroe's were trading bullets, and it was a complete war zone.

Throughout all of the chaos, Monroe and Zyir were busting shots at each other, trying to kill one another. In the meantime, bodies were dropping like flies. The pastor even caught a stray bullet to the abdomen as the two sides went all out against each other.

The shootout went on for seven minutes straight as the killers tried to kill the killers. The gunfire gradually thinned out, and only two guns were being shot—Monroe's and Zyir's. They traded bullets with each other, neither of them hitting anything. Zyir used the corner of the outhouse as a shield, while Monroe ducked behind the stage and used that as his fort. They were trying to take each other's heads off.

Zyir looked around and saw all of the dead bodies. Some of his soldiers were dead, and some of Monroe's were too. He saw Fly Boogie hiding behind a tree with his gun close to his chest. Zyir looked over and they made eye contact. Fly Boogie signaled that he had no more bullets, and Zyir nodded his head and signaled for him to stay put.

Zyir looked at his gun, which was jammed back, and realized that he had run out of bullets. He was a sitting duck at that point, and it would be damn near impossible for him to escape without someone covering him. Zyir, out of pure adrenaline, stepped out in the open with his arms out.

"Monroe!" he yelled. "Bring yo' bitch ass out right now!" Zyir was now in the middle of the floor, stepping in between all of the dead bodies. Just as he figured, Monroe popped up with his gun drawn. He knew that Monroe's ego wouldn't let him stay hidden behind the stage.

Zyir racked his gun back and made it seem as if he had more ammunition, but he was taking his chances bluffing.

Monroe and Zyir slowly walked toward each other, meeting in the middle of the floor. They both had their guns pointed at each other, both of them out of bullets while trying to bluff the other. As they both looked down the barrel of a gun, so much hatred was in their hearts as they stared intensely at the man who stood before them.

"You come in here on my wedding day trying to kill me?" Monroe asked through his clenched teeth. He was burning with anger toward Zyir for having the audacity.

"Yeah, and I'm not done yet," Zyir said smoothly as he gripped his gun tightly and returned the screw-face toward Monroe.

Just as Monroe was about to respond, they had guests walk through the door. Leena, his son, and Breeze walked in and witnessed the bloodbath that was supposed to be a joyful day.

"Oh my God," Leena said as she placed her hand over her mouth. Leena quickly grabbed little Monroe and rushed him back out, not wanting him to see the gory sight.

Breeze was frozen in terror as she stopped in her tracks. It reminded her of her father's funeral. It was a complete massacre. Breeze then focused her attention on the two men at the center of the floor, both with guns drawn on each other.

"Zyir! Monroe! No! Stop right now!" Breeze yelled as she stormed toward the two. "Put the guns down now. Please, I'm begging the two of you! Look at all of this. Look what you two have done," she said as her voice began to crack. She was pleading with all of her heart.

Monroe was the first to look away, and when he saw Breeze crying, it hurt him deeply. She fell to her knees and folded her hands in a praying position.

"Please stop, you two. Please! I have lost everything and everyone. I can't take it anymore. I can't!" she said as the tears began to flow down freely and in abundance.

Zyir briefly took his eyes off of Monroe and looked at his wife crying. It broke his heart to see his wife in so much agony. His heart softened temporarily, and he looked back at Monroe, who was in the same spot.

"I'll see you again," Zyir whispered in a low tone that only Monroe would be able to hear.

"Indeed, bitch-ass nigga," Monroe responded with a smile.

With that, Monroe fled the scene. Zyir watched him leave and then lowered his gun. He immediately went over to Breeze, who was completely broken down, sobbing. Zyir walked over to her and tried to console her. He helped her to her feet, and she immediately hauled off and slapped him.

"How could you!" she yelled. Zyir stumbled to the ground and fell on one knee. Breeze knew that she wasn't that powerful, so she looked closer and saw a bloodstain forming in Zyir's abdominal area. He had caught a bullet from the crossfire, and due to adrenaline, never noticed it. "Zyir!' she yelled as he grimaced and held his stomach in pain.

Miamor sat across the table from Murder, frustrated with her plastic fork and butter knife. She tried to cut the steak that Murder had prepared for her, but the utensils broke for the second time. "Can you at least cut the fucking steak up for me since I can't have a knife?" she asked as she looked at Murder with hateful eyes and resentment. Murder shook his head in disbelief and reluctantly got up and walked over to Miamor. He cut her steak into pieces for her and quickly returned to his seat.

"There you go, eat up," he encouraged as he slid a piece of steak into his mouth.

"You could have given me the knife. I can cut my own steak," Miamor said as she shook her head and took a bite of her food.

Murder chuckled and shook his head. "Really? You think I would give you a knife right now? If it were any other chick . . . maybe. But you can make a knife a deadly weapon. I'm not letting that growing belly over there fool me. You're not some weak pregnant chick, li'l mama. I know how you get down, Miamor. Remember, I taught you," Murder said, killing any thought of Miamor doing any slick stuff that she was conjuring up in her mind.

Abruptly, Miamor doubled over in pain, grabbing her stomach. Murder smiled and ignored her, knowing that she was trying to be deceiving. But when she yelled out in pain and knocked her plate to the floor, causing it to shatter, he grew concerned.

Miamor fell to her knees while cupping her baby in agony. Murder looked at her face and saw that she began to sweat profusely, and at that point, he knew that she wasn't faking but being sincere. Murder instantly got up and went over to Miamor's aid. Although he was holding her against her will, he wanted nothing but the best for her. He couldn't stand to see her hurt.

She was on her hands and knees, grimacing in pain as she breathed heavily. Murder then dropped to his knees and removed her hair from in front of her face.

"What's wrong? Are you okay?" he asked as a look of concern was plastered all over his face.

Miamor was sweating and drool was sliding out of her mouth as she attempted to look in Murder's eyes.

"Are you okay?" he asked again as he put his hand on her back. He never saw it coming. Miamor had grabbed a sharp piece of the shattered plate, and with all her might, she jammed the sharp end into Murder's neck.

She let off a roar as she plunged it as deep and hard as she could. Murder instantly grabbed his neck with both hands, and blood began to leak from his mouth. He gagged, not being able to breathe, as his eyes got as big as two golf balls.

Miamor scurried away from him as he reached for her, almost as if he was saying, "help me." She stood to her feet and quickly grabbed the keys that were on his belt buckle. Murder was dying slowly, and Miamor had tears well up in her eyes as she snatched the keys from him and ran to the door.

Murder repeatedly gasped for breath as he slowly crawled over to Miamor as she tried to figure out which key went to each lock. The piece of glass lodged in his throat blocked his airway, and he began to slip in and out of consciousness.

Miamor finally got the locks unlocked and exited the house and ran for dear life, all while Murder was choking on his own blood. Just before he reached his last breath, he mumbled four words. It was four words that he meant with all of his heart. "I love you, Miamor."

Chapter 23

"If the shoe was on the other foot,
I'd be in the basement morgue."

—Zyir

Things seemed to move in slow motion as Breeze sat with her face in her palms, bent over in worry as blue scrubs rushed in numerous directions around her. She hated everything about the hospital. Its sterile scent made her stomach turn, the pale white walls were numbingly disgusting. She had seen one too many hospitals, laid in one too many electric beds, met one too many nurses. If she never stepped foot inside another hospital again she could die a happy woman.

She had been sitting for hours, waiting impatiently as her foot did a tap dance against the tiled floor. A mixture of anger and concern brewed inside of her chest. There had been so much blood. Zyir had been in so much pain. *God, please be with him. If something happens to him, I'll die. . . .*

"Are you the young woman that came in with Zyir Rich?"

Her prayers were interrupted by a young black girl with a fresh doobie wrap and a friendly smile. Breeze looked up.

"Yes, I'm his wife . . . Breeze," she said quickly, eagerly. Her desperation was apparent. "Is he okay? Is he out of surgery? Please tell me something. I've been sitting here for hours. No one will tell me anything."

"I'm Nurse Jackie," the girl responded. "Zyir is out of surgery, and the doctors did a wonderful job. They removed the bullet and repaired most of the damage. He will need to stay here for about a week, but he is very lucky."

Breeze placed a hand over her chest and breathed a sigh of relief.

"Can I see him?" she asked.

Before she received an answer, sirens rang out and a group of nurses and doctors rushed to the ER doors.

"Jackie, get over here. We've got one coming in!" one of the doctors yelled to the young girl standing before Breeze.

"I'm sorry. I've got to go. Someone will come for you when you can see him," the girl yelled as she ran across the room.

Breeze walked toward the commotion as she watched the girl jump into the action. The doctors and nurses transferred a body from the back of an ambulance onto a gurney and wheeled it quickly past Breeze.

"This woman is in pre-term labor and the baby's heartbeat is weakening. We've got to get this baby out of her now!" a doctor yelled.

Breeze looked at the face on the gurney and her mouth fell open in shock. She chased after the group of doctors and nurses. "Wait!" she yelled.

"Please, ma'am, someone will be out to inform you about your husband," Nurse Jackie said urgently.

"But wait! I know her! She's my—"

Before Breeze could finish her sentence, they had wheeled their patient into a restricted area, leaving Breeze standing in the hallway distraught. She stormed out of the hospital and into the parking lot, where she pulled out her phone.

"Please answer, please answer," she mumbled as she dialed Carter's number.

"Hello?"

As soon as she heard his voice, she began to cry. "Carter! You have to come home. Everything is out of control. Money shot Zyir. There was a big shootout. We need you here. I found . . ." She swallowed the lump in her throat. "I found Miamor."

Carter boarded his jet with urgency as he nodded a greeting to the pilot. "Let's get her in the air as soon as possible. I need to get back to Miami immediately," Carter instructed.

"I think they might slow things down," the pilot responded. Carter turned to him in confusion, and the pilot pointed to the red and blue lights that were racing toward Carter's jet.

The unmarked black vehicles were filled with federal agents, and Carter's worst fear had come to fruition.

Visiting Polo had been a mistake. There was no doubt in his mind that Polo had kept his promise by not speaking about The Cartel to the Feds, but just by showing up at his door, he knew that he was now on the radar of the government. Carter had been down this road before. He wasn't trying to catch another case, especially a fed case.

"Start the engine," Carter said as he stepped off of the plane.

One agent approached him, yelling over the whir of the plane's propellers. "Carter Jones!" he shouted as he flashed his badge. "Agent Cooper. I can't let you get on this plane."

"Considering that your cuffs aren't out and your men don't have their guns drawn I'd say that you don't have a warrant," Carter said calmly as he tucked his hands in his designer slacks and stood shoulders squared in front of the agent. "Now I'm going to get on this plane and fly back to Miami, and you will forget that you ever saw my face, if you know what's good for you. Do your homework, Agent Cooper. You can't beat me." Carter patted the agent on the shoulder as if to say, "Better luck next time." He then turned and ascended the steps to his jet without ever letting the pig mu'fuckas below him see him sweat.

Carter could face a thousand-man army, stare down the Feds, or take on any other kingpin without batting an eye, but when it came to seeing Miamor, he couldn't handle it. He walked into the dark hospital room and saw her resting peacefully. He didn't understand exactly what had occurred, but he was grateful to see her nonetheless.

He looked at her flattened abdomen and knew that she had told the truth in her letter. She had aborted the baby, his baby, and he had to bite his inner jaw to contain his sadness. Why couldn't she just be the woman he expected her to be? What was it that made her so cold, so disloyal when it came to him? And despite all of this, why couldn't he ever let her go? He couldn't get her out of his system. Whenever she beckoned, he came running to her rescue, no matter what kind of hurt she had put on his heart. Carter couldn't figure out why his heart wanted her so badly.

Nurse Jackie walked into the room.

"She's strong," Nurse Jackie said.

Carter nodded his head. "She is," he agreed with a sarcastic scoff.

"You must be the child's father? He's in the nursery. He's small and very fragile, but he's strong, too. Not many babies survive being born three months early, but he's a fighter. Would you like to see him?" the nurse asked.

Carter looked at her as if she were speaking French. He looked back at Miamor and then to the nurse. "She had the baby?"

"Yes, she had him a few hours ago. That's why she's so exhausted. She's probably on Mars right now because of all the pain medication she's on, but she'll wake up when she's good and rested. She did good today. She almost lost your son, and she cussed the doctors out every step of the way, until she heard his screams," Nurse Jackie said.

Carter leaned over and kissed Miamor's forehead then whispered in her ear, "Thank you."

"Come on, I'll take you to see him," the nurse offered.

Carter followed the nurse to the neonatal intensive care unit where the premature babies were taken care of, and as soon as he rounded the corner he saw Breeze. She sat in a rocking chair, holding his son, singing softly in his ear.

Carter could barely keep his composure. He fought tears of joy as he approached his sister. Breeze looked up and smiled. She put a finger up over her lips to request silence.

"Congratulations, Carter, I'd like you to meet your baby boy," Breeze said as she handed the tiny bundle of joy to his father.

The connection that Carter felt when he held his son caused his heart to swell. "He's so small," Carter said.

"He'll grow big and strong. We'll have to keep him here for a while—"

"No, he's coming home. I'll hire the best doctors and nursing staff to be with him around the clock if I have to, but when his mother leaves the hospital, so will he," Carter said with authority. He looked down at his trooper with all the love and happiness in the world. He had never felt so complete. The little dude was a true blend of his parents; he was the perfection that resulted from all of their imperfection. Out of all the bad that they had done in their lives, he was the one right that fixed them all.

"Daddy loves you, man," Carter said with sincerity.

The nurse took him and placed him back in the incubator, handling him with the gentlest of care.

"This will keep him away from things that can harm him. He's very delicate, and his lungs still have to mature. We'll keep him hooked up to machines that will help him breathe and monitor his heart rhythms until we're sure that he can function without them," the nurse explained.

"Can we have him moved to Miamor's room? I want them together at all times," Carter explained. He looked to Breeze. "And call up Fly Boogie. I need a man on her door around the clock until I can get her home. How is Zyir?" Carter asked.

"I haven't been in to see him yet," Breeze said.

"What?" Carter exclaimed, surprised.

"He and Money would have killed each other if Leena and I hadn't shown up. You should have seen them, Carter. I can't even look at Zyir right now or Monroe," Breeze said as she shook her head in disgrace.

"I'll go in and have a talk with him first, but he needs you right now, B. So get yourself together. The last thing he needs is his wife against him too," Carter said. He kissed her cheek and then held her hand as they walked toward Zyir's room.

Carter entered the hospital room and saw Zyir lying with his head against a pillow, eyes open, face solemn.

"What's good, Zy? How you hanging in there?" Carter asked.

"Shit hurts like a mu'fucka, fam," Zyir stated. "They talking about keeping me for a week."

"You need anything? You comfortable in here? I can send you home, set you up with a nurse and everything if you want. Just say the word, li'l homie," Carter offered.

"Nah, the way B is acting, home might be a little chilly, nah mean?" Zyir replied.

Breeze opened the door and stepped inside, keeping her distance as she looked at Zyir.

"You alive?" Breeze asked.

"Yeah, B, I'm breathing," Zyir answered with a charming smile and a wink.

Breeze shifted uncomfortably in her stance. "If I hadn't stopped you, would you have killed him?" she asked.

Zyir knew that his answer could change the course of their relationship, but he didn't want to lie to Breeze. He owed her more than that. He had spoken nothing but truth to her since they first met. He wouldn't start lying now. "If I had the best draw, yes. If the shoe was on the other foot, I'd be in the basement morgue," he said.

"I won't stay around and watch you put my brother in a casket, Zyir. I will not bury another person with the last name Diamond, and if you make me, I will hate you until the day I take my last breath. You end the beef with Money and I'll come home," she said as she slipped her five-carat wedding ring off her finger. "Until then you can have this back." She set the ring on the foot of the bed and rushed out of the room before he could see her tears.

Zyir grimaced as he reached down and picked up the ring. He held it inside his hand as he brought his closed fist to his mouth and kissed it. He looked at Carter, who gave him a gentle pat on the back.

"Looks like I don't got a choice, fam. I better get comfortable in this hospital bed, because I may not have a home to go back to."

"Get off of me!" Leena screamed as she snatched her arm away from Monroe as he ushered her into the house.

"I want niggas all around the house," he shouted to his three most trusted henchmen as he breathed hard and his eyes lit up in anger. "Niggas on the roof and around the perimeter. If Carter or Zyir even drive past this house, blow them straight to fucking hell!" he barked.

Leena covered her son's ears as she rocked him in her arms. "Money, just stop it! Do you hear yourself? You sound insane! Have you lost your fucking mind?" she asked. Her once beautiful white dress was covered in blood. What was supposed to be the happiest day of her life had turned into the worst. "This was our wedding day!"

"The nigga Zyir is out of his league. He ruined your day, not me! He started it, but I'ma finish it and snatch the fucking crown off of his dead head. I'm going to hang the disrespectful nigga from the fucking streetlights," Monroe barked.

Leena stormed out of the room enraged as she carried her son to his room. She marched into the master bedroom and pulled out a suitcase, stuffing clothes, jewelry, and shoes inside sloppily as tears flowed down her cheeks. She was fed up. The people she loved were fighting like enemies on the street.

She grabbed the Louis Vuitton luggage and wheeled it back to the living room. Monroe turned toward her, confused.

"I know you're mad, Lee, but where you going? Huh? You're not going anywhere, baby," he said, softening his tone.

Leena smirked and snaked her neck like only a black girl can do. "You fucking right I'm not going anywhere. You are. Take your shit, Money, and leave. You want to beef with Zyir. You two want to kill each other, you can do it without me. I won't watch that. I won't stick around for the bullshit," she said.

"Lee, there are some things you don't understand."

"Just leave, Money," she said with hurt eyes and with defeat lacing her tone.

"Leena," Monroe said more sternly this time.

"Get out! And take your goons with you!"

Monroe stormed out of the house, and it took everything in Leena not to call him back. He didn't even turn around before slamming the door to their home, and as soon as he disappeared from her sight, Leena dropped to the floor in devastation. She cried her woes of despair, drowning in a heap of lace and sadness as she prayed for a resolution to a winless war.

When Miamor opened her eyes, Carter's was the first face that she saw.

"Hey, you," she said with a lazy smile as tears came to her eyes. "I didn't think I'd ever see you again."

Carter leaned down and kissed her dry lips. "Why did you run from me?" he asked.

Miamor frowned and shook her head in protest. "I would never run from you, Carter. A nigga snatched me off the street in broad daylight. My old boyfriend. Someone I knew from my past took me," she whispered.

"Did he touch you?" Carter asked. "What old boyfriend, ma? What's the nigga name?" Carter spit venom with each word he spoke as Miamor saw flames of anger dancing in his eyes.

"He didn't touch me, but I don't think he had any intention of ever letting me go," she answered honestly. "We used to be close. He went to jail years ago and I forgot about him. I met you, and I left him in my past. I guess he didn't want to stay there."

"What's his name?" Carter asked again.

"Murder," she replied.

"What about the letter?" he asked. "He made you write that too?"

"I don't know anything about a letter," Miamor replied. "The first opportunity I got, I ran. I stabbed him and I took off. I didn't look back. I don't know if he's dead or alive. I just kept running until I couldn't anymore. He's the only person besides Mecca that I've ever been afraid of. What if he's not dead?"

Carter was livid as he saw the fear and heard the anxiety in her voice. "Don't worry yourself, ma. I'll handle it. He won't ever touch you again. Just lay back and rest. You've done enough work. You did good, kid. You gave me the greatest gift . . . my son. I'll protect you both at all costs. I love you."

He kissed her once more then sat back in deep contemplation as she drifted into a restless sleep.

Chapter 24

"No Guns. No Goons. Just me and you."

—Carter

Carter looked in his rearview mirror and noticed that the same two cars had been following him for blocks. At that moment, he knew that the Feds were on him. The white boys who were driving the cars that were tailing him were a dead giveaway. Carter immediately put the pedal to the metal and bent a couple corners to shake them. With his foreign car and world-class speed, there was no competition.

Carter checked his rearview mirrors after a couple corners and brief stretches and just as he expected, he was in the clear. He headed toward the hospital for Zyir. It was a must that they shook out of town until things died down. The heat from the authorities was too much to bear.

As Carter made his way toward the hospital, his phone began to ring. He looked down at his caller ID and noticed that the call originated from Los Angeles, California. He picked it up, only to hear another person breathing on the phone.

"Hello," he said again and still received no answer. He then knew that the call was coming from Polo. It was a discreet way of telling Carter that the Feds were about to move in on him.

Carter hung up his phone and shook his head in frustration. He knew that if he stayed around, it was only a matter of time before he went down. First and foremost, he had to get his li'l man out of the city too. Zyir was his right-hand man from day one, and he refused to flee the city and leave Zyir hanging out to dry.

Carter arrived at the hospital and immediately knew that he would be walking into a trap. He could spot unmarked cars from a mile away, and the entrances were swarmed with them.

"Fuck!" he said as he hit his steering wheel with force and aggression. He picked up his phone and called Zyir.

"Hello," Zyir answered in a low, raspy tone.

"Listen, who is in there with you?" Carter asked, cutting straight to the point.

"Just me and Fly Boogie," Zyir said as he slowly sat up in the bed while grimacing.

"Listen closely, because we don't have a lot of time. The Feds are coming in. Do me a favor. Tell Boogie to look outside the door and see if there are any agents outside your door," Carter said as he pulled off and looked at the cop cars filing into the hospital through his rearview mirror.

Zyir immediately told Fly Boogie to check, and he poked his head outside of the door and came back.

"It looks clear. Just a couple of nurses," he said as he stood there wide-eyed, trying to figure out what was about to go down.

"Shit looks normal," Zyir said to Carter.

"Okay, good, good. That means that they are on their way to you right now. Listen, you have to get the fuck out of there, Zyir. Like right now," Carter said.

"Damn. Okay, cool. Where are you at?" Zyir answered.

"Meet me at the take-off spot. You already know what it is," Carter said, not wanting to tip off anyone, just in case he had wiretaps on his phone.

"On my way," Zyir said as he began to snatch the wires off of him that were monitoring his heart rate.

"Yo, Zyir," Carter said as his tone dropped.

"What up, big homie?" Zyir replied.

"I'm not leaving without you, so make sure you get there," Carter said with all sincerity in his voice.

"I'll be there," Zyir confirmed just before he hung up the phone.

Carter headed in the direction of Monroe's condominium. He had unfinished business with his brother that needed to be handled.

Carter made sure that there wasn't anyone trailing him before he turned into Monroe's place. Carter took his gun from his waist and exited the car. He threw the gun in the seat, not wanting to even have it on him when approaching Monroe. He didn't want to go that route with Monroe. Carter just had to tie up loose ends.

Carter walked to the doorstep and knocked. He didn't know what to expect on the opposite end, but he was prepared for whatever God had in store for him.

As Carter waited for someone to answer, he got a bad feeling in the pit of his stomach. He took a deep breath and then exhaled, trying to calm his nerves.

The sounds of locks being unclicked sounded, and Carter stood strong as he waited for the face of his brother to appear. Once the door was open, he realized that it wasn't a face that he was staring at, but it was the barrel of a double pump shotgun that Monroe was holding about five inches from his nose.

"I come in peace," Carter said as he put both his hands up. Carter walked toward the gun, pressing his chest against the barrel and slowly walking Monroe backward. "I don't want no smoke, bro. Just want to talk," Carter pleaded as he spoke softly, slowly, and collected. There was no hostility showing in his voice or mannerisms. He knew that he was playing Russian roulette at that point, but he knew it had to be resolved.

"You come to my house after you sent ya li'l mans to get me? You must be out of your mind," Monroe said as he stopped and dug the barrel into Carter's chest even deeper.

"You're right. But if I recall right, you sent Buttons' niggas to kill me in Rio. Remember that? Look, we both have been at each other, but this shit has to stop," Carter said with no malice in his heart.

Monroe was at a loss for words.

"I'm tired of the killings. I just want this shit to end. Honestly, I would prefer if you get this gun out of my chest. If you want, I'll shoot you a fair one and we can handle it like men," Carter said, referring to a one-on-one fight. "No guns, no goons. Just me and you," Carter suggested.

Monroe paused as if he was in deep contemplation and then released a small smile, gladly wanting to take Carter up on his offer. Monroe slowly lowered the gun and then tossed it on his couch. Carter stepped completely in the house and closed the door behind him. He then took off his shirt, exposing his chiseled body and ripped abs.

"I thought you would never ask, playboy," Monroe said as he snatched off his shirt and put up his hands. They were both the direct bloodline of the most fearless man who ever walked the earth: Carter Diamond. So there was no fear in either one of their hearts.

Carter also put his hands up, and the men began to circle each other in the middle of Monroe's living room.

"This ass whooping has been a long time coming," Carter said as he began to inch closer to his brother.

Monroe threw the first punch. Carter side-stepped to the left, just barely missing getting hit by Monroe's punch. Almost simultaneously, Carter snapped a quick jab to Monroe's kidney.

"Too slow, li'l nigga," Carter said as he smiled and swiped his nose, taunting him. This enraged Monroe.

Monroe began to throw haymakers at Carter, trying to knock his head off. Carter caught a couple of them, but the majority of them he dodged artistically.

Carter saw that Monroe was getting tired, and he knew it was time for him to put in work. He went after Monroe relentlessly. Left hook, right hook, jab—sending Monroe flying onto his back. Carter then pounced on Monroe, straddling him while wrapping both hands around his neck, trying to choke the life out of him.

Monroe fought for air as Carter gripped his neck tightly. Monroe felt that Carter was much stronger than him and knew that he needed help getting Carter off of him. He reached for the lamp and grabbed it. He then smashed it against Carter's head, making the lamp shatter into pieces and temporarily getting Carter off of him.

Carter flew to the ground as the world began to spin. He temporarily saw stars and tried to get up, but couldn't keep his balance.

Monroe, on the other hand, was panting on the ground, trying to catch his breath. Blood leaked from Monroe's swollen lip, and Carter had a huge gash on the right side of his head. It was an awkward moment of silence as both of them leaned their backs against the wall and tried to regain their composure.

"We could have been a dynasty. We . . . could . . ." Monroe tried to say in between breaths as he steadily held his throbbing neck.

"That was the plan," Carter said as he sweated profusely and sucked air, trying to get his wind.

"You let that nigga Zyir take my place," Monroe admitted as he expressed his true feelings. He was envious of the place that Zyir held in his brother's life. They were close, and Monroe felt as if he had missed out by being away from life for so long.

"Zyir is my nigga. He's been there with me from the start. He wasn't taking anyone's place, because he always had a place of his own. So that's what this is all about, huh?"

"I just believe in blood over everything. I was raised in this drug game, and what I learned is that anybody will cross you for the right price. But family, family doesn't have a price. Family is forever. Diamonds are forever."

"Diamonds are forever. We have to end this, Money. We have to," Carter said as he looked over at Monroe. Neither of them wanted the beef to go any further. It was as if them saying that Diamonds are forever released the tension out of the room.

"I've lost everybody from this game. This game has no love for anyone. I don't want to lose the only brother I have left behind this," Carter admitted.

"I want this shit to be over too, bro. I swear to God I do. It seems like it's at a point of no return," Monroe replied.

"It's never too late, my nigga. All we have to do is let it end here," Carter said as he slowly stood up, sneering at his aching headache. He reached down his hand to Monroe and looked at his brother in the eyes.

Monroe paused and took a long, hard thought about what he was about to do. He took a deep breath and reached out his hand, letting his older brother help him up. They embraced and rocked back and forth, both of their souls being cleansed in the process.

"Now we have to go. The Feds are coming," Carter said as he went to the window and looked down over the street cautiously. "We have to go. They will be here any minute."

"What?" Monroe asked, trying to grasp what was going on.

"They're on to Estes, which means they're on to all of us. Just come on! I don't have time to explain, but I have a jet waiting to take us to Bermuda. All we have to do is make it to the airstrip. We have to go!" Carter said as he fled out of the door.

Monroe followed closely behind, and just like that, they were gone out of the door.

***

Zyir looked at the dashboard and saw Fly Boogie pushing over 120 miles per hour. Zyir then looked in his rearview mirror and saw the trail of police cars and flashing lights. They were on a high-speed chase, and Zyir knew that it wasn't looking good. He looked at Fly Boogie and noticed a grin on his face. He was actually enjoying the high-stakes car chase. A helicopter was hovering above them, keeping up with their every move. Zyir shook his head and had no choice but to smile. He gripped his wounded stomach and felt his phone vibrate. It was Carter.

"I'm on my way, but I have a couple friends with me," Zyir said, knowing that it didn't look good for him.

"I'm waiting for you, homie. You have to get here. I am not leaving without you, Zyir. Make a way," Carter said confidently. He heard the sirens in the background and knew that Zyir wasn't looking too good.

Carter hung up the phone and took a deep breath. He and Monroe were sitting on the jet, waiting to go. Carter looked at his watch and took a deep breath. "He'll be here," he assured Monroe as he looked out of the window. "Come on, Zy," he whispered to himself.

Fly Boogie jumped off the highway, pushing almost 150 miles per hour. He had created about a thirty-second lead on the cops, and he had an idea. He saw a tunnel and knew that that was their only chance. With the helicopter still on their tail, Fly Boogie raced into the tunnel and stopped about halfway through it.

"Look, big homie, you go that way and I'm going to shoot out this way, taking all them Feds away from you."

"Damn, Boogie. I'm not going to let you go out like that. Fuck it. I'm rolling with you. Let's get it," Zyir said bravely as he steadily clutched his stomach and frowned.

"Naw, I got you, big homie. They want you, not me. I have zero strikes and they have nothing on me. This shit going to make me a legend in the hood," Fly Boogie said as he kept a childish grin on his face.

Zyir shook his head and returned the smile. "You a crazy li'l nigga. You know that?" Zyir said as he held out his hand and gave Boogie a pound.

"And you know this!' he said playfully as he dapped up his mentor.

Zyir got out of the car and began to walk the opposite way. Fly Boogie put the pedal to the metal and shot out of the tunnel like a bat out of hell. He shot out of the tunnel and the helicopter got right back on his tail.

The federal agent in the helicopter called in Fly Boogie's location, and a mile down the road the cops were back on him. This time it was double the amount of marked cars chasing him. Fly Boogie was about to go down like a G.

Zyir casually walked into a gas station that was nearby and used the payphone to call a cab. Within thirty minutes he was pulling up at the jet strip where Carter was waiting for him.

Carter helped him into the jet, and Zyir was startled when he reached the door and saw a hand reaching to help him in. It was Monroe.

Zyir got onto the aircraft, and Carter immediately shut the door. "Okay, let's go!" he yelled to the pilot as they took off.

Carter looked at Zyir and then Monroe. He was determined to bring his family back together, and he was not taking no for an answer. Before they would kill each other, Carter would kill them both. He wanted the war to end for good. They had other problems ahead of them—problems that they could have never forseen. The three biggest gangsters in history were on their ass: The F—B—I.

The jet lifted into the air and disappeared into the clouds as three of the realest niggas in Miami flew off into the sunset. Carter directed the pilot to head directly toward the Bermuda triangle—a no-fly zone where many aircrafts have vanished in American history. He instructed Zyir and Monroe to sit back and relax until they reached their destination. He had a plan—a master plan.

Carter sat back in the luxury chair and stared out of the window. Just before they entered the Bermuda triangle, he smiled and whispered, "Diamonds are forever."

Final Chapter

"I'm numb to the death around by now.
It doesn't even matter."

—Breeze

Weeks Later

Leena lay in bed, holding her son to her chest as she cried her eyes out over Monroe. She had lost him once before, and now she was reliving the horror of his death all over again. *How can a plane just fall out of the sky without anyone noticing? God, please keep them. Bless their souls,* she prayed silently.

The minutes on the clock ticked by, torturously slow as she waited for the sun to break through the dark sky. She needed to speak with Breeze and Miamor. They were all that she had left. Leena felt more vulnerable than ever, and they were the only women in the world who could relate to her pain. Widows of The Cartel, they had more in common now than they ever had before. Through circumstance they had been made sisters, and everything that their men had left behind was now in their hands. Power, paper, prestige . . . an entire empire now lay at their feet.

Leena kissed her son's head, grabbed her cell phone off the nightstand, and rose from the bed. Putting on her silk kimono robe, she walked out onto the balcony that overlooked the entire estate. Monroe had her living in the lap of luxury. Their mansion rested on a ten-acre compound on the outskirts of the city limits. He provided her with the best of everything. From labels to diamonds, she was afforded her heart's desires, but the material things seemed so pointless now. None of it mattered. She would burn the multi-million dollar walls she dwelled in to the ground if it meant Money could live again.

What she wanted most was time with the man she loved. It seemed as though life always tore them apart, and for a second time she was mourning his loss.

Her mind was so full and her heart so heavy that she could barely breathe. She felt weighted with emotion, and she needed to get some of it off her chest.

Leena dialed Miamor's number. Full of tension, she didn't even realize that she was holding her breath.

"Leena, why are you awake? It's so late," Miamor answered.

Leena exhaled loudly and chuckled slightly. "I could ask you the same thing. Doesn't sound like you're getting much sleep either."

"The baby is restless. To be honest, so am I. I miss him. I can't believe he's gone," Miamor admitted. "He was all I had left. So what the hell do I do now?"

Leena's heart went out to Miamor. To see Carter and her together was to see true love. Leena knew that not even her own relationship with Monroe could rival the one she witnessed whenever she was around them. "Have you spoken to Breeze?" Leena asked.

The sound of sirens broke through the silent night, and Leena looked around in confusion, and then she looked at her security cameras.

"The police are here," Leena announced. Unmarked black cars were pulling onto her property. "They must've found the plane," Leena whispered as she rushed back into the house, tightening the belt on her kimono as she raced through the massive mansion. "I'll call you back," Leena said.

"Lee . . . wait . . ." Miamor began to protest, but Leena ended the call.

Her feet slapped the cold tile floor as she headed toward the front door, frantically, as hope began to rise in her broken heart. She flung open the door and ran out into the yard, meeting the officers in front of her home before they even got out of their vehicles. She was taken aback when she saw how many had come. By the time she realized something was wrong it was too late. Twenty federal agents exited their vehicles swiftly with automatic weapons aimed toward her face. Red beams appeared all over her upper torso, and as

Leena looked down she realized that all it took was an itchy trigger finger to end her life.

"Let me see your hands! On the ground now!"

Leena went deaf as the thunderous hum of a helicopter roared above her head. The windstorm that it created as it circled above her, shining a bright spotlight on her, caused her hair to blow wildly.

"What? What is going on?" she shouted frantically.

"Hands up! On the ground now!"

Leena was manhandled to the cement as she resisted their demands. She watched as the Feds swarmed her home. "Wait! My son is inside! My son is in the house!" she screamed as she tried to stand.

One of the men put a forceful knee in her back, causing her to grimace in pain as he cuffed her wrists tightly. The metal bit into her skin, and her wrist snapped from the agent's brute force. They held no sympathy for her as they made their arrest.

"You can't do this! I've done nothing wrong! My son! If you touch one hair on his head, I will have your fucking head!" she screamed as she resisted arrest. She lunged, kicking and screaming as she tried to break free. All she could think of was her son. Leena had no idea why she was even under arrest, but the Feds had come at her so heavy that she could only assume the worst.

Leena's heart broke in half as they forced her into the car. She looked out of the rearview window and saw her son crying hysterically in the arms of one of the men. She broke down instantly. She had no clue of what would become of her and her child.

"Please, just tell me what is going on. What will happen to my son?" she asked as snot and tears wrecked her pretty face. There was no keeping her composure. Leena was distraught. She knew that the tides of life were changing. With the death of the men, the Feds had grown balls of steel. They would have never come at The Cartel with such arrogance and disrespect otherwise.

"Your son will be placed in temporary custody of the state," one of the Feds said as he drove away from her home.

"No, please! You can't," she said with a gasp.

"We can and we will, unless you can tell us something that will make us change our minds and set you free. Your cooperation will make all of this go away. So do yourself a favor and tell us what you know about the murders, the cocaine, the dirty money laundering that The Cartel is involved in. It's in your best interest to start talking."

"I'm not telling you anything," Breeze stated as she sat with her hands behind her back, handcuffed to the hard chair.

"We have evidence against you and everyone affiliated with The Cartel. We've got you for drug trafficking, running a criminal enterprise, fraud, tax evasion, the list goes on and on."

Breeze kept her eyes on the wall in front of her, barely blinking as she blocked out the voice of the federal agent. The olive-skinned man leaned in menacingly over Breeze, using intimidation tactics to get her to break.

Zyir had trained her well. Breeze knew better than to volunteer any information. They couldn't even get her prints on a coffee cup, she was so seasoned. Growing up in the folds of the largest organization in the South had prepared her for this moment.

"We found pieces of an aircraft, scattered throughout the Atlantic Ocean, about 150 miles off the coast of Bermuda. Too bad the cowards left their ladies to take the fall for their bad deeds."

Breeze's eyes turned dark at the insult and her heart wrenched. "You don't have anything on me," Breeze said.

"We have everything on you. You recognize this face?" The agent tossed a photo of Estes onto the table in front of her, and Breeze turned green as her stomach turned.

"Let's just say family doesn't mean much these days. He's singing like a canary and has implicated not only your husband and brothers, but you and over a hundred other mid- and low-level dealers across the state," the agent said. He noticed that Breeze's demeanor had changed.

"Not so cocky now, huh, princess?" he mocked. "We picked up over thirty people directly affiliated with The Cartel. You're standing tall, but do you honestly think all of them will too? Now the way this works is whoever talks first gets the deal. There is only one way out of this."

"Magdalena!" Miamor yelled in urgency as she quickly dressed. The Spanish housekeeper appeared in the doorway. "I need you to watch the baby. Do not let anyone into this house under any circumstances. I don't care if God himself knocks on the door. You don't let anyone in. *Comprende?*"

"Sí, sí," Magdalena replied.

Miamor placed a call to Carter's attorney and within minutes she was headed to the federal building. She knew the game, and now that the Feds felt The Cartel was weakened, they were coming in for the kill. There was no way that Miamor was letting all that Carter had built be destroyed. She had watched him closely, studied the way that he reigned, and just as she had in life, she would now hold him down in death. She already knew that Leena had been arrested, and when she couldn't reach Breeze, she had a gut feeling that she was being held too. Surely they had intended to come for her next, but Miamor moved to her own beat. She wasn't being taken into custody without representation.

She rode in the back of the plush interior of the Maybach as her driver guided it through the city's streets. Miamor's chest heaved as anxiety crept into her bones. Today her worst fear was coming true. She was about to go up against the law. Most who did it had no wins, but with the team of sharks that Carter had left her with she was confident that she could come out of things unscathed.

The car arrived at her destination and Miamor saw that Carter's legal team was waiting at the top of the steps. Steve Rosenberg, the best esquire in the city, was already on retainer. Standing confident and dapper as ever in a Brooks Brothers suit, he waited with a briefcase in hand. Miamor waited for her driver to open her door, then she emerged from the vehicle.

"Ms. Matthews, I'm glad you were smart enough to call me," he said as she shook his hand.

"Thank you for coming, Mr. Rosenberg," she replied anxiously.

"Looks like they're reaching a bit. They do have extensive
evidence on Carter, Zyir, and Monroe, but seeing as though
they are now deceased, that pigeonholes their investigation.
They're using scare tactics to try and get an informant out
of you ladies. The Cartel has been responsible for drugs and
crime in this city. They need a kingpin to tie it to, but in this
case they are willing to settle for a queen pin. Since they can't
get your men, they now are gunning for the three of you."

"They have Leena and Breeze. Have they turned them?"
Miamor asked as she bit her inner jaw, hoping that the ladies
could stand tall under pressure.

"Not yet, but let's go get them out of there before one of
them do. The DEA has been known to flip the most hardened
of criminals."

Just seeing the face of such a prestigious defense attorney
turned the tables in the girls' favor. Within an hour Breeze
and Leena were released, but the struggle was far from over.

"They'll keep coming for you. As long as they have Estes's
cooperation, it's only a matter of time before they bring indict-
ments down on anyone he's naming. I'll do more research in
the morning to find out what we're up against. I'll be in touch,"
Rosenberg said.

"What about my son?" Leena asked urgently.

"I've already made arrangements to have him returned to
you. As soon as they process the paperwork, a caseworker will
drop him off to your home. Shouldn't take more than a few
hours."

He bid adieu to the ladies, and they each watched him pull
away.

"They found the plane," Breeze informed sadly as tears
flooded her eyes. "It crashed in the middle of the ocean.
Divers are still looking for their bodies."

"What are we going to do? Everything is falling apart,"
Leena whispered.

The three women formed a small circle and put their arms
around one another, creating a circle of power . . . street
royalty. They were the queens who would inherit the throne.

"We do what we have to do. We take over The Cartel," Miamor replied. "And the first thing on the agenda is to clear our names." She turned sympathetically toward Breeze. "I know that Estes is your grandfather, but—"

Breeze put her hand up and interrupted. "Do what needs to be done. If he's talking, it'll be well deserved anyway. I'm numb to the death around by now. It doesn't even matter."

"Do you guys know what this means? We can't just step in their shoes. I just sat back and spent the money. I'm not in the streets. I don't know the first thing about running anything . . . I can't do this," Leena protested.

"You can and you will. For years we've sat back and watched the throne. It's time we inherited it. It is our time now, ladies, and we either do this together or watch the entire Cartel fall. The vultures will pick everything our men established apart until there's nothing left if we don't assume our roles," Miamor schooled. She knew the streets. She had come up in the trenches, and her murder game was official. There was nothing in her that was scared of this opportunity. She was reveling at the chance to continue Carter's legacy.

"We have no muscle," Breeze said.

"Some will stay loyal; others will test us. Niggas gonna learn a hard lesson when they buck, but they not knocking us off," Miamor assured.

"First we memorialize our men. Give them a homegoing that the streets will never forget," Leena whispered.

Breeze nodded and added, "Then the takeover begins."

The Cartel 5

Chapter 1

*"I've been to a funeral where
there was a body but no death."*
—Miamor

Lost in the morning sky, Carter was silent as he stared out
of the window, his mind full of a million thoughts and his
heart conflicted. The billows of white clouds gave him a sense
of serenity. At 30,000 feet in the air he felt as if nothing could
touch him. Fuck a fed, he was flying high. No case could bring
him crashing to the ground, or so he hoped. Running from a
fight wasn't really Carter's style, but things had happened so
quickly that he didn't have a choice. If he and his brothers had
stayed in Miami, they would be in federal custody right now.
He needed time to make these problems disappear. His mind
drifted to Miamor and his newborn son. Guilt-ridden by his
sudden departure, he tortured himself with the fact that he
wouldn't be around to take care of the ones he loved. He didn't
know how long he would have to stay away and it killed him
that he wouldn't be around to get to know the life that he had
created. He wouldn't be there to see Miamor transform into
the woman she was born to be. He had confidence that she
would be a great mother, but to see her playing the role that
every woman was made for would have made his heart loyal
to her forever. He was missing all of that and it left him with
a disgruntled soul. They were half way across the Atlantic, as
the private jet ate away at the distance between the States
and Bermuda. They were out of U.S. airspace so they were
safe. Their escape had been executed flawlessly. He just hated
that they had left their families behind. He was confident that
Miamor could handle herself in his absence. Unlike Breeze
and Leena, she knew the game. Miamor would be just fine

until he returned . . . of that much he was certain. Carter looked over at Monroe and Zyir, grateful for his right and left hand. Although they had been at odds, there was nothing like a common enemy to make men come together. The federal case against them was enough to make them put their differences aside for the time being. Carter only prayed that the peace lasted because if he had to choose between the two of them, even he couldn't call how it would turn out.

"Everything good?" Zyir asked, noticing the wrinkled brow of his mentor. He knew that whenever Carter grew silent and his eyes distant that there was something in the air.

Carter pinched his chin as he rested his elbow against the armrest. He rubbed his five o'clock shadow as he nodded his head.

"We left something undone," Zyir stated, knowingly. Carter didn't have to disclose his thoughts in order for Zyir to know what was wrong. "The women."

Carter confirmed with a nod, still deep in thought. Zyir sat up in the leather seat and rested his elbows on his knees as he rubbed his hands together. "They don't know anything, they can't be touched."

Monroe interjected, "That don't mean shit. The Feds will catch em' up with RICO. Just from spending the money they can build a case against all of them. Then what? Li'l Money ends up where? Li'l Carter goes to who? There is no more family left. We are all we got."

"If the Feds go after the ladies the case won't stick," Carter said. "I know Miamor. She'll handle it and I left a bank account full of money with the lawyers. Nothing will happen to them, they're protected."

"I hope you're sure," Monroe said.

"I am brother," Carter confirmed.

Zyir raised his head. "Is there a chance we could go back?" He had left without a good-bye, without warning. One moment he was with Breeze, the next he was not. He had done so many things that he had yet to apologize for and still had so many I love yous that he wanted to express to her. He felt as if he had left his home unstable. He could only imagine how she felt at the moment.

"I don't know," Carter admitted. "Right now, this brother-hood here . . ." He pointed between the three of them. "This is all we have. This is the family that we can rely on. We left Leena, Breeze, and Miamor with enough money to last a few lifetimes. The Feds took some of it, but there is so much more that they will never trace. Our families are set. They will survive. Miamor is a shooter with a reputation behind her. Niggas won't run up on her without thinking twice. She can hold down The Cartel. They are safe. The question is are we?"

"The Fed case is solid," Monroe said dismally. "If we get caught . . ."

"We can't get caught," Carter said with finality.

He stood and walked up to the captain's cabin. The mid-dle-aged white man had large headphones on his head and aviator shades covering his eyes. He focused intently on the sky before him. The serene look on his face was understand-able. As Carter looked out of the front window he realized that the pilot had the best view. Nothing but white clouds filled his vision. It was easy to get lost in the sky and Carter stood mesmerized for a moment at the incredible sight. It was one that not many people got to see. He placed a hand on the captain's shoulder. "It's time," he announced. "Turn off all communication. As far as the government is concerned this plane should drop out of the sky. We're all dead to the world from this moment forward. You do understand that you can never go back to the States?" he grilled.

"I understand. A million dollars is enough to make a new life somewhere else," the pilot responded.

"Good," Carter said. He gave the pilot a pat on the back and then watched as the man made the flight disappear from airspace.

The ocean below them sparkled many shades of blue and turquoise as the plane descended out of the sky. They arrived in paradise as the plane's wheels touched the ground with a gentle thud. The cabin rocked slightly as the pilot slowed and taxied to a stop on the private clear port. The three men emerged, suited, and unscathed as if escaping federal custody was a simple feat. When the federal scope fell upon most empires it fell instantly, but The Cartel would survive. Carter was smart. He had prepared himself for the scrutiny. It was his ability to foresee the government's attack that had allowed him to elude it. Carter shrugged on his suit jacket as he frowned from the bright sun that shined into his eyes. A titanium briefcase was gripped tightly in his hand. The three men stood at the bottom of the steps and waited for the pilot to exit.

"Safe and sound in Bermuda! Just like I promised you boys. Now where's my million dollars," he said as his face pulled outward in a wide, gap filled, smile. He was already spending the money in his head. His greedy palms couldn't wait to feel the tax-free dollars flipping through his fingers.

Carter passed the man the briefcase and shook his hand firmly. "Stay out of the states. Go anywhere but there," Carter instructed.

"You've got it, you're the boss," the pilot replied. Carter nodded at the warehouse that sat adjacent to the airstrip. "There's a mechanic waiting inside there. He will get you refueled and make sure you're good before you take off."

"Take-off? I though Bermuda was the final destination?" he asked.

"It is our final destination, you will be going elsewhere," Carter answered sternly. The pilot nodded in reluctant understanding as Carter, Zyir, and Monroe walked away.

They looked like Mafioso as they strutted powerfully across the clear port in their expensive Italian suits.

"You know he is going to go right back to Miami right?" Monroe stated. "There is no telling who he's going to run his mouth to. We need to dead that nigga."

"He'll never make it. The mechanic is going to make sure of it. The Feds will find the plane at the bottom of the ocean, assuming that we were on it," Carter replied. He swiped his nose arrogantly, feeling no remorse for double-crossing the pilot. He knew that the man would not be able to resist returning to Miami. He had just come into a million dollars. He wouldn't want to be rich alone; he would want to share it with the people who knew him. There was no point in getting money if you couldn't floss in front of the people that you were once broke in front of. He would disobey Carter's orders and surely attempt to return to Miami. Unfortunately for him Carter had anticipated this. The man would be half way across the Atlantic ocean when the engines on his plane gave out. It was cold blooded, but the men couldn't afford any slip-ups. The pilot was a casualty to the game. No one, not one witness to their escape could remain alive. No one needed to live to tell the story of how they had evaded the law. A black, tinted, Escalade pulled up directly in front of them with two Arab men in dark suits inside.

Zyir instantly reached in his waistline, but Carter grabbed his wrist, halting him. "They're allies," he informed. "Polo arranged for us to hideout in Saudi Arabia. We'll be safe there."

"The Middle East? That's not an easy move bro. We don't have friends there. We don't speak the language. This is the plan?" Monroe protested unsurely.

"Your father," Carter paused. "Our father, had friends there. He put in work that is protecting us today. We will be well taken care of. It's our only play right now, unless you have a better idea. We can't stay in Bermuda. The Caribbean will be the first place that the Feds look. Its too predictable."

"The way you're talking we ain't never going back," Zyir interjected solemnly. "My lady is in Miami. You have a new baby in Miami? Li'l nephew is there . . ."

"What about family?" Monroe finished for Zyir. Zyir shook his head unsurely.

"I'm not going to leave her unprotected fam. You talking about letting them think we're dead," Zyir stated. The thought of never seeing Breeze's face again, or hearing the sweet tone of her voice sickened him. He knew what his "death" would do to her. She would crumble.

Carter sighed in frustration. "Look. I would like to move as a unit but we're all grown men. I'm going to Saudi, but if this is where the road separates for the three of us I understand. I'm not worried about Miamor. I know her. She is more than capable of holding things down while I'm away. Until I can get word to her that we are safe the girls will just have to go through the pain of our loss. Eyes are on them right now anyway. Their grief will make it look real."

If Zyir could think of any other solution he would have offered it. The situation was just bad from all angles. Zyir may not like the plan but he trusted Carter with his life. It was time for loyalty to kick in. Everybody in the crew couldn't be chief. It was Zyir's turn to take the back seat so that anarchy didn't divide them.

"I'm with you my nigga," Zyir conceded.

Carter turned to Monroe. "What about you? We've got another flight to catch. What's it going to be?"

Since Monroe's return he had been the rebellious soul. Carter half expected him to buck against him once again. Instead Monroe nodded. "I'm with you bro."

Good. Carter opened the back door of the truck and climbed inside. Zyir and Monroe piled in behind him. "By this time tomorrow we will be half way around the world."

Breeze's heart felt frozen. A plane crash. The moment she had heard those words her heart had stopped beating inside of her chest. It was like the blood refused to flow through her veins. Her fingertips were ice cold, her eyes void of emotion, and her mind blank. How could this have happened? Zyir, Carter, and Monroe were three of Miami's most powerful men and they had been killed. Not by a bullet, a war, a rival or even a cop . . . but by a mechanical error on a private plane. She sat still, staring out of the window as the chauffeured Benz truck pulled up to the church. It was the same church that her father's funeral had been held in. Now here she was years later, burying not only the love of her life, but her brothers as well. She rode alone. It was how she preferred it. Since hearing of the tragedy she had wanted no one around her. She needed time. Space. Silence. She and Zyir had been beefing before he fled town. Their last words had been hostile ones and it was a regret that she would live with for the rest of her life. What had once felt like not enough time, now felt like too much. With Zyir by her side it seemed like life was not long enough to love him, to be with him. She had wanted a couple of forevers to bask in the joy he gave her. Now with him gone, she didn't want to go on another day, another year . . . let alone a lifetime without him. She was beginning to think that her family was cursed. No one she knew, no one with whom she shared blood had ever lived without looking over their shoulders. She was the last one standing. The only Diamond left of her generation. A heavy burden had been placed on her shoulders and she could feel it weighing her down already. As the driver sat silently in the front seat, waiting for her command to open her door she sighed deeply. Once she stepped out of the car all eyes would be trained on her. News cameras, the ghetto grapevine, friends, foes . . . they would all be awaiting her reaction. She had been young when her father had been murdered. She hadn't known the rules. Now she was well versed in the ways of the underworld. She remembered how strong her mother had been during her father's funeral and she vowed to be that strong today. If she was going to do that however, she needed to get it all out now because there was no way she was going to let the world see her cry. She cleared her throat. "Please lift the partition," she instructed. The driver nodded and as soon as Breeze saw the dark glass slide up her soul bled through as a gut wrenching cry came over her.

Leena held Carter Junior in her arms as Monroe's heir rested his curly head in her lap. Her red-rimmed eyes cloudy as she sniffled slightly. She wasn't ready for this day. Burying Monroe. It was too soon. Life was not supposed to come to this. She had done this routine before and he had promised her that she would never have to see him lying in a casket again. She couldn't help but be mad that he had broken their pact. She hadn't bothered to put on make-up. She knew that her sorrows would do nothing but wash the charade of happiness away. She was shaken to her core. Her baby, their baby was left without a father and Leena didn't know if she could do this alone. She had gone through a lot being first Mecca's, then Monroe's girl but nothing had ever made her feel more alone than this. "Where is daddy?"

When her son asked the question her entire body quaked. He was old enough to realize that Monroe wasn't around. He missed his father and Leena's lip quivered as she searched for a response. "Daddy's . . ." she paused, unsure of what to say. She gripped her son's hand and took a deep breath. *Get it together. You have to keep your shit together for your baby. You're all he's got now. Do not break down in front of him,* she told herself. "Remember when I told you about God and how he has angels by his side baby?"

Her son nodded innocently. "Well God loved daddy so much that he needed him by his side baby. Daddy is resting now. He lives with God and we won't be able to see him anymore. More he's always with you. He's your guardian angel and if you close your eyes and listen to your heart you'll feel him. He is always watching over you baby. Do you understand?"

Monroe Jr. nodded and smiled as he closed his eyes, squeezing them tight as he said, "I feel him mommy! I feel him!" He opened his eyes excitedly. "Close your eyes too mommy! Hurry, hurry!"

When Leena closed her eyes she felt the tears drop out of the sides of them but she didn't make a sound. Her heartbeat increased and she sobbed silently, not wanting her child to hear her grief. "Keep them closed baby. Just be with daddy for a little while," she said. She opened her eyes and saw her driver extending a handkerchief to her. She mouthed the words, *thank you,* and wiped away her tears. Taking a deep breath she said, "Okay baby. Its time to go inside now. I love you."

"I love you too."

The smile of her child put the strength in her legs that she needed to stand on her own two. She reached into her bag and pulled out the Xanax she had been prescribed. She needed to take the edge off a bit. She placed it inside of her mouth and took a swig of her son's apple juice before she readied herself to face the world or rather the underworld of Miami.

Miamor sat behind the windows of the tinted Maybach. She was last in the procession of fancy escorted cars. The fleet had cost them almost $50,000 but she had spared no expense. Bulletproof everything was not a luxury it was a necessity and she took an extra measure of security by putting Leena in a car with the kids because she knew that no one would target her. They saw her as a grieving widow not a member of the Cartel. Leena would be the last to be hit if anything did go down.

Miamor hadn't actually gotten time to process the plane crash just yet. She was in shock. So many things had fallen apart simultaneously that the only thing she could do was go into autopilot. She was handling the Feds, the organization of the memorial, a newborn baby. It was all so overwhelming and time consuming that the fact that Carter was never coming home to her had not yet hit her. She would never see his face again and still no emotion had materialized within her . . . not just yet. Miamor knew that once she allowed herself to feel that she would feel it all and falling apart was not an option at the moment. She would mourn him in private, after the memorial was over, but right now she had to protect his legacy. She had to protect his seed, his sister, and what was left of their family. She clicked her gun off safety and placed it inside of her Chanel bag. She wanted to wear it on her body, but the black Herve Leger dress left no room for her to tuck it inconspicuously. Miamor hoped she wouldn't have to use it but in any case she would be prepared to pop off. She herself had once walked into a Cartel funeral with the intent of murder so she didn't put it past anyone. The Cartel was weakened by the death of their men, it was the perfect time for infiltration. She looked out of the window at the massive crowd that was filtering out of the church. Even the mega church wasn't big enough to accommodate the amount of people that had come out to pay their respects. Everybody was there, but not all that attended came out of love. She was sure a few enemies lingered in the crowd to confirm the deaths. The Feds were lurking. She could sniff out the pig bastards from a mile away. They were so obvious that she almost wanted to go and say hello. But the majority of the attendees were Cartel affiliates. Wives, girlfriends, hustlers, runners, muscle, groupies. Everybody was out and dressed to impress. If the mood wasn't so somber it would have been a hell of a party. Even in death Carter commanded respect. It was one of the many things she had loved about her man. She climbed out of the car and watched as Leena, Breeze, and the kids did the same. The bodyguard that Miamor had assigned to Leena and the younger ones escorted them in first as Breeze and Miamor trailed behind. Concealed behind designer shades they all made their way into the church and with heavy hearts they said good-bye to the men that had ruled not only the streets of Miami, but their hearts like no other before them.

"It didn't feel like a funeral," Leena said. "Their bodies. Where are they? Am I the only one that feels like maybe this is a mistake? Maybe they're alive?"

"They're not alive," Breeze said. "No one could have survived that wreckage."

"And I've been to a funeral where there was a body but no death," Miamor said, reminding them of Monroe's fake funeral years prior. "We just have to accept what is. The kids are asleep. I'm going to bed. You're more than welcome to stay the night if you want. Choose a room," she said, motioning to her massive mansion. She secretly hoped they would stay. With Carter gone it felt ominously empty . . . void of color . . . of life . . . of hope. She used to dream of filling every room with Carter's bobble head babies. She imagined that their girls would have long, curly coils, and big brown eyes. Their boys would be dark and strong with serious temperaments like their father. Now, she saw nothing. She couldn't even imagine what tomorrow would be like let alone foresee far into the future. Time stood still. Death would do that to you. She remembered the healing process when her sister was murdered. It had taken years for her to get over the loss. Feeling hurt every moment of everyday made days feel like weeks and weeks like months. It was all just so unbearable. It was worse than any physical torture that she had ever encountered. She would need something to help her sleep through the night and a bottle of wine was the only remedy. She walked into the finished basement and then down another set of stairs where Carter had insisted on building a wine cellar. She would have preferred a gun chamber but his incessant passion for fine wine had quickly rubbed off on her. She grabbed a vintage bottle. It was one that he would have never allowed her to open had he been alive. She pulled it down as she thought, *you shouldn't have died on me.* A tear fell down her face as she carried it up to the basement. She couldn't wait until she got upstairs. She sat at the basement bar and frantically uncorked the bottle as she poured herself a full glass. As the bitter redness entered her mouth she felt her emotional dam breaking. She lowered her head as she gripped her wine and let her tears flow. Finally, it hit her. Carter wasn't there to chastise her over his expensive bottle of wine. He wasn't there to hold her. To love her. To help her find her way as a new mother. She was by herself. It was how she had started out. She almost wished she had never loved Carter because losing him was worse than never having him at all. She wished that she had a fast forward button to push her past this part. When she felt pain she liked to inflict pain, but as a new mother she could no longer follow that pattern. Miamor was in unchartered territory. She didn't know how to be this girl. She didn't know how to live this life without Carter there to guide her. She had become the type of woman he could trust, but now that he was gone she didn't trust herself. She had loved him so hard that she had lived her life in accord to his liking but he was gone now. *Where does this leave me?* She thought sadly.

Before she knew it the entire bottle of wine was empty and she had cried so many tears that her eyes burned. She hated being so weak, it didn't suit her. She walked upstairs, bumping the walls along the way from her drunken state. She wasn't for this sulking shit. Her emotions were getting the best of her and she didn't like it. She located her Chanel bag and pulled out her pistol. She was glad that the memorial had gone peacefully but the pop off queen in her needed a release. She found Breeze sniffling quietly on her living room sofa.

"You're still awake?" Miamor asked.

"Can't sleep," Breeze responded with a shrug. The evidence of her loss was written all over her face.

"Come on," Miamor said. She went into the hall closet and pulled down a case that held a 9 mm inside. She passed it to Breeze.

"What are you doing?" Breeze asked, confused.

"Showing you the perfect stress reliever. Follow me," she answered. Miamor led Breeze out of the back of the house and out into the vast yard.

"Where the hell are we going?" Breeze asked.

"Whenever I feel overwhelmed I come out here," Miamor said. The amount of land that they had was unbelievable. Huge lots weren't common in Miami, but Miamor had acres. Carter had wanted a large yard and a big house to raise his family in but today it hurt to even breathe the air inside. When they were far enough away from the house Miamor stopped walking and pointed to a ledge that held bottles on top.

"Pulling a trigger is a stress reliever for me," she admitted.

"Figures," Breeze shot back with a smirk. "Let's go ahead and test your theory." Breeze aimed.

BOOM!

She hit nothing.

Miamor chuckled. "We need to work on your aim. I thought Zyir taught you how to shoot."

"Not in the middle of the night," Breeze said. "Give me a break. You're drunk. You probably can't do any better."

Miamor aimed.

BOOM!

The glass broke as Miamor hit her mark effortlessly.

Breeze threw up her hands incredulously causing Miamor to laugh out loud. Her laughter turned into cries as Breeze's eyes watered. The two women embraced, leaning on each other. They were sisters, not by blood but by street law and at this moment all they had was each other.

Chapter 2

"D.E.A is all over us. The workers are snitching, they have photos, and evidence . . ."

—Breeze

Four Weeks Later

Miamor sat in her son's nursery as she swayed gently in the wooden rocker. Her emotions were all over the place. Here she was holding the newborn child of the man that she was supposed to spend the rest of her days with, yet he was gone. It seemed as if they had just reunited. They hadn't had enough time together before Carter was taken away. "A plane crash," she whispered still in disbelief. She was still getting used to being a mother. Her body, her emotions, her view on the world . . . it had all changed the moment she gave birth. She had prepared herself for her life to alter drastically, but not in this way. She would never get used to raising her child alone. All she wanted was forever with Carter but it seemed that forever was elusive. Miamor wanted to break down, but everything seemed to land on her shoulders. With the absence of the male heads of The Cartel, the empire was in need of leadership. Breeze had come up around the game, but she had never been a player in it. She was a pampered princess. All she knew was the money and the reputation that she got from being affiliated. She knew nothing of the stripes that it took to lead an army of street niggas. Then there was Leena. A pretty face who had stood on the arms of made men for years. She had been around, but Miamor was almost sure that she was just like the average hustler's wife, she knew no details. Leena wasn't street, but could still prove valuable because she was sharp, and she seemed to be loyal. Still, she lacked the raw courage that it took to run things. In an organization as infamous as The Cartel, there couldn't be weakness. Miamor was used to running with a pack of thoroughbreds. Leena and Breeze were a far cry from The Murder Mamas. Miamor had trusted them with her life, she wasn't sure if Breeze and Leena could compare.

The doorbell rang causing Miamor's body to tense. Her son was so in tune with her body that he erupted with cries simultaneously. "Shh!!" she whispered as she stood to her feet, her maternal instincts to protect kicking in. "Shh, its okay." She ran into the panic room that was attached to the nursery and put in a code quickly, her hands shaking violently. Miamor was normally so rational, so meticulous, but having another life to look out for besides her own made her emotional. Just the ring of a doorbell scared her. Normally the security cameras would have announced the identity of whoever was ringing her bell, but the Feds had disarmed all of her cameras when they had hit her with the warrant. The streets knew that Carter was gone. There was no telling who would come to her door trying to usurp her kingdom. Miamor was on edge. She placed her baby in the bassinet inside of the panic room and then rushed to the safe. With her hands free she calmed herself slightly as she punched in the combination. She grabbed the loaded .357 out of the safe and rushed out, locking her crying child securely inside. It was two o'clock in the morning. Nothing good could possibly come to her at that hour and whoever was at the door was about to feel her wrath. Miamor rushed to the door and pulled it open swiftly, ready to pop off, her gun aimed, arm steady.

"Whoa!! Whoa!"

Miamor popped off, shooting past the kid's ear only missing his head by an inch.

"Who the fuck are you?" she asked.

The kid grimaced as his mouth fell open from the deafening ringing in his ear. "Whoa ma, chill out. Fuck! You gon' blow my fucking eardrum! Who are you? Femme Nikita or some shit! You busting at niggas," the guy responded with his hands still raised to show he had come in peace.

"You've got five seconds to tell me who you are and why you at my doorstep in the middle of the night," she demanded, voice cold, finger wrapped securely around the trigger.

"I'm a friend. My name is Fly Boogie. I was with Zyir the day that he ran from the Feds. I distracted the cops so that Zyir could go meet Carter and Monroe. I swear on everything I'm a friend. I ran one of the trap spots," Fly Boogie said. The words flew from his mouth so quickly that Miamor knew they had to be true. He was fearful of his life. He wanted to give her no reason to pull the trigger. "Can I put my hands down now?"

Miamor eyed him suspiciously and then grabbed his collar and put him against the brick wall. Her pistol kissed the back of his skull. She felt his waistline for a gun. He wasn't carrying. "I don't got shit on me. I just got out of county. They locked me up for the high-speed chase I took them on the day it all went down. Look, I know it's late and I shouldn't have come but I came straight here as soon as they let a nigga go. I received this post card in prison. Your address was the return address but there was no message written on it. I know the game. Seems like I was supposed to deliver this to you."

Miamor lowered her gun and Fly Boogie lowered his hands while breathing a sigh of relief. She snatched the post card out of his hand. She knew that he was right; this was no incident. She hadn't sent the post card and there was only one other person who could have. *He's alive,* she thought. She looked down at it and saw a Desert Oasis printed on the front of it. Her hand shot to her mouth, covering it in disbelief. *Are they in Saudi Arabia? Could this be for real?* she thought as she read the wording on the front. Her worry transformed to relief as the ball of tension that her body had become melted. She looked up at Fly Boogie, unable to stop the tears from glistening in her eyes. "Thank you," she said.

"Thank you for not blowing my brains out," he replied with a sense of humor before walking off of the porch. Miamor closed the door, locking it securely behind him. She rushed upstairs, heart pounding, eyes clouding with tears of uncertainty. *Oh my God please let him be alive. Let this postcard mean what I think it does,* she thought as hope flared in her chest. She rushed up the stairs to retrieve her son and then picked up her phone to call Breeze. She paced back and forth, child in one hand, as she held the cell to her ear.

"Miamor?" the rasp in Breeze's voice cracked in the late night hour and she cleared her throat.

"I can't speak to you over the phone. Call Leena. Come now. It's important," Miamor said. She hung up the phone before she could receive protest. She wouldn't have taken no for an answer. She was used to leading and if Leena and Breeze wanted the legacy of the Cartel to continue they had to get used to following.

Within the hour Breeze and Leena arrived with little Monroe in tow. Miamor took the sleeping toddler from Leena's arms. "I'll put him upstairs in my bed," she whispered. After ensuring that he was comfortable she joined the ladies in the kitchen. The smell of mocha thickened the air as Breeze grinded fresh coffee beans. "We'll need it," Breeze said when Miamor entered the room. "Seems like it's going to be a long night."

Leena leaned over the island that sat in the middle of the room. She folded her hands atop of the counter as she looked up at Miamor anxiously. "What's going on Miamor?"

Miamor pulled the post card out of the pocket of her Ralph Lauren plaid pajama pants. She slid it across the counter.

Leena picked it up and turned it over, surveying the front and back. Frowning in confusion she said, "You made me pull my son out of his bed at two in the morning to look at a postcard. What we doing? Taking a vacation?"

Breeze crossed the room and took the postcard out of Leena's hands. "Saudi Arabia," she read. Her brow furrowed.

"A li'l nigga named Fly Boogie dropped it off here," Miamor started . . .

Breeze nodded. "I've heard Zyir mention the name before . . ."

Miamor continued, "He said it was sent to him anonymously. I think Carter is in Saudi Arabia with Monroe . . . and Zyir."

The entire room seemed to freeze as Leena and Breeze looked up at her, eyes wide, mouths open in shock from the possibility.

Leena shook her head in denial. "They found a plane in the middle of the ocean Miamor," she whispered. "They couldn't have survived a plane crash."

"What if they were never on it? They didn't recover any bodies," Breeze said hopefully.

"I know Carter. He's reaching out to me. This postcard says nothing but says so much all at the same time. It isn't flashy, it isn't loud . . . it isn't anything that can be traced, but its enough. It's a whisper that only I can hear. I think Carter is alive. They all are but they can't come back here, unless that case goes away."

Exasperated Breeze flopped down on one of the bar stools that lined the kitchen island. "D.E.A is all over us. The workers are snitching, they have photos, and evidence . . ."

"The case is strong," Leena finished. "If their return depends on that we'll never see them again."

"The case has to go away," Miamor said.

"And then what?" Leena asked. "I'm so tired of this life. This isn't how I envisioned my life. Even if this case goes away and they get to come back . . . it is only a matter of time before something else tears this family apart. I don't know about the two of you, but I've had enough of the drug business. We have money. We have respect. It's time to move on from this."

Breeze was quiet as she pondered Leena's words. The Cartel had been her life for as long as she could remember. She had been born into it. Continuing the legacy allowed her father to live on, even in death, but was it worth it? By honoring their father, their family was diminishing before Breeze's very eyes. The streets would eventually make the Diamond clan extinct. *She's right, it's time for a change,* Breeze thought.

"The guys aren't here to guide our footsteps ladies. It's time that we made the decisions that we think are best for this family. It is time to take The Cartel legit. I don't want to lose any more loved ones. I want to live without worry and as long as we're in the drug business that will never happen."

The three women sat in silence, each haunted by their own thoughts. The ache in their hearts from their missing partners resonated within them.

Miamor looked around at their fractured group. They needed their men back.

"I'll make this case disappear, one way or another. After we bring the men home we'll talk about getting out of the game . . . for good."

Chapter 3

"Day or night, I'm available to you."

—Yasmine

Nothing had ever been so foreign to Zyir. He was Flint bred and Miami crowned. He preferred to stay where the native tongue was one that he understood. Call it closed minded, but Zyir just called it smart. He was a young man who liked to be aware of everything moving around him. As soon as he stepped off of the private jet an uneasiness settled into his bones. It was instinctive for him to reach out to Breeze. He missed her. The fact that they had been at odds ate away at him the entire flight. He knew that she was suffering because he could feel her strife. He was across the globe and was still emotionally connected to his shorty. She was his rib, he just wished that he could tell her that everything was going to be okay. Stone faced, he emerged from the plane and the first thing he saw was men carrying assault rifles lined up in front of two luxury SUV's. They were dressed in traditional, long flowing cloaks made of the most beautiful fabrics. Their heads were wrapped as well, only revealing their menacing facial expressions.

"They don't look too friendly fam," Zyir whispered to Monroe as they made their way down the stairs.

"You strapped?" Monroe asked.

"You know it," Zyir replied.

They were ready to go out guns blazing. It wasn't like them to tread lightly, but they followed Carter's lead. He was the captain of this ship and as long as he appeared comfortable they would remain that way too. Should he even show the slightest wrinkle of concern on his face, they would get it started. They were clearly outnumbered but Monroe's marksman aim evened the playing field a bit.

The door to one of the SUV's was opened and a distinguished man with a full beard exited. He wore gold garb and held out his arms in receipt of his guests. "Welcome to Saudi Arabia," he said in perfect English. He stepped forward and met the men halfway, showing good faith. He walked right up to Carter. "You must be Carter," he said as he held out his hand. "You're the spitting image of your father. He and I had some good times in America as young men. Before the wives and the children." The man paused and inhaled long and deep as he reveled in the fond memories. "To be young and rich again," he said. Carter gave him a firm handshake.

"You must be Mr. Baraka," Carter replied. Polo had made the connection so Carter knew that they were in safe hands. "This is my brother Monroe and my good friend Zyir. Thank you for extending the invitation."

"A son of Carter Diamond is a son of mine. I owed your father my life. He was a good man. I was very saddened to learn of his death," Baraka stated.

"As were we," Carter replied, keeping it short. "Thank you."

"Shall we?" Baraka said, extending his arm toward their awaiting vehicles. "Monroe and Zyir can ride in the first truck while I discuss specifics with you on the way to the resort."

"Resort?" Monroe questioned.

"Yes. I own Saudi Arabia's largest resort and casino. Five star. I have a penthouse set up for each of you," Baraka revealed. "It will be most comfortable."

Monroe nodded and headed for the truck as Carter climbed inside with Baraka.

The scenery outside of his window was mesmerizing. He was in a desert Oasis. It was so hot outside that he could see the heat waves creating a hazy view on the other side of the glass. The tan sand dunes around him made him feel out of place. This was unfamiliar territory but it was also a safe haven. He was out of reach of all of his enemies, legit and otherwise. He felt the tension dissipate from his chest. Fear of capture had been real until this very moment, but now that he had touched Saudi soil he realized exactly why Polo had suggested this place. He was worlds away. The air didn't even smell the same on this side of the planet and despite the fact that he missed Miamor and his son, he welcomed the change.

"I couldn't get any details from Polo as far as the troubles you are in," Baraka said. "Please tell me."

Baraka was mild mannered but Carter could see nothing but boss status and old money when he looked at him. He didn't know many old men who walked around with armed guards on a regular. Baraka was important and the rubies sitting on his ringed fingers told Carter that he came from extreme wealth. Carter had every intention on laying low but he was like a sponge. He soaked up knowledge and stored it for future use. He was all about expanding and building a usable and influential network. Something told him that Baraka was someone that he wanted on his team.

"The D.E.A. is trying to prosecute us on drug charges. They have evidence, mostly circumstantial and witnesses. There was no time to hinder their case against us. They want us behind bars to try to contain our influence over Miami. If we were free than their witnesses would never testify. We had no choice but to flee. We need time to regroup, maybe establish some networks over here," Carter said smoothly opening the door for potential business.

"Well you are welcome to stay here as long as you need to," Baraka said.

"Thank you," Carter replied. "I don't come empty handed however. We aren't in the business of taking handouts. Any business I conduct is mutually beneficial. There's a saying that in a good deal both parties walk away feeling like they sacrificed a little bit." Carter handed Baraka the briefcase that he had carried off of the plane. "A million dollars to show our appreciation for your hospitality."

Baraka gave Carter a chuckle as he took the case. "You are your father's boy," he commented.

"So I've heard."

The word penthouse did the accommodations no justice. They were being put up in mini-mansions in the sky. Each one came with a group of personal hand maidens, butlers, and a personal chef, not to mention the private plunge pool. This was the luxe life and Carter could appreciate the fact that the hideout felt more like an escape. He hadn't been expecting much but this set up exceeded his wildest dreams. He had seen opulence in his day but nothing quite like this. The Cartel reigned in the fields of drugs, war, and even real estate, but it was apparent that they hadn't amassed wealth on this level . . . yet. If Carter had anything to do with it they would make the transition soon, after his legal troubles subsided. After finishing the tour of Carter's penthouse Baraka turned to his guests. He stood tall, strong, with his hands clasped in front of him. "I hope you find your accommodations most suiting," he said. "Each penthouse is identical."

Monroe nodded and Zyir spoke, "No detail was left undone. Appreciate it."

Baraka smirked. He could spot a protégé in the making. Zyir was a chip off of Carter's block. Their swag was almost identical. They may not be brothers by blood but they were definitely family. Always had been . . . always would be.

The sound of a key card opening the door to the suite caused everyone in the room to look over their shoulders. When they saw her, they became breathless. The foreign beauty was the most beautiful creature that God had ever created. Her Miss Universe smile illuminated the room as she walked confidently past the group until she was tucked safely under Baraka's arm.

Damn, Carter thought. He ran his hand down his goatee and exhaled as he shifted his stance. Her long, butt length hair was dark and mysterious, matching the charcoal colored eyes that pierced upon first glance. She was slim with a model's physique. Her only curve was the perky c-cups that sat up out of the custom tailored Dolce pant suit she wore. Her skin looked like honey and Carter couldn't help but wonder if it tasted just as sweet. He shook the thoughts from his head as Baraka spoke. "This is my daughter Yasmine," Baraka introduced. "She knows my hotel better than I do. She is the hospitality manager. If you need anything she can take care of it for you. No matter how sensitive the matter, she can handle it and keep it in strict confidence. Do not hesitate to ask."

"Good to know," Carter replied as he extended his hand to her. "Nice to meet you."

There was seduction in her eyes as she took his hand. He could practically feel the heat of her touch melting into his skin as she rubbed his hand slightly. "I look forward to pleasing you," she said with a hint of mischief dancing in her eye. "Day or night, I'm available to you."

Carter smirked as he cleared his throat, bringing a balled fist to his mouth.

"I know your journey has been long. We will let you gentlemen rest," Baraka said. He led Yasmine out of the suite. The handmaidens remained stationed in the corners of the room, ready to serve.

Monroe and Zyir stepped up next to Carter. "This shit is wild bro," Monroe said. "Servants, butlers, and shit . . ."

"Don't take advantage," Carter instructed.

"From the looks these Arabian women been throwing our way, I'd say we are the ones at risk of being taken advantage of," Monroe replied with a handsome grin.

Zyir smirked but remained silent. He had caught the vibes as well and knew that this would definitely be an interesting trip. *An interesting trip indeed,* he thought.

Chapter 4

"We are the law Aries. You're a Murder Mama. This suburban neighborhood with manicured lawns got you confused ma."
                                                                    —Miamor

The serene country street was void of all threats as Miamor sat in the rental car outside of a modest two-story home. The small city in middle of nowhere, Idaho, was quiet, peaceful, and completely off the map. Miamor completely understood why it had been chosen. It was where you would go to run from your past. It only existed to its own residents. Outsiders had no knowledge of the place whatsoever. She secretly wished that she could find a place that she could run away to with her family. How nice it would be to leave it all behind. Solace. She watched as children rode their bikes up and down the paved streets. The houses all matched. The lawns were perfectly manicured as automatic sprinklers swished sounds of home ownership into the air. Miamor saw no sign of trouble, no sign of drugs, guns, murder. There was absolutely no mayhem on these Idaho streets . . . just good people, living normal, safe lives. *Must be nice,* she thought. She exited the car and hesitated as a car passed her on the street. The driver smiled and waved. *People are friendly here,* she thought as she waved back. She crossed the street and approached the house that sat on the end of the block. It was beautiful and well taken care of with flowers planted around the perimeter of the large country porch. The creaking of a swing whistled in the wind as a little boy sat with shoulder length dreadlocks, rocking slowly as he played with toy trains. He kicked his feet joyously as the swing creaked with every movement.

Miamor gasped at the sight of him and then her heart filled with warmth.

"Hi," she greeted. "Is your mom home?"

The boy stopped swinging and on cue the front door opened with a gun immediately pointed at her face. The mother inside was so on point that she knew that an intruder had interrupted her son's habitual swaying back and forth. Miamor stared down the barrel of a .357.

"Miamor?" a voice of disbelief rang out, but the recognition didn't cause the gun to lower. It was aimed at her, steady, unflinching, and ready.

"Hello Aries," Miamor greeted. Aries held the gun firmly in her grasp as she stared into the eyes of a cold-blooded killer. Miamor was the devil in a dress and she hesitated before she decided to take a chance and lower the gun. Confusion filled her eyes.

"Miamor . . ." Her brow furrowed.

The little boy stood up and ran to his mother, clinging to her leg. Aries peeled her son off of her. "Go to your room sweetheart. Lock the door and watch cartoons," she instructed, her voice stern.

The little boy nodded and disappeared inside of the house.

"You think I'm going to hurt you? I would never bring harm to you Aries. You're my friend." Miamor's voice didn't reveal the stab of anguish she felt in her heart. If her own friend feared her, she must have been a monster. *How did it come to this?* she thought.

"Yeah well I thought you were dead and I don't let my guards down these days . . . for anyone. Even friends," Aries replied.

Miamor looked down at her body. "I'm wearing Prada and five inch heels Aries. You really think I came to put in work looking like a super model?"

Aries icy demeanor chipped away a little bit and she smirked. "Bitch nobody said you look like a super model. I see we're still arrogant huh?" Aries cracked. Her face melted into a smile. "You look great for a dead woman," she cracked. Aries put the gun on safety and embraced Miamor. "You have a lot of explaining to do," she said.

"I know," Miamor replied. "Are you going to invite me in?"

Aries stepped back into the house and Miamor followed.

"I'm proud of you," Miamor admitted as she looked around the home. Everything was in its place. Modest, but extremely beautiful, Aries house felt like a real family lived in it. Plush carpet absorbed her feet, beautiful venetian blinds shaded the windows, while leather furniture sat on top of an opulent French rug. A stab of jealousy vibrated through her, but it only lasted for a moment. This was the life and she was glad that one of the Murder Mamas was blessed to live it. It wasn't about the money or respect, it was about peace of mind. After the sins that they had committed Aries was lucky to find it. "You made it out. You have a home and a child. I assume there is a man?"

Miamor sat down at the kitchen table as Aries went to the cupboard to start a pot of tea.

"There used to be someone," Aries said. "He was killed. The past knocked on my door and he got mixed up in some bull-shit. I bounced around from place to place. Went back home to the Islands, then to Montana to settle a score, to Arizona, and finally decided to settle here. I ditched the accent to blend in and I started over. This place felt the safest."

Aries filled the kettle with water and placed it over the blue and orange flame on the stove. Miamor admired her. *She's so normal now,* Miamor thought. She then took a seat across from Miamor. "What happened to you Mia?" A dark cloud seemed to shift over their heads as the mood changed. The reunion had turned dark as the thought of their dead friend loomed over them.

"I was in hiding," Miamor admitted. "Running from Mecca. I only came back after Carter killed him."

"But we got your hands sent to us in a box," Aries whispered.

Miamor shook her head. "It's a long story but they weren't my hands."

"You left us," Aries whispered. "We were in the middle of a fucking war and you just dipped. You left us stuck. Where were you when they took Robyn's life?" The reunion between the two of them was bittersweet. Miamor had been their leader. Aries couldn't help but think if she had stayed things may have turned out differently.

"I cried for a week straight when Robyn was executed. I'm sorry Aries. I should have been there," Miamor whispered. "You all were my sisters."

Tears accumulated in Aries eyes. "They put her down like a dog," she whispered. She quickly swiped the emotion away. "You have a child?" she asked.

Miamor frowned. "How do you know that?"

Aries chuckled. "You put on some weight. The bad bitch I know don't play that. You wouldn't gain a pound. A baby is the only explanation. Can I assume that you're back with Carter?"

Miamor smiled. She missed this intimate interaction with Aries. No one had known her better than the Murder Mamas. They were family. Despite her love for Carter and her growing bond with Breeze and Leena, she was never as intimate with anyone as she was with her crew. "I am. Which is why I'm here. I need your help Aries. There's a case against Carter, Zyir, and Monroe . . ."

"Monroe?" Aries questioned in shock. "What the fuck? Everybody is just rising out of their graves in Miami?" The revelation hit her the same way it had everyone else when they first found out Money was alive, like a ton of bricks. "I saw that man in his casket."

"He's alive," Miamor confirmed. "He lay in a coma for five years but he breathes just like you and me. The case that the Feds have brought down on The Cartel is solid enough to send everyone away for life. They're on the run . . ." Miamor wouldn't have shared that information with anyone else, but she had trusted Aries with much more. Miamor hid no truths from this old friend. They had done and seen it all . . . together. "I'm being watched or I would put the work in myself. This fucking prosecuting attorney would love to catch me up in the RICO case. You're not on the radar though Aries. You could get in and out. Help me make this go away."

"You want me to murk a P.A.? Have you lost your mind Miamor?" Aries asked. They had gotten away with their share of murders in their day, but this situation reminded her too much of the one that sent Robyn to the death chamber. "You know this is how Robyn got caught up. We aren't bigger than the law."

Miamor's gaze toughened. "We are the law Aries. You're a Murder Mama. This suburban neighborhood with manicured lawns got you confused ma? Anybody can get it. Niggas, bitches, children . . . white, black, fucking purple. I will do anything to bring my man home."

"Yeah but you're not Mia. You're asking me to and I just can't. I'm out of the life," Aries protested firmly.

"Maybe but this certainly isn't living Aries," Miamor's tone softened as she sympathized with her friend. "You have to be lonely here. You have no family, no friends . . . just you and your son. Come back to Miami with me. I want to be a part of your son's life. I want you to be an aunt to mine. We are the last two standing," Miamor said genuinely.

"Miami is Cartel territory Miamor. You can forgive and forget because you love the nigga that's in charge of it, but I still remember. I remember the war. The beef . . ."

"They are good people," Miamor interrupted. "And I need you there. Carter's half way across the world and he won't ever come home unless I make it happen. I need you to help me get this case off his back."

Aries shook her head. "Nah, Miamor. That's your problem, not mine. I'm not ever coming back to Miami."

Miamor wanted to press the issue but out of respect she didn't. They had done a lot of dirt together and it wasn't Miamor's right to push Aries into re-entering the life. "Okay," she said. She stood to her feet thinking that there was nothing left to say. Miamor needed Aries, but she did not blame her for declining the proposition. Aries was loyal, she always had been; Miamor knew that it would not be easy to get her to change how she felt about The Cartel. Love had caused Miamor to become soft, but Aries was still Aries and she would forever throw the middle finger to the organization who killed Anisa. It was just the way that she was built.

Miamor began to walk toward the door but was halted by the sound of her name. "Mia . . . you want to at least meet your nephew before you leave?" Before Miamor could answer the whistle of the teapot erupted in the air. Aries went to the stove poured two cups as steam drifted from the spout. She handed one to Miamor. "Come on," she said. Miamor followed Aries up to the little boy's room and when they opened the door they found him fast asleep on his bed.

"You don't have to wake him," Miamor said. She walked over to the bed and knelt over the small child. "Auntie loves you." She planted a kiss on his forehead.

"His name is Tre," Aries said.

Miamor stood and went into her clutch. She removed a piece of paper and pen. "Take care of yourself Aries. I am so proud of you. If you ever need anything just call me." She wrote down her number and address before handing it to Aries.

"Thanks for coming by Mia," Aries responded. She took the paper but they both knew that she would never use it. She was shutting the door on her past life and silently Miamor wished that she could do the same.

"I love you Murder Mama," Aries whispered sadly.

Miamor closed her eyes for a moment and thought back to when they all were together; there had been five of them at a point in time. She was flooded with instant grief at the fact that three of them were no longer breathing. *Did I lead us here? Are their deaths my fault?* She thought. It was a burden that she would always carry on her shoulders. The loss of her sisters weighed heavily on her conscience. "I love you too Aries. Always." Miamor opened the door.

"Mia . . ."

Miamor turned around to Aries.

"Don't try to kill the P.A. or the judge or none of that. It's too dangerous. There's more than one way to skin a cat. A dead public official will only make the government go for more blood. You need leverage," Aries said. She shrugged. "But hey what do I know? I'm just a suburban housewife. Good-bye friend." Miamor nodded and walked out of the house filled with hurt. It was a pain that she had never felt before because she knew this was the final good-bye. She was headed back to Miami to fix her problems on her own, but not in the way that she had intended. Aries had given her some words of wisdom, ones that would prove valuable in time.

Chapter 5

"He on that real suit and tie type shit."
—Fly Boogie

Two Weeks Later

Murderous thoughts filled Miamor's mind as she thought of ways to tamper with the federal case. The role of motherhood had settled her a bit. It forced her to think first and react accordingly, but it did nothing to scratch the itch she had to make bullets rain from the sky. It was like a junkie craving a fix; when Miamor had a problem she solved it, period. Erring on the side of caution was like pulling teeth to her. As much as she wanted to reinstate her murder game, she could not. Miamor had to think about her son and if she went off the handle she wasn't sure she would ever be able to recover. Murder was like heroin for her. The familiar feeling of revenge was hard to shake. Once she got a taste of her old lifestyle it would be hard to revert back to a normal life. Motherhood and the game didn't mix and Miamor desperately wanted to get that part right. She wanted to be the wife and mother that her family needed, not the goon that streets required. She had to fix things. It was up to her to put her family back together but there were certain risks that she wasn't willing to take at the moment. Although she didn't see them, she knew that there were so many eyes on her that if she so much as jay walked they would bury her under the jail. In the past this problem would have disappeared already. It would have been nothing to tie up a wife or kidnap a kid to make a judge throw the case out, but in those days she had lived recklessly. Now, she had a child who depended on her and she would not sacrifice him in order to save Carter. She had to play it smart this time and use caution before she proceeded. She hadn't heard anything further from Carter and she knew that she wouldn't. It was too risky. Any communication between the two of them could cause exposure. Her mind spun with worry as she thought of him. He consumed her every waking moment. *I have to make this go away.* The doorbell rang and Miamor arose from her seat. Her housekeeper Magdalena had quit after being interrogated for hours by the D.E.A. so she was left to take care of the massive estate on her own. She hastened her steps to stop the guest from ringing the bell again. She couldn't have the sound intruding on her infant son's sleep. She pulled open the door and stepped aside as Fly Boogie walked inside. Neither she, nor, any of the girls could move freely so she had put Fly Boogie on the prosecuting attorney. She had eyes on him at all times as she slowly gained information about him.

"What do you know?" Miamor asked, cutting directly to the point of his visit.

"Not much. This mu'fucka is squeaky clean. He on that real suit and tie type shit," Fly Boogie said as he dug his hands in his pockets.

"Nobody is completely clean," Miamor responded. "Everybody has dirty laundry, we just have to find the closet he's hiding it in."

Fly Boogie shook his head doubtfully and handed her his phone. "Take a look for yourself. I've been stalking this nigga for days. This is all I've got, a bunch of pictures . . . but nothing stands out."

Miamor swiped her finger across the screen as she flicked through photos. She peered at the images with a critical eye. She sent each one to her email before moving to the next shot.

"I'm telling you there's nothing there. You should just let me get at the niggas who turning state. No witnesses, no case," Fly Boogie said.

"I don't know what you're talking about," Miamor said quickly. She hadn't told Fly Boogie her exact agenda. She didn't know him well enough to trust him with the details. He was Zyir's man and off of that strength she decided to use him to her advantage.

"Yeah a'ight. Look I know a nigga young and fly and all that, but one thing ya' boy Fly ain't is dumb," he answered. "You trying to find something out about the prosecution to shake shit up. When all you got to do is cut off a few pair of loose lips, nah mean? A nigga with no lips can't do no talking."

Miamor smirked at the young hustler's remarks. He was confident as if he had a cloak of invincibility. That type of bravado came with youth. She had lived many days with that same cockiness, but she was older and smarter. She knew better. She couldn't kill everybody. This case was sewn up tightly. Too many low level hustlers and mid-grade buyers were exchanging testimony for deals. Most were hidden away in witness protection. One witness in one safe house was feasible, but multiple murders without the aid of her old crew was impossible.

"Again, I don't know what you're talking about," she reiterated.

Fly Boogie nodded and then proceeded to the door. "I can put in work and I'm not like these other li'l homies out here. Zyir is my man. Whatever I got to do to prove my worth, I'm with it. You can trust me."

"Good-bye Fly Boogie," she said with a half-smile. The kid was growing on her and his charismatic personality paired with his knack for the streets was appealing. He was a young goon, and a hustler by any means necessary. He was Carter Jones before the Italian cut suits, drug kingpin status, business acquisitions, and overseas connects. Fly Boogie was gutter but had so much potential. He was ride or die. If they ever came out of this she would definitely tell Carter how helpful Fly had been. *And if Carter never comes home, I'll put Fly Boogie on my team,* she thought, preparing herself for the worst.

The sound of the grandfather clock ticked slowly as the pendulum swung back and forth. Leena tapped her nude, manicured, nails against the wooden arm of the office chair as she waited patiently. The nude jumpsuit she wore along with six-inch heels, stood out amongst the poorly dressed businesswomen around her. Their cheap threads paled in comparison to the immaculately styled attire she wore. While well composed in appearance, she was unraveling on the inside. She had become acquainted with the night hours since Monroe had gone away. Worry and stress etched permanent lines on her once youthful face. She was no longer a young girl in love with a bad boy. She was a grown woman, dealing with the consequences of loving a man whom conflicted with the law. Her choices had led her to this point. The choice to stay involved with The Cartel had been hers and now she was suffering, heart empty, future unpredictable. She was a dope man's wife and to a young girl it was a dream . . . to a grown woman it was a nightmare. The position was glitzy on the surface but dulled the person she was within. Leena wanted out and as she sat waiting for the Diamond family accountant to summon her, she was determined to find her exit.

"Leena Deveraux, Mr. Odom is ready for you now," the receptionist announced.

Leena stood and followed the thin, brunette to the back office. She nodded gratefully as the woman stood to the side and extended her arm so that Leena could bypass her. Mr. Odom stood, clad in a Brooks Brothers suit. He was distinguished with smooth, black, skin and a clean baldhead. The dark features of his goatee and thick eyebrows stood out on his face, perfectly groomed. His persona yelled wealth and he had a presence that made everyone around him attentive. He was the complete opposite of what Leena had expected. A rich, successful, black man paving a way in a legit atmosphere was so foreign to her. All she had been around for years was men involved in the game. This black man in front of her was refreshing. He smiled and extended his hand. The scent of his clean cologne awakened her senses.

"Thomas Odom," he introduced. "You must be Ms. Deveraux,"

"Call me Leena," she replied.

She sat down and placed her handbag in her lap as he walked around his desk to take his own seat. He folded his hands on top of his desk, the lines of the suit hugging his broad shoulders.

"What can I help you with?" he asked.

Leena cleared her throat before she spoke, trying to swallow the lump that had formed. She wasn't a dumb girl. In fact, she had a bachelor's in business, although it did very little besides collect dust in a box. She had allowed herself to be sucked into the lifestyle of the rich and infamous. Leena had completely abandoned the concept of a normal life, but there was only so much she could take. After the catastrophe of her wedding day and Monroe disappearing into the sky, she could no longer take this life.

"My fiancé was Monroe Diamond," she started. "I'm here to speak to you about Diamond enterprises. I know that he along with Carter and Breeze have a lot of money put into that corporation. I'd like to talk about investment opportunities. The family is interested in going in a different direction."

Odom studied her as she spoke, admiring her beauty. "First let me express my condolences to you and your family. I'm sure this is a very hard time for you, but I can not speak to you about Mr. Diamond's financial affairs. He wasn't a client of mine. He was a loyal client of Jamison Wildes. Perhaps you should be speaking to him about the Diamond affairs."

Leena went into her Birkin and removed a manila envelope. "I thought you may say that Mr. Odom . . ."

He waved his hand. "Thomas," he said, dismissing the formalities.

"Thomas, well Jamison Wildes only handled the domestic accounts for Monroe. You are far better versed in foreign money, which is why Monroe hired you to handle any international transactions, including Swiss and Cayman accounts. Here is Monroe's living will," she said as she passed it to him. "As you can see he left his third of Diamond enterprises to me. Along with that is the living will of Carter Jones. I already have his beneficiary along with Breeze on board. We want to change the way that our money is earned. I know that Monroe trusted you with his money because of that I trust you."

Odom pulled his tie and sat back in his seat, crossing his leg over the other. "I have done business with the Diamond family for many years. I tried over a decade ago to steer Carter Sr. away from his way of business. It saddens me that it took so much loss to come to this," Odom said. "Unfortunately the government has seized all accounts associated with your family. There is no money."

Leena smirked. "That's funny. What you have to understand Thomas is that our men prepared us for this day. You don't fall in love with a man like Monroe Diamond without preparing for the inevitable fall from grace. I want the money that's tucked away in the Swiss and Cayman accounts. I want it in cash and I know exactly how much it is so please don't try to short change me."

Odom smiled as he got comfortable in his chair. Intrigue danced in his eyes. Leena's hard exterior covered up a bleeding interior as her heart beat rapidly. She hadn't had a sleep filled night since the Feds had come around. Leena needed the money to take The Cartel corporate. She didn't know how yet, but she knew that the move was completely overdue and absolutely necessary.

"Stand please," Odom said.

"Excuse me?" she asked, suddenly thrown off.

He motioned with his fingers smoothly for her to stand. She put her hand bag down on the floor and stood, as did he. He rounded the desk, his tall figure walking toward her. Fragile and heart broken Leena's thought drifted to Monroe. Until now, she had never had to take the lead. She was so comfortable following. Thrust into power, it was her place to now manage the money that Monroe had left behind. She needed to square her shoulders, put fire in her eyes, and boss up her entire life but instead all she felt was emptiness.

As Odom stood in front of her he seemed to see through her. "You're beautiful Ms. Devereaux. It truly pains me to see a woman like you so broken. You are worthy of much more."

Leena sucked in a sharp breath. *Am I that transparent? S*he thought. Odom was handsome and she had his full attention. Leena silently wondered what life would have been like had she met a man like him. He was what Monroe would have been had the war with the Haitians not happened. Instead she had been caught in a web of drugs, lust, and money. She had fallen for not one but two Diamond brothers. She hadn't stood a chance.

Sensing her discomfort he switched the subject. She was clearly mourning. She smiled demurely. "I'm fine. A bit uncomfortable standing in six inch heels when I could be sitting comfortably," she replied.

He cleared his throat. "I'm sorry. I just need to be sure. Please hold out your arms."

Leena frowned but did as she was told. His hands began to roam. "You think I'm wired?"

Odom didn't answer, but he continued to search her. When he was sure that she was clean he nodded.

"I apologize. The IRS and other bureaus have been combing through my records trying to make me an accomplice in this case. I can't be too careful. Now let's talk about the money . . . perhaps over dinner?" Odom asked.

Leena was stuck for a moment. *Did he just ask me out?* She thought. He sensed her hesitation. "I realize that you are basically Monroe's widow. I was in attendance at the wedding turned massacre remember. It's just dinner and good company while attending to business."

"Okay," Leena said. She wanted to say no, but until she got the money in her hands she decided to keep things comfortable between them. He wouldn't be the first accountant to clean out a client, so she decided to play it safe to hinder any foul play. "I'll send a car for you tonight at 7:00 p.m."

Odom's eyes widened in surprise.

She chuckled slightly as she grabbed her bag. "I'm the Cartel Mr. Odom. I have to control my surroundings. Guess I picked up a few tricks to the trade being around Monroe."

"Apparently," he quipped. The way he eyed Leena, she knew that she would have to be careful with him. He had never met a woman like her and she knew that she never would. She was one of a kind and held a power that even she did not yet realize. Her mind was so sharp that she could outthink the majority and now it was her time to come into her own. A new regime was emerging. The streets had forced Miamor, Leena, and Breeze into a sisterhood. Together, they would takeover.

Chapter 6

*"I forgave you because my brother loves
you but I don't fuck with your clique."*
                                                    —Breeze

Breeze stepped out of the chauffeured Maybach with over-sized Bulgari shades hiding her true emotions from the cameras. She was the surviving child of the infamous king of Miami, Carter Diamond. She was a living legend and everyone wanted a piece of her. Controversy circled the family like vultures waiting for death. The news reporters stayed on her particularly. Everyone wanted a comment, an interview; even Time Magazine had offered her money for a sit down. Street fame was turning into actual fame for Breeze; she wanted none of it however. The only thing Breeze craved at the moment was Zyir. Loneliness consumed her days while the only companionship she had at night was grief. Leena and Miamor were lucky. They had the seeds of the men they loved to cultivate. Even in Carter and Monroe's absence, the children they left behind provided comfort. Breeze was alone. Breeze was not a mother. She had no piece of Zyir, besides her memories and even those weren't enough. She wanted her man. She was skeptical about his well-being. A part of her didn't believe that he was alive, but Miamor seemed so sure that it kept a tiny spark of hope blazing in Breeze's chest. Breeze was the weakest link but she hid it well. Sunglasses were a permanent veil to cover her red, puffy, eyes. Her expensive clothes distracted the masses from her hunched shoulders. She disguised her burden well because she made sure she was always put together right. It was how her mother, Taryn had raised her. "You have to always be a bad bitch." It was words she had lived by her entire life, but in the absence of all the people who had sworn to be her protectors, they never rang more true. The hired goon stood suited in Italian threads while concealing American metal in his holster. His six foot five inch frame pushed the reporters out of the way as she trailed him into the building to meet the federal prosecutor.

"Ms. Diamond, how does it feel to be the last member of The Cartel standing?"

"Is it true that your family is responsible for seventy percent of the murders in Dade County?"

"Ms. Diamond can you comment on the mysterious plane crash that killed your brothers and live-in boyfriend?"

Breeze kept her head low as she held onto the back of her bodyguard's shirt. The thirsty media was so focused on breaking open the story of the largest crime family in the South and they were relentless in their tactics. Relief came as she stepped inside of the rotating doors.

"Wait here for me," she instructed.

The average person would have been shaken by a request to meet with the law, but Breeze was fully prepared. She had a pit on a chain in the form of her attorney, Rosenberg, and like a loyal dog ready to bark he stood waiting for her in the lobby. He had represented the family for years, dating back to Big Carter and Polo. He knew of their dealings intimately and had protected them from persecution for a few decades. He had attended family barbecues, holidays, and birthday parties. Breeze felt completely safe in his care.

"Breeze, how are you?" he asked as he greeted her with a firm handshake.

"I'd be better if I didn't have to be here. What is this about?" she asked as they made their way to the elevators.

"This is a fishing expedition," Rosenberg replied. "You can let me do all the talking. That's what you pay me the big bucks for." He gave her a wink and she smiled, feeling relaxed as she followed one of her father's oldest friends into the lion's den.

Rosenberg led her directly into the office of Daniel Broome, the P.A. assigned to take down her family. Her internal alarm immediately went up.

"Rosenberg, I didn't realize you would be joining us," Broome said.

The two guests took a seat without being asked and Breeze folded her legs, making herself comfortable.

"You should know better by now Daniel," Rosenberg replied, showing disrespect by using his first name.

Daniel Broome was an American bread golden boy. Son of a senator and an ivy-league grad, he came out of law school with a readymade position. He had assisted on many cases, including the original case that the Feds had brought against Carter Diamond. When they didn't convict, Broome had a hard-on for The Cartel and now that the children of the man whom had eluded the law were in his clutches he was determined to bring justice. He was a young, ambitious, lad . . . too ambitious for Breeze's taste.

"Why am I here?" Breeze asked.

"Breeze as you know I've been following your family for quite some time. This case is strong, completely rock solid. Before the death of your brothers and your boyfriend my focus was on convicting them. Their deaths don't mean that this case goes away. Someone still has to pay for the damage that has been done to the streets of Miami."

The P.A. pulled out a manila folder and began to pull out still photographs. "Your family, your father, your brothers have destroyed this community," he said. He placed a picture of a young boy laid out in his own blood before her. Breeze didn't flinch. He then placed a picture of a young toddler who had been hit by a stray bullet. Again, Breeze was unmoved. There were casualties in war. "Innocent people have lost their lives behind the melee of The Cartel."

Breeze felt badly for the people in the pictures, but she was raised up in a game where death was an everyday factor. She had lost everything and no one was sitting back mourning for her . . . feeling sorry for her. Breeze had experienced it all and she was still here, standing tall. She gave no fucks about anybody who was outside of the scope of The Cartel family. If her brothers had executed anyone, they had deserved it. As many losses as The Cartel had taken, she felt no qualms about the losses of others.

"These are sympathy tactics you use on a jury Daniel. Cut to the chase. What do you want?" Rosenberg asked.

"I would like to put a deal on the table," Broome said. "When I get the jury to convict, you will go away for the rest of your life. You are a young woman Breeze. You don't want to grow old in prison. If you give me the cocaine supplier we can shift the focus of this case to a larger entity."

Breeze remained stoic as she sat back judging the suit and tie, white-bred, lawyer. *He has no idea what he is up against,* she thought. *I'm never going to cooperate. This is a waste of my fucking time.* Snitching wasn't an option. Emilio Estes supplied The Cartel so she would only be freeing family to enslave family. It was a catch 22.

"Can I have a moment with my client?" Rosenberg asked.

Breeze raised her hand. "We don't need a moment. There's nothing to talk about. We'll pass," she said.

Breeze stood to her feet, signaling that the meeting was over. Rosenberg followed her lead. "See you in court."

Breeze walked out of the office and bumped directly into a girl.

"Excuse me," the girl said. She quickly turned her head and kept walking but her presence made Breeze freeze in her steps as she watched the girl make a hasty retreat.

Goosebumps formed on her arms as her heart beat rapidly as her fight or flight instincts kicked in. It was as if she had seen a ghost. The girl had only spoken two words to Breeze but that was all that was needed for Breeze to recognize the voice. There was a murder mama in town and as Breeze high tailed it out of the office fear chilled her to the bone.

"Breeze! Is everything okay?!"

Rosenberg didn't even get a response. All he saw was Breeze's shaken facial expression as she disappeared behind the closing elevator doors.

"Miamor!!!"

Leena and Miamor stood to their feet in alarm as they heard Breeze's distressed voice break through the mansion.

"What's wrong?" Leena asked as Breeze entered the kitchen, where they had congregated for lunch with the children.

"Ask her," Breeze said as she pointed toward Miamor.

Miamor frowned as she withdrew the bottle from baby Carter's mouth. "Lower your voice please before you scare the kids," Miamor said with authority. "Have a seat, pour yourself some wine, and calm down before you talk to me."

"Fuck the wine. I saw your friend today at Daniel Broome's office. She walked different and she talked different but it was her. The bitch who helped kidnap me was in his office! I bumped right into her."

"My bitch," Miamor said with a smile.

"What? You knew she was here?" Leena asked distressed.

"Let's pour some wine. Let me explain," Miamor said. "But first are you absolutely sure it was her?"

Breeze shot Miamor a look that could kill. "It was her but why is she here?"

"I went to visit Aries to see if she could help me get to the P.A. She turned me down, but I guess she's had a change of heart," Miamor replied.

"Listen Miamor, I forgave you because my brother loves you but I don't fuck with your clique. I don't know them. They brought harm to the people I love. She is not welcome in Miami. If I have to I'll put money on the problem to make it go away," Breeze said threateningly. Had Breeze been any other person making any other threat Miamor would have bodied her, but Breeze was her sister. She had to remedy things between Aries and Breeze in order for everything to work.

"I need you to trust me Breeze. You are my family and I love you as such. She is not here to bring any more harm to you. I promise you on my son's life that she is here to help," Miamor reasoned.

"I don't care what she is here for. I don't rock with Aries," Breeze said. "And I don't deal with people who deal with my enemies."

Breeze stormed out of Miamor's home livid as hot tears burned at her eyes.

"Breeze?!" Leena called.

Miamor sighed. "Go after her. Make sure she's okay. Li'l Money can stay here with us. You have to meet the accountant tonight anyway. You can pick him up in the morning."

Leena kissed Miamor on the cheek. "I hope you're right about your friend being in town to help. We don't need anymore betrayal amongst us."

Miamor watched as Leena departed. She immediately picked up her phone and dialed Aries' number. Her presence could only help bring Carter back home . . . that's if Breeze didn't put her newfound power into play first.

Candles flickered and the scent of sea salt filled the humid air as Leena walked into the five-star restaurant. White clothed tables and couples in love filled the space as Leena made her way to the table where Odom was seated. She was conservatively dressed in a flawless vintage Chanel pant suit. She didn't want to give the wrong impression, but her beauty made it hard to hide her appeal. Her curves were sharp and as she walked she turned the heads of everyone around her. She came up behind Odom and said, "I have to say, I don't appreciate the change of venue. I was expecting a more appropriate environment."

She shifted uncomfortably, visibly displeased. Odom stood and placed his hand on her back as he guided her to her chair. He pulled it out for her before reclaiming his own spot. "I'm a fan of the steak," Odom dismissed.

"Hmm," Leena smirked. "We're here to talk about business. Lets be clear."

"Relax Ms. Devereaux . . . Leena, I understand your position. That doesn't make me any less intrigued by you. I must be honest. You seem more like a woman who prefers legitimate money."

"Money is money," she responded.

"I guarantee you Leena it isn't. No cop, no district attorney, no enemy can come and take my money away," Odom said. "My wife will be secure forever."

His words evoked something within her because she completely understood what he was saying. Just because it was truth didn't take the sting out of the words.

"An accountant's money can't afford me," she replied, slightly offended.

Odom smirked as the waiter walked up with a tray full of food. "I took the liberty of ordering."

"You don't even know what I like," Leena said.

"That's why I got a little bit of everything. It's good to try something new every once in awhile Ms. Deveraux. You never know, you just might like it," Odom answered suavely. She cut her eyes at him but the scent of the five star-cuisine invaded her senses as the waiter set the meal out in front of them. If this had been a date, she would have surely been intrigued by Odom. He was an eligible bachelor . . . charming, handsome, and well-off but he was too slow for Leena. The white-collar job was too safe to ever make her panties wet. While his efforts were flattering, they were in vain. In the end, all she wanted was the money. Odom thought that Monroe was deceased, otherwise he would never have the moxie to push up on his lady. While Leena was determined to draw a professional line clearly in the sand, Odom seemed insistent on crossing it.

"Tell me Leena, how does a woman like you end up in such a delicate predicament?" he asked.

"What's delicate about it? I have access to more money than people see in two lifetimes. Monroe left no stone unturned. My son and I will be well taken care of," she reminded. "Once you hand over the funds that is."

"It is very hard to produce that much money in cash without implicating myself. It would be much easier if I could arrange a trust for the three of you and your children," Odom said seriously.

"We want cash. Cash is untraceable," Leena said.

"Liquid cash is also dangerous. A trust makes you legitimate. That's what you want for The Cartel am I right? Legitimacy," Odom countered. Leena's mental wheels turned as he spoke. She was savvy when it came to business and she knew that he was right. If he set up the trust correctly, he could make it appear as though it was earned from legal sources. Cash would be risky. Every purchase would be scrutinized and they would be able to secure no lines of credit. The cash would make them hood rich but Leena and the girls were trying to establish an empire that could rival the likes of the Trumps and the Rockefellers.

The sounds of Nina Simone cut through the air as a live band began their set.

"Dance with me," Odom said, his white smile decorating his face nicely.

Leena cleared her throat and reached for her wine glass. She took a sip, extending her long neck upwards as she took her time responding. Her red lipstick left a kiss of seduction on the glass.

"That would be inappropriate," she answered.

"Maybe, but it would also be fun." Odom stood to his feet and extended his hand to her.

Leena smiled. She would have to watch this man. He was too smooth for his own good. "You gone leave me hanging. Don't make me tuck my tail in embarrassment. One dance," he said.

Leena rolled her eyes and gave him her hand while simultaneously throwing her napkin on the table.

"One dance," she shot.

She stood and he escorted her onto the floor with the other patrons who were gently swaying to the music.

Odom pulled her close, but still left space between them so that she was comfortable. "When is the last time you had fun?"

Leena's mind went down memory lane but she knew that it had been so long ago that she couldn't recall exactly.

"Every day of your life should be fun Leena, carefree, comfortable," he said. He lifted his hand and spun her, then pulled her back close.

"Maybe in another lifetime," she said. "I'm sure you are a very good man. In fact you seem like the perfect man, for a different type of woman. I am flawed. My life isn't black and white. I've been living in the gray for so long that I could never go back. A square life doesn't suit me."

Leena let go of his hand as the music faded. "Now if you don't mind, let's talk more about this trust . . ."

The water parted like the red sea as Monroe's hands moved rhythmically as he swam with aggression. 50 laps had become light work for him. The early morning sun was just rising.

He could feel it warming his muscular back. He came up on the edge of the pool, panting as he finished his a.m. workout. He admired the orange rays of morning light as they slowly seduced the slumbering earth into awakening. He eased his body out of the water and stood in tight swim shorts, the V-cuts of his lower abdomen toned and defined. Monroe was built like a Greek God. He was completely conscious of what he put into his temple. After surviving a near death experience he wanted to take care of himself and live as many years as he could. He was still playing catch up for the five years he had lay in a coma. Feeling his pulse racing as he pushed his body to the limit made him feel alive. He did any activity that made his heart pump blood to his organs. Yoga, swimming, basketball, golf, weights, it didn't matter . . . movement made him feel most alive. He grabbed the towel from the Saudi Arabian woman who awaited poolside. Draped in beautiful fabric she was his personal assistant. The Saudi's had been very accommodating to them and he felt completely comfortable in the far away land. Carter had instructed them to put home in the back of their minds but being the control freak that he was he always kept an eye on Miami, even from Saudi Arabia.

Monroe walked over to the poolside spread that lay out for him. Breakfast and a USA today were neatly placed out for him. It was a routine that he had done since leaving the states. It was his way of staying abreast in a world that was now so foreign.

"Shall I set a place out for Mr. Jones?" his lovely assistant asked, causing Monroe to raise his head. He saw Carter emerging from the immaculate resort and headed toward him. He wore a casual confidence on his face and a controlled arrogance led the cadence of his footsteps as he approached. For the first time in years Carter wasn't strapped. He was completely carefree in Saudi. No one posed a threat. They were amongst allies and it felt good. The only thing that was missing was his Miamor. In her absence one thing was very certain, the ladies still swooned over him. Even within a society where religion was so thick and women were held to a higher standard, he still turned their panties to puddles whenever he entered a room.

"Yes, you can set up a place for him. Thank you," Monroe replied. "Its kind of early for you huh bro?" he greeted. "I know you ain't trying to join me with the morning routine. From the looks of things Saudi is treating you good. Nigga getting a gut and all."

Carter chuckled. "I don't do that sweating shit bro. I leave that for you. I'm feasting like a king, this that money gut play boy," he cracked jokingly.

Carter sat across from Monroe and graciously accepted the coffee that Monroe's servant poured for him. "Is there anything else you need Mr. Jones? I would love to oblige any request," the girl cooed as she batted her eyes.

Monroe smiled as Carter shooed the girl away, requesting privacy.

"Get your own desert girl. That's all me," Monroe said.

"Ladies recognize real muscle. That gym shit ain't working bro," Carter teased. The men shared a friendly laugh but Monroe could see there was something Carter had come to get off his chest.

"I know you ain't up at the crack of dawn to banter. What's up fam? Speak your piece," Monroe invited.

"I know I've told you and Zyir to dead all communication back home, but I've kept my eyes and ears open to the circumstances of The Cartel . . ."

"As have I," Monroe admitted.

Carter pulled a burner phone out of his pocket and pulled up a picture before passing it to Monroe.

The average person wouldn't have been able to see the anger that suddenly struck Monroe but Carter noticed the tension that had filled his jawline. As Monroe stared at Leena dancing closely with their accountant Odom, he was livid.

"Apparently, Odom hasn't given up the money in the Swiss accounts yet. I'm told that Leena is being compliant to his dinner requests, his impromptu business meetings, just to keep things running smoothly until he turns over the cash. He thinks your dead. Leena is a beautiful woman."

Monroe slid the phone back over to Carter. "Don't worry about it," he said arrogantly. "That square ass nigga don't got a chance with my girl. If a nigga can pull my bitch he can have her."

Carter nodded. "Just wanted to let you know what Leena and the girls are up against."

"Who do you have as your eyes in Miami?" Monroe pondered.

"F. Boogie, who else?" Carter answered, matter of factly. "Miamor doesn't even know that I'm in communication with him yet."

Monroe nodded. "He's a smart kid. Definitely need to promote him for his loyalty when we return," Monroe said. "I'll get with you later fam."

Monroe headed up to his penthouse suite. Although he didn't wear his heart on his sleeves he was highly bothered by Odom's blatant lack of morals. He hadn't been "dead" long enough for anyone to push up on his lady, especially not a close family friend. There were two things that Monroe didn't play games about. His money and his woman.

Chapter 7

*"The young diamond princess always
has been easily shaken."*

—Aries

Miamor knew Aries well enough to know that when the time was right she would make her presence known. After Breeze's spotting Miamor decided not to call her old friend, but instead to give her room to work. *What the hell do you have up your sleeve Aries?* Miamor wondered. She looked at the text message she had received from an undisclosed sender. Anonymity did little to hide the identity of the sender, it was Aries. As Miamor went to the place she used to call home so many memories flooded her system. Miamor was headed to her old condo in Miami. It was the one that she had sat in with all of her girls, including her sister, plotting in. It was the place where she had first realized that her love for Carter was real. It was familiar to Miamor and when she pulled in front of the building she smiled. It was nothing like the castle she lived in now, but at one time in her life it had been home. She left her car on the street and fed the meter before heading up. She was cautious because she feared being under the federal scope. She drove around in circles for at least an hour before heading to her true destination. She took the steps, an old habit from her hit-woman days. She never liked closed off spaces. Elevators left her vulnerable. She would rather go up and down a million stairs than to be a sitting duck in a confined space. Her calfs burned until she conquered the fifteen flights that led to her old doorstep. A light sweat had formed under her clothes and she gave herself a moment to still her racing heart.

"It's a lot of steps right?"

Aries voice echoed in the stairwell causing Miamor to spin around. Aries was one flight above her. She was the only other person in the world who would have opted for the hard route. They were one in the same.

"Bitch I should have known," Miamor said. "Now you mind filling me in on how you weaseled your way inside the P.A.'s office? You nearly sent Breeze on a tirade after she bumped into your ass. Thanks for the heads up!"

"The young diamond princess always has been easily shaken," Aries recalled. "Let's go inside, I'll explain everything. I think I have something that can help you."

Miamor watched as Aries unlocked the door and walked inside. The apartment was white walls and white carpet; bare with the exception of a blow-up mattress that filled the space.

"What made you decide to help me?" Miamor asked.

Aries placed her hands on her wide hips and shrugged. "I knew your crazy ass would have tried to do it yourself if I didn't help. Through it all Miamor you are my sister. We are the only ones left."

"Where's your son?" Miamor asked.

"Somewhere safe," Aries said shortly. "I'm not here to stay. I will never move him to the place where I have done so much dirt. Once the job is finished I'm going back into the shadows."

"Understood," Miamor replied. "How did you get a job at the prosecuting attorney's office?"

Aries reached into her skintight jean pockets. They hugged her thighs so snugly that her hand barely fit into the pockets. She pulled an ID badge out and handed it to Miamor. "Shit I don't work for the prosecuting attorney. I snagged an ID badge, clipped it to my shirt, and walked in the building like it was home. There are so many interns running around there; fetching coffee and making copies that no one even batted an eye. They just think I'm another face to do their odd jobs and make lunch runs."

"You are a bold bitch Aries, I'll give you that. If one finger print is traced . . ."

"It won't be. I'm careful," she asserted.

Aries pulled out her phone and opened her email. "I've been around the office for a few weeks now and at first I couldn't find anything. The fact that Broome was so squeaky clean is what made me determined to keep digging. Nobody has no dirt. There is always something. A cheating spouse, a kid or parent on dope . . . your homeboy Broome was pulling up too clean."

"So how does this help me?" Miamor asked, impatient.

"I started clocking his movement, his emails, his calendar and on Thursdays at 4:00 p.m. there is a firm meeting he leaves the office to attend. I logged into the system with his ID but I couldn't get an idea of who he was meeting, so I followed him," she said. Aries went into the hall closet and retrieved a leather MCM back pack. She removed a DSLR camera, unscrewed the expensive lens, and then passed the body to Miamor. "Flip through the pictures," she instructed. "You know who that is?"

Miamor went through the still images. "I can't tell. You don't have any of his face. Is he gay? He's meeting with his lover? I don't understand . . ." She kept moving the images until finally, Timmy "Two Time" Bono appeared on the screen.

"He's meeting with the mob," Miamor whispered as her brow furrowed and her fingers clicked the buttons anxiously, while she gripped the camera tightly. She was speeding through the pictures so fast that they began to play in front of her like a movie. Broome was passing Timmy Bono a stuffed, yellow, envelope but before she could inquire about the contents the next flick showed Timmy Bono pulling money out and thumbing through it.

"Are they paying him off for a case?" Miamor asked.

"He's placing bets," Aries said. "He's into horse racing bad."

"How can you be sure?" Miamor asked with a gasp and a glint of mischief in her eyes.

"Gamblers have a language of their own. My husband used to gamble. If you sit back and listen they don't talk about favorite sports teams, they focus on the numbers. The over, unders, the spreads. They talk about the breed of a horse, its bloodline. I know an addict when I see one. Timmy Bono is the biggest Italian gangster in Florida. He retired here from Chicago. He's not into the drug scene, but he's head of the largest underground gambling ring on the East coast.

Everybody places bets with him. Athletes, actresses, rappers, and apparently prosecuting attorneys."

"The question is what is he betting on?" Miamor asked.

"The races," Aries replied, matter-of-factly. "The Kentucky Derby is coming up and he's preparing to put it all on the line. I told you. He's got a bad itch for horses."

"Than let's put him in a position where he has everything to lose," Miamor whispered as she painted a beautiful picture of deception in her head.

The smell of money laced with cigar smoke and manure filled the air. Elaborate hats with feathers and jewels sat atop the heads of the women in attendance and everyone had brought out their finest wears. Aries and Miamor blended with the eclectic crowd. They didn't want to gain attention so they kept their presence demure.

"The entire front row around the entire track is big fish," Aries schooled. "Mostly Asian. They always have the most money in the pot."

"This shit is unreal," Miamor said as she looked around the massive track. She had thought the Miami championship crowds were thick. The entire city came out whenever the popular team played, but the entire world seemed to show up for the derby. She bumped into so many people that her shoulder was beginning to feel sore. Miamor had to check her temper and keep a level head. *Everything is riding on today,* she thought.

Inside of her Birkin she had an envelope filled with 75k. More money than any stable hand would ever see at one time. Miamor was sure that this would get her next to Mona Lisa, the prize winning, legendary horse that Broome had placed $100,000 on. When Miamor found out that Broome was a gambling man, she knew she had him. The question was, how had he come up with such a hefty sum of cash to place the bet in the first place. After much digging, Aries discovered that Broome had borrowed the cash from the evidence locker in a federal case. His horse was what the gambling world would call a favorite. All of the odds fell in its favor. Once Broome collected his winnings he would be able to replace the cash while keeping fifty thousand that he had flipped in the race. The plan would have been foolproof had it not been detected. Now Miamor was about to ruin his life.

They were oblivious to the festivities. Miamor and Aries kept their eyes on the horses. They watched the jockeys. They watched the people behind the gates as a horse retired after its race. Their eyes caught everything, until finally Miamor chose her mark.

"Her," she said with certainty.

"How do you know?" Aries asked.

"I just know," Miamor said.

Aries had seen the determined look on Miamor's face many times before and she trusted her friend's intuition. She shrugged with indifference. "All right. Let's do it."

The duo waited for hours until they finally noticed the woman they had seen earlier at the track, emerging and headed toward the parking lot. Her long hair fell in one length past her middle back and was pulled into a sloppy ponytail. Her dirty clothes revealed the fact that she had worked closely with the horses all day. The woman slightly hunched over, her posture poor as she walked tiredly to her car.

"Follow her," Miamor instructed Aries and like clockwork they pulled out of the parking lot right behind their mark. Miamor and Aries worked like two hands, one washed the other. It was as if they had fallen right back into their old ways. They were parts of a well-oiled machine. Their work was efficient and flawless. "Hurry, don't lose her," Miamor urged, anxiously.

They tailed her for half an hour before pulling across the street from a small blue house with worn shutters and peeling paint. The front screen door was hanging half way off the hinges, but the woman beamed gratefully as she got out of her car, as if she was going home to a palace.

Miamor waited until the woman placed her key in the lock before she exited her car. Aries looked left, Miamor right. The streets were bare. Cloaked in the night's shadows, their identities were concealed. It was the perfect stage for treachery, but Miamor hoped that things played out smoothly. Miamor hurriedly walked up the walkway and just as the woman was pushing her door open, Miamor was forcing her inside.

"Agh!" the woman yelled startled.

"Shhh," Miamor said as she cupped her mouth. "Is there anyone else inside this house?" she asked.

The woman's eyes were filled with terror when Aries brandished her .45 while she looked around cautiously. She shook her head.

The home was barely the size of a small apartment and Aries checked it quickly. "No one is here," she informed.

"Good, that'll give us privacy to talk," Miamor said. "I'm going to take my hand from over your mouth. You can't scream. If you scream then my friend here is going to have to silence you . . . permanently. Nod your head if you understand me."

The woman nodded frantically and Miamor let her go.

"What do you want? I'm a poor, old, woman, I don't have anything of value," she said.

"You have something that is of great value to me," Miamor said softly. "I'm not going to hurt you. I'm here to offer my help in return for yours."

The woman stood clutching herself as her eyes danced back and forth between Miamor and Aries.

"I . . . I don't understand," she stammered.

"Please sit," Miamor said. The woman did as she was told while fear corrupted her heart.

"You have access to the horses in tomorrow's 6:00 p.m. race," Miamor started.

The woman nodded nervously.

"I need the Mona Lisa sabotaged and I'm willing to pay $75,000 for your assistance," Miamor said bluntly.

Flabbergasted the woman immediately shook her head. "I . . . I can't . . . I could never . . . I love those horses."

Miamor looked down at the stack of bills on the entry table. "It looks like you could use the money. No offense but this is hardly living," she said, referring to the house. She was trying to get what she wanted by using sugar before the situation turned to shit.

The woman stood. "Please, you have to leave. I don't want your money. I'll get by. Please I'm not interested" the woman pleaded fearfully. She was obviously frightened as she tried to usher her unwanted guests to the door. Miamor hated to put this burden on the woman's heart. She seemed nice and Miamor knew that she had grown soft. In the past she wouldn't have cared about her mark, but today she felt compassion for the disheveled woman before her. Not many people would turn away from such a large sum of money. The woman had principles and Miamor respected it. It wouldn't help the woman out of the situation, but still Miamor gave the woman a few points for trying to stand her ground.

"Okay remember I tried it the nice way first," Miamor said, her voice suddenly cold. She walked around the living room as if she owned the place until her gaze fell upon a mantel of framed pictures. "What do we have here? Children? I'd bet you would hate to see anything bad happen to them."

"Please . . ." the woman's eyes were wide and filled with tears as her bottom lip trembled.

"Look bitch let me make this perfectly clear," Aries interrupted as she placed her gun to the woman's head. "You're going to inject Mona Lisa with a shot tomorrow directly before the race. Simple, quick, and easy. If you refuse by the time you leave the tracks little miss blondie up there . . ." Aries pointed to the picture of the woman's daughter. "and those two ugly little grandkids of yours will be dead before you get home. Don't think we can't find them. We've done this for quite some time. I assure you, we're quite good at it," Aries threatened.

Miamor stepped up. "All you have to do is inject one shot. It'll be the easiest $75,000 you ever make," Miamor finished. "Do we have a deal?"

The woman nodded in trepidation as her tears finally broke free and fell down her face.

"Relax. You do this and you'll never hear from us again. You don't and we'll be back, next time for blood. You tell anyone about this little visit and you'll be burying your entire family by the week's end," Aries threatened. Miamor handed the woman a shot of a drug called Lasix. Some breeders used the drug to stop their horses lungs from bleeding while racing. It was three times the normal amount that breeders usually give their horses before a race. It would dehydrate Mona Lisa so badly that the horse would most likely die before ever meeting the finish line. Once Broome was broke and desperate, Miamor would have him right where she wanted him. It was only a matter of time . . .

Odom pulled his Aston Martin out into traffic as he loosened his necktie. The day had been long and stressful. Gathering the money that the Cartel had stacked for a rainy day had required all of his focus. He had needed to ensure that he didn't leave a paper trail that would lead him to the big house. He had set up two trust accounts, one for Miamor and the other for Leena. Because they weren't directly related to the Cartel he could create whatever financial history he wanted them to have. Since Miamor had practically lived under the grid since her teenage years, her credit was non-existent. Leena had worked in cash so her credit was neither good or bad. It was easy for him to manufacture perfect credit scores for them both. Breeze on the other hand was another story. Her family was deeply rooted in the drug game and any trust that he set up for her would have been immediately seized. Her money was placed in Leena's account for safekeeping, but he wasn't ready to hand over the key to their new fortune just yet. Odom was smitten with Leena and wanted nothing more than a shot to court her. She had accepted the dinner invitation but he knew that once she had access to her own money she wouldn't need him anymore. He needed a little bit of time to show her that a legit life wasn't so bad. His attraction was strong and he was trying to get to know her. The late night text messages that he would send her were always politely returned. His early "Morning beautiful" lines answered immediately, but always safely. He understood her hesitance. She was a new widow. Her last relationship had left her lonely, overwhelmed, and hurt, but Odom was determined to crack her. He wanted to introduce her to something new. Her consistent no's only made him more persistent. A man of the upper class, he was used to getting his way. Most women let him have his way with them with just the flash of his black card. He was attractive, successful, important, but he lacked the raw edge that Leena was drawn too. In the end when she was around him she didn't feel that familiar pulse in her pussy. Mecca had made her feel it at first sight and Monroe had made her wish she didn't. Odom knew that he had his work cut out for him, he was up for the challenge. He was hoping that the unexpected bouquet of roses he had sent over to her home would at least be rewarded with a call. He had been anticipating her response all day. He picked up his phone and saw that he had no missed calls.

"Fuck it," he whispered to himself as he took matters into his own hands. *There's nothing wrong with going after what I want,* he coached himself.

The phone rang twice before the husky melody of her voice filled his ear.

"Hello?" she answered.

"Just the sound of that voice brings so much joy to what has otherwise been a shitty day," he said.

"Oh really?" Leena replied. He smiled because he could hear the laughter in her voice. "It couldn't have been that bad. You had the time in your schedule to send flowers to my door."

Odom chuckled and replied, "You're quite a distraction Ms. Devereaux. You don't quite seem like the roses type of girl, but they are beautiful all the same. I thought I'd play it safe."

"They aren't my favorite flower," she admitted. "But the arrangement was beautiful. Thank you. When can we expect to have our affairs in order?"

"We can arrange an affair anytime you are ready," he joked.

"Odom . . . you are a really nice man, but I'm . . ."

"Easy Leena. Don't stick me with the fork yet. I'm not done. It was only a joke. I understand your situation. I just want it to be known that I plan to wait. As long as it takes for you to get over your loss. I'm very interested in making you mine."

Her sigh was heavy on the other end of the line.

"Maybe I can take you to lunch. We can discuss the trust. All of the money is in two accounts. I can explain everything to you tomorrow. Maybe just maybe you will tell me your favorite flower. That way next time I know what to send. You pick the place this time and I promise I'll stick to your plans."

"I'll think about having lunch with you," she said after a long pause. "After we close out our business. I'll meet you at your office at noon."

"I'm looking forward to it," Odom said, flirtatiously.

"Good night Odom," Leena finished.

Odom could hear the sweetness in her tone and he ended the call with a half smile, feeling hopeful. Hope quickly faded into alarm when he saw the hooded figure rise out of his backseat.

"I don't know what the fuck you smiling for playboy. That little lunch date ain't happening," Fly Boogie retorted as he pressed cold steel against the back of Odom's neck. "You was putting all your game down too. My bosses feel that is a bit disrespectful. Slime-ball mu'fucka."

"Look you can have whatever you want. I have money . . ."

"I don't want your money. I have a message from Monroe Diamond," Fly Boogie said "His bitch ain't on the market."

Odom's eyes doubled in size as he realized this goon had been sent by a ghost himself. "I meant no disre . . ."

Fly Boogie hit Odom hard against his skull causing him to wince as his head jerked forward and the car momentarily went off course.

"Pull this mu'fucka over!" Fly barked.

"Please . . ."

"Dig this," Fly Boogie said calmly as the car rolled to a stop on the side of the road. "Tomorrow you're gonna hand over the money to Leena and cut off all communication with her going forward. If not I'm going to visit your mama out in Aventura off of Biscayne Blvd. Am I clear?"

"Crystal," Odom replied. He didn't have to ask how Fly knew his mother's address. He knew exactly who he was fucking with. The caliber of the Cartel's reign hadn't been seen since the days of the New York and Chicago Italian mobs. The Diamond family was heavy in Miami. He didn't know what he was thinking approaching a widow of The Cartel. He had let his little head get him into a beef when in actuality he wasn't built for that life.

"Good, now get out of the car," he ordered.

Odom stepped out of the car and out into the shower of rainfall that fell from the sky. Fly Boogie got out, gun trained on Odom.

"Please don't kill me," Odom said calmly, realizing that he was fucking with an entirely new type of drug dealer . . . one that neither the Feds nor death could catch.

"Get on the ground," Fly Boogie hollered as he kicked in the back of Odom's knee causing it to buckle. He fell to the wet ground, gritting his teeth and kicking himself for being so unaware of his surroundings.

"Better cut Leena loose tomorrow mu'fucka or its lights out for you," Fly Boogie said. "Sincerely, Monroe Diamond."

Fly Boogie climbed into the driver's seat and rolled down the window. "Ol' pussy ass nigga," he spat an insult before pulling off recklessly. Water back splashed onto his expensive suit as he watched Fly Boogie speed away from the scene.

"Fuck!" Odom shouted as he climbed to his feet throwing his fists at the air in frustration. He had clearly fucked with the wrong man's wife.

Chapter 8

*"I've got a thing for a woman
with aggression."*

—Carter

Carter erupted out of his sleep, immediately reaching for the handgun that lay at his bedside. It was instinct for him, especially during times of high stress. He would rather pop first and ask questions later than to be caught slipping. Only this time it was only Yasmine's face he saw. Her expression was fearless and held a bit of impatience as she raised an eyebrow at him. "You're going to shoot me?" she asked.

Carter lowered his weapon and swiped his tired eyes with his hands as he shook his head to wake himself up. *What the hell was she doing in his suite?*

"My fault ma. Its habit," he said as he climbed out of the comfort of the plush bedding, exposing his shirtless body. "You don't knock huh?"

"People knock when they are guests. I own this entire property. No need for me to tip toe around my own establishment," she replied with a smile. "I didn't mean to alarm you."

He could see the amusement in her eyes. "I'm funny?"

She shook her head. "Not at all Mr. Jones," she replied. "I find you quite intriguing. Men here, don't carry the same air of confidence that you do. You're . . . dangerous." She said.

"You shouldn't sneak up on dangerous men than," he replied.

"I happen to like danger," she answered flirtatiously. "How did you sleep?"

"Well."

"My father explained to me the circumstances that brought you here. I can only imagine the stress that you've built up. I've arranged something for you and the others. I think you'll find it very pleasing Mr. Jones," she said.

"Call me Carter," he corrected.

She nodded. "Carter," she said. She walked up on him, standing closely as she placed a finger on his chest. "Shower, get dressed, and then follow these instructions. It's my job to fulfill your needs."

He felt his manhood jump at the insinuation of her words. He would have to tread lightly around this siren. Images of her petite body bent over in front of him flashed through his mind, causing him to harden. It had been awhile since he had been inside of a woman. Miamor had been recovering from the delivery of their child. He had been on the run for his life. He hadn't realized how backed up he was until he felt his desire building in this moment. She stepped closer, pressing her body against his, feeling his wanting. "Hmm," she moaned softly. "You are definitely not like the men in Saudi Arabia."

Not one to let his little head do the thinking for him, Carter stepped back, putting room between them.

"I'll see you in half an hour. Monroe and Zyir have already received their invitations," she said. She turned and strutted out of the room and Carter couldn't help but wonder about what was underneath the clothes that she wore. He shook his head, hoping that he hadn't just run from one problem only to bump right into another. It was obvious that Yasmine was trouble just waiting to happen. He wasn't a young man. The potential for lust didn't distract him from the task at hand. He needed to lay low and he was interested in finding out more about Baraka's business practices. He wouldn't allow a woman to get in the way of a potentially fruitful partnership. He would keep her at arm's length because he had a feeling if she ever got her hands on him, he wouldn't want her to take them off. She was a temptress but he was a man of principle. He didn't shit where he slept which meant that the beautiful Arabian women around him were off limits, especially Yasmine Baraka.

The smell of vanilla filled the air as the smoke from the lit incense floated mystically into the air. The lights were dimmed as Zyir walked into the suite, surveying his surroundings. Women were everywhere. Hedonistic, sexy, uninhibited, as they partook in various sexual activities. A magnificent spread of food was presented on a long dining table. Fruits, wines, cheeses, meats . . . it was a king's feast.

"I hope this is to your liking."

He turned to see Yasmine enter the room with a friendly smile as Monroe followed her. "I arranged a bit of convenience for you gentleman. These harems are here to service you in any way. Your every desire, your every wish is their command," she said.

Zyir was led away by a naked woman just as Carter walked into the room. It was a full out orgy of woman on woman action. The scent of sex lingered in the air, hidden by the musk of the vanilla fragrance. Monroe looked back at him with a raised brow. "You see this shit?" he asked. "They treat us like kings over here."

"You are a king Money. Make sure you act like one. Take care of those who take care of you. Tip well for good service. These women work hard for their money fam," Carter said. Paying for pussy wasn't his thing and although this was being gifted to him, he still wasn't too interested. He liked to pursue a woman, wine and dine a woman, sweet talk the panties off a woman as she tried her hardest to resist. He enjoyed the art of the chase. This wasn't his vibe. "Enjoy brother, we all could use a release. Strap up," he warned.

He turned to leave.

"You don't like?" Yasmine asked.

"Its not my thing," he responded.

"What is your thing?" she asked curiously. The moans that filled the air caused him to look over his shoulder. Two of the most beautiful designed women he had ever seen were feasting on one another. One of them capturing the other's swollen clitoris in her mouth, sucking gently. Carter definitely needed a stress reliever but this wasn't his idea of a conquest. These women were following orders for the sake of a dollar. They weren't his type. Physically they were flawless but mentally they were weak.

"I've got a thing for a woman with aggression," he replied.

"Well I'll have to see if I can accommodate that?" she said. "Since this isn't your type of party, maybe you'll join me for the evening. I can show you around."

Carter reluctantly agreed. The last thing he wanted was to offend Baraka's daughter. They were his hosts and if it hadn't been for them he would be in police custody by now. He nodded and followed her out of the room. She led him to the front of the resort and out to the valet where an armed body guard waited for her.

"I don't think I'll be needing you tonight Aki," she said to the six foot nine inch, threatening presence. "I think Carter can protect me just fine. Although you will have to drive."

"Why is that?" he asked.

"Women aren't allowed to drive in Saudi Arabia. I have an SUV and a driver to escort me at all times, but I thought you would like to test out my Lamborghini?"

"Your father instructed me to escort you whenever you leave the property Ms. Baraka," her bodyguard spoke. He was a mammoth of a man and Carter didn't doubt that he provided excellent protection. His menacing looks alone would probably deter anyone from pushing up on Yasmine.

"I've got it homie," Carter said coolly as he placed his hand on the small of her back and guided her into the car. He walked around and jumped into the driver's seat before speeding away from the resort.

"Why do you have a lamb if you can't even drive it?" he asked.

"Because I can ride it," she responded seductively. "Big toys, fast toys, they're *my* thing. I get off on the finer things in life." She maneuvered in her seat as if her thighs were on fire and in actuality they were. She yearned to be touched by a man like Carter. The darkness of his skin, the confidence in his stride, the smoothness in his words . . . it all made her panties wet. She wondered what it was like to be the girl on his arm, to feel his hands on her ass as she rode him slowly. Saudi men were too damned docile. She wanted a man that would pull her hair as he slid into her from the back. One who would bust his gun if another lusted after her too openly. She desired a man with swag and Carter Jones was dripping with it.

"You're bad ma," he said with a chuckle.

"I'm so good at it too," she replied.

He shook his head and increased his speed, feeling the horsepower of the engine. "These ain't the kind of problems

you want ma, trust me," he said, his thoughts flashing to
Miamor. She was a live wire and he loved it. It was her touch,
her companionship, her wit that he was craving. Even if he
used Yasmine in the bedroom, she could never make up for
the other roles that Miamor served in his life. Without her he
felt a void . . . sexually and otherwise. He was missing his lady
and it showed.

Yasmine noticed the look of concern on his face and couldn't
help but to pry. "Did you leave a girlfriend behind? Perhaps a
few?"

"There's only one," he responded. "And she's not up for discussion," he replied vaguely. He didn't want to bring Miamor
into his thoughts too much. She was his weakness and he
didn't want to expose that fact.

The look of pure adulation in his eyes couldn't be hidden. A
man who truly loved his woman couldn't deny it if he tried.
Yasmine didn't know Miamor, but she couldn't help but envy
her slightly.

*She's not here. What a fool of a woman to let him venture
so far away from home. Especially when there is a woman
like me, waiting for her to slip up,* Yasmine thought.

Yasmine guided him to the local market where rows and
rows of the cities finest craftsmen set up shop each day to sell
their goods. Carter stood out amongst the sea of cloaked men
and women. The heat beat down unbearably on him, causing
him to remove the jacket to his Gucci suit and unbutton his
Oxford shirt slightly.

"I should have warned you about the temperatures," Yasmine
chuckled. "This isn't America. Its like a melting pot in this
desert climate." She removed a linen scarf from her purse
and reached up to wipe the sweat from his brow. Their eyes
connected and she gave him a coy smile before withdrawing
her hand and leading him through the rows of vendors.

The people of Saudi Arabia flocked to him as he walked
the streets. Barefoot kids ran behind him offering to sell him
goods that he didn't need, or even wanting to perform tricks
for tips. Carter's heart went out to all of them. He purchased
from every one who stopped him because he knew that the
small change he was spending meant nothing to him, but so
much to them.

"America! America!" they called to him, trying to lure him over to their shops and small stands. They spotted him from a mile away. His ritzy Rolex and shiny shoes gave away his wealth. He didn't mind spreading it however. He was having the time of his life. He held babies, and shook the hands of the local men as if he were the president himself.

"They like you," Yasmine said. She was highly impressed by the humility of this man. Not only was he a boss, but he had compassion and it only made her infatuation for him thicken.

He shot her a smile as a little boy behind him fell down suddenly. "Oww!!" his yelp was ear piercing as Carter turned his attention toward him. The kid couldn't have been older than six or seven. He had been trampled by the older ones trying to keep up. He was holding his bare, dirt covered, feet in agony. Carter bent down, resting his elbows on his knees so that he was eye level with the kid. The rest of the kids circled around the two of them as Carter helped him up. "You okay li'l man? Looks like you could use some shoes," he said. The boy looked at him in confusion and Yasmine quickly stepped up to interpret for Carter.

When the boy responded, Yasmine relayed the message. "He said his mother doesn't have money for shoes."

Carter picked up the young kid and placed him on his back, not caring that his thousand-dollar suit was now soiled in sweat and dirt. "Tell them all to follow me," he said.

Carter took over the streets of Riyadh Providence as he led a bunch of street kids from booth to booth picking them out whatever they wanted. He made sure that each child left with a pair of shoes.

He was so distracted by the crowd that had accumulated around him that he never saw the men that had been lurking in the distance. Saudi Arabia was known for its oil. Many households lived in extreme wealth because of the industry but in this part of the city they were surrounded by nothing but poverty. It was where the poor resided and with him coming around flaunting his money, he became a quick target. Kidnapping was the name of the game. Wives of rich men were often held for extreme ransoms and with Yasmine as his escort she was in jeopardy. As the crowd thickened he lost

sight of her. It wasn't until he heard her screams of distress
did he realize that something had gone drastically wrong.

"Carter!"

Her voice broke over the crowd as Carter instantly turned to
look for her. He spun left then right as he pushed through the
crowd. It wasn't until he broke the edge did he see her being
stuffed inside a raggedy van. She was fearless as she resisted
the entire time, kicking and screaming as the man tried to
force her into the car.

"Shit," he uttered as he ran, full speed back to the lambo. If
he lost sight of the van there would be no getting Yasmine back.
This wasn't his country, he didn't know the land or the language.
All it took was for them to get away from the scene of the crime
for her to be lost forever. He couldn't afford to have her abduc-
tion on his conscience. He would be solely to blame and the
hospitality Baraka provided would quickly turn to hate, putting
not only himself but his brothers at risk. He hopped into the car
and sped off recklessly, burning rubber as he pushed the gas
to the floor. Carter was sweating like a pig and he was slightly
irritated. It had been a long time since someone had come at
him on some rah rah shit but even though he was out of practice it was like riding a bike . . . he always remembered how to
pop off. His temper flared as he caught up with the van with
ease. There was no way the raggedy contraption could outrun
the half-a-million dollar car. He passed the van and cut it off,
stopping sideways in the middle of the deserted street. The van
came to a screeching halt and before the driver could reverse in
the opposite direction Carter hopped out of the car and let his
canon bark.

BANG! BANG! BANG!

He couldn't really see through the nasty windshield of the
van but he knew exactly where the driver was supposed to be
sitting and when he heard the horn blare out of nowhere he
knew he had hit his mark. Suddenly a second man hopped out
of the van, holding Yasmine at gunpoint.

She was already gagged and bound as the man held a pistol,
point blank range at her head.

His face was wrapped in Arabic garb, concealing everything but his menacing eyes. He screamed at Carter, making

demands that Carter couldn't understand. There wasn't time to think, no time to do anything but react and as Carter pulled his trigger his heart stopped momentarily.

The bullet lifted the man off his feet and laid him flat. He rushed to Yasmine's side, snatching off the blindfold to find her hysterical underneath. It wasn't until he looked down did he see that he had hit the man between the eyes. Yasmine clung to him as he picked her up and carried her back to the car. "Let's get out of here," he whispered as she hugged his neck tightly. She pulled back and looked him in the eyes before placing her lips on top of his. His adrenaline pumped as sparks flew between them. A few seconds passed before Carter turned away.

"I can't," he whispered as he placed her in the passenger seat. He cupped her cheek. "You okay?"

She nodded and turned her feet inside as he closed the door. Carter ran his hands over his neatly waved Caesar cut and blew out a sharp breath. *What the hell am I getting myself into?* He thought. He hopped inside and pulled away from the bodies that he had left leaking in the middle of the street. He was supposed to be lying low, not adding to his body count. As he glanced over at Yasmine he realized that he was putting himself at risk in more than one way. *Its time to press chill,* he thought. *Today could have ended badly. It could have easily been me circled in chalk.*

"Please don't tell my father," she whispered as they pulled back up to the resort. "I just want to forget that today even happened and if he finds out he'll increase my security. They suffocate me as it is."

"How old are you ma?" he asked, curiously.

"Twenty-five," she responded. "Too old to have a babysitter."

Carter looked at her seriously and replied, "Men protect priceless possessions. You're irreplaceable. It's important to keep you safe."

She blushed and replied, "Thank you for saving my life today. If you hadn't been there . . . "

"You wouldn't even have been there if it weren't for me. I appreciate you taking me down there and showing me your city, but don't jump out of character for me. I get the feeling that you've never shook the hands of a poor person in your life. You were put in danger because you were out of your element," he replied.

"Yeah well everything about you is out of the ordinary for me Carter," she said. "and I don't plan on staying away."

Carter sighed and began to respond but was interrupted when the valet opened his door. He exited as did she and he guided her back into the comforts of luxury. As soon as they entered the sound of slot machines rang out in the air.

"Have a good night," she said. She wanted to kiss him and he knew that she wanted to, but they both also knew that he would stop her.

"You too," he said before retreating to his suite.

Chapter 9

"I'm attracted to the bad boys."

—Leena

BANG!

The sound of the loud bell sent the beautiful horses bolting as the race began. The beautiful stallions were like well oiled machines as their strong bodies darted around the track. Dirt kicked up from beneath their hooves as each jockey swatted their individual beast, pushing them to their limit. The crowd was loud, rowdy, and watching in pure marvel Miamor and Aries sat back, watching anxiously as the jockeys rode the horses with expertise around the track. Timmy "Two Times" Bono stood to his feet as he and his cohorts cheered along the sidelines, in the first row of the stadium seating. Miamor had no doubt that they stood to make a pretty penny on the race, or at least they would have if she hadn't tampered with the odds. Despite the 85-degree weather, various members of the Italian mob were dressed to the nines in expensive suits. Miamor's heart raced in rhythm to the sound of the hooves hitting the dirt. She could hear the stampede in her ears and feel adrenaline pumping in her chest as she fisted the guard-rail in front of her. Mona Lisa was in the lead and Miamor had to admit it was an exquisite animal. It was strong and determined as its nostrils flared while its legs moved swiftly. Miamor was enthralled. She anxiously stood to her feet. "Why isn't it working?" she wondered as she watched as Mona Lisa neared the finish line. "Aries . . . its not . . ."

Before she could finish her sentence Mona Lisa suddenly bucked and raised on its hind legs. The entire crowd stood and gasped as the horse seemed to freeze in mid-air, kicking its front legs in distress. The jockey struggled to hold on but was thrown off as Mona Lisa fell with a loud thud to the ground. The stampede of other horses raced right by the champion bred animal. No one seemed to focus on the winner as an underdog stole the race and an emergency team rushed out onto the track.

Miamor glanced at the Italian mobsters and saw not a trace of jovial excitement in their expressions. They each had lost a fortune, as had most of the people in attendance. She had to force herself to keep the sly grin off her face. "Let's go Mia," Aries whispered.

Miamor tore herself from the scene as she thought of the next part of her plan. Now she had to set-up the proposition to get Broome to drop the case against The Cartel.

Leena sprayed her Dolce Blue perfume as she stared at herself in the mirror. The emptiness that occupied her eyes was undeniable. As much as she wanted to tell Odom he was wrong, she knew that he was right. He could see through the fancy clothes, chauffeured cars, and queen on the throne, persona. Leena craved normality. If she were a normal girl in a normal world, her man would still be with her. He wouldn't be faking his death or running from federal cases. Sadness was paralyzing and she had been forcing herself to live in a fog ever since Monroe had first disappeared from her life. Mecca and Monroe had consumed her with lust, with love, with money, and power . . . she had been sucked in by it all. Like a moth to a flame it all was so enticing. Now she had been burned and Odom was there, saying all the things that she wanted to come from Monroe's lips. No, she didn't want Odom, but she would love to experience life on the right side of the law. She stepped into her Donna Karan dress and maneuvered her arms awkwardly to zip it to the top. She placed a blazer over it and slid into six-inch heels. She exited her bedroom and descended the steps to find her son playing boisterously with Breeze.

"Thank you for keeping him," Leena said.

"He's my nephew Leena. This isn't considered a favor. We are family," she replied. She turned her focus to Monroe's son. He looked so much like him, but his demeanor was mischievous like Mecca's. Li'l Money might have been Monroe's seed, but he had a piece of Mecca inside of him as well. Breeze recognized it even at such a young age. "What did auntie teach you? Huh? Diamonds are . . ."

"Forever!" the three year old quipped loudly with nothing but youthful innocence. He had no idea how deeply rooted that statement was or how true it rang. He was born, Monroe Diamond II, he would grow into a powerful man. "We'll be fine. Just get the money, finish this business and tell Odom to quit stalling you."

Leena nodded and then kissed Breeze on the cheek before leaving. The attention that Odom showered Leena with was flattering, but instead of making her feel good, it made her feel uncomfortable. She wanted Monroe to do those things, she wanted him to say the things that Odom said so eloquently. She wanted a square life. She could not endure any more of the streets. Although they came with many perks, if Monroe wasn't there to enjoy them with her, it wasn't worth it. Leena smiled at her driver as he held open her door and she slid into the back seat.

Her thoughts were so plentiful that they distracted her and made the thirty-minute drive fly by. Before she knew it she was pulling up to Odom's office. Passersby stopped as they attempted to see who was pulling up as the driver hit his hazards and hopped out to open her door. All they saw was legs for days as she stuck her Manolo out first to steady her balance. Leena exited smoothly, ran her hands over the fabric of her dress to smooth the wrinkles and then double stepped it into the building. Oddly, butterflies filled her stomach. So much weighed on her shoulders. She had to be coy enough to not disrespect Monroe's legacy but open enough to Odom's flirtation to keep him from turning snake. *I'll be glad when he come up off this money,* she thought to herself. She was tired of the charade because honestly it left her confused at the end of the night. Odom seemed to spot the empty spaces of her life and put them under a magnifying glass. He made her question Monroe's love for her. *If he truly loved me would I even be in this position?* She thought. "Stop it, of course he loves you," she whispered, scolding herself. "This man is about to stop playing with my money. I'm not leaving here today until it's in my possession."

Leena's step was more confident as she marched into Odom's office with determination. "Good morning Ms. Devereaux," the receptionist greeted at first sight. The many calls she had been instructed to place and flowers she had ordered for Leena on Odom's behalf . . . the woman was very familiar with Leena. "Please go right in. He's expecting you."

Leena gave the woman a gracious smile and headed into Odom's office.

She went to close the door, but Odom interrupted her. "Leave it open," he said with a direct tone. Leena paused and looked at him. "Sit."

He passed her two manila folders, sliding them across the table. "This concludes our business. The account numbers and trust information is inside the folders. Thanks for coming by."

Leena was taken aback by his tone and change of attitude. *Just last night he was sending flowers . . .* she thought. She was confused. He was abrupt with her, almost rude. He didn't even look at her in the eyes as he spoke to her.

He looked up from his desk. "You're still here because . . ." he let the words linger and Leena jerked her head back, insulted. She flipped through the pages of the manila folder and saw that all of what she needed was inside. The jig would have been up anyway. Now that she had all of The Cartel's assets in her possession she no longer needed to play nice. Leena stood to her feet abruptly. There was a weirdness in the room as if there was an invisible elephant between them. *Fuck it, I've got what I came for,* she thought. She turned on her heels but the nagging feeling that something was awry wouldn't let her leave without finding out what the hell was going on. She stopped as she reached the threshold of the door. Turning to Odom she opened her mouth to speak, but Odom held up his hand to stop her.

"Just leave Leena. I don't want that kind of trouble. You're off limits," Odom said, visibly shaken as he lacked his usual confidence. He was abrupt, almost rude, and obviously intimidated. This wasn't the flirtatious Odom that she had come to expect. In fact, it was almost as if someone had set him straight and she only knew one man that would do such a thing on her behalf.

Leena smirked as her entire chest warmed. She knew that Monroe had sent a message to Odom. He had reached all the way across the world to put a man in his place for coming at his lady. It was then that she realized that no matter the burdens, she loved the swag of being with a dope boy . . . especially one that had risen into infinite power. Monroe had status and because of that so did she. Odom never stood a chance.

"You see Odom. That's why you would have never been able to get even a whiff of this. I'm attracted to the bad boys and the fact that you were so easily scared off shows exactly how much bitch you have in you," she said with a laugh. "And to think . . . I almost bought what you were selling." She shook her head back and forth before adding, "Good-bye Odom."

Leena strolled out of the office with complete confidence that her man was alive and well. She just hoped that Miamor and Aries did what they had to do so that he could finally come home.

Chapter 10

"Stop bluffing."

—Yasmine

Carter shook his head in disdain as the blackjack dealer swept up the losing hand. Saudi Arabia had given him a new ritual. He spent his mornings at the card tables trying to beat the odds but today he was nothing but bad luck. He felt a presence behind him as the scent of Yves Saint Laurent invaded his space and Yasmine came into his peripheral view.

"Looks like you need a break, the tables are murdering you," she said in her husky tone. Carter looked up at her and she flashed him an amused smile.

"You find my losses funny," he cracked with a half-smile.

She pinched two fingers together and scrunched her face. "Just a little bit. I've been in the camera room watching you lose all morning," she said. She chuckled and reached down to pull him from his seat. "Let's go. Join me for brunch," she said.

Carter stood to his feet and pulled a wad of money from the pockets of his Brooks Brother slacks and placed three hundred dollar bills on the table. The dealer broke change but when he went to hand Carter the chips, Carter waved his hand. "Keep it," Carter said. He always tipped the dealers well and they loved him for it. "See you tomorrow morning Mr. Jones," the dealer said, never losing count as he dealt a new hand to the remaining players.

Carter nodded and then placed his hands in his pocket as he followed Yasmine out of the casino. The blare of slot machines filled the massive space and the smell of tobacco smoke clung to his clothing.

"I need to get out of these clothes, take a quick shower. I don't want to ruin your meal by smelling like an ashtray. I can meet you in a half hour," he said.

"Nonsense, we can stop by your penthouse on the way," she said.

Carter nodded. He didn't know her well but from what he could tell, she wasn't accustomed to the word no. The pampered Arabian princess always got her way.

"Fine," Carter said. "You remind me of my sister, Breeze."

"Well Breeze must be fabulous," Yasmine responded. "Now let's get you changed before I starve to death."

They laughed as they conversed on their way to the top floor. When they arrived Carter's two hospitality servants stood ready to wait on him, hand and foot.

Each woman was equally beautiful, but Carter made sure not to take advantage. "Mr. Jones is fine for the time being ladies. You are dismissed for the day. I promise to take good care of him," Yasmine said.

Their disappointment was apparent but they didn't dare object as they left the room. "I think your staff is quite fond of you Carter," Yasmine said in amusement.

"They are just doing their job," Carter responded as he unbuttoned his shirt, revealing his chest and stomach.

"Oh don't tell me you don't notice the affect you have on women? You're quite intriguing," she said. Her eyes revealed her own interests and Carter shook his head with a smile.

"You're trouble," he said.

"Men like trouble," she said with a wink.

Carter disappeared into the bathroom. "I'll make this quick," he said. He showered, the warmth of the water easing the tension from losing as steam filled the bathroom. As he placed both hands against the shower walls he lowered his head beneath the stream. Making it quick he lathered his body and rinsed. He reached for his towel and exited, wrapping it securely around his waist. Carter dripped water across the floor as he made his way to the large walk-in closet that adjoined the master bath. Surprisingly Yasmine was already inside.

"I thought I'd choose something debonair for you to wear," she said. "You have great style."

Carter smirked and walked around her. "Thanks but I can piece my own shit together ma. Women like to incorporate too many colors, too many fabrics. I'm simple. Black Ferragamo pants, black button up, nice Mocha shoe, preferably, Prada," he said as he pulled each item down.

"Nice choice," she commented.

"Glad to have your approval ma," he said with a wink as he held his towel in place. "Now do you mind?" he nodded toward the door.

Yasmine gave him a flirtatious purse of the lips as she turned on her heels. "Don't make me wait too long. I lose interest easily," she said and somehow he knew that she wasn't talking about brunch.

Carter knew that he would have to tread lightly with Yasmine. She had been very hospitable during his time in Saudi Arabia. He spent more time with her than he did anyone else and he enjoyed her company. She flirted, he enjoyed it, but he would not cross that line. He was grateful to her father for his assistance in their hiding out and thought that in the future he could make a great ally. Pussy wasn't worth the destruction of a great business relationship. No matter how pretty the face it was attached to may be.

"Good morning daddy," Yasmine greeted as she looked up from her mimosa to see her father approaching over Carter's shoulder.

"Somehow I knew I would find you here," he said as he leaned down to kiss his daughter on the cheek. "I'm sorry to interrupt, but I thought I'd invite Carter here to a game of poker."

"I'm not much of a card playing man," Carter admitted.

"Then you must learn," Baraka insisted. "It's the kind of table that you want to have a seat at. Not everyone is accepted to play."

"Count me in," Carter agreed.

"Very good," Baraka said. "Seeing as how the two of you spend so much time together, Yasmine may as well teach you. She's quite the accomplished poker player. Maybe it will keep her out of the city and safe behind the walls of comfort I've built for her, eh?"

Yasmine's mouth dropped as she realized that her father knew about the attempted kidnapping. "Father, I . . ."

Baraka raised his hand to silence her and turned his attention to Carter. "I appreciate you taking care of her and bringing her back unharmed. For that, I owe you a debt. We can discuss more this evening. It seems you are a good man to

have around. Just like your father," he said. He shook Carter's
hand and gave him a pat on the back before walking away.

"How did he know?" Carter asked.

"He runs this town. He knows everything," she shot back.
"And everyone worth knowing. The card game is important.
Dignitaries, kingpins, investors . . . very powerful men come
to my father's monthly game."

Carter licked his lips and replied, "Then you better show me
what you got ma."

I'll show you all right, she thought. While Carter was trying
to learn the game, Yasmine was trying to learn him. She loved
being in his presence and the more time she monopolized of
his, the more she wanted him for herself. *Forget his girlfriend.
He is here and she is all the way there. Its not like she is his
wife,* Yasmine thought. *By the time I'm done with him, he
won't remember her name.*

Yasmine had a poker table set up in her suite and dismissed
the dealer so that she could teach Carter one on one. After
hours of drinking and lessons she finally said, "I don't think
there is anything more for you to learn. You're kind of horrible
at this." She laughed and he shook his head in amusement.

"You know you are the only person who I've let laugh at me in
years. You know that right?" he replied with an embarrassed
smile.

"Oh, well perhaps you have soft spot for me in there after all,"
she concluded.

"Perhaps," he whispered back as he lifted the glass of cognac
to his lips.

She came from behind the table and said, "Don't worry.
Poker is all about the bluff anyway and you are very good at
that."

"I don't bluff ma," he shot back.

"You most certainly do," she replied. "You've been telling
yourself that there is nothing between us since the day you
met me. That's the biggest bluff of all."

He eyed her as he stood, challenging her words as he moved
closer to her, invading her space. "You're very good at bluffing
but you can stop now." She leaned in and kissed his full lips
and it felt so good that her legs buckled slightly. She creamed
in her panties instantly as his strong hands lifted her off of the
floor. She wrapped her legs around his body and pressed her

pelvis into his manhood. It was big and bulging against the zipper to his designer slacks. The friction alone threatened to make her explode. He laid her across the poker table as he ripped open her blouse, popping every button until her voluptuous honey colored breasts were revealed.

"I can't," he said, tormented as he pulled away, but she wasn't letting him get away this time.

"You can," she whispered lustfully. "My pussy is so wet Carter. Stop bluffing." She pulled her panties to the side and rubbed her blooming clit. It was swollen and he could swear that he could see it pulsating in desire. It was begging him to conquer her. "Nobody has to know Carter. I can be your little secret."

Carter loved Miamor, but he was a man and the sight before him was too much to resist. He undid his belt and stepped out of his pants quickly. She wanted it. She had been begging him for the dick since he had arrived. She was a beautiful girl. He had to. Carter couldn't stop himself as he slid into her wetness.

"Oh shit. Damn ma," he groaned as her walls formed around him like saran wrap. She threw the pussy up at him as if she were an all star pitcher and he knocked it out of the park every time. She smelled so sweet and felt so good that the remorse he felt was overshadowed by the pleasure. He hated to say it but this was the best he had ever had and she was willing to take it any way. The veins popped out of his manhood and she felt his girth as she moved her hips, bucking against him as he grinded. This was the type of sex she had craved. He was hitting her spot and commanding her body. She had known that he would make her go crazy and now that he was finally inside of her she was in complete bliss. She was sure that now that he had gotten a taste of her, he wouldn't be able to stay away and eventually their lust would transform into a love that no average chick from Miami could compete with. What Yasmine didn't realize was that Miamor wasn't an average chick. While Yasmine was relying on sex to keep Carter's interest, Miamor was putting in work to prove that she was the only woman in the world who could ever truly hold him down.

Carter didn't fare well at poker. He lost $75,000 in the course of an evening but it was the price to pay to get into a room full of prestigious men. The table of ten ranged from a Saudi prince to an oil tycoon to a Wall Street banker from New York City. He was the only dope boy in the room and it worked to his advantage. By the time the games were over he had made connections with those whom he felt would be useful and had exchanged contact information with those whom felt he could be useful to them. Baraka was impressed and as they exited the private playing room he said, "Once your legal affairs are in order, we should do business. I don't make many trips to the states anymore. My wives aren't fond of the long trip, but I want to expand my casino into the Nevada market."

"Las Vegas," Carter said.

"Yes, I'll need a partner. In fact, I just want to invest and see a return. I've seen the way that you handle the dealers, your wait staff," he paused and looked Carter square in the eye before he added, "my daughter. She listens to no one but she minds you. If you two weren't worlds apart and your line of work wasn't so dangerous I would find you quite suitable for my Yasmine."

"She's a lovely girl Baraka, but it's not rocking like that between us," he replied. "I don't like to create potential conflict in business and your backing is something that I highly value. Nevada could be a great look for The Cartel."

"I can't get in that market alone. Las Vegas is old mafia money, built up. I don't have the muscle to fight my way in, but you do," Baraka said. "Let's table this discussion until you figure out your affairs with this government case. Just keep me in mind. When the time is right to make the transition, you have my support."

With the shake of a hand the deal was solidified. All he had to do now was figure out how to get his neck out of the federal noose so that he could get to the money. Drug money was like peanuts in the scale of things. Owning a casino would legitimize him in a way that the streets never could. *Not bad for a young nigga from Flint, MI.* he thought. He adjusted his cufflinks and headed toward the elevator bank with a smirk on his face. *Not bad at all.*

Chapter 11

*"Take the bass out of your fucking voice before I let you hear
a tiny whisper that'll leave you speechless."*
—Miamor

Daniel Broome rolled out of bed when the smell of fresh
bacon frying hit him in the early morning hour. His bare chest
was muscle-less and hairy, accompanied by a slim frame, and
small waist. He wasn't much of a man. But what he lacked
in stature, he made up for in reputation. His tenacity and
ambition had gained him an excellent conviction rate at work.
He was the most fast tracked prosecuting attorney the region
had seen in quite a while. He ran a hand through his messy
hair and made his way out to the kitchen where his wife and
young daughter were already seated around the table.

"Morning honey," he said as he gave her a soft swat on the
behind and a kiss on the cheek. She never turned from the stove
as she prepared breakfast.

"Mornin'," she responded. "Breakfast will be done in a sec.
There's coffee in the pot."

"I just need to grab the morning paper first," he replied. He
stepped out onto his porch and retrieved the Miami Herald.
Wandering back into the house, he grabbed the hot cup of
brew that his lovely wife now had waiting at his seat.

"Morning daddy," his daughter piped, finally looking up
from her coloring project.

"Morning sunshine," he answered. Making himself comfortable, he unrolled his paper and took a sip of the brew.

Before he could even dive into the reporting he frowned as
a photo fell from within the pages. He gasped when he saw an
image of himself handing money to Timmy "Two Time" Bono.

"Is everything okay?" his wife asked as she turned briefly
from her cooking.

"Uh . . . yeah," he stammered as he quickly stood and grabbed the picture. "Yeah, yeah. Everything is fine. Look I'm going to head in early for the office. I've got a heavy case load today," he lied, eager to get out of the house. He rushed back to the bedroom with the newspaper and photo in hand. "Fuck!" he cursed. He tossed the paper on his bed and noticed a bet slip from the horse race. He picked it up. On it in big bold letters he read the words . . .

GOTCHA!

Thoughts ran through his mind a mile a minute as he fumbled with his clothing. He didn't even bother washing off yesterday's stink before dressing and rushing out of the door. Before he could even reach his car a black sedan pulled up at his curb. He paused, his car key grasped between his thumb and pointer finger, as he diverted his attention to the vehicle.

Honk!

The beep of the horn made him eerily aware that the surprise visitor was for him. He looked around and then unsurely made his way down his driveway and toward the tinted car. The back window rolled down and Miamor sat wrapped in an expensive silk scarf. The large Chanel sunglasses she wore hid the intention that shone in her eyes.

"Get in," she said, the tone of her voice leaving no room for him to decline. She popped open the door and moved over to the other side of the car. Broome fisted his hair and sighed heavily before hunching down to enter.

"It seems you're in quite the predicament Mr. Prosecuting Attorney," Miamor began. "You lost money, evidence money, on a horse race. It was supposed to be a sure bet, but it wasn't. Now you have to come up with the money to replace the borrowed evidence before anyone realizes its gone missing."

Daniel Broome, the young cocky P.A., with his American boy wit was speechless. He turned beet red as he realized Miamor had his balls in a vice grip. "I don't know what the hell you're talking about!" he roared. His heart felt like it would implode as an ache of devastation vibrated through his chest. He could see his entire future being flushed down the drain. His college boy gambling fun had turned into a nasty habit, one that had led him straight into the arms of the devil.

"Simmer down Mr. Broome," Miamor said as she looked out of the window without a care in the world. "You feel that? Your tie feels like it's cutting off your oxygen and your hands suddenly became moist. Your stomach is a bottomless pit and your throat as dry as the Sahara," she described. "That's how I felt when you brought a case against the man I love. It felt like the walls were falling in around me. You had all the power, but now . . . I have the power and I'm a ruthless dictator . . . I don't rule fairly. The only thing that stopped me from running in your house and tying up your kids and slitting your wife's throat while you watched . . . was the fact that you had so many fucking Feds watching me. So consider this route the easy one. You can keep your career and no one has to know about the missing evidence if you play this by my rules from this point forward."

Broome's entire body was tense and he was pressed so closely to the door that Miamor thought he would fall out of the car. She recognized his fear. He was afraid of her. Many had been before, but she had never felt satisfaction like this until now. Before her murder game had been a job. This time it felt personal. Part of her wanted to say the code word so that Aries could fill Broome with bullets from the place where she rested in the trunk, but she held her composure. She needed him alive, at least for the moment. She needed him to drop the case.

"You are threatening an officer of the court! I will . . ."

"You will take the bass out of your fucking voice before I let you hear a tiny whisper that'll leave you speechless," Miamor said as she placed a chrome pistol with a chrome silencer in her lap.

Broome's eyes watered as he was instantly brought back to reality. "I'm here to make you an offer. I'll give you the money you need to replace the evidence."

"Your accounts are frozen," he whispered.

"You're a fool if you think we don't have access to greater assets," Miamor laughed. "If you drop the case against us, our men and the entire Cartel syndicate, I will give you the money in cash. You can replace the evidence and no one will ever have to know that you took it. If not, I'm going to ruin your career."

"I can't just drop the case, there are witness statements, evidence . . ."

Miamor interrupted him. "Give me the locations of the witnesses. I can make them disappear. The statements will be recanted or silenced. Carter, Zyir, and Monroe aren't dead. Once you drop the charges they will come home. You can reduce the charges if dropping them seems too fishy. Reduce them all the way down. I'm talking slaps on the wrist, a few months in jail at the max. No real jail time."

Broome was in a state of shock as his chin hit his chest. It was at that moment that he realized that he was in over his head. How three men had evaded federal arrest was beyond him. Not only that, they had been smart enough to make the government stop pursuing them. He wanted to stay on the right side of the law but there was no way he could get out of an evidence scandal without ruining every-thing he had worked for.

"Do we have a deal?" she asked. The car stopped moving and Broome peered out of the window to see that they had pulled right back to his house.

"How do I know you won't cross me after the case is dropped," Broome said.

Miamor reached into the front seat grabbed the bag off of the passenger seat. She passed it to Broome. "There's your evidence money. The rest, you'll just have to trust me on. The fact that I have something over your head will keep your cross hairs off of The Cartel. If we ever go down, you'll fall with us," she assured.

Daniel Broome nodded his head in understanding and then exited the car. As he watched the sedan pull away his wife came up behind him, taking him by surprise.

"Holy Hell! Donna!" he screamed on her, jumpy as ever.

"Who was that?" she asked.

"Nobody," he mumbled. "I've got to go to work."

He hurried into his own car and pulled off, leaving his wife standing in their front yard watching him leave in concern. He drove all the way to the end of the block before the stop sign halted him. Gripping the steering wheel with two hands he lowered his head and sobbed like a baby. He had just gotten in bed with Satan and he knew that no matter how the situation played out, he would eventually be burned.

Chapter 12

"That Murder Mama shit is sexy."

—Carter

"Hmm," Carter moaned as the feeling of warmth tightened around his strength. He could feel the veins popping out of his shaft as his manhood grew inside of her mouth. Being awakened out of his sleep to the best head of his life was like heaven. Yasmine was good for not knocking before she entered. He had meant to pull her to the side and discuss what had happened, to prevent it from going further. In a conscious state he would have been able to decline this favor, but she had caught him off guard. She had slipped into his bed while he was asleep and wrapped her pretty lips around his dick. As he brought his hands to her head he fisted her hair as he straightened his legs while curling his toes in ecstasy.

"Shiit," he whispered. He had so much tension built up in him that he could feel himself pulsating in her mouth. Her tongue circled his head causing every nerve ending in his body to awaken. Her hands reached up and rubbed over his chest while her head traveled south as her tongue massaged his loins. Carter sucked in a sharp breath when he felt her tongue dip too far and he tightened his grasp on her hair to pull her up. He finally opened his eyes and lifted his head to the most beautiful sight he had ever seen.

"Hey you," she said with a smile.

"Miamor?" he whispered. He wanted to think that he was dreaming . . . that she was a figment of his erotic imagination but the pleasurable feeling she was giving him felt too real . . . too familiar to be fake. "What are you . . ."

"Shhh," Miamor whispered as she placed a finger over his lips and pushed him back onto the luxurious sheets. Miamor pulled her dress over her head and spun her body so that she mounted Carter backwards. She snaked her hips and his eyes followed as her waist and behind winded to a silent beat. By the time her depth drowned him he could barely hold off the orgasm. A rush washed over them both as her mouth fell open in an O and she drew in a sharp breath as he stretched her walls. He was thick and strong. The feelings of his hands on her hips set the tone as she began to rock and roll, slowly. Carter had a front row seat and he had to bite into his bottom lip to keep himself from losing his cool and moaning too loudly. Miamor rode him like she was the star cowboy at a rodeo show. Each time she bucked back he saw the pink of her pussy bloom as her voluptuous ass cheeks spread. It was a beautiful sight to behold. He reached out and palmed her backside, massaging it as she made his length disappear and reappear, again and again in her slippery abyss. She was warm and the honey scent that invaded his senses was the sweetness that only a woman could possess.

"Let's play a game," Miamor whispered as she turned her neck and looked back at him. The coy look in her eyes was seductive yet flirtatious and as she subtly looked down at her own ass she twisted her hips simultaneously. Carter smirked because she knew that he loved every moment of her sex play.

"I ain't been inside this pussy in months baby, later for games," he whispered. Miamor tightened her walls until her muscles shook, begging for release, but she kept them locked around him. "Have you given my dick away?" she asked.

"You know this your shit ma," Carter replied as he sucked his teeth, toes curling. Miamor eased up the pressure, manipulating her grip on him while winding. She tightened again as she rose upwards. "Did a bitch have her mouth on this dick?" she asked.

"Never that, all I want is this right now. What's with all the talking?" Carter asked.

Miamor lowered her hips, rocking slowly, sensually. "That's too bad," she said as she tightened once more. She sped up her pace, turning their love making into passionate fucking as sweat glistened on her body. This was carnal. It had been too long for them both. "If you had said yes, I would have told you to let me watch," she whispered. The image of himself intertwined in the depths of one of the foreign beauties as Miamor sat and watched was too much for him to handle.

He roared and his entire body tensed as he released himself inside of the woman he loved. Miamor kept her pace despite the fact that she was spent. She was too close to her own orgasm to stop now. Carter sat up and reached around her body to thumb her clit. The friction of his hand was all it took. He stroked her swollen knob until it pulsated. Her back arched and her head flew back as he grabbed her neck, then her breast. "Give it to me ma," he whispered.

Miamor rained all over him and her body went limp as she leaned against him. His manhood went limp and easily retreated out of her as he pulled her backwards until she lay beside him against the sweaty silk sheets.

"How did you know where to find me?" he asked.

"I'm resourceful when I need to be," she said as she stared at the wall as they spooned, while he ran his fingers through her hair. "I used to hunt niggas for a living. Hunt and kill. Finding you wasn't hard, especially after you sent the post card clue."

"Were you followed?" Carter asked seriously. "Does Leena and Breeze know where you are?"

"Breeze is home with the kids. Leena is in Monroe's room I'm sure doing something very similar to what we just did," Miamor said with a laugh.

"This was stupid ma," Carter said sternly in her ear, but he couldn't help but to nuzzle in the crease of her neck. "Damn, I missed you."

Miamor savored the feeling of his touch and she closed her eyes, planting the moment in her memory. Now it was hers forever. She turned to him.

"I came to bring you home," she whispered.

He sat up on one elbow. "You know that can't happen."

"I took care of it," she whispered as she stared at him intently. "The charges have been reduced. You, Zyir, Money, you all can come back to Miami. You can come home Carter."

His eyes turned cold. "What did you do Mia?" he asked. "My son needs a mother."

"And your son's mother needs you. I need you Carter. I look at our son and I cry because he doesn't know you yet. He's a baby yes, but I want him to have you. There was no way I was sitting around while you ran for the rest of your life. Like it or not you're in love with a murder mama Carter. When shit pops off I react. Now I couldn't make it go completely away. I tried, but to avoid suspicion you guys will have to do some time. 5 years. That's lightweight though compared to the life sentences they were trying to throw your way. You come home, you knock out the fed time for tax evasion, and I'll be waiting for you when you get out. I just want you back," she professed. As she spoke tears fell down her cheeks and Carter could see that his absence had taken a major toll on her. They had spent years apart and had vowed never to separate again. Carter didn't want to see the inside of any prison but for his family, he would do those five years. If that's what it took to get back to Miamor and Carter junior, he would.

He wiped the tears from her eyes. "Don't ever put yourself at risk for me ma. I'm not worth your freedom. I'm not worth tearing a mother away from her son. You hear me? I can take care of myself. Our li'l man can't. That's your job while I'm away. He is me and I am him. He is my weakness Miamor. So make him strong. Make him your first priority from now on. I come after that, you understand?"

She nodded. "Yes and that selflessness is one of the many reasons why I'm in love with you," she whispered.

Carter smiled and gave her a small laugh.

"What?" she asked as she frowned in confusion.

"That Murder Mama shit is sexy," he whispered. "You rode out for yo' man."

"Always," she replied with a laugh. He watched her as she gave him a mischievous grin and disappeared under the sheets. They had been apart for too long. She had to remind him of all the things about her that he loved so much. It was time for round two.

Monroe stared out of the window of the penthouse suite as he leaned his head against his forearm. The sun was rising indicating a new day, yet Monroe still hadn't let go of the old one. His mind was restless. Sleep didn't come easy for him these days and the beautiful servant massaging his shoulders did little to calm his worries. A constant burden rested on him. It was the cause of all of his tensions. No amount of rubbing would make those go away.

"Can I do anything for you?" the Arabian goddess asked sweetly.

Out of nowhere a voice responded. "You can remove your hands before you find yourself without any."

The servant immediately let go of an astonished Monroe as he turned to see Leena's not so sweet face. Her scowl was harsh as she stood with her arms folded across her chest.

"Really?" she asked as she cocked her head to the side.

Monroe didn't justify her displeasure with a response. He rushed her, picking her up, his arms wrapped under her behind as he lifted her. His excitement couldn't be contained as he pushed her against the wall, knocking expensive French paintings to the floor. Their kiss sent them to another world as the servant stood awkwardly, watching them. She cleared her throat.

"Hmm, hmm."

Monroe waved his hand, dismissing her without ever losing focus of Leena and the servant fled the room. As his hands explored her body, he realized he hadn't been homesick. Monroe had missed his woman. He lifted her skirt and ripped her panties as she fumbled with his pajama slacks.

He filled her up to capacity as he pulled back, moving her hair out of her face gently. Her mouth was slightly open and he slid his tongue inside as he made love to her against the wall.

"I missed you," she whispered. "Oh God, I missed this."

Monroe had so much anger, so much emotion, so much love, so much everything . . . built inside of him that he was more passionate than he had ever been with her. Monroe had left Miami on bad terms with Leena. They had fought, they had been beefed out when he had been forced to go on the run. Leaving her while they were in distress ate him up inside. He didn't like to leave loose ends untied and it had been weighing on him. The last time they had seen each other, hateful words had been spoken. He needed her to feel his love for her and he was trying to give it all to her in that moment. Her legs were wrapped around his waist and he pinned both wrists above her head, with one hand. He placed the other hand around her to pull her love into him. Her wetness soaked him as his hips went in and out. Leena was a prisoner to his stroke. At his mercy, she could do nothing but close her eyes and let him take her on the orgasmic high. Monroe moved from her lips to her neck, to her breasts, as he kneeled before her. He kissed her belly button, her stomach. She gasped. She held his head and braced herself because she knew where he was headed. He found her throbbing clit and took it between his moist lips. "I'm sorry," he whispered. "I'm so sorry."

Before he even said the words, all had been forgiven, but she didn't tell him that. She let him pour all of his woes into her as he licked and sucked her gently. "Agh," she moaned. "Money, wait."

"No baby, just cum," he said.

Leena brought her knees up and pushed it into his chest, sending him onto his back. Straddling him in a Sixty-nine, she placed her flower back over his face as she eased his manhood into her mouth. She could taste her sweetness on his tongue as she pulled on him with her tongue. Deep, then shallow, then deep, and wet . . . oh so wet, until finally he reached his peak. He sucked her clit mercilessly as he pulled her hair, causing her to lift her head as his seed spilled. He knew she had gotten hers as well when he felt the tremble of her thighs.

She climbed off of him headed toward the bathroom. "Come shower with me?" she asked.

Monroe arose and followed her into the bathroom. The steam from the shower quickly filled the air as they stepped in together. "How are you here right now?" he asked.

"I could never stay away from you Money. I love you," she said. She took the soap and squeezed some on a towel and began to wipe his broad chest.

"I'm sorry ma, about everything. I don't want to fight with you. This shit has eaten away at me since we left Miami. I couldn't reach out to you, couldn't hear your voice. The last time I saw you, we were yelling and saying shit that

we should never say to each other. I love the shit out of
you Leena. I want you to know that, every minute of every
day. I just got ghost on you and I didn't know if you knew. I
needed you to know . . ."

Monroe gripped the back of her neck as he spoke. Their
faces, inches apart, their soapy bodies close. They just wanted
to be one.

"I knew," she replied in a husky whisper.

"No ma, you don't know," he said as he looked in her eyes. "I
can see it in your soul. You couldn't feel me. You didn't know
because I didn't show you good enough. Marry me."

"What?" she said as she pulled back.

"You heard me ma, I'm not speaking French," he laughed.

"When?" she asked.

"Now," Monroe replied. He eased her under the stream of
water as the remnants of their lovemaking circled the drain.
Cleansed and feeling pure Monroe didn't know if he was
caught up in the emotion of their reunion or if this had been
his plan all along. All he knew is that he wanted her to be his.
He wanted her to know that what they shared was nothing less
than authentic.

"Let's go," he pulled her out of the shower. "I want to be married tonight by the time to sun sets you will be a Diamond," he
said.

"What? Money!" she exclaimed. "This is crazy! We can't do
this. Not here."

Monroe paused. "Is this what you want?"

Leena was suddenly breathless but her smile was infectious.
"More than anything in the world."

"Then that's all that matters," he said.

Miamor looked over at Carter and smiled. He gave her
a wink causing her to blush as they sauntered through the
desert atop of the humps of brown camels, wearing all white.
Monroe rode in front of them and Zyir behind them. The day
was slowly slipping away as the sky transformed from blue
to beautiful mixtures of orange and red. The tan sand dunes
around them served as the only backdrop. Dusk was upon
them and happiness was in the air.

Leena rode last. She was carried on a canopy-covered plat-
form, escorted on the shoulders of four men. Her identity concealed as they made their way into the desert where her wedding ceremony awaited. She couldn't believe that this was
happening and so suddenly at that. She peered out of the can-
opy to see the imam, who stood patiently, waiting for them to
arrive. Although she wasn't a practitioner of Islam, the Muslim
religious leader, was the only option. There wasn't enough
time to fly her own priest out so she would be wed under the
blessings of the Muslim tradition. Her heart beat out of her
chest. She was nervous but nothing about her was unsure. The
connection that she shared with Monroe was incomparable to
anything that she had ever felt for another human being. Their
friendship was deep like a bottomless ocean. Not even they
had explored all of its depths and secret places. She looked
forward to embarking on the journey of intimacy together
in the years to come. *Damn, I'm about to become someone's
wife,* she thought. A few tears built up in her eyes. She had
never been a princess. She didn't know what it felt like to be
entitled, to be royalty. Her entire life she had always dreamt
of the day that her prince would come. The reality was so far
from the dream that it made her emotional. She always envisioned marrying into a traditional family. She imagined baking cookies with her mother-in-law or giving corny sweaters
to her father-in-law for holidays and birthdays. Monroe's family was incomplete however. His mother, his father, and Mecca
were pieces to the family puzzle that would forever be missing.
In a perfect world, they would have been front row at the wedding but today their absence was blatant. She could only imagine how hurtful that was to her man. She wiped her eyes. She
didn't want to ruin her flawless make-up or put a damper on
the day but she couldn't help but wish that they came from a
more traditional world. A world where street wars and chaos
didn't exist. She let the fabric close and took a deep breath as
she felt the four men who acted as her carriage, stop moving.
This is it, she whispered. "You're about to be Leena Diamond,"
she whispered. Leena knew how big of a responsibility came
with the name. Carter Diamond's children had been raised
to believe that diamonds were forever. The name rang bells

in the streets of Miami. She was about to take on the legacy of another man . . . of her husband, and while it was one of the most joyous things she had ever felt, she also felt overwhelmed. She realized that she was about to make this thing official and that there was no turning back. Once she was in, she was in and the only out was death. Leena wondered if she was making the right choice. Their love wasn't perfect, but life was not a fairytale. It was time for them to solidify as one. She couldn't ask for a better mate. The curtain opened and she stared into the eyes of Zyir.

"Hey Lee," Zyir greeted with a smile.

"Hey Zy," she replied with an equally dazzling grin. She was a woman in love and it showed. She was truly glowing on this day.

"You ready?" Zyir asked.

She nodded. "Doesn't feel quite right doing this here without Breeze and the babies. My parents," she admitted.

"Right now all that matters is that you and Money are here. Everyone else is just extra," Zyir schooled as he extended his hand.

Leena placed her hand in Zyir's. For years he had acted as brother to Leena and uncle to her son. He was truly loyal and Leena was glad that he was there to escort her to her awaiting groom.

"Here goes nothing," she said as she beamed while Zyir reached up and lifted her into the air before placing her on her feet. Her Carolina Herrera dress was long, made of soft silk. It was simple. No poof, no train; just a long flowing fabric that hugged her body just right. The thin straps held it up against her lean yet curvacious frame. She stood next to her Zyir as she hooked her arm within his. All eyes were on her. Carter and Miamor stood lovingly to the side while Monroe stood beside the imam. If she had any qualms before they were all erased the moment she saw his face. He calmed her soul with just one glance and she knew that it didn't matter who wasn't in attendance. All they needed was each other. That's what true love was all about. Zyir escorted Leena all the way to Monroe. A sense of peace washed over her. The closer she got to him the more her smile brightened. Zyir stopped and extended his hand to Monroe.

"Congratulations . . . family" he told Monroe with a nod.

"Thank you bro," Monroe replied. The gestures were a far cry from the bullets that had been flying at each other the last time Leena had attempted to wed Monroe.

Monroe turned toward Leena and grabbed her hand as they stepped in front of the imam. Her fingers merged with his as if they were two pieces of one puzzle coming together. They turned to one another as electric compatibility sparked through them. The imam cleared his throat and began speaking in Arabic. The English translator who stood behind him brought clarity to his words.

"We stand here under the laws of Saudi Arabia and the blessings of Allah to join this man with his first wife. The couple has requested to recite their own vows as they enter into this union," the translator expressed.

Monroe stepped toward Leena closing the small space between them as he gently caressed the side of her cheek. His eyes drank her in, admiring her. "You've never looked so beautiful," he said. He was overcome with emotion as he peered at his bride and she could see tears accumulating in his eyes. She wiped them away for him as he began his vows. He pressed his head against her forehead as he cupped her face and closed his eyes. He was visibly overwhelmed. "No woman has ever given me what you give me Lee. I promise to protect you and keep you well because when you are safe, I feel whole. When you hurt, I hurt, and I promise to never do anything to hurt myself. You give me a reason to breathe Leena. You're the air in my lungs. You fill my spirit. You steer me straight and bring morality to the world of wrong that I live in. You have intrigued me from the first day I met you. I promise to never let that intrigue die. To always reinvigorate our love and keep it fresh as the years go by. I promise to appreciate you, to nurture you, to support you, to honor the woman that you are. I will cherish you and walk with you faithfully. I vow to never burden your spirit with disloyalty. You have my fidelity until the day that my body fails me and I am no longer of this world. Even still my spirit will always walk with you. I will forever love you ma, from day one until the death of me."

Leena was filled to capacity with joy. His words were so heartfelt and unrehearsed. They weren't perfect, but they were Monroe. They symbolized everything that embodied the man he was and she loved them. No vow had ever sounded so sweet. His words sent the sentiment of love into the air.

Leena's mouth fell open. At a loss for words, her tears finally freed themselves. It was his turn to wipe hers away. "I don't know how to follow that," she said overcome with a small chuckle, causing Monroe and everyone witnessing the ceremony to laugh and erupt in applause.

"I'm simple Lee. You know what I need to hear," he whispered while gazing lovingly at her.

"I will love you," she whispered. "I vow to love only you until I die."

"That's my girl," Monroe said with a coy grin. "That's enough. That's all I'll ever need from you. I've got the rest." He turned to the imam and nodded his head.

Again in Arabic he spoke as the translator assisted. "By the powers given to me by Allah, you may kiss your lovely bride."

Monroe's lips graced hers so delicately that she melted into him. They were now husband and wife. A new family, a subsidiary of The Cartel, had just been forged . . . not by blood, not by money . . . but by love.

Chapter 13

"Kiss good-bye to our freedom for
awhile gentlemen."

—Carter

Monroe and Leena were surprised by the elaborate reception that had been paid for and gifted to them by Baraka. Although they didn't know most of the guests there, they partied all the same. There were belly dancers, and flame spitters, and more presents than they could possibly open. The day couldn't have been more perfect, but as it wound down, they all knew that sunrise would bring about a new era. Carter sat alone at the bar as he watched Miamor dance happily with Zyir. She looked so carefree and genuinely at peace, even if it was only temporary. Carter knew that she deserved this feeling of contentment to be permanent, and he vowed to give it to his lovely Miamor.

"So that is your girl friend?" Yasmine said as she slid into the barstool next to his.

Carter smiled. "That's her."

"Looks average to me," Yasmine commented as she sipped from her champagne glass. She was obviously irritated and slightly intoxicated, equaling a loose tongue.

Carter smirked as he removed her champagne flute from her hands. "I think you've had enough," he said. "You're talking reckless. Besides, green doesn't look good on you ma. You're bigger than that."

Yasmine cut her eyes at him playfully. "Everything looks good on me Carter, even nothing, but you know that already, don't you?" she asked seductively as she rolled her eyes and walked away, clearly pissed.

Zyir and Monroe approached him next as they all watched Yasmine make her exit. "You better be careful with that one bro," Monroe said.

"And you better reign her in before Miamor catches wind," Zyir added.

"There's nothing to catch wind of," Carter assured. He looked at the glass of champagne that he had taken from Yasmine and downed it.

"Just watch out for that one. She's been at your side since we got here and she don't seem too happy to find out about Miamor," Monroe said.

"I've got it under control. Luckily this is our last night in Saudi. Tomorrow morning we will be on a plane back to Miami. We've got to be prepared for the arrest. Get your heads together. We'll be going inside for a few years. Doesn't sound like much compared to the life sentences they were trying to throw at us, but I promise you it won't be a cake walk. We'll need protection. In prison its all about numbers and reputation. I'll make sure we have that," Carter said. "I need you two to be on the same team . . . we don't have time for division from within."

"That's water under the bridge. We're good," Zyir said as he extended his hand to Monroe. Monroe pulled Zyir in for a hug and Carter nodded his head.

"Good," he said. "Kiss good-bye to our freedom for awhile gentlemen. Tonight will be the last night you'll enjoy for a long time."

"Zyir," Breeze whispered as she saw the caravan of black, chauffeured, SUV's pull into the gates of Leena's home. "Thank you God." She held her nephew, little Carter in her arms. Monroe Jr. clung to the ends of her skirt. "Come on boys, your daddies are home," she said happily. She was so eager to see them all that she could barely contain herself. When the cars stopped before her in the circular driveway she descended the steps. Miamor and Carter emerged from the first car.

"Welcome home brother," Breeze greeted with a wide smile.

"Thank you B," Carter replied. He reached down and scooped his son from her arms. "He looks like me," he whispered. The infant had grown in the months that Carter had been away and now his features were clearly visible. Carter felt pure pride as he admired a mini-version of himself. It was every man's greatest desire to have a son and Miamor had given him that. He would be forever grateful to her for such an amazing gift. This little person he held in his arms was his heir . . . the carrier of his last name, of his legacy. Miamor stepped to Breeze's side and kissed her cheek. She then bent down to pick up Monroe Jr. knowing that Breeze was eager to get to Zyir. "Go get your man," Miamor said with a wink.

Zyir emerged from the second vehicle and Breeze ran to him full speed. He picked her up and kissed her lips sensually. "I should kill you," she whispered as tears flooded her eyes. "I really thought you were dead. Do you know what you did to me?"

"I know," Zyir replied as he held her tightly. Nothing but love pulsed through him as he realized how incomplete he had felt without her. "I'll never make you a widow Breeze," he promised. He moved her hair out of her face and placed her on her feet. "I love you."

As soon as the words left his mouth they were followed by the sounds of sirens. Breeze peered over his shoulder in alarm as she saw the many police cars pulling onto the property.

"Why are they here so soon?" Monroe asked as he emerged from the car. He rushed over to his son and pulled the toddler into a warm embrace.

"Daddy!" his son shouted in excitement.

"I love you Money," Monroe said. Tears built in his eyes because the short lived reunion was hardly enough. He had hoped to spend a few days with his son before turning himself in. "Take care of mama for me okay? You're the man of the house. Daddy has to go away for a little while longer, but I'm always thinking about you man. I'll always come back for you. You're my strong man?" he asked. His son nodded his head. Monroe knew that the young boy couldn't comprehend exactly what was happening, but he felt obligated to say all these things before he was taken away. Monroe was becoming emotional at the fact that he was about to miss the next five years of his son's life. It was a long time to miss of a young child's upbringing. This was a long good-bye and he only hoped that one day his son would understand. Leena knelt down next to them.

"Tell daddy you love him Money," she said. She grabbed Monroe's hand as they embraced their son.

"Love you daddy," the toddler spoke.

"We both love you Monroe and we'll wait . . . for however long it takes," she promised.

Monroe kissed both of their foreheads and then stood to his feet. Carter and Zyir came to his side as the wives and children stepped back.

Carter handed his son off to Miamor and etched her face into his memory. He kissed her lips. "Everything will be okay. I'll be there, visiting you, writing you, whatever you need," she assured. Carter nodded and in that moment held so much respect for her. A lot of women made the promise to ride it out but very few actually came through. He knew that this was one thing he didn't need to worry about. If Miamor said it, she meant it and suddenly he was plagued with guilt for betraying her with Yasmine. A part of him wanted to confess his sins to her but he knew her too well. She would hate him forever because while she had been back in Miami fighting for him, he had been fucking the next chick. That resentment would only grow while he was locked up and it would tear them apart. He needed her. He loved her, even when his actions spoke otherwise. Miamor would be his motivation to keep his nose clean inside. Prison was a whole new world. Once you went behind the wall there was never a guarantee that you would emerge. five years could easily turn into forever if they caught a new charge. Miamor nodded her head and blew Carter a kiss as he was taken into federal custody. It was now up to the three of them to keep The Cartel afloat and to move them into the next era.

Leena picked up her son and turned around. "I'm not staying to witness this. We're done with this street shit," Leena said firmly. "When they get out, I want them to come home to something legit. I never want my son to see his father off to prison again."

Leena stormed into the house as Breeze and Miamor shot each other a glance of sympathy. The two women huddled close to each other as Miamor cradled her son. It was a new day and as their men were carted away like common criminals Miamor knew that Leena was right. It was time to move forward in a different direction. It was time for maturation.

Chapter 14

"This feels like the end Mia."

—Carter

Miamor sat next to Carter as she clasped his shackled hand. Their attorney, Rosenberg spoke on his behalf. Money and Zyir had already signed their plea deals. Carter was last up and although in her heart Miamor knew that this was necessary, it still didn't feel right. *Maybe it would have been better to let him stay on the run,* she thought. *At least than he would be a free man.*

As Broome ran down the terms of the plea bargain Carter was stoic. His expressionless face was hard to read. He almost appeared numb to it all. Prison was a place that he had promised himself to never go. He would have much rather let his legend die in the streets, under a hail of bullets, than to let it become obsolete in a prison cell. He didn't want to be another hood legend forgotten. The steel bars and brick walls had a way of keeping you out of sight and out of mind. He feared that the most. Everything that he had built, everything that The Cartel had accomplished would become a memory. For an inmate, life froze in place. The only two days that mattered was the day you went in and the day you got out. On the outside, however, life moved on and he knew that eventually even his woman would disappear. He wanted to think of her as the exception, but time waited for no man. Miamor was beautiful and smart, not to mention cunning. Another boss with another organization, perhaps in a different city would eventually spot her and claim her as his own. She was a kingpin's perfect prize.

"Carter," Miamor whispered, sensing something was wrong with her man. He looked up at her. She frowned because in all the time that she had known him, she had never seen him look so unsure. Indecision, was not a quality that he often exuded.

"Please clear the room," she said. "I'd like a moment alone with Carter before he pleads out."

"That isn't protocol," Broome began.

Miamor shot him a look so deadly that it silenced him into submission.

"You have two minutes," Broome said as he stood and escorted Rosenberg out of the room.

"This feels like the end Mia," Carter admitted. "The end of The Cartel, the end of us, the end of it all. Shit is fucked up. There is no way I can keep control from the inside."

"This is the beginning Carter. Five years is not long enough to scare me away. You don't worry about anything. I will keep it all together. You just have to trust me," Miamor said.

Carter nodded and kissed her lips. "Whatever you do you keep it out of my ear. I don't expect you to wait, but I expect you to be respectful. Don't tarnish my name ma," he stated seriously. He was a realist. He had seen this same situation play out too many times before not to know how it ended.

"I only want you," she reassured. What he didn't realize was that he was it for her. She truly only had eyes for one man. "I don't want you to doubt me Carter. I'll do whatever you need me to do, in order for you to trust me. Let's get married. Right here, today. You know me. I'll never break that vow."

"And you know me, I'd never trap you with that vow," Carter replied. "When I marry you, you'll be in a white dress. You'll have the violins and white doves and hundreds of guests . . . because you deserve that. I'll never trap you. I don't want you stuck with me because you have to be . . ."

"I want to be stuck with you forever Carter. Whether you're next to me every night or not. I'll wait and I don't need no fancy shit to do that. I just need your promise to love me and to be faithful to me," she said sincerely.

"I'm about to be property of the federal government for five years ma. You realize that?" he asked.

"I will ride with you through whatever," she promised. "If this is what I have to do to prove that than let me. Or am I just not the type you think of when you think of a wife?"

Carter leaned into her, but the handcuffs that bound him to his chair stopped him from fully reaching her. She met him halfway. When they kissed Miamor could have sworn she heard angels singing. That's how pure their love felt. "You know better than that," Carter replied. "No other type could ever be my wife. It's always been you."

Broome opened the door and entered with Rosenberg on his tail, interrupting their brief moment. Miamor realized it would be a long time before they ever truly had privacy again.

"We want to fill out an application for marriage. We'd like to make it happen before he goes in," Miamor said.

Broome loosened his tie. She had him by the balls and all of her requests were making him appear weak to his colleagues. She was pushing the limits of their arrangement, but what could he do? Since Carter had not yet pled guilty, the approval of the marriage request was up to Broome's discretion, not some warden. Before he could respond Miamor said, "Make it happen, we'll wait. After we are married, Carter will sign your deal and enter his guilty plea."

Carter was amazed at how Miamor was running the show. She had the P.A. jumping through hoops at the drop of a dime. As a judge was summoned, the couple stood in front of one another. "Are you sure this is how you want to do this Miamor?" Carter asked.

She nodded. "I've never been more sure of anything. I love you. I don't need the pomp and circumstance," she assured.

Her answer held nothing but truth and as they stood two people reciting vows in a downtown federal building, they became one. It didn't matter if it wasn't as she had imagined. They were perfect for each other and it didn't matter that they were being thrust into imperfect circumstances.

"I now pronounce you, man and wife," the judge said dryly. It wasn't perfect or romantic, but it was official and that's all that either of them wanted. Miamor smiled. "You may kiss your bride."

They didn't even give Carter the ability to wrap his hands around his new wife. They kept him handcuffed, but it didn't matter. His mouth found hers anyway and this one kiss elevated their bond to the next level. She could feel his energy pulsing through her body as if suddenly she knew what true love felt like. Broome gave them no time to celebrate before he got back to the task at hand.

"Hmm, hmm," he cleared his throat and slid the paperwork across the desk.

Carter felt Miamor's hand rubbing his back softly in support as he leaned over, fumbling with the pen because both of his hands were locked by the cuffs. He put his John Hancock sloppily on the paper in front of him and was instantly whisked off.

"I believe this ends our business," Broome stated as he looked at Miamor smugly. "Hope you have some frequent flier miles," he said. "I'm shipping those sons of bitches to a federal institution in Colorado." It was his way of making things difficult.

Miamor turned and walked out of the office. She wasn't angry, she had anticipated some type of kink in the plan. As she slid into her chauffeured SUV she dialed Aries.

"Miamor, is everything good?" Aries asked.

"As good as to be expected right now," Miamor replied. "I need you to put me in touch with Timmy Bono."

"Sure, but what do you have up your sleeve bitch?" Aries asked with laughter in her voice. She knew Miamor too well and could only imagine why she needed to be put in contact with the notorious Italian mobster.

"Nothing beats the cross," Miamor started.

"Like the double cross," Aries finished. "Consider it done."

Chapter 15

*"Look around. You're the only one of
your kind for a reason."*

—Man at the bar

The dimmed yellow light illuminated the smoky bar as incoherent chatter filled the air. The exclusive spot may as well have had a no-blacks allowed sign on the door because as soon as Miamor stepped foot inside, she was out of place. All conversations ceased as she walked toward the bar. Her expensive heels crunched peanuts under her feet as she made her way through the down home establishment. She slid into a stool next to a young Italian man. He gave her a once over and then poured the remainder of his drink down his throat in one swig.

"You lost sweet heart?" he asked.

"No, this is exactly where I need to be," she replied.

"Look around. You're the only one of your kind for a reason," the man said. "Although I must say I don't mind the view, you know what I mean?" He raised his hand and motioned for the bartender. The older Italian man had skin as rough as leather. His greasy, black, hair was slicked back off of his face, his top lip completely covered in a bushy mustache. Miamor could see the depth in his eyes and she would put her life on it that the hunch of his back was caused by the many secrets he had weighing down his soul. *These four walls have probably witnessed some crazy shit,* she thought.

"What can I get you?" the bartender asked as he glanced at Miamor.

"When's the last time you saw someone like this in the bar? Eh, Fred?" the man beside her asked.

The bartender tapped his finger on the bar and said, "A black girl in a bar is the least of my worries Sonny. Don't be a jackass," the bartender said sternly. He turned to Miamor. "What can I do for you sweet heart?"

Miamor lowered her voice. "I need to see Timmy Bono," she said

The bartender grabbed the bar rag and began to clean the countertops as he shook his head back and forth. "I don't know what you're talking about toots. I don't know anyone by that name. Sure you got the right spot?" he asked.

Miamor had expected to hit this roadblock so she had come prepared. She slid an envelope out of her handbag and placed it on the bar. She tapped it with her blood red fingernail. "After he sees this, he'll want to see me too," she said calmly.

The bartender discreetly grabbed the envelope and then disappeared without saying a word. Miamor kept her hand in her purse as she palmed the .45 that rested at the bottom of it. When she saw the wooden door that was hidden in the back shadows of the bar open up she knew that Timmy Bono was there. The bartender returned.

"Go through that back door there," he said.

Miamor arose from her seat and walked into the back. As soon as she stepped foot inside the door closed behind her. She spun to see two goons posted on the sides of the door. She looked at the man sitting behind the wooden desk in front of her . . . Timmy Bono.

"Please have a seat," he offered.

"I'd rather stand," Miamor said as she shifted uncomfortably.

"My men are going to search you," Timmy Bono said.

She held her hands out at her sides while gripping her bag in one of them as one of the goons stepped up. His hands searched her body gropingly, but he was so distracted by her curves that he neglected to go through her bag. "I'm clean, I'm not a cop," she spat harshly when she felt him palm her behind.

"So, what brings a pretty little thing like you into my bar?" he asked.

"I'm here to extend my friendship," Miamor said. She removed another envelope from her bag and placed pictures before him. "Daniel Broome has been building a racketeering case against you. All of the illegal bets that you have placed for him were caught on wire taps."

"Who are you? How do you know all of this? And what do you have to gain by telling me all of this. If I've learned one thing in my line of business it is that people who come in the form of friends are often truly enemies," Timmy Bono responded with dark eyes.

"I'm neither," Miamor answered. "I'm a woman with information," she said. "I choose my alliances very wisely and carefully. I'm sure you are familiar with The Cartel."

"The Diamond family," Timmy Bono said. "We call them the black mafia." Bono laughed heartily and his voice boomed loudly in amusement. "I am familiar with The Cartel."

"I am the head of The Cartel now and like I said, I would like to be friends," Miamor said.

"The head of The Cartel?" Timmy Bono asked. "What type of show are yous running over there?"

"That is not your concern. All you should know is that you have a problem with P.A. Daniel Broome. Don't say that I didn't try to warn you when the Feds come kicking in your door," Miamor said.

She turned and headed for the door.

"What's your name? Ms. new head of the cartel?" Timmy Bono asked.

"Miamor," she replied with a smile. "Don't let the good looks fool you Mr. Bono." She nodded toward the pictures on his desk. "Don't take my warning lightly."

Timmy Bono nodded as he watched Miamor walk from the room. She sighed in relief, but didn't release the hold on her bag until she was tucked safely in the car. As she collapsed in the passenger seat she looked over at Aries.

"Everything smooth?" Aries asked.

Miamor shook her head. "I don't know," she replied. She wasn't sure if Timmy Bono would act on her advice, but if he was anything like her he would eradicate Broome just to be safe. Revenge would be hers and she wouldn't even have to lift a pretty finger . . . all Miamor had to do was sit back and enjoy the show.

Chapter 16

"You're my world, Zyir."

—Breeze

Carter heard the sliding partition of his cell open and as he sat up out of the twin sized bed, he watched as a manila envelope was dropped inside. He stood and met the eyes of the C.O. who had acted as delivery boy. He gave him a nod, but said nothing as he walked over to retrieve the package. He bent over and scooped it from the floor but when he stood the C.O. was gone. It didn't matter however, Carter had already committed his face to memory. He was someone that Carter could use to communicate with the outside. Should the need ever arise, he now had a dirty officer that could do his bidding . . . for the right price of course. He opened the envelope and frowned when he pulled out a folded up newspaper. There was a lipstick print right next to the title.

THE MIAMI HERALD

He read the headline.

Prosecuting Attorney, Daniel Broome found dead.

"That murder mama shit is sexy than a mu'fucka," he muttered with a chuckle as he shook his head in disbelief. A sexy grin crossed his face as he rubbed the stubble of a beard that had begun to grow. "She wild."

He knew that Miamor was somehow behind the hit. She was more reliable than any hired hand and more gangster than the goons that made up the Cartel. She was his lady and although he knew that she could hold him down, it bothered him that she was still taking risks on his behalf. They had a son. She wasn't supposed to still be pulling triggers. He had failed her, but he promised himself that once he got out he would never disappoint her again.

Being locked up made him feel like he was weak and it made his family touchable. It wasn't the shackles that bothered him . . . it was the fact that he was so far away from everyone he loved. He couldn't protect his family if he weren't around. *I can't even send a kite to my niggas to let them know how to move because I'm in the middle of fucking nowhere,* he thought. The Feds had hidden him away in the mountains of Colorado and to make matter worse they had separated them. Zyir was in upstate New York . . . Monroe was tucked away in California. They had divided them in an attempt to conquer them. Without one another to rely on, the five-year stretches would feel like forever. Each day would be a hard one lived. Carter Jones was considered the leader, head of the criminal syndicate, The Cartel. Therefore he was shipped to a maximum-security facility. He was locked down for Twenty-three hours of the day. He only showered twice a week and the measly hour that he was allowed to leave his cell was spent under extreme scrutiny. This type of time would drive a man mad. He knew the intention of the judge and he was determined not to fold under pressure. His mother had always told him that when life got too heavy for him to hand his problems over to the Lord. It was something she had said repeatedly when he was a young boy and he never truly under-stood what she meant until now. This jail shit was for the birds and if he didn't get his mind right he would never survive. He worked out his guilt by getting familiar with God. Praying for a resolution to the things that ailed him . . . the biggest thing being that he was missing out on baby Carter's life. He was a father to a black son and because of some bullshit case he was forced to be absent. He was missing everything and it pained him deeply to know that he had left the love of his life to raise his seed by herself. *What kind of man does that to his wife? To his son?* Behind steel and concrete Carter now realized that none of the millions he had touched had been worth his freedom. He had always thought he would die in the streets before he would ever let a pig take him to jail, but having a child had changed that for him. He couldn't blaze out with the

Feds because he had a son to look after, but what good was he to anyone now. Caged like a rabid animal, Carter's head was all over the place. He wasn't young anymore. He was pushing thirty. He had done all of the things that he had set out to do in the game. He had reigned over the streets of Miami. His name rang bells and put fear in the hearts of many. It was over for all of that. He no longer needed the street life because when it was all said and done the streets didn't love him back. He made a vow to himself that when he emerged from behind the wall, he would go legit. He would take Baraka up on his offer and relocate to Las Vegas. In fact, he would put the plays in motion beforehand. There was nothing left in Miami for his family but bad memories. It was time for Miamor to pack up their estate and make the trip west. Las Vegas was much closer to Colorado than Miami anyway. It would make the trek to visit him more convenient. It was time to reorganize his entire empire from the ground floor up.

Books. That's what got Zyir through his days. He buried his head in all of them. From the bible, to philosophy, to the street classics, it all fed his brain. He needed the words to take him on a mental vacation because his physical body was trapped behind the wall. If he stopped reading long enough his captivity haunted him. The only time he ever put the books down was when he was sleeping and even that he did with one eye open. Being shipped off solo to upstate New York, he was up for a challenge. He was locked up with a bunch of Tony Montana types. Every inmate in the joint walked around like they had something to prove. He wasn't even six months in and he had already been tested. These five years would pass by slowly because he didn't have the privilege of flying under the radar. His reputation had beat him there. Everyone knew he was affiliated with the infamous Cartel and they either wanted to be down or to challenge him.

The stretch ahead of him was daunting but he was no fool. He would eat the five because he knew that he was supposed to be serving life. He was no saint. The crimes that he had committed during his reign on the streets should have gotten him buried under the jail. His hood resume was official and he secretly missed the action of the everyday grind. He was like a caged bird and he knew that until he was free he wouldn't be able to rest easy. He would have to get used to the anxiety that now weighed him down. He only hoped that he survived his time. Prison life was unpredictable. No one knew what the next day held. Five years could easily turn to ten, even twenty if he made the wrong move. He would have to be careful how he handled niggas inside. A man serving life had nothing to lose and hated to see a young nigga like Zyir eventually go free.

"Rich stand up."

The unexpected visit from the C.O. caused him to stand.

"You've got a visitor," he said.

Zyir frowned. He wasn't expecting anyone, but he didn't mind taking a walk. The air in the visiting room was easier to breathe than the musty, muggy, stinking atmosphere where the cellblocks were located. He turned around and placed his hands behind his back, then backpedaled so that he could stick his wrists through the slot on his door. Every time the metal cuffs bound his hands he cringed. This was slavery. He was in bondage and it hurt his pride as he grit his teeth.

"That's a little tight bro," Zyir stated with impatience as he shot a warning look over his shoulder. The C.O. didn't respond but he loosened the cuffs slightly. He opened the door and Zyir stepped out.

As they walked him through the cellblock the inmates peeked out of their holes, trying to get a glimpse of him. Some looked at him with hate in their eyes, others with respect, but either way they all looked. He made eye contact with no one.

When he saw her face his cold heart melted. Her smile always warmed him.

"I didn't think you would come," he said as he leaned into her, kissing her neck and inhaling deeply as the smell of her perfume intoxicated him. She was his Breeze. Only she had the power to blow the negative thoughts out of his mind and brighten his day without effort. All it took was her presence.

"Of course I came," she replied. "You're my world Zyir."

Breeze was effortlessly beautiful and the faded skinny jeans she wore and crop top fit her body like a second skin. The other inmates in the visiting room couldn't keep their eyes from straying from their own guests. They were too busy ogling over his wife. She was like a piece of meat and Zyir's temper flared as he asked the inmate next to him, "Fuck you looking at my nigga?"

Breeze noticed Zyir's aggression. He was wound tightly and wore his stress all over his face. She reached across the table, gripped his chin and turned his face back to her. "Hey, look at me Zy. Just focus on me. Forget what they're looking at. It's me and you. An hour is hardly long enough so lets make every single minute count. Okay?"

Zyir nodded as he rested his face in her palm, becoming emotional. Tears accumulated in his eyes but his pride would let none fall. "I hate being away from you B. I love you so fucking much. I'm sorry for leaving you."

"It's okay," she whispered. "It's okay. It's hard but I'm fine. We will be fine and I'll be here every visiting day. I'm thinking of getting a place in New York until you're free."

There was nothing he would have enjoyed more than to see her face twice a week, but he wouldn't burden her with that expectation. "Nah B, don't do that. You stay with the family. You, Leena, Miamor. It's important that y'all stay together. Wherever they go, you go. That's the only way I know you'll be safe. I don't want you to come here again B. These niggas eye fucking you and shit. I'll catch beef over you ma and you deserve better than to have these bitch ass C.O.'s feeling you up every time you visit."

"I'm coming Zyir," she protested adamantly.

"Promise me you won't Breeze. You're my wife. You have to trust me. I want you to live. Don't fuck with no nigga because I swear to God when I get out I will put him in the dirt, but don't become a jailbird running up here to see me all the time. That's not who you are. Write me letters. Send me pictures, but my queen won't grace these walls again. Stay on your throne. You're too good for this," he said.

A tear rolled down her cheek and he brushed it away. "I love you."

"I love you more Zy," she responded.

Zyir spent the next hour enjoying the melody of her voice and drawing a mental picture in his mind because it would be years before he saw her again. He touched her, stroking her hand, her face, inhaling her scent. He didn't want to forget one detail. In five years she would be different. It was a long time to be away from someone, there was no way that either of them would be the same and he secretly feared what that change would mean for their relationship. He loved her, like no one he had ever loved before and he hoped that this bid didn't destroy the bond that they shared.

Monroe was a part of the black La Cosa Nostra, it was a known fact. Even behind bars he was royal. There was no such thing as being low-key for Monroe. His face was known worldwide and because he was the surviving son of Carter Diamond and the blood born heir to Emilio Estes, his story was not easily concealed. He wasn't like Carter. He couldn't hide behind an illegitimate name. No one knew about Carter Jones except for those that needed to know. Everyone knew about the infamous twin sons of Taryn and Carter. Mecca was no longer here. Monroe was the last official son standing. He was a Diamond. He was Monroe Diamond. As soon as he was taken into custody, the media went mad. *The New York Times, USA Today, Miami Herald,* and all the bloggers covered his story. He was a modern day mobster and when Time Magazine plastered him on the cover he became famous. His name suddenly became a synonym for 'gangster'. The hottest rappers dropped his name in lyrics, his mug shot was printed on a popular t-shirt line. He became ingrained in pop culture but he never confirmed anything. He kept his mouth closed and ignored the speculation. He wasn't a fool. The Feds were just waiting for him to get cocky and confirm some of the illegal activities that had made him so popular. They would slap a case on him faster than he could bat an eye. Monroe Diamond would never be able to outrun his past because it had now been noted in the history books. It was a gift and a curse. The streets would forever mention his name but when he finally got out of prison he would never be anything but a drug dealer to everyone he met going forward. His future was already ruined. He was and would forever be a kingpin. On top of that he was a king pin that stood tall. He hadn't snitched, he hadn't turned state's evidence to get himself off of the hook. He lived by principle and he never did anything that he couldn't stand behind. He had sold dope on the streets of M.I.A. He had murdered on the streets of M.I.A. If that was his legacy, so be it. He had done it so there was no point in being ashamed now. His father had always taught him to stand behind his decisions. It didn't mean that he didn't have regrets because his head was filled with many, but he was man enough to live with the destruction that he had caused. Diamonds didn't fold. So these five years he would eat like chocolate cake.

As a result of his newfound fame, the inmates around him showed nothing but respect whenever he graced them with his presence. Prison life for Monroe was far different than what Carter and Zyir were experiencing. He did what he wanted, when he wanted. The locks and chains were merely a façade. Even the prison guards wanted to keep him happy in hopes that when he got out, he would remember the favors they bestowed. He was like a king inside. Being locked down only intensified his network. The Feds were better off letting him be, because when you put him with other wolves he ended up leading the pack. The relationships he was building behind the wall would only strengthen his muscle when he was finally released. At first his reach was slightly limited to Miami but he was locked up with criminals who had run their own enterprises, shaken down their own cities, murdered under their own circumstances. Once Monroe recruited and took them under his wing the Cartel would emerge better than ever. The Feds had tried to stop him but they had only helped to decorate his crown because he was picking up some valuable jewels while being locked away. It was only a matter of time before he put them to use.

Let the five-year bid begin.

Chapter 17

"Our reactions depend on your actions."

—Breeze

Year One

"We're moving to Las Vegas," Miamor said to the ladies as they moved around the kitchen, preparing Sunday dinner. It was a tradition that they had started as soon as the men went inside. It had only been a few months but Miamor knew that it was of utmost importance that they remain strong . . . united. When Miamor got the go ahead from Carter to transition out of Miami she knew that it would be a hard move. She was reluctant to leave all that they had built but she trusted Carter. If he said it, than it was law. Las Vegas it was. It was up to her to get all the pieces put in place. Upon release, Carter and the men would be convicted felons which would automatically black ball them from the Nevada market. Anything they owned would be put in the names of their women.

"Las Vegas?" Leena asked. "No offense but I'm not moving across the country to jump into the pit of another fire. We know these streets. Why would we go somewhere else where The Cartel name has no clout?"

"In business you don't need clout, just money. When we move we'll be clean. Carter wants to open a casino," she informed.

"A casino?" Breeze questioned.

Miamor nodded. She was just as unsure as them, but it didn't show. She knew that if her skirt showed than they would worry. She had to appear as if she had it all under control. She didn't, but they didn't need to know that.

"What do we know about the casino business?" Breeze asked.

"Not much, but we have friends who know it well. Baraka from Saudi Arabia will invest. I have a meeting with him this evening. While I'm setting up shop, Breeze you need to liquidate our assets here in Miami. Sell it all. The realty company, this house, your houses."

"I'm not selling my house," Breeze said. "And I'm definitely not selling my parent's old home. This is where I grew up. This is where the next generation of our family should grow up."

"Where you grow up isn't usually where you grow old Breeze. There's too much history here. Miami won't give you a chance to grey. This city would rather see you dead. Keep the old Diamond estate if you like, but sell the others. This transition will be hard but I have a feeling that it will be worth it. Leena we'll need somewhere to stay when we get to Vegas. Think you can handle that?" she asked.

Leena nodded. "Yeah, I'll get on it right away."

Miamor approached her next subject tactfully. "There is someone else I need to bring in on this." She paused because she knew that conflict was to come. "I need Aries."

"No," Breeze replied without hesitation.

"Miamor!" Leena protested.

"Look without Aries, neither of you would have ever seen your husbands again. She helped bring them home. I can't run The Cartel without some bite behind my bark and I don't see the two of you putting in that kind of work. We need people like Aries to do our dirty work. She's loyal and I trust her," Miamor said, arguing passionately on her behalf. Breeze shook her head and rolled her eyes in disbelief.

"Breeze just give her a chance. Talk to her. One time. If you don't like it than I'll leave it alone, but remember that there are a lot of niggas in line for the thrones. With the three of us sitting on top this empire, we have to prove that we are not to be fucked with. If not, there is only a matter of time before niggas begin to test us. If everyone does their part we will be out of this city by the month's end and will have some loyal soldiers following us. Just let Aries do what she does best."

"Murder?" Breeze shot back sarcastically.

"She's protection Breeze and she's loyal. If she is on your side she is on your side. You don't have anything to worry about.

The days of Ma'tee and that beef are long over," Miamor tried to convince.

"I'll meet with her, but I'm not making any promises," Breeze shot back.

"That's all I can ask," Miamor said. "Now which auntie is watching baby Carter while I take this meeting?"

"That's nothing," Leena said with a flip of the hand. "You know I got you."

"Pack a few days worth of clothes," Miamor instructed.

Leena frowned in confusion.

"The meeting is in Saudi Arabia."

After a long and tiresome flight, Miamor emerged from the private luxury jet a bit fatigued. The thick heat that seemed to blanket the air was the first thing she noticed as she made her way down the stairs. A driver waited at the bottom and he greeted her with a smile.

"Mrs. Jones, welcome to Saudi Arabia," he said.

Miamor nodded and placed her Versace shades over her eyes as she stepped into the vehicle. Miamor took a deep breath as she rested her head on her closed fist while propping her elbow on the windowsill. She would never admit it, but she was exhausted and completely overwhelmed. Since giving birth it seemed that her life had been moving at a rapid rate. She hadn't had a moment to breathe. Her emotions were all over the place and some nights she barely slept. If she didn't know any better she would have thought she was battling with a bout of post partum, but she was a 'Murder Mama' . . . nothing had ever gotten the best of her. She wouldn't start to accept defeat now. She wished that she lived in a world where everything was black and white; where she could be a mother to her son without worry of her past coming back to haunt her. A woman with a body count like hers was never supposed to bear a child. The child always paid for the sins of the mother and she feared that eventually her murder record would catch up to her. She could only hope and pray that it never did.

Lost in her thoughts, the hour long ride passed her by in no time and when she arrived at the resort she was escorted to the gardens, where a private luncheon was set up strictly for the occasion.

Baraka had a guard waiting at the entrance and she spread her arms out wide as she was searched thoroughly. He walked up to her wearing a tan cloak and matching head wrap. A friendly smile decorated his face.

"I have heard many tales about the infamous Miamor Holly, but your legend does not do you justice. It fails to mention how lovely you are," Baraka said.

She smiled. It never failed. It seemed that no matter their ethnicity, men always fancied her. Men found her irresistible.

"Thank you but apparently my legend hasn't been updated yet. My last name is Jones now," she replied, letting it be known that his flirting was in vain.

"Carter's wife?" Baraka said, obviously shocked.

She nodded confirmation but the sound of clicking heels caused her to turn her attention to see who was approaching from behind.

"Father, you didn't tell me we had a guest."

Baraka extended his hand to his daughter. "Miamor this is my daughter Yasmine. Yasmine this is . . ."

"Carter's girlfriend," Yasmine finished for him without a smile. She clearly wasn't happy to see her. "I know who she is."

"Appraently you don't," Miamor replied, sensing ill vibes from Yasmine. "I'm his wife," Miamor corrected, giving no smile of her own. Her intuition was in overdrive as she eyed Yasmine intently.

"Funny, he never mentioned that," Yasmine shot back.

Miamor scoffed. She wasn't going to discuss her man with a woman that was irrelevant. There would be no playing badminton with snide remarks. This wasn't a competition and if it was Yasmine would lose . . . Miamor killed the competition, literally. *You don't want to see any part of me little girl. Keep it moving,* Miamor thought. She focused her attention to Baraka, blatantly dismissing Yasmine.

"Shall we discuss business?" Miamor asked.

"Absolutely. I look forward to meeting with your representative," Baraka said. Arab men held women in low regard when it came to business. The men wore the pants. Period. Point blank. In Baraka's eyes Miamor's place was to be seen but rarely heard. "I assume since Carter is not available you have a family member, perhaps a brother, or consigliere to do things on your behalf?"

Miamor smiled, realizing the difference in cultures made her presence awkward. "I'm fully capable of handling this independently. Until Carter is free, I am the only person who has the authority to negotiate on his behalf. It's a bit different for you, I understand, but I think I can hang with the boys," she said charmingly.

A woman with such a strong presence was uncustomary to Baraka and the way she used her femininity to enamor him left him with a stiff one. He was taken aback by her instantly. He had fallen under the murder mama spell. "I think that you can," he replied. "I like a woman who knows how to get what she wants," Baraka said. He held out his bent arm for her to latch onto. "Shall we?" She embraced him as he escorted her onto the grass until they reached their table.

Yasmine followed closely behind. There was no way she was sitting out of this meeting. If it concerned Carter, she wanted to be involved. She would do anything to be in his presence again.

The three of them sat and ate while having casual conversation. Yasmine did most of the questioning . . . too much for Miamor's taste. *This bitch wants to know more about Carter than anything else. The fuck?* Miamor thought. Her patience was wearing thin so she fast-forwarded to more serious matters.

"I know that you originally had planned to open a casino with Carter. As you know Nevada gaming will never approve a license to him now that he has a criminal record. I on the other hand am squeaky clean," she said.

"I find that hard to believe," Baraka replied quickly and with intrigue.

"Where it counts Mr. Baraka," she added with a laugh. "On paper I'm as legit as they come. My credit is impeccable and I have no record besides juvenile stuff that was sealed long ago. Carter trusts me to be the front woman for this new venture."

"As do I," Baraka admitted. "You are sharp and fearless if everything that I hear is true."

"I'm sure that some of it is embellished," she said coyly.

"Tell me," Baraka leaned up, intrigued. "Is it true that you once severed a man's . . ."

"Don't believe everything you hear," she interrupted, not wanting to cop to anything. She didn't want her reputation to scare off his business. How the story had traveled all the way across the world she had no clue. She had to chuckle slightly to herself. She had been a wild girl before Carter had calmed her slightly. He really did bring stability into her life. *The good old days,* she thought.

"Besides that is something only a disgusting woman would do. Its quite barbaric, don't you think? Certainly not the type of woman that Carter would take as a wife," Yasmine shot.

"Sometimes barbaric is necessary when people don't stay in their place," Miamor replied with an underlying tone. "My husband can be quite brutal himself when the situation suits it."

"I will put up fifty million to finance half of the new resort and casino in Nevada. I take it The Cartel can come up with the other half," Baraka suggested.

"We can," Miamor said.

"Nevada isn't an easy town to takeover. I'm sure you are quite skilled in the art of war, but you will need an entire army. I don't have that type of support. This is where The Cartel would be beneficial," Baraka insisted.

"It's where we excel," Miamor replied.

"I'll write you a check and have my lawyers draw up the paperwork. In the meanwhile . . ."

Miamor cut him short, "In the meanwhile you can get the money in cash." She pulled a folder from her Birkin bag and slid it across the table. "I had the liberty of having our attorney draw up the agreement. All you have to do is have your people look it over and sign."

Baraka laughed heartily at her wit and handed the paperwork off to Yasmine. He stood. "Please Mrs. Jones, enjoy a suite, rest up, do a bit of gambling if you prefer. We have excellent spa facilities. Whatever you would like. I will have the contract and the money returned to you by the time your wheels are up tomorrow. When you speak to Carter be sure to tell him that he is a very, very, lucky man," Baraka stated.

"He knows," she smiled graciously.

"Well than give him my best," Baraka replied.

When he walked away Miamor felt like jumping for joy, but instead she kept her cool. The financing was the hardest part. Now that she had gotten the ball rolling there wasn't much that would stand in her way to getting Carter's casino.

"Where d' fuck is dis' bitch?" Aries muttered as she sat inside of the restaurant waiting for Breeze to arrive. The waiter walked up and refilled Aries drink.

"Slow day?" Aries asked.

The waiter gave a slight smile and a shrug before walking away.

Being back in Miami had brought the accent right back out of her. She was in her element and right back in the mind frame of a stone cold killer. She had forgotten completely about the suburban housewife and mother that she had forced herself to transform into. "De bitch is lucky I'm agreeing to meet her at all." Aries was losing patience. Breeze was twenty minutes late. Aries had already let the spoiled princess choose the time and place. She was feeling a type of way about being made to wait. *If it twasn't for Miamor, I would slit de' bitch's pretty little throat. Arghh! Waiting tis' for the fucking birds,* she thought. Aries had always had a temper problem when it came to anyone with the last name Diamond. She had a bitter taste in her mouth over Anisa's death. Their entire crew had fallen apart the day they set their sights on The Cartel. Distracted by her thoughts, Aries didn't notice the two large men heading toward her. She had been too busy looking for a carefree, sun-kissed, impeccably dressed socialite that was Breeze Diamond. What she didn't realize was that Breeze had grown up and life had hardened her. She didn't move without thinking nowadays. In fact, the place where they were meeting, Breeze owned. It was empty for a reason. Breeze had ordered it to be. She never left anything to chance anymore and as the two goons parted Breeze became visible. Aries motioned to stand but Breeze stopped her. "Sit down. If you make one move too quickly my pits right here," she paused as she nodded toward the two men who stood faithfully at her side. "They'll put a bullet in your head. Do we understand each other?"

"You grew balls," Aries stated with a smirk.

Breeze flew across the table and slapped Aries across the face with all her might.

Aries temper flared as they faced off.

"Jump bitch," Breeze instigated.

Aries' trigger finger itched uncontrollably as she bit her inner cheek. "Guess you not de' weak one anymore. If you brought me here t' kill me I would be dead already. I'm not your enemy girl."

"You aren't my friend either," Breeze replied. She rolled her eyes and continued, "The only reason why I haven't had my men kill you is because of Miamor. Sit down."

The two women eyed each other harshly as they both took a seat. Aries used the white linen napkin to wipe the blood from her lip. "This is the thanks I get for saving your ass from the Feds."

"Oh come on! You kidnapped me and tried to kill my entire family. I think we're even," Breeze stated. She crossed her arms over her chest stubbornly. "I don't trust you. You're Miamor's people but you're not like her. You can't be saved."

Aries laughed incredulously. "I'm just like Miamor. That's what you don't get. Mia and me. We're built exactly the same. She just happens to be on your team now."

"I had nightmares every night for a year. Ma'tee . . . he . . ."

Breeze paused and closed her eyes as the horrible memories came flooding back. She hadn't thought of it in years, but in the blink of an eye terror gripped her as if it had happened just yesterday.

"Ma'tee was a psychopath," Aries whispered. "Not everything dat I've done I'm proud of." Aries noticed how Breeze had seemed to fall into a daze as she thought of her torment and she immediately felt sympathy for the role she had played in her kidnapping. She had contributed to her fear. "Look Breeze. You might never like me. I get it but it wasn't personal. You may not relate to me but your father, your brothers, Miamor . . . dey all can. We are killers, Breeze. We live the street life. We live by de gun, we die by de gun. We don't think about de target. We just do de job. It was about de money, not about you."

"Why did you help set up the prosecuting attorney?" Breeze asked, slightly rattled as her hands shook. These old memories haunted her. She had forgotten the impact that they had over her until now.

"Because Miamor loves your brother and I love her. She is my sister. She needed my help. I was out of de life. I have a son. I had moved on and prayed for forgiveness for all de lives I helped destroy. But loyalty ties me to Miamor. I'm a Murder Mama and you don't walk away from that. She is aligned with you now. I don't like it. Your family took from me . . . from Mia too. We lost someone we loved from a bullet dat your brother fired. A war has two sides Breeze. Your family is far from innocent. You just happened to be the only good one caught in de middle," Aries schooled.

"I don't trust you," Breeze said clearly, not mincing words.

"Trust is earned. De feeling is mutual," Aries replied, frankly.

Breeze stood up from the table and leaned over Aries. "How do I know you won't cross my family as soon as we let you on the inside?"

"Miamor may be your family now, but she was my family first. I would never hurt her. Some loyalty you just don't break," Aries said.

Breeze grabbed her Louis Vuitton and turned on her heels. "Bring your son by the house. If you're family of Miamor's he may as well meet his cousins. Monroe has a young son he can play with." She began to walk away but stopped again. "I still don't like your ass though and I don't trust you as far as I can throw you. If I even feel like you're plotting on anyone I love, I'll have you put down the rabid beast you are."

"Touche'," Aries responded. "We all have dat one family member dat we can't stand, guess I'm the black sheep."

A truce had just been called. Aries was just the experienced gun that Miamor would need to help her conquer a new city. Las Vegas wasn't ready for the type of tyranny that The Cartel was about to bring.

***

The abandoned warehouse was eerily silent as Miamor stood, staring out over the fifty men she had assembled. It had taken a bit of time to weed through the massive following that their organization had. From runners, to shooters, to the cook-up crew, Miamor had observed them closely and cut the fat from the bone. Only the most thorough, the most gangster, the most loyal had been chosen. Now they stood before her for one specific reason . . . to witness her gangster so that they would never test it. This was a 'town hall' meeting in a sense. With a change of leadership, new laws needed to be laid down and she wanted to make sure there was no confusion. She could see the skepticism in their eyes as they looked at the women who stood before them. Breeze and Leena were at her side. They were aesthetically gorgeous and the men were distracted. They were too busy ogling over them. Yes they were beautiful, but to cross them would be deadly. Miamor needed that point to be made here and now.

"The Cartel is transitioning out of Miami. Las Vegas is the next move gentleman and there is a place for each of you if you choose to accompany us as we expand out West. Carter, Zyir, and Monroe are still very much the heads of this organization. Consider us their mouthpieces. If you had loyalty to them, we have now inherited that. If that is a problem, leave now because treachery will not be tolerated. There is a punishment for going against the grain," Miamor said. The doors behind her audience clanged open as four, hooded-figures, were escorted in at Aries' gunpoint. The sniffling cries underneath revealed that there were women underneath. Miamor pointed up to the sky, where four men stood on rafters, a noose hanging around each of their necks.

The women were lined up in front of Miamor and as she walked past each of them she snatched the hoods off of their heads.

"These women have done nothing wrong. Their only crime is marrying snitch ass niggas who folded under pressure instead of standing tall. The case that was brought against us, was held up on the backs of those men," Miamor stated as she pointed up to the sky where Fly Boogie was waiting for her signal. "Their testimonies helped the D.E.A. to gather evidence against us. I don't show mercy. Anyone that professes loyalty to the Cartel and then betrays us in any way will pay. I don't give a fuck about your wife, your kids . . . they will either suffer or be rewarded depending on your allegiance."

She looked up at the sniffling men. "Jump," she ordered.

Breeze turned her head and Leena just stared off into space as the men plunged from the rafters. The sound of them struggling to breathe as their bodies fought against the inevitable was sickening and it took everything in them not to flinch. This was the part of the game that they had not been exposed to. This is how the money was made. Order had to be established or anarchy would occur. The gruesome details had always been hidden from them, but Miamor knew the real. She knew that the necessary had to occur, but since becoming a mother something in her had changed. She had no sympathy for the men who had chosen their fates, but the women in front of her had done no wrong. Their only offense had been falling in love with the wrong type of man. They were probably mothers, just like she was. Her heart silently ached for them, but her face showed no emotion as she turned to Aries too and gave her the nod.

Aries went down the line. One bullet each, to the back of the heads of the women. The men shifted uncomfortably in their seats as they watched the cold-hearted sight. "Your family can either eat with us or die at our hands. It's all up to you."

Out of nowhere Breeze stepped up and began to speak. "We do not enjoy murder," she said, her voice a bit shaky. She paused to stifle her fear before she continued. "But it is a part of the game that we all know exists. My father, Carter Diamond, ruled with love and because of that he found himself in an early grave. My brother Mecca ruled with fear and he too met the same fate. So we will rule with both. Our reactions depend on your actions. Act accordingly and you can all avoid putting on those black suits. There is no need for flower bringing. Loyalty is all we ask." Breeze looked over at Aries. "Choose a few men and clean this mess up. We will cover the funeral expenses."

Miamor smirked as Breeze walked out of the room. She was like a proud mama because although Breeze didn't like it, she had finally come into her own. *Maybe she can help me run this thing after all,* Miamor thought. "We depart for Vegas at the end of the month. We'll be in touch."

She walked out and Leena followed suit as their stilettos clicked on the concrete floor as they made their exit.

Miamor's conscience had never played tricks on her but she couldn't get the faces of the women she had ordered killed out of her mind. As she sat in her son's nursery, watching over him as he slept, she wondered how many kids were now motherless because of her. Miamor was evolving. Ever since she had given birth and Carter went away she had been experiencing a vulnerability that was so foreign to her. She heard the ringing of her phone and she quickly answered it, to stop the sound from waking up her son.

"Fly Boogie?" she said in surprise as she checked the time. It was nearly three a.m. "Did something go wrong?" she asked.

"Nah, nothing like that. I'm at your door. I didn't want to ring the bell. Last time I did that you stuck a gun in my face," he said. "I kind of like my face." She could hear his smile and she shook her head as one melted across her face too. He had a way with her . . . he reminded her of what it was like to be young . . . reckless . . . brave. "I'll be down."

She eased out of her son's room and hustled to the front door. She checked the peephole to make sure that Fly Boogie was alone. She paused because a part of her knew that she should send him away. Whatever he wanted could wait until morning, but she didn't want to.

"Remind me again why you're at my door this late again?" she asked, placing a hand on her hip as she leaned her head against the doorframe.

"The bodies were taken care of," Fly stated.

She wagged a finger as she raised an eyebrow. "You talk reckless," she replied. "Take off your jacket and lift your shirt."

"You think I'm police ma?" he asked. I just put eight people in the ground for you for turning state's evidence and you think I'd turn around and set you up."

She didn't respond. She just looked at him as he sucked his teeth and lifted his shirt, revealing his toned abdomen. She eyed the V-cuts in his pelvis and the .45 he had tucked in his waist as she pursed her lips. Fly Boogie was young and thugging it. She remembered the good old days and she found his carefree attitude appealing.

"Satisfied?" he asked.

She nodded. "You have blood on you," she said.

"That's cuz I put in work. Don't insult me ma, I'd never switch up on you," Fly Boogie stated seriously.

She pinched the bridge of her nose feeling conflicted. "Sorry. I'm tripping. I don't know what's wrong with me. I've never felt remorse after murking anybody, but tonight it made me sick to my stomach." She didn't know why she was telling him this. Perhaps she needed to vent. Carter was usually her listening ear, the one person that she could express her true feelings to. With him gone, she had so much pent up emotion that it felt like she would burst.

"You're human. It can't be easy being a woman and in your position," he said. "I know you're official and everything, but you don't got to be tough all the time."

"Come on," she said as she started down the hall. "Let's clean you up." They walked into the bathroom and she wet a towel with hot water and wiped it across his strong chest, cleaning the blood spatter and dirt off of him.

"You're beautiful," he whispered, causing her to tense up and stop. "Everything about you Miamor. You're dope as fuck."

"Fly you shouldn't . . ."

Before she could even finish her sentence he covered her lips with his. It had been so long since she had felt a man against her that she fell into the rhythm. She knew that she should have stopped him, but she didn't. She melted into this young tenderoni, allowing him to pick her up and place her on the sink as he cupped her face with both hands. It felt so good . . . too good. It was reminiscent of the way that Carter used to touch her. *Carter* . . . as soon as his name appeared in her thoughts she froze, pulling back. "We can't. I can't," she whispered. "This is a mistake. You can't look at me like that."

"Any man would look at you like that," he answered.

Miamor picked up the towel and wet it once more as she sighed. "Fly you're young. You need a young girl. I'm pushing thirty," she chuckled. "There's nothing fresh about me. You need to get you a good girl." She dismissed.

He went to speak and she placed a finger over his lips. "Don't Fly. You got one kiss. Let's just leave it at that. I like you. I don't want you to go down that road. It wouldn't end well for you. Carter is away, but he'll be back and when he gets here I don't want your loyalty to be tainted. Just forget it ever happened okay?"

He nodded, but still stared intently. "Yeah, okay," he replied.

"Here let me clean you up," she said, starting again. She stopped when she felt the temptation of his hard body. She passed him the towel. "I'll wait in the living room."

When he came back out she stood against the wall with her arms folded "There was so much blood. You were covered in dirt. What did you do with the bodies? Dig a grave?"

"I dug four," Fly Boogie replied. She looked up at him in shock as he continued to explain. "I threw the bitch niggas who ratted in with the sharks. I buried the women in an old field. Nobody's going to find them don't worry and if they do they won't be tied to us. Tossing them in the ocean didn't feel right to me." Miamor looked up at him completely understanding where he was coming from. His compassion made him even more attractive. In her younger days she would have made him hers, but what she didn't know was that she had ruined love for him. Fly Boogie would never give too much of himself to any other woman all because of Miamor. She had him mesmerized without even trying and if he couldn't be her man, he would be her illest soldier. No questions asked.

"Have you ever killed anyone Fly?" she asked.

"I've hit a nigga off before for coming at me. Nothing like tonight though," he responded truthfully. "If that's what I've got to do, I'm with it. Whatever it takes to keep you on the throne ma. Anybody who got a problem with it can get it. You need a finger wrapped around the trigger, I'll pull it every time." She realized why he had come to her home. He was feeling the hangover of homicide and he wanted her to coach him through it. She took his hand in hers and placed them under the running stream of water as she cleansed him. She hated that she had tasked him with the burden of death. Fly Boogie wasn't a murderer. He would do it if he had to, but he didn't prefer it. He was just a hustler . . . a damned good one at that. She made a vow to herself not to turn his soul black. What she didn't realize was that Fly Boogie was committed to protecting all that Carter, Zyir, and Monroe had left behind, including their women . . . especially her. Although she was the one holding everything together he saw through her visage. Miamor hid her weaknesses well, but she wasn't superwoman and until Carter was home to hold her down, he would have her back.

Chapter 18

"I know a few Italians in high places."

—Miamor

Year Two

"It's so damn hot here! I thought Miami summers were bad, but this is almost unbearable," Leena huffed as her driver helped her out of the SUV.

Lisa Matthews, owner of Vegas' most prominent real estate agency, chuckled as she led the way into the condominium. "Living in the middle of the desert takes some getting used to. I've been here ten years and it still gets to me sometimes." She waved her hands around at the buildings around them. This is city center. It is the most luxurious property in the entire city. I think you will love it," she said as she led the way.

The beautiful Aria hotel was inspired by Chinese architecture and took her breath away as soon as she stepped foot inside. Everything was high quality, from the marble floors to the floating candles hanging from the fifty-foot ceilings. It was amazing and immediately excitement about this new venture filled Leena's chest. "If the condos are anything like this casino, I'm already sold," she said.

"I think that was the designer's intention," Lisa laughed. "Let the casino sell the real estate. This way please," she directed, walking swiftly.

They took the residency elevator all the way to the top floor where the elevator opened up to a plush, 5,000 square foot, two-story, condominium. It came already furnished, with the best view of the strip, and a private plunge pool to match. Leena smiled. This was living. *Maybe Vegas won't be so bad,* she thought.

"I love this," she admitted.

"I have two other ones just like it. One sits atop of the Mandarin Oriental and the other atop of the Vdara. Both the same size, different layouts, but equally nice. Designed by the same person. All you and your sisters would have to do is move in," Lisa said.

"It's a done deal," Leena said. "Let's talk price."

Leena was all about the numbers and by the time she was done negotiating she had walked the price down by a quarter million dollars for each condo. Lisa left out of the deal with only a fifth of her normal commission after Leena was done with her.

"We're also interested in commercial real estate . . . casino's in particular," Leena said.

Lisa stopped walking. She had been defeated in negotiations with Leena over the condos but the word casino renewed her. She had never been involved in the purchase of one, but she knew that it was the cash cow. She silently wondered if this lovely black girl in front of her even had enough money to enter the ball game. Vegas was a 'pay to play' type of city.

"I'd be happy to help you. I know of a few properties that are on the market but we aren't talking about million dollar properties here. You would have to have capital in excess of at least a $100,000,000," Lisa informed. "There are many moving parts when it comes to the casino business. I can handle the real estate side, but you'll need legal representation and you'll have to set up a board of trustees, amongst many other things. I can get in touch with a few colleagues of mine that can help me execute this type of deal, but the money would have to be readily available."

"That's not a problem," Leena replied cockily.

Lisa stammered, unable to form words. She had clearly underestimated Leena. She had assumed that she was the girlfriend or wife of some famous athlete.

"P-perfect," Lisa said, getting excited about the potential commission to be made. "I just need to see your purchase permits, liquor and gambling licenses as well to get the process started. It takes ninety days to even hear back from the gambling commission. Acquisition of a casino requires a letter of loan approval as well from the financial institution that's financing you. I'll write down this information and when you are ready, you can contact me. I'll be happy to assist you with the purchase of the casino, but I must warn you honey. You don't have the right color skin or the right jewels between your legs. That alone will stop you in a city like Vegas. Old Italian money runs that industry." Lisa handed Leena her card.

Leena placed it in her Louis Vuitton clutch and replied, "Yeah well new black money is moving to town. I would suggest they make room."

"Magdalena, please prepare a bottle for CJ," Miamor said as she walked around her new home. It was immaculate. All white with floor to ceiling glass windows and her view was amazing. The entire strip could be seen below her and the mountains were in the far distance. "Auntie Leena really out-did herself," she cooed to her baby boy as she bounced him in her arms. She looked at him. She was completely in love with her son. The past year and a half of her life had been pure hell without Carter. She missed him on a daily and discovering her way as a mom on her own had not been easy, but she had finally found her groove. With the help of Magdalena, she was doing just fine. She wasn't the typical Susie homemaker but she loved him all the same. There was something to be said about motherly instinct. Even the most wretched soul could be saved when it came to loving a child and Miamor completely adored hers. CJ was a perfect mix of his parents and he reminded her of Carter so much that she couldn't help but be completely putty in his hands. He was now one and a half and the bond they shared amazed her. She had been hardened by life's circumstances but when it came to her son she was a soft cookie. She couldn't wait for Carter to finish his bid and rejoin their family. Life would be so perfect. Until then she had to fill his shoes and command an army of goons as they took over a new town. The doorbell rang and Miamor carried CJ with her as she went to answer the door. Breeze and Leena were the only ones who knew where she lived. The rest of The Cartel members had been put up in Summerlin, a safe distance away from where the bosses actually rested their heads. The only members that were allowed to be close were Aries and Fly Boogie. They took up residence in rental apartments in the hotel portion of the resort.

"Hey," she greeted as she allowed them entry.

Breeze immediately scooped her nephew from Miamor's arms. They shared a bond like no other. Breeze loved on her nephews constantly, spoiling both Monroe and Carter's sons as if they were her own. "He's getting so big! I can't believe he will be two in a few weeks," Breeze said as she held him above her head while making love faces at him. "I'm throwing him a party," she said.

"Glad you have so much time on your hands," Miamor shot back with a smile. "While you're doing that, I'll be dealing with the gaming control board and gambling commission. They denied my application."

"We have to have that. You're being boxed out by the Italians," Leena said as she lifted Monroe Jr. up and sat him on the kitchen island. She removed his shoes, kissed his cheek, and then placed him back on the floor. Miamor shook her head as she realized that the three of them were truly multitasking. Raising children, running an empire, and holding down their men was no easy task but through sisterhood, they were making it. In that moment she was truly grateful for Leena and Breeze. It had been an unlikely sisterhood, but somehow it worked.

"We will get it. I'm going to make sure of it. I know a few Italians in high places," Miamor replied.

Miamor had known that she would need Timmy Bono sooner or later. A business alliance between the two of them could only prove to be fruitful. He owed her a favor and she was smart enough to only use it when it was absolutely necessary. *This greasy, olive oil smelling, mu'fucka is just what I need to get by in this town,* she said. Timmy "Two Time" Bono was old mafia and he had much respect in the game. Just because he had never been to Las Vegas didn't mean that the Italians who ran the city had never heard of him. They knew exactly who he was so when he requested a sit down, they obliged. They just didn't know that he was bringing a guest along with him.

"Let me do the talking toots," he said as he smashed out his cigarette on the brick exterior of the butcher's shop that they were about to enter. "Just stand next to me and look pretty."

She smirked but didn't respond. She would let him think that he was running the show . . . for now. As soon as she entered the shop the smell of blood overwhelmed her. Italians were all about their produce and fresh meats and cheese lay behind the glass freezer cases. It smelled like a slaughterhouse and her stomach turned as they bypassed the front, walking directly into the back.

A bulky, overweight, man stood off to the side and allowed Timmy to pass, but he stopped Miamor dead in her tracks, pushing her chest slightly.

"This is Gucci you fat fuck," she said in irritation as she slapped his hand away.

"She's with me," Timmy Bono said. His words were like magic. He might as well have said 'abracadabra' because suddenly the big man magically had a change of heart, letting her walk by. A card game was taking place inside a walk-in deep freezer and to her surprise a man hung in the corner, hog tied and hanging by his hands as he shivered uncontrollably. Miamor didn't flinch. She had done worse in her day so the bloodied man before her was all in a day's work. This wasn't some rival drug crew in Opa-locka, or a hustler on the come-up in Carroll City. The Italians weren't running an amateur show. They were a crime syndicate that had reigned over Las Vegas for years. She was well aware of her adversary . . . but they were unaware of theirs.

"Who's the girl?" one of the men asked as he filled the air with putrid cigar smoke.

"A friend," Timmy Bono stated.

"Timmy "Two Time" you are always welcome in Las Vegas. Chicago is where the bosses reside. They've spoken highly of you. Your rank is recognized here. This mouliano we don't know. You shouldn't have brought her here."

"This mouliano's name is Miamor and I run The Cartel from Miami," she said, speaking up for herself.

The silence that fell over the room let her know that they had heard of The Cartel before.

"You're a long way from Miami," Mr. Cigar said as he held his cards close to his chest. He didn't give her the respect of looking at her as he spoke, but the other men at the table stared intently.

"I'm here to buy a casino. After being denied a license, I was told to come here. Apparently the gambling commission has a commission. I take it that this is it," she commented. "I come in peace and offering five percent of my earnings to you Mr. . . ."

"Salerno," the old man huffed.

"In addition to my five percent I come with a gift," she said. She placed a suitcase in front of him. "A million dollars. No pressure, just a gift. I hope that my application can be reconsidered. I've done square business with Mr. Bono. I know that it is necessary for me to have an Italian presence in my casino. I'm prepared to offer him a position on the board, to represent the interests of the Italian community."

"Smart girl," Salerno stated. He didn't even pop open the briefcase. He simply slid it to the man sitting at his left and said, "Put that up. We done here or you gonna interrupt my card game all day?"

Miamor contained her smile because she knew that by accepting the money he was accepting her terms. Had Carter walked into the joint they would have never done business with him. Italians hated black men, but they loved black women and Salerno could get used to the pretty young thing with attitude that had waltzed into his butcher shop. He had a hard on for Miamor. Her skin tone, the contours of her hips, her breasts, even her pretty face . . . he lusted after it all. There was no way he was turning her down, at least not until after he had sampled what was between her legs.

"Have a good day," she said as she turned around.

"Bono, pull up a chair. Deal him in," Salerno stated. "Oh yeah and toots . . ." he said to Miamor just as she reached the door. She rolled her eyes. Apparently it was the nickname that all Italian men had reserved just for her. "Make that ten percent and if you ever cross me I'll cut your pretty fucking tongue out of your mouth and lick my balls with it, eh?"

Miamor smirked before turning on her heels and walking out, completely satisfied. She was one step closer to fulfilling Carter's dream. By the time he came home, his casino would be up and running.

"This is all you get in Las Vegas for $100,000,000," Leena asked skeptically as she turned up her nose at the old, musty, hotel and casino. The machines were old and outdated; the furniture rickety and rusty. Breeze, Leena, and Miamor looked around slightly taken aback.

"It was scheduled for demolition," Lisa Matthews said as she held out her hands. "You didn't pay for the building. It was the location that cost you. You are right on the South end of the strip. Your location alone is worth at least three times more than what you paid. A little TLC will have this place up and running." The real estate agent tried to sound optimistic but even she wasn't buying the load of crap that was falling out of her mouth. "All the three of you have to do is sign right here on the dotted line and this property will be yours."

Miamor breathed deeply as a heavy feeling sank into her chest. This was the moment that they all had been waiting on, but she couldn't help but feel overwhelmed. She had never had to make moves on behalf of anyone but herself. She wished Carter was free. Letters and phone calls weren't enough to fill the void that he had left in her life. She had been making plans, executing plays, and moving on his behalf. There was no way to let him know about every thing that went down before she did it, so she was playing so much by ear in hopes that she was acting in accord to what he wanted. Was this the property that he would want? Would he be displeased that she had to cut a deal with the Italians in order to make it happen? Miamor was so unsure about so many things, but it was too late to back out now. She took the pen from Lisa's hand and reluctantly provided her signature. Leena signed next and then Breeze.

"Congratulations," Lisa said as she tucked the paperwork securely in her briefcase. "You are now the proud owner of . . ." The woman paused and said. "What are you going to name it?"

"The Davinci," Miamor replied.

"Has a nice ring to it," Breeze stated. "How did you come up with that?"

"Because I'm going to make this a work of art," Miamor answered surely. Leena pulled a bottle of Champagne out of her oversized bag and popped the top. The girls squealed in excitement as the bubbles overflowed.

"We don't have glasses," Breeze said.

"Than hit it like a thug B, stop being so prissy," Leena teased. Breeze laughed as she tilted her head back as Leena poured champagne in her mouth. The girls laughed as they each drank a bit in honor of their first official day as owners of The Davinci Resort and Casino.

Chapter 19

Three Years Later

Carter emerged from the prison and looked up at the sky. It was the first time that he had seen the sun without wires and barbs interrupting the picture. His appearance was different. He had grown a full beard and his body was chiseled to perfection from the time he had dedicated to his body. His face held a scar from a fight that had broken out on the yard, but still his swag was the same. His walk was still powerful, his stare still deadly, and his mind sharper than ever. The past five years had changed him and for the better. He looked back at the prison as he thought, *I'll never let a man put me back in a box. Ever.*

As he strolled over to the black Maybach that awaited curbside he frowned as he removed the prison issued shirt, revealing a white wife beater underneath. He was relieved to see Brock, his old driver. It wasn't the first face he wanted to see, but seeing as how he had been released 6 months early and wanted to surprise Miamor he would have to be patient.

"Good to see you Boss," Brock stated.

Carter slapped hands with the seven-foot killer and pulled him in for an embrace before stepping into the car. He smiled when he saw the Cubans waiting for him in the seat. He quickly clipped the ends and sparked a match as he puffed the cigar to life.

As the smoke danced in his mouth he savored the feeling of freedom as he melted into the leather seats. "I thought that would be your speed boss."

"My nigga you thought right," Carter said.

"Where to?"

Carter tossed the prison shirt out of the window as the car pulled away from the curb. "Take me to the nearest Neiman's my nigga. It's been four and a half years since I've seen my bitch. I want to walk back into her life and be the same as she remembered," Carter said.

Time seemed to stand still when he saw her. Five long years had passed and he sat back admiring her as she walked through the beautiful casino, smiling graciously at the players. The dealers seemed to fawn after her. He could see the admiration in their eyes as she blessed each of them with a bit of her presence, even if only for a second. The casino and resort was flawlessly designed. He saw Miamor's personality throughout the entire establishment. She had chosen every detail from top to bottom and its modern vibe was impressive. She had gutted the place completely and if the crowd was any indication than business was booming. He couldn't be more proud. Miamor moved around the casino like a fish swimming through water. This was where she belonged. She was in her element and he found her incredibly sexy. The way she commanded respect. The way her beauty stood out amongst the sea of people. She was radiant and in that moment he didn't think it was possible to love anyone more than he loved her. His eyes scanned the room and he immediately peeped Fly Boogie, sitting back hawking Miamor's every move. She was protected and he made a mental note to hit Fly Boogie off with some bread for being so on point. He didn't want to interrupt. Instead he turned around and walked back out of the door. Miamor was busy right now . . . busy holding him down . . . busy being the boss and he wouldn't interrupt that. He would re-enter her life when the time was right.

Miamor felt the hairs on the back of her neck stand and she turned around, scanning the room to see why she was suddenly paranoid. She felt eyes on her. It was the murder mama in her. She always knew when something in the universe was off. She felt like she was being preyed on. She tensed and as soon as her smile turned into a frown Fly Boogie was out of his chair and across the room at her side.

"You good?" he asked.

"Yeah, yeah," she said as she shook her head. "It just feels like someone is watching me."

"The entire room is watching you ma, you're the star of the show," he said.

"This feels different. I just need to go upstairs for awhile and regroup. I'd feel much more comfortable if I wasn't naked down here," Miamor said.

"You don't need your strap ma. You're protected within these walls. Anybody breathe on you too hard, I'm plugging em'," Fly Boogie stated. "Relax. Nobody's here to hurt you. The people come here to see you, because you make them feel like you know each one of them. You're like a drug ma. They can't get enough and as long as they see your face them wallets stay open. Do you. I got it."

Miamor nodded and continued to seduce the room, but she still couldn't shake the eerie feeling that had suddenly killed her vibe.

She saw Leena coming through the casino. Impeccably dressed and cuffing legal documents in her hands. "Hey, where are you headed?" Miamor greeted her. They kissed once on each cheek.

"I'm headed to financial to drop off these insurance papers and then I'm conducting interviews for a housekeeping manager," Leena said.

"Where is Breeze?" Miamor asked as Leena began to walk away, obviously in a hurry.

Leena shrugged. "If I see her, I'll tell her you're looking for her."

"And the kids?" Miamor asked, yelling after her.

"They're with Aries."

Miamor nodded and tried to go about her day but something was nagging her. She had no idea that Carter was free but she would soon find out.

As soon as Miamor stepped into her suite the overwhelming aroma of fresh flowers invaded her senses. Her mouth dropped in an O of surprise as she looked around. She was baffled. This was a romantic gesture and although she was aware that Fly Boogie was fond of her, he knew his place. *He would never cross that line. Would he?* she thought, confused. She picked up her phone to call him. If he was responsible for this she had to correct this problem. She didn't like how good the gesture felt. It was time to create some space. *I've got to put some distance between me and his charming little ass,* she thought with a smirk as she shook her head. Perhaps being her personal goon was becoming a bit too personal. She was flattered but she was also taken. She would give nothing but heartbreak for the young kid. She hit the dial button and placed the phone to her ear as she made her way further into the suite.

"Hello," he answered.

"Fly, we need to . . ." she halted her step and stopped mid-sentence when she looked out on the balcony. A shadowy figure stood, overlooking the strip. Alarm shot through her. If Fly Boogie was on her line . . . *who the hell is that?* She thought.

"Hello?" he asked again.

"There's someone in my suite," she whispered. She hung up the phone and tip toed to the couch where she kept a gun tucked under the cushions. She removed the small .22 and let the gun lead her to the balcony. It was dark. The only light that illuminated the space was the glitzy lights from the streets below.

"The only reason I'm talking first instead of plugging you with holes is because my suite is full of flowers. Who the fuck are you?" she asked.

"Ask questions last next time ma, never give a nigga a chance to catch you slipping."

The gun fell from Miamor's grasp as she cupped her mouth in complete shock. "Carter?" she whispered. He turned toward her, his hands tucked in his Gabbana slacks. "Oh my God," she whispered as tears filled her eyes. Suddenly Fly Boogie's boyish charm was the furthest thing from her mind. Carter Jones was a man . . . her man . . . and he was 100 percent all man. The way he hung the Italian cut suit made her heart swoon as she ran into his arms, their lips meeting while his hands roamed all over her body.

"I missed the shit out of you Miamor," he said, practically growling into her ear. She could hear his need and feel it too as he pulled her behind into him.

His kisses stopped her from speaking and his fingers ripped her panties to shreds as he lifted her leg, leaning her against the balcony door. When he filled her she gasped. It had been so long since she had felt him inside of her and she fit him like a glove. He grinded and she bucked hungrily, his face buried in her neck as lust took over them. His dick hadn't been wet in five years and it was too long for him to do any real damage. When he came, he didn't pull out. He spilled his seed inside of her. He would give her ten babies if it meant their souls could unite. Panting, he placed her on her feet and rested his forehead against Miamor's. Her hands touched his face, to make sure that this was real. She had dreamt of their reunion so many times that it felt like she was in a daze. "If you ever leave me again, I'll kill you," she cried, her tears burning her eyes as they slid down her cheeks. "Five years was too long. It felt like a lifetime." She wept. Finally, she was able to free the turmoil that she had concealed since the day he had been taken away. There was no better feeling than his embrace as he wrapped her in his arms.

"Shhh, I'm back Mia. I'm home and I'm never leaving again. The only thing that will ever take me away from you is death," he promised.

KNOCK! KNOCK! KNOCK!

"Who the fuck is that?" Carter asked as he adjusted his clothes. She pulled her skirt down and followed him inside as she wiped her eyes.

"It's probably Fly," she said. "I called him when I saw you standing on the balcony."

"My *murder mama* called Fly Boogie?" he asked. "He your body guard or something?" Carter asked.

"He's not the same kid he was five years ago," Miamor said. "He's put in a lot of work for me over the years. I trust him."

"Yo Miamor!" Fly Boogie's voice came through the door.

Carter pulled it open and Fly Boogie's eyes widened. He was caught off guard at Carter's presence. "Oh shit, my bad fam," he said. "I thought there was a problem up here. I didn't know you were home. When you touch down? Welcome back."

"Just now," Carter replied.

"You good?" Fly Boogie asked Miamor directly. She nodded, giving him a half smile. She could see that his feelings were slightly hurt by Carter's presence. They had spent a lot of time together over the years. Now that Carter was home that would surely cease. She was recognizing the signs of a crush from Fly Boogie, she hoped that Carter wasn't getting the same vibe.

"She's good," Carter confirmed, answering for her. "We can chop it up tomorrow li'l homie. I hear you've helped hold shit together in my absence. I'll get with you. Have a good night."

Carter closed the door dismissively and turned back to Miamor. "Where's my son?" he asked anxiously.

"He's at home with Magdalena and Aries," Miamor said.

"This ain't home?" Carter asked looking around.

"No, this is just a suite that I keep here at the casino. I'm usually here all day. I like to rest or switch clothes without having to leave the property," she revealed. She grabbed his hand and pulled him into her. "The home that we've built here is amazing Carter. It took so much work and so much time but we did it. I did it . . . for you. I'll show you everything tomorrow. We might as well spend the night here. C.J. is already asleep and you and I have a lot of catching up to do," she whispered seductively. She planted a kiss on his full lips and then dropped to her knees. Carter's head fell back in bliss as she went to work. She was determined to show her man just how much she had missed him. Tonight would be all about his pleasure.

Chapter 20

*"Sparkly diamonds and foreign cars
are some of the pros."*

—Leena

"I'm so proud of you Carter. Tonight belongs to you," Miamor said as she stood in the doorway, watching as the resort tailor hemmed Carter's pants to his Gucci suit. He looked exactly the same. The five years away had done nothing to age him. The only change she could see was the scar that ran along the side of his face. Even still he was the most handsome man she had ever seen. If anything, the scar added character. The years apart had almost made her forget how much his presence filled the room. Carter Jones didn't even have to speak. His aura was simply boss and Miamor felt a silky wetness building between her legs just from looking at him. Carter shook the Asian man off. "Thank you Xuan," Carter said, calling the man by name. He was making it a point to learn each one of his employees and considering that Xuan did excellent work, he used him every day. He adjusted his steel grey jacket and twisted his cufflinks as he stared at his reflection. Retrieving his money clip from his inside breast pocket, he removed a hundred dollar bill and handed it to the elderly man.

"Thank you, Mr. Jones."

Carter nodded and Xuan left the room. Miamor came up behind him, wrapping her arms around his shoulders as they stared at the perfect image of their reflection in the full-length mirror.

"I couldn't have come this far without you ma," he said.

"Neither could I," she replied. "Just because you missed the past few years doesn't mean that anyone has forgotten the work that you've put in. You are the king, Carter. It's time that Vegas witnessed your crowning."

"What's the status on Zyir and Monroe?" Carter asked.

"Everything's fine. They will be here. Tonight the Cartel will be whole again. There are no missing pieces. It will go perfectly . . . trust me," she said. She kissed the back of his neck and then walked out of the room, leaving him to his thoughts. She had an entire glam squad waiting for her at home.

Breeze could barely breathe as she waited for Zyir's plane to land on the private clear port. Loneliness didn't quite describe the despair that had fallen over her while he had been locked away. She had fallen into a state of depression . . . one that she had hidden well but depression all the same. She didn't have a child to look after or to substitute for the love that Zyir gave her daily. So without him, it was just her and it had been a struggle to get through every single day. Letters and phone calls did nothing for her soul. Over the past few years her heart had deflated but as she saw the lights from the incoming plane she knew that all of her pain was about to be erased.

She had driven herself. She didn't want anyone to witness their first moments together. It was intimate . . . private . . . and she wanted Zyir all to herself. She got out of the car . . . too anxious to wait inside the captivity of her BMW X5. *Why am I nervous?* She thought. Butterflies danced in her stomach. As the plane gently touched its wheels to the ground it brought a forceful wind with it. Her expensive dress and flawlessly silked hair blew all over the place, but she didn't care. She held her breath as the plane's door slowly opened and a staircase was attached to its side.

He emerged, suave like a model out of GQ magazine. He was already dressed to escort her to the grand opening. A man in a suit had never looked so good. He stood at the top of the steps, mesmerized at her beauty. It had been so long since he had laid eyes on her that the image had become fuzzy in his head. He had forgotten how truly radiant she was. His memories had done her no justice and when he saw her kick off her red bottom heels and start running to him full speed, he smiled. He walked down the steps and she jumped into his arms, practically tackling him to the ground. His usually prissy princess didn't seem to mind that her custom Alexander McQueen gown was covered in dirt from the unpaved landing strip. She cried a river as he fisted her hair, while kissing her passionately.

"Welcome home Zyir," she whispered. "Never ever do that to me again."

"I won't B. That is my word," he replied. He stood to his feet, attempting to dust off his clothing. "I take it we're not going to the grand opening?" He reached down to help her up and then scooped her into his arms as if she were a new bride.

"The last place I want to be is around a bunch of people. I want to go home and I want you to put a baby in me tonight," she whispered. "I want a piece of you that I get to keep forever. It's time to plant seeds Zyir. It's time to grow our own family. I'm not comfortable in Las Vegas. The Cartel doesn't feel the same. Aries is here and as long as she's around I don't want to be." Breeze had held her tongue about Aries because she knew that her presence was necessary. Zyir was the only one she could speak openly with and she had no problem admitting, "she is not and will never be on my team. She scares me."

"You telling me you want to leave?" Zyir asked. "Did she threaten you B?" It took quite a bit to get Zyir angry, but the thought of malicious intent against Breeze was all it took.

"It's not what she says," Breeze replied. "It's what she doesn't say. She has a vendetta against The Cartel. She tries to hide it, but I will never fully trust her and I don't feel safe. She's too close for comfort."

"Don't worry about that tonight. As a matter of fact I'm home. Don't worry about that ever again B," Zyir said as he placed a hand around her shoulder and pulled her in for a kiss. "Consider it handled."

"Daddy! Daddy!" Monroe II was a replica of his father and as the eight year old came rushing to him with the speed of a young athlete, Monroe felt emotion burning his eyes. It wasn't until this very moment did he realize how much time had gone by. *Damn, I've missed too much,* he thought sadly. When he had been locked up his son was a toddler . . . three years old to be exact. Now he was a big kid and Monroe was feeling conflicted about how he hadn't been around to raise him. He remembered the lessons that Big Carter had drilled into him. There had never been a day that his father had not been there. He couldn't remember one time that he had wondered, *Where is papa?*

As his son wrapped his hands around his waist Monroe held him tightly as he stared at Leena from across the room. She didn't see him but he admired her as he spoke to his son. "I missed you man," Monroe stated. "You been taking care of your mama, being the man of the house?"

"Uh huh," Monroe answered.

"You held it down like a G, I'm proud of you son," he said. "I know I've missed a lot, but I won't miss another day. That's my word and if a man don't have his word he . . ."

"Don't have nothing," Monroe II finished. Monroe nodded. His son had a roughness about him that reminded him of his brother Mecca and it took everything in him not to drop a tear. There were cameras all around him. The media had covered his release as if it were a red carpet event, but his goons kept them at bay. He didn't want anyone to get too close as he reunited with his family. This was a personal moment. "Ma will be glad that you're back. She was sad while you were away," Monroe II said.

Monroe frowned and looked his son in the eyes. "Why do you say that son?"

"She would cry every night when she thought I wasn't listening. After she put me to bed, she would go in her room. She said your name in her prayers all the time," his son informed.

Monroe pulled his son in for a hug and then straightened out the collar to his oxford shirt, making sure his son was put together well. "You will never hear your mother cry another tear over me."

"Your word?" Monroe II asked.

"My word son," Monroe responded.

He stood and watched as Leena talked to a group of people. The casino was impressive and he sat back admiring what their women had built as pride filled his chest. Leena had held up nicely under pressure. Ironically, the weakest link of them all had turned out to be a diamond after all. The grand opening was a success as the massive crowd slightly obstructed his view, but he maneuvered until he had come up on her from behind.

Leena smelled his signature perfume before she saw his face and she interrupted her conversation with the mayor to turn around to search for him. She was breathless when she spun and found him staring her directly in the eyes.

He caressed her face with both hands, cupping her cheeks as he gave her a single kiss on the forehead. "Hey you," he greeted as if no time had passed.

"Hey you," she responded.

He pulled her onto the dance floor.

She giggled slightly, feeling as if this were a dream. "Gangsters don't dance," she said.

"Yeah well this gangster has some making up to do, so dancing, holding hands, midnight strolls through the park, I'ma be doing all that sucker shit until I've made up for my absence," he said with a charming smile. Happiness melted all over her face. "You like that cornball shit huh?" he laughed.

She shook her head, "No, but I love that you know that you have some ass kissing to do. The new G-series Benz truck will do just fine," she replied.

"Oh really?" he asked, finding her incredibly sexy. She had changed . . . grown . . . come into her own during his time away. He loved this new version of her.

"Absolutely. A prison bid is one of the cons of being married to a kingpin. Sparkly diamonds and foreign cars are some of the pros," she replied. She planted a seductive kiss on his lips and whispered in his ear. The cameras from the paparazzi flashed all around them but the couple was in their own little world. "I missed you Monroe Diamond. Welcome home daddy." She pulled his hand and led him off of the dance floor. "Now let me show you around your new casino."

Chapter 21

"I get everything I want."

—Yasmine

Miamor smiled as she danced with her baby boy, holding his hand as she bent down to kiss him on the cheeks. He was clad in a Ralph Lauren suit and as she turned her head to see Carter watching them closely, she realized that life could not get any better. She held out her hand for him to join them and Carter shook his head to decline but gave her a wink instead.

Carter had never imagined that the fruit to their street labor would be so abundant, but Vegas seemed to be the reward. For all the loss . . . the blood shed . . . the misery that The Cartel had endured, they had finally reached the ultimate goal. Legitimacy. As the live band switched tunes he checked the presidential on his wrist. It was almost nine o'clock. It was time to send the children home with Magdalena so that a night of true celebration could begin. He motioned for Miamor to come off the dance floor. She was now grooving with CJ and her nephews Tre and Monroe Jr. She left the boys to entertain themselves as she went to her husband's side.

"Have Magdalena take the kids back to the condo," he said.

"Cool, you want me to send Aries?" Miamor asked.

"No, she needs to be here. She helped build this. The men, their families . . . the entire Cartel gets to enjoy this night," Carter said. Miamor kissed his cheek, recognizing his nostalgia before walking away to dismiss the kids.

He watched Miamor hustle out of the room but tensed when the feeling of soft hands covered his eyes.

"Guess who Mr. Jones?"

He turned, stepping back to create some distance. "Yasmine? What are you doing here?" he asked. He was cool under pressure as he rubbed his freshly lined goatee.

"You think my father would invest in a casino without protecting his investment. I'm his eyes and ears," she replied. "After hearing that you were out, I couldn't help but make the trip. We have unfinished business Mr. Jones."

Carter smirked at her persistence. Even after five years Yasmine didn't give up. She was a lioness on the prowl and she was looking for a king. She was prettier, more mature, and more glamorous. In another lifetime perhaps she would be his lady, but in this one the competition for his heart had already been won.

"What business is that?" he asked.

She stepped close, standing next to him as she leaned into his ear. Carter kept his eye on the crowd, not even looking down at her as she whispered, "No one has fucked me quite right since you and I know that little ghetto girl of yours can't suck your dick like I can. She's trash."

"Watch your mouth," Carter warned, still keeping his eyes straightforward.

She cut her eyes at him. "You know you don't love her Carter. If you did, you would have never slept with me. Silly man," she said with a mischievous grin. "If you think I came here to be turned away you're mistaken. We both know the connection we shared while you were in Saudi Arabia. If you like, I can refresh your memory."

She caressed Carter's hand but he quickly gripped her wrist tightly and pulled her across the room until he found a corner of slot machines that was practically empty. He cornered her against the wall. "Look ma, this is my life. Shit was good in Saudi, I'm not gone play you like it wasn't but it isn't laying like that between us over here. I have a wife now . . . a family."

Yasmine reached down and massaged his print, feeling his thickness through the fabric of his pants. He shook her hard, slamming her back against one of the machines. "What the hell is wrong with you ma? I said it's not happening." He thumbed the center of her forehead. "Get that shit through your head."

She reached out to him, grabbing at his lapel but he dusted her off of him as if he were removing a piece of irritating lint. He was trying to save her. The way she was acting she would blow up her own spot and get herself whacked. *My bitch ain't bout them games,* he thought, shaking his head as he walked away briskly.

He didn't realize that his face was scrunched until he found Miamor. "What's wrong?"

He straightened his brow and took a deep breath as he replied, "Nothing ma. Everything's good."

"Good because it's time for the ribbon cutting ceremony and for you to make your speech," she said.

Monroe made his way to Carter's side and they hugged jovially. "We made it bro," Monroe said.

"We'll always make it," Carter replied. He looked around. He had his left hand, now he was only missing his right. Zyir was his hitter and it wouldn't be right to bust this cherry without him. The casino symbolized their rise into greatness. He had helped to achieve it. It was important that he be a part of this moment. "Where is Zyir?"

"Breeze isn't going to let that nigga come up for air anytime soon," Monroe replied. "We can get started without him."

Miamor walked up on the small stage where the live band was playing and signaled for them to stop playing as she took the microphone.

"Good evening everyone. First I would like to thank you all for coming to the official grand opening of The Davinci Resort and Casino. I would like to introduce you to the owners of The Davinci, my husband Carter Jones, and my brothers Monroe Diamond and Zyir Rich. Let's give them a round of applause ladies and gentlemen."

Miamor walked off stage as Carter and Monroe stole the spotlight. As she stepped off she was yanked into an empty broom closet. She protested, but her hands were held tightly at the wrists as a hand quickly covered her mouth to silence her scream.

"Chill Miamor, it's just me," Fly Boogie stated.

Miamor snatched away from him violently. "What the fuck is up with you?"

"I had to talk to you ma," Fly Boogie said. "You haven't fucked with me since Carter been home. It's been days Miamor. I've called you like a hunnid times ma."

Miamor shook her head. It was now confirmed that she had him lovesick. He was handsome, paid, hungry, and she had trained him to be a killer but he wasn't for her. He didn't have enough teeth in the game to even look her way. Her resume trumped his. Even if she wasn't in love with Carter she didn't have time to grow Fly Boogie up. They weren't in the same league. "Fly, my man is home. My husband," she said.

"I know and I respect big homie, but I'd be lying like shit if I told you that I haven't been thinking about you. I'm feeling you ma. I know it ain't supposed to happen like that but its true. Seeing you on this nigga arm is making me sick," Fly Boogie stated as he cornered her. He reached down and seconds before his lips touched hers she turned her face, causing him to kiss her cheek.

"Stop, just stop Fly," she protested. "Carter will murder you in this bitch. If you've never believed anything before please believe that. Just do your job Fly. Remain loyal. I'm not the girl for you and these are not the kind of problems you want."

"Look at this shit ma," he said, pulling up his sleeve to reveal a tattoo of her name on his wrist. "I'm riding with you Miamor. Everything I do is for you. I'm stacking my paper for you."

"Have you lost your mind? What if Carter sees that? What does that mean " she asked. "Fly, get a hold of yourself before you put yourself in a position you can't get out of."

"You didn't feel nothing. When Carter was away and it was just me and you? Tell me I'm imagining it," Fly Boogie challenged, wearing his heart on his sleeve. Over the years Fly Boogie had fallen for Miamor. She was the only type of woman he could see himself with. Carter coming home had thrown him off. He couldn't stand the sight of them together. It pained him greatly despite the fact that he knew what it was.

She looked into his handsome face and thought, *If Carter was any other nigga I would give you what you asking for little boy. But he holds the key to my heart.*

Miamor didn't respond, she simply walked out of the closet while shaking her head in disgrace. She wasn't a liar and she didn't want to insult Fly Boogie's intelligence. They had connected. She even enjoyed his company. Many nights they had stayed up until the sun came out, talking about the game . . . about life . . . his presence had made things a little less hard. She couldn't tell him that she hadn't felt anything, but she wouldn't confirm that she had either. Even thinking it made her feel like she was betraying Carter. With her thoughts running rampant in her head, she bumped straight into Yasmine.

"I love your dress. What is it? Yves Saint Laurent?" Yasmine asked, playing nice. "I had one just like it *last* season."

"I know one thing you didn't have last season," Miamor shot back. She wasn't even going to pretend to like this girl. She had no time for games. Not when Fly Boogie had her flustered and bothered.

Yasmine pursed her lips as she waited for the punch line. Miamor pointed her manicured finger up at the stage where Carter charmed the crowd. "That's all mine," she said. Yasmine rolled her eyes as Miamor joined her husband on stage. By the end of the speech and the ribbon cutting ceremony, Carter had made all of the attendees fall in love with him.

"What is Yasmine Baraka doing here?" Miamor asked, leaning into him so that no one could overhear her disdain.

"Her father sent her. She's here to stay so play nice ma . . . for me," Carter stated.

"I don't play at all. The sooner she learns that the better. I have no problem shipping her ass back to the middle-east in a box," she spat. Carter was already feeling the heat from the mistake he had made years ago. He only hoped that it didn't come back to haunt him. He had to make sure that Yasmine could keep a secret, because if his infidelity ever got out he could lose it all.

"Why exactly were the Italians brought in on the deal?" Carter asked. It was the first words out of his mouth as Miamor walked into their condo. She was carrying a sleeping CJ in her arms. It was the first day that she hadn't had to rely on Magdalena to play 'mommy'. She had spent the entire day with her four year old and she was exhausted. In so many ways being a regular wife and mother was more taxing than running an entire staff at the resort and casino. The last thing she wanted to do was come home and go over every single move she had made while Carter had been away.

"That's the first thing you say to me? I haven't seen you all day!" she said as she pouted playfully. She carried CJ into his room and laid him across his bed before rejoining Carter at the dining room table. He had requested that every contract that had been acquired during his absence be copied and sent to him. It was all laid out in front of him as he tried to wrap his brain around the entire operation. He couldn't be a boss without knowledge. He didn't want to have to go to Miamor every time someone asked him a question. He was playing catch up and it was overwhelming.

"Okay Mr. Jones . . . the Italians?" Miamor said rhetorically. "Well Jim Salerno runs this town. He's old school. Mafia. I could not get the gambling commission to approve my license application unless I cut a deal with him. He has a ten percent stake in The Davinci. I'll make the introduction if you like?"

Carter nodded and pulled her into his lap as he kissed her shoulder. "I'll set it up for the morning."

Carter and Miamor stayed up half the night as she filled him in on business. She was thorough and ran through it all, leaving no detail up in the air.

While she had him talking Miamor's thoughts drifted. She didn't like how Yasmine suddenly had a vested interest in The Davinci. *Where the hell was she when I was building it from the ground up?* "Can I ask you something?" she asked.

"Anything ma," he replied, distracted. Miamor used her forefinger to turn his chin toward her.

"I need you to be honest with me Carter," she replied. "And I need to see your eyes when I ask you this."

Her tone worried him and he gave her his attention. "You ain't got to tip toe around anything Miamor. I'll tell you whatever you want to know," he said seriously.

"Have you ever fucked with Yasmine?" she asked.

The question caused his heart to stop but his face remained the same. He wasn't one to lie but he couldn't admit to that. To dig up skeletons from years ago would only bring trouble. He didn't want to upset Miamor or give her insecurity about Yasmine. He had told himself that it would never happen again and he had meant it. "No, I wouldn't have her here, around you everyday, if I had. I wouldn't disrespect you Miamor," he said. As he spoke he felt like scum because that's exactly what he was doing. Yasmine had an inside joke on Miamor and he knew how catty women could be. *I got to take care of that,* he thought. "You don't have to worry about that okay?"

Miamor wanted to believe him but her intuition was telling her otherwise. He had never lied to her before. It was she who had been the deceiver in their relationship. Even if she didn't want to she had to extend the benefit of the doubt. "Okay," she replied.

Carter saw the doubt in her eyes. The fact that she couldn't hide it told him that life was about to get real messy for him. Straightening out things with Yasmine would have to be the first thing on his agenda. *Fuck the Italians,* Carter thought as he shook his head. *They're the least of my worries. I've got to get this shit together before it blows up in my face.*

Carter, Zyir, and Monroe sat in the aficionado bar, sipping cognac and puffing the finest cigars as they absorbed all that had occurred.

"It took a lot to get here bro, but we made it my niggas," Monroe said as he raised his glass in the air.

"Indeed," Zyir agreed as they all touched glasses.

"There are a few things that can be fine tuned but over all the girls held it down. If it weren't for them . . ."

Monroe didn't even get to finish his statement before Carter interrupted. "We would have been stuck in Saudi Arabia."

"Saudia Arabia wasn't so bad though my nigga. The bitches over there . . ." Monroe replied, shaking his head.

"Speaking of," Carter said as he leaned forward and rested his elbows against his knees. He lowered his voice. "I need the two of you to run interference on Yasmine. Keep her away from Miamor. I don't know why she is here but the heat is hot at home. She thinks Miamor is some regular chick, but my li'l mama don't do the catty shit. She will set that trap and have Yasmine plugged. That would be bad business for everybody."

"I told you that one was bad news," Zyir said. "The smartest thing to do would be to send her ass back to Saudi Arabia."

"Baracka wants her here and we kind of need her. She has experience running a casino. If she can keep her head on straight it would be a good look," Carter said.

As if they had spoken her up Yasmine came waltzing into the bar. Her presence was like a magnet and the men in the building immediately turned their attention her way. She was a beautiful woman. That much couldn't be denied.

"Here you are," she said with a smile as she stood. "Hello gentlemen," she added, nodding at Zyir and Monroe. "Do you mind if I borrow him?"

Monroe nodded as he grinned, knowing the delicate position that his older brother was in. Carter gave him a stern look and then followed her up to her office.

He was glad that Miamor had played the back that day. Since his return he knew that she was trying to let him find his footing in the casino. Today her absence gave him the perfect opportunity to iron things out with Yasmine. As soon as they were inside the privacy of her office Yasmine was all over him.

"I missed you Carter and ever since I saw this desk, I've imagined you fucking me on top of it," she whispered.

Her seductive ways enticed him. He hated that she was so damn sexy. A lesser man would have taken her up on her offer, but he wasn't a dog. He wasn't in the business of lying. Cheating took too much effort. He grabbed her wrists as she tried to undo the buttons of his shirt while rubbing her body against his.

"Yasmine. Stop," he said sternly in a low no nonsense tone.

"Hmm," she moaned as if she couldn't help herself. "You know I'm never going to stop."

"I'm married ma. It was different when we were in Saudi Arabia. Things have changed," he said. "We can't do this."

"Oh we can," Yasmine stated. "And we will . . . as often as I want. Because if you don't, I'll ruin your marriage. You wouldn't want that little black bitch to find out about us now would you?"

Carter placed his hands in his pockets to stop himself from

laying hands on Yasmine. His jaw tightened instinctively. He didn't take kindly to threats and she was testing him. Just for getting flip at the lip he wanted to wring her pretty little neck. She was too comfortable, too close, and he wasn't feeling the thin line she was dancing on. "Perhaps I'm not making myself clear," he stated his voice dangerously low. "I eliminate anything and anyone who poses a threat to my family. There is no way I'm leaving my wife or allowing you to embarrass her. So do your job, lets make this money together, and forget about the past."

Yasmine chuckled. Carter's threats only made her want him more. It was his gangster that she loved the most. "Forget about the past? You wish you could Carter. How many times did you think of me at night while you were locked up? The way I wrapped my lips around your dick? Or the way my body molded to it as I rode you? You probably see my face when you're fucking that average wife of yours."

"We're done," Carter insisted.

"We'll see about that now won't we?" she said as she licked her lips. "Because I'm just getting started." She reached down to stroke his manhood and it jumped. She was like a snake charmer, commanding it at her will. He gripped her hand but she was insistent as she massaged his rising manhood harder as she undid his slacks. He didn't even feel her slide his cell out of his pocket, he was too focused on the arousal she provided. "Maybe I'll just get rid of your bitch of a wife altogether and then I'll have you to myself." Everything in him wanted to bend her over and punish her. She was right . . . he had fantasized many times before just off her memory, but it was only a physical attraction for him. The more she played this game, the more she put his family at risk, the more she held their tryst over his head, the more his mental despised her. Carter pushed her off forcefully, causing her to stumble as she crashed into her desk. He glared at her as he adjusted his clothes. "You're biting off more than you can chew. Stay the fuck away from my wife."

"With pleasure, as long as I don't have to stay away from you," she replied. She hopped on her desk and spread her legs as she moved her panties aside, massaging her swollen clit. "Join me?"

It was a temptation that not many men could resist, but Carter knew that dipping into Yasmine was like sinking into quick sand. An affair with her would drown him. He fumed as he slipped out of her office, shaking his head in dismay because he knew that Yasmine was a problem. She was playing hard body and it seemed that the only way to control her would be to comply. Otherwise her slick talk would get him caught up. A part of Carter wanted to just come clean to Miamor. The secret keeping and covering his tracks was boggling his mind. He needed a clear head to take hold of the casino operations and to move the resort into a new direction. He couldn't focus on business when his personal life stood on rocky ground. If Miamor uncovered the truth on her own, her wrath would be severe. Yasmine thought she had control of this little game but what she didn't realize was that she was playing Russian roulette. There were only so many times she would be able to pull the trigger before Miamor popped off.

Miamor sighed in frustration as she was sent to voice-mail for the fourth time. "Where the hell is he?" she whispered as she slipped into her shoes. An impromptu meeting with the mayor of Las Vegas had popped up and she needed Carter to be there. She was supposed to make the introduction. Right now all of the major players in the city were familiar with Miamor. They knew her as the owner . . . the face of the casino. Easing Carter into prominence was important. He couldn't officially be on the deed because of his prison history, but it was the unofficial business in a city like Las Vegas that made the world go round. She wanted to be the lady on his arm, but his presence was required in order to make that happen. She was beyond irritated.

"Relax, he will be here. I'm sure he's just busy. His phone is probably in his desk. When he gets to it, he'll be here," Breeze said. "In the meantime, Money and I will take C.J. for the night."

"Thanks Breeze," Miamor said. "You're a lifesaver. I already packed his bag." She walked into her son's room to find him sitting in the middle of the floor playing with his toys. She loved her son, more than life itself. She couldn't wait until things were settled. She just wanted to be a wife and a mom. She could hang her holster and her business hat up. She would be completely content with being Mrs. Jones forever and ever. "You ready to go with Auntie Breeze and Uncle Money?" she asked.

"Yeah!!!!" he shouted. He hopped up and ran to Breeze who was standing behind her.

"Can I get some love first?" Miamor said with a laugh. Her son ran back to her full speed and kissed her on the cheek repeatedly, inciting laughter. He knew exactly how to fill her with joy. He then rushed out of the door, following Breeze.

"Good luck tonight!" Breeze shouted as she eased out of the door.

Just as she made her exit the telephone rang. Miamor rushed to answer it. "Hello?"

"I'm downstairs, buzz me up ma," Fly Boogie said.

"What are you doing here?" she asked.

"You forget about the deposit? I was late going to the bank. Didn't want to keep that much paper on me," he said.

Miamor went to the door and buzzed him up.

He walked into the penthouse with a Gucci book bag slung over his shoulder. He held it out for her.

"I take it there is no need to count it?" she asked.

"I'm never short ma, you know that," he replied. "Where you going?"

"Carter and I are supposed to be meeting with the mayor but it looks like I'm being stood up. Carter has been unavailable all day. I can't get in touch with him. Did you run into him at the casino?" she asked.

"Nah, I ain't seen him," Fly replied. "The nigga slipping though. If he let you leave the house looking like that and you not on his arm, he's crazy."

Miamor laughed as she shook her head. "You need a girl Fly. I worry about you. You can't trap all day and night without someone to go home to," she said. She grabbed a bottle of wine and cracked it open as she poured two glasses.

"Before your boy got out you left me no room to get a girl. You took up all my time," he replied with a charming smile. "Had a nigga around twenty-four/seven. A bitch would have had a problem with that," he said.

"I needed you," she admitted. "I couldn't have held every-thing together while Carter was gone without you."

"I'ma always be here ma. No bird can get in the way of that," he said. "You're the priority. My loyalty is always with you," he said.

Miamor was speechless. She didn't know if Fly Boogie was loyal to her for business or in a more intimate sense. She knew that she should establish limits with him, but he was too good to her. He was good for her. She didn't mind having him around. Loyalty was hard to find. She handed him a glass.

"Have a drink with me while I wait?" she asked.

He took the glass and then downed the wine before handing it back to her. "I'ma get out of here. It's late," he replied. He stepped closely to her, dangerously close, making the temperature in the room increase. He smelled good, looked good, and his youth made him fear nothing, not even Carter. Miamor could feel his attraction. The more they interacted the more it grew. Fly had a thing for her. They both knew it, but they both were aware that it could never be. She would have to be very careful how she handled him. She didn't want to mis-manage his young heart. Young boys were loyal but they were also reckless when wounded. He kissed her cheek. "Goodnight beautiful," he said. "If it were me, I'd never keep you waiting."

"I believe you," she replied. "But its not you Fly. Carter would kill you for even having the thought. He's out, things are getting back to normal. I need you to be okay with that . . . with my husband. You're loyal to The Cartel, not to me."

"Nah ma, just you," he answered.

He made his exit leaving Miamor's heart racing and she grabbed the entire bottle of wine, drinking straight from the bottle.

Where the hell is Carter? She thought, flustered and over-whelmed. While he had her waiting he had no idea that there was somebody in line just dying to snatch his lady.

"Mr. Jones, I have your messages," his secretary said as he entered his office. His day had been long and stress-ful. Thoughts of Yasmine filled his head, distracting him, tormenting him all day. He had never been one to tolerate blackmail, but she was Baraka's daughter. Baraka owned half of The Davinci and on top of that his power was unlimited. He couldn't handle Yasmine like he would any other chick, because she was far from ordinary. He would have to handle the situation with extreme delicacy. "Mrs. Jones wants to meet for drinks. She's waiting for you in your suite upstairs."

Carter nodded, deciding that he would handle the rest of his business later. He headed out. The thought of seeing Miamor's face instantly soothed his troubled soul. She was his safe haven, his peace, and his guilty conscience made him feel like he could lose her at any moment. He made his way upstairs, knowing exactly what she had in store. He inserted his key card into the lock and pushed the door open. He opened it and walked inside, finding his favorite cognac already prepared. A note accompanied it.

Have a drink and relax. Tonight is about us. Turn off your phone. I'll be up in five minutes.

After the day he had endured he could use a drink and he downed it in two large gulps before searching for the open bottle. He poured himself another, took it to the head and then finally slow sipped a third. Finally he felt the tension melt from his shoulders as he settled onto the couch. There was nothing like a good cognac to unwind but tonight he was feeling exceptionally loose. He licked his lips as he imagined the things he would do to Miamor. He wanted to taste her on his lips and the thought alone caused his manhood to brick. He lay his head against the couch as he adjusted his hard-on in his pants. The distress of his day had worn him out. He was more tired than he had realized. He hated that Yasmine had something over him. The pressure to live according to her terms was too much. *I'm not playing the blackmail game. I'm going to come clean to Miamor. If she has to hear it, it should come from me,* Carter thought. He heard the click of the lock and then the lights went out as the sound of stiletto heels click clacked against the tiled floor.

"I love that you set all of this up for me ma, but I need to talk to you about something important," he said.

"Shhh," was the only reply he got. The room was so dark that all he saw was the silhouette of her trench coat and when she lowered onto her knees and fumbled with his belt he knew what was next. He closed his eyes as she licked his length. He was throbbing and she could feel him pulsating in her mouth as she took him in. No gagging, no shallow throat, she was a pro as she worked his shaft with her hand while sucking the life out of him. It wasn't until she said, "I told you Carter. I get everything that I want."

When he heard her voice he jumped up, pushing her off of him. "What the fuck?" he exclaimed as he tripped all over himself while backpedaling away from Yasmine. He was stumbling all over the place. Suddenly he had turned into a clumsy oaf. He couldn't seem to gather his bearings as she advanced on him.

"Don't fight it Carter, just take me. Take me any way, every way, you want to," Yasmine said as she pushed him toward the bedroom. Either he was light as a feather or she had suddenly become he-man because he couldn't evade her as she aggressively pushed him onto the bed. His mind was screaming no, but his dick was clearly in the game as it stood to attention as she lowered her body onto his girth.

"You drugged me?" he asked in disbelief as he placed his hands on her hips. He didn't have the strength to lift her off of him. She hadn't meant for him to drink three glasses back to back. She had spiked the bottle with Ropyhnol, hoping to keep him submissive through the night. The amount he had drank had him completely sedated. He could feel everything, but even now remembering how he had gotten to this point with her was beginning to fade away. All he felt was the pleasure as she bounced on his dick.

"Damn," he whispered. The fact that he had fallen for her okie doke had him feeling like a sucker. She was in control, at least for the night and with him incapacitated there wasn't much that he could do. In his mind he knew that this would be the straw that broke the camel's back. In a situation where the truth sounded like lies, Miamor would never believe him. As he blacked out the last thing he heard was Yasmine whispering in his ear. "You should have just gone along with me Carter. You know you love it."

Chapter 22

"We all followed you out here. The Cartel of Miami belonged to Carter, but The Cartel of Las Vegas belongs to you."
—Fly Boogie

Miamor's heart instantly froze in her chest and then splintered like an icy windshield right down the middle. Blind rage. Unrivaled pain. Unending sickness. That's what she felt. The sex-capade in front of her was so intense that Carter didn't even realize that she had entered the room. Her first thought was to wreck havoc. She wanted to beat the breaks off of Yasmine. Throwing, swinging, biting, punching . . . it all would have felt so good at the moment but she couldn't. Her grief rendered her helpless. Suddenly the ring on her finger seemed so heavy. It weighed her down. She couldn't breathe, she couldn't think straight. She couldn't do anything but stand there . . . watching. She waited for him to come to his senses and push Yasmine off of him, but the look of pleasure on Carter's face confirmed that he had wanted this. He had betrayed her. After all that she had done to hold him down. After all that they had been through. All it took was a skinny, privileged bitch from Saudi Arabia to get him to switch up on her. She walked over to the bed, walking slowly as she clenched her stomach. The smell of another woman's sex filled her bedroom making her want to vomit. She took her wedding band off and when she was within eyesight she tossed it on Carter's bare chest. Before she could stop herself she grabbed Yasmine by her hair.

"Bitch!" Miamor shouted as she flung her to the floor, her rage giving her the strength of a madwoman.

"Oh shit!" Carter exclaimed as he stood to his feet. The room spun around him and he stumbled as he reached for Miamor. *What the fuck happened?* He thought. The paraphernalia that was strewn about the room told a story of a night of lust and he grimaced, cursing himself. He truly had a limited memory of what had gone down, but one thing was blatantly clear, he had fucked up. There was no stopping Miamor. She was locked on like a pit as she viciously delivered blows to Yasmine's face.

"I . . ."

PUNCH.

"TOLD . . ."

PUNCH.

"YOU . . ."

PUNCH.

"NOT . . ."

PUNCH. PUNCH. PUNCH.

"TO FUCK WITH ME."

Carter tried his hardest to get between the two women but his world was moving in slow motion. He could barely move. He was weak, legs wobbly, head unclear, stomach churning. He was incapacitated and could barely remember what had happened the night before. Images of what had occurred flashed in his mind. His body intertwined with Yasmine's, his fingers fisting her hair, her mouth kissing all over him. He saw it all. He had fucked up. No matter how unintentional his actions were, he had betrayed his woman. He could only imagine the sting that plagued her heart. "Mia chill!" he barked as he tried to pry Miamor off. He tried holding her back, but in his current state she shook him with ease. Miamor was relentless. "You're going to kill her!" Carter felt woozy and he didn't have all of his strength, which allowed Miamor to get the best of him. He was surprised she didn't turn on him with her blows. Miamor was going for broke.

What the fuck? He thought as he shook his head while pinching the bridge of his nose as he tried to steady himself. "Miamor!"

Hearing him scream her name with such aggression caused her to stop, fist raised in the air as she panted over Yasmine. The girl groaned beneath her, nose busted and crying. Yasmine covered her face as she rolled left to right in agony.

"You defending this bitch?" Miamor asked. She was so upset that she could barely catch her breath. It felt like she was hyperventilating as she leaned over, resting on her knees as complete agony took over her body. Carter saw the hurt in her face and it almost brought him to his knees.

Damn, I fucked up, he thought. His mind couldn't piece together the part of the night where Yasmine had drugged him. All he knew was that he had messed up and now the fall out was about to begin.

"Let me talk to you for a minute ma. Let me explain," he whispered. He went to touch her but she cringed as she slapped his hands away. He stumbled. *Get your shit together. Tell your wife something before you lose her,* Carter told himself. But what could he say? She had caught him . . . hand in the cookie jar. *How the fuck did I slip up this much?* he wondered. *This shit is just sloppy. Hitting Yasmine in the suite that Miamor has complete access to.* There was no lying his way out of this and even if lies would get him off the hook, he wouldn't tell them. It wasn't in his character. He was tired of telling half-truths. He had done it. Why? He still couldn't make sense of it. How had he let himself take it this far when he had been so determined to keep her at arm's length? He had no recollection of the night's events and his head spun as he tried to piece it together. *Damn,* he thought, legs weak. Head clouded with confusion. He needed to sit.

"Mia," he said.

Yasmine rolled onto her knees then slowly climbed to her feet. "Fuck this Carter! Don't lie to her. We don't have to hide this anymore. Tell her! We've been together since you came to Saudi Arabia five years ago!" she shouted as she wiped the blood from her nose with the back of her hand.

"Yasmine chill!" Carter shouted.

"No! I'm not hiding it anymore! She should know!" Yasmine screamed, hysterically, filling the air with falsehoods and fanning Miamor's emotional flames.

Miamor shook her head in disbelief as tears fell down her cheeks. Her soul was heavy. It felt like she was suffocating as shame fell over her. She looked at him, wrapped in the bed sheet, basking in the afterglow of his rendezvous with another woman. *Damn why does this hurt so bad?* She thought.

"Mia, I fucked up. Let me talk to you ma. Let me . . ."

"Talk to her," Miamor said. It was like the sun had fallen out of the sky and the world had come to an end. "I'm done," she whispered. Carter swiped his face with his hands. Her hurt was hurting him. He wanted to say something to make her stay, but even he was lost. How could he defend what he didn't understand. He loved her. He loved every single thing about her. How had he fucked this up so badly?

Before he could respond she was gone and he was across the room in a flash, knocking over the lamp because he could barely keep his bearings.

"Carter I'm . . ."

Before Yasmine could even get the words out of her mouth Carter wrapped his hand around her throat, pressing her into the wall. It was like his rage gave him strength as he held her thin body in place. He wanted to choke the life out of her, but he knew that this wasn't her fault. He had done this. If he hadn't wanted to sleep with her it never would have happened. No one had forced him into this situation. Somewhere deep down he had allowed her to get into his head. His attraction, their flirtation, their deception was the gasoline that fed the fire. It had started years ago between them in Saudi. He should have stopped it then. He had made this bed, now he had to lay in it. He released her and then punched the wall beside her head. "Just get out," he whispered. He lowered his head in disgrace. He had been at a crossroads with Miamor before but never over another woman. He knew her well enough to realize that this was one transgression that she would never forget.

Miamor's tears blinded her to the point where she stumbled through the casino as she made her way to the front door. She was distraught and a snotty mess as people turned to look at her. She was a walking spectacle. No one had ever seen her so torn apart. Something had permanently broken inside of her as soon as she saw Carter inside of another woman. She had given him too much of herself, holding nothing back and trusting him to take care of her psyche. Now that he had dropped the ball she had nothing reserved for herself . . . no strength . . . no faith . . . no love. Carter had taken it all. *Selfish ass nigga! I hate him, I hate him. I will never forgive him for this,* she thought.

Her heart was raw and she clenched her chest wishing that the pain would ease. It felt like someone was pouring alcohol over a bleeding wound.

"Miamor!"

She heard Breeze call her name. "Mia! Oh my God! What the hell happened? What's wrong?" she asked.

Miamor gasped as she tried to tell her but she couldn't even speak the words. She was weak and the trauma too great. She didn't even want to hear the words fall out of her mouth.

"Miamor!" When she heard Carter's voice she shook her head and broke away from Breeze. She rushed through the crowd and out of the door. Fly Boogie was the first person she saw. He was pulling up to the hotel and like always, he was right there whenever she needed him.

"What's wrong?" he asked in confusion as she rushed into his arms.

"I've got to get out of here," she said. "Get me away from him."

Fly Boogie nodded as he opened the passenger door for her and tucked her safely inside. Just as he got inside himself, Carter and Breeze emerged from the hotel.

"Miamor!" Carter roared. She didn't even look at him as Fly Boogie pulled away.

"Aries bring me my son!" Miamor screamed into the phone.

"I can't Mia," Aries replied. "Carter's here and he won't let me take him anywhere. He's afraid you're going to disappear on him again and take CJ with you. Are you okay?"

"Tell him I will murder him in his fucking sleep if he doesn't deliver my son to me!" Miamor's rage was real and all she wanted was to see her baby boy. She knew that his love would be like a dressing to a wound. He could stop the bleeding of her heart.

"Come home ma . . ."

Carter's voice filled the phone as he intervened on their conversation. She could hear his worry and regret in his tone. Miamor instantly hung up in his face. She knew that if she listened to him for too long she would become dumb to the truth. She wanted him to justify his actions and she would become one of those women who believed bullshit and accepted disrespect. No, she couldn't talk to him. Ever. Her legs gave out as she collapsed to the floor, sitting in her own misery with her head buried in her hands.

Fly Boogie swiped his face, unsure of what to do. She hadn't eaten or slept in two days. She just cried. She was the most official chick he had ever met and with the negligence of one man she was now broken. Carter had mishandled her. Fly Boogie walked over to her and scraped her off of the floor as he carried her across the hotel room. He had checked her into a room under his name because she knew that if she used her own, Carter would find her. Normally, Miamor would never let anyone see her so weak, but she couldn't help it. Life felt over. It would be less painful to put a bullet in her brain and call it a wrap. She was thankful for her son, because had it not been for his existence she was sure she would have done so by now. Murderous thoughts, suicidal thoughts . . . plagued her. She was a woman who had been hurt by a man. Fly Boogie laid her across the bed and turned to leave the room.

"Don't go," she whispered.

Fly Boogie nodded. "I'm right here. I'm not moving until you move ma. You can lay here and cry that shit out until your system is dry, but if you trust me and you take a ride with me . . . I think I know something that will make you feel better."

"I can't," she whispered as she lay, face stuck to the comforter while she squeezed her eyes shut.

"Well when you're ready, I'm here. Try to rest," he replied.

Miamor was grateful for his presence. Having him with her, so loyal, and accommodating didn't take the hurt away but it did help.

BANG!
BANG!
BANG! BANG!
BANG!

"I told you to trust me. Every time you're feeling a type of way you go to the range," Fly Boogie stated.

"How do you know that?" she asked, shocked.

"I've been with you for five years ma. A nigga notices you," he replied with a wink. She gave him a small smile as she re-aimed her gun.

BANG!

BANG!

His effort was sweet but not even the sound of Miamor's gun relieved her stress. This time her burden was too great. Shooting practice wasn't enough to make her forget her problems. She had a fetish for murder and right now she wanted to body something.

"You're like a surgeon with the burner ma," Fly Boogie stated as he leaned against his Range Rover, one foot propped up on the fender. There was no one around for miles. The only thing around them was mountains and desert air.

She flipped her hair out of her face and sighed. "This isn't helping," she replied. "I just feel like dying. How did this happen?" Her voice was a whisper. A rhetorical question that not even she could answer.

Fly Boogie was silent as she fisted both hands through her hair and closed her eyes as she fought back tears. Carter had blown up her phone all night, along with Breeze, Aries, and Leena. They all had been trying to reach her. Although she didn't want to be available for anyone, she knew that she couldn't hide forever. She had a child. It was only a matter of time before natural instincts would lure her home. She felt like she was losing her mind. Her mood was up and down. Her stomach was constantly queasy. She had to get her mind off of Carter. He was all that she could think about. She walked up to Fly Boogie and kissed him out of the blue, melting into him as she pushed him against the hood of his car. She had caught him off guard, but he didn't resist. He grabbed her ass roughly and then picked her up as she wrapped her legs around him. He was the perfect distraction. He was fly, young, and living the thug life. After doubting herself, wondering what she lacked, or what Yasmine had that she didn't, it felt good to have a man want only her. His kiss melted her as their tongues danced slowly, passionately. It surprised her when he pulled back. With her still in his arms he whispered, "Damn ma, I could love the shit out of you if you would just let me." He placed her back on her feet and brushed her hair out of her eyes. "You're only doing this to get back at your man. I think its time I took you home." He was so honorable, so thorough, and in that moment she knew that if it hadn't been for her fated romance with Carter, she probably would be Fly Boogie's girl.

"I would think that you would enjoy this," she said. "He fucked up. You're feeling me. Isn't this when most niggas make their move?"

"Lame niggas," Fly Boogie responded. Despite the fact that her body felt so good against him, he moved as he hit the unlock button on his keys. "Anything you do right now is out of character. This is all about him. I would be playing myself if I jumped on you. I can see the hurt in your eyes Miamor. I'm the last nigga you got to worry about taking advantage. I'ma get my shot at you ma, but this ain't it."

Miamor smiled, slightly embarrassed as she walked up to him once more. She kissed his cheek. "This kiss you earned." She blew out an exasperated breath and shook her head to try and gain some clarity. "I have to go home," she whispered. "I need to get my son and pack some things. I'm not beat for this Vegas shit. He wanted this life. I'm going back to Miami."

"Nah ma. I'll take you home but you pack up his shit. You built all of this out here. We all followed *you* out here. The Cartel of Miami belonged to Carter, but The Cartel of Las Vegas belongs to you. You got a gang of niggas that'll ride on your command," Fly said. He opened the passenger door for Miamor. He had given her something to think about and as she climbed inside the car, plots of revenge flooded her brain. Hurting the one who had hurt her sounded like poetic justice and she knew that the only way to get to Carter would be to take what he treasured most. She was going to hit his pockets, his empire, take his throne . . . she wanted it all . . . not because she needed it, but because he wanted it too much. He wasn't afraid of her gangster and she didn't know if she could ever hate him enough to handle him the 'murder mama' way. She couldn't intimidate him with her reputation, but she could handle him like a wife scorned. She would divorce him and take everything, including the Cartel. He wouldn't be expecting her to play hardball and by the time he realized what was happening, it would already be done. She was going to take him to the cleaners and while she was at it, she would send Yasmine straight to hell.

Chapter 23

"I think I just started another war."

—Miamor

Three Months Later

"Dig deeper," Miamor stated coldly as she stood over the two burly men that were unearthing the desert soil. Their shovels clanged loudly against the earth as their grunts filled the air. "It can't be shallow. We don't want any mangy coyotes coming along and digging the body up." Miamor was livid and her heart pumped violently as her emotions went haywire. Her Cavalli sunglasses masked her watery eyes as she thought of the motivation behind her actions. She had murdered many times before. Fuck it. It was nothing for her to go boom on a nigga. She was in the business of extinction, but when business became personal it always played a tug of war with her mental.

Her judgment hadn't been this clouded since she had lost her sister at the hands of Mecca. She had promised herself that she would never let her emotions get so tangled again, but yet here she was . . . devastated . . . heartbroken . . . confused all over again. She should have been taking her aggression out on the root of the problem. Her man. Carter 'muthafuckin' Jones. He was the perpetrator to the crimes that had been committed against her heart. It was he who deserved to be buried in this shallow grave but instead it was his pretty little mistress who was in her crosshairs. Miamor saw red when the blacked out SUV pulled up a few yards away, because she knew who was hidden inside. They were in the middle of nowhere . . . Thirty miles into the Mojave on uncharted land. It was an unofficial graveyard. Many a mobster had held court in these deserted lands. There was no telling how many bones were buried beneath the hot sands. Miamor was about to host a funeral and the guest of honor was a Persian bitch named Yasmine.

The most dangerous thing in the world was a woman scorned, but a Miamor scorned was deadly. No one had seen the kind of damage that Miamor could do. She hadn't had to deal with groupies in Miami. Carter had always walked a straight line. Their love story had been so complicated that he hadn't found the time to entertain anyone but her. Even during her absence from his life he had remained true, but Yasmine . . . Yasmine had distracted him. She had seduced Miamor's man and there was a price to pay for that. *The bitch clearly doesn't know who she's fucking with,* Miamor thought, her temperature rising as she stalked across the desert. She was heated . . . not from the sun that blazed down on her, but from the hatred that burned in her heart. As an unsuspecting Yasmine climbed from the backseat of the car, Miamor approached.

"What the hell is the meaning of this?" Yasmine asked.

Miamor was feminine as ever in designer clothes and five-inch heels. She hadn't anticipated getting too dirty. She had men who followed orders at her discretion now. When she wanted someone to bleed, it never dripped on her shoes now. But this bitch Yasmine was a bit too pretty for her tastes. The smug, entitled, expression she wore irked Miamor to the point where she couldn't stop herself from slapping the taste out of her mouth. Before she could stop herself she struck her violently and muscled her to the ground. Miamor's vice grip on Yasmine's jet black hair caused the girl to scream in alarm as she tried to tear Miamor's hand from her scalp. Sweat started to form on Miamor's forehead as she spoke through gritted teeth. "There are plenty of men in Vegas. You should have chosen somebody else's," she said. She didn't even care about getting her hands dirty anymore. When her temper flared it took nothing less than murder to calm her down. She was on ten, it was too late to be rational now. She pulled Yasmine through the desert, destroying along the way, the all white dress that the girl wore.

"Agh!!" she screamed as she clawed at Miamor's wrist while kicking her legs violently as she tried to break free.

Miamor mustered strength that she didn't even know she had and she didn't stop until she had pulled her from the car to the hole that was now complete.

As soon as Yasmine laid eyes on the ditch, terror filled her. She turned to Miamor. "Do you know who I am? You can not get away with this!"

Miamor smirked as she shook her head incredulously. "I know exactly who you are. You're nobody. You live off of your daddy's name to get by. You think because you're a pampered little bitch from Saudi that you can do whatever you want, but you made one mistake. You didn't know who you were offending. You didn't check my resume. You see me in the casino in my fancy clothes, prancing around as Carter's arm accessory and you got me confused. You thought I was just a wife . . . just a mother perhaps? You didn't do your homework. Should have checked my resume."

"Please! You can have Carter . . ." the girl began to plead.

"Bitch I already have Carter. There ain't a woman alive that can take Carter away from me. I own that nigga. That's my dick, my houses, my cars, my everything."

"Okay, okay. I won't even look at him. I swear to you," Yasmine pleaded as she held her hands out in front of her. "Just let me go. This isn't necessary."

"You fucked my nigga. This is very necessary. I hope it was good," Miamor said. Suddenly she snatched one of the shovels from her bodyguard's hands and swung it full force, hitting Yasmine in the side of the face. She fell to the ground as blood poured from her ear. Miamor's rampage exploded as she hit her repeatedly, again and again and again and again. She showed no mercy as she took her frustrations out. Miamor knew that ultimately it was Carter's fault for sleeping with Yasmine. She wasn't married to Yasmine. Yasmine owed her nothing, but the fact that she was so smug about it had earned her this fate. Miamor didn't care that she was literally beating the life out of the girl. Yasmine's efforts to block the blows were futile. There was no protecting herself from this ruthless assault and as the excruciating beating continued she could do nothing but pray. Miamor's chest heaved as she felt her clothes begin to stick to her skin. She held the shovel high above her head as she prepared to bring it down once more, but the sniffling, bloody, mess of a woman before her was no longer worth the effort. This beating wasn't making her feel any better. It didn't dull the pain that plagued her. She was still aching inside. The unbearable emotion haunted her, making it hard for her to breathe. Tears clouded her vision as she tossed the shovel to the ground. "Should have never crossed me," she said. She turned to her men. "Put the bitch in a box and bury her while she's still breathing. Leave a little air hole for her. I want it to be slow. Let her feel every single moment of what's left of her miserable life." Miamor left two of her men behind to clean up her mess as she headed back to the car with her driver. She had a meeting to attend. Yasmine was only the first to be punished. Carter would feel her wrath as well. As she climbed into the back of the car she knew that no matter what fate she delivered to him . . . she would always suffer behind his betrayal. Nothing she could do to him would ever make this right because even when she hated him . . . she loved him.

Carter was a man of little patience and as he checked the presidential that occupied his wrist he had to contain his anger. Tardiness was a sign of disrespect and Carter clenched his jaw as he folded his hands, placing them on the conference table in front of him. He was all business as he sat with a stern expression. The tailored Tom Ford suit he wore proved that he had graduated from the streets. He was no longer chasing hood fame; he was chasing them M's . . . the legal way. Owner of The Davinci, Las Vegas' newest resort and casino, he was a man with little free time. He had no hours in the day to waste. Miamor knew that. She had been by his side for so long that he already knew that her late arrival to their meeting was intentional. She was purposefully showing him that no matter how large he became, she would always run the show. He had given her the throne beside his. She was his queen and because of that he was on her time, like it or not. Carter leaned into the attorney that sat to his right. "We need to wrap this up."

Einstein looked across the table at the opposing counsel. "Mr. Levie, if your client doesn't show up in the next five minutes, we will have to reschedule this mediation session," he spoke. "Clearly she isn't taking this situation very seriously. Mr. Jones has asked her numerous times what she wants. We have yet to receive a response and today she doesn't even show up . . ."

Davison Levie drummed his fingers on the oak table as he leaned back in his chair with one hand placed underneath his chin. "She will be here . . ."

"I am here."

Miamor's voice caused all three men to turn their attention toward the door. Standing in a Carolina Herrera bodycon slip dress and five-inch heels, each of them were mesmerized by her beauty. Her hair fell in an asymmetrical bob around her face. Beautiful wasn't quite the right word to describe Miamor. She was dangerous, enticing, and alluring. Miamor was simply a bad bitch. The curves of her body were so sharp that they were deadly. Her face so pretty that it was deceptive. She was like a black widow. It was easy to get caught up in her web and very few escaped it. She took a seat beside her lawyer, sitting directly across from Carter. Her heart thundered in her chest. Seeing him made her blood boil, but oddly she loved him so much all at the same time. She could not believe that she was sitting across from him, when her place had been next to him for so long. Once lovers, they were now adversaries and it was still so hard for Miamor to believe. As she sat silently, soul bleeding, love dying, she wished that she could turn back the hands of time. Her eyes were cold, dark, and distant as she sat stiffly, trying to remain strong. There was no way she would give Carter the satisfaction of seeing her break, not over him, not over his infidelity and lies. She had thought he was so different. Carter had promised her a unique love, but in the end he had turned out to be just another nigga. He had broken her heart and now there was no turning back. They had survived many things, but his one mistake had brought their love to a screeching halt. Now they sat, at the divorce table, enemies as they each watched their love slip away.

"Glad you could make it," Carter said sarcastically.

Miamor nodded her head but didn't respond with words. She had nothing to say to him. She knew that if she opened her mouth to speak that nothing but tears and sobs would fall out. No, it was best if she remained composed and let her attorney do the speaking. She and Carter were beyond words at this point. She leaned into her lawyer and whispered, "Lay out my demands."

Levie cleared his throat. "Mrs. Jones wants everything. She wants to keep the fifty percent stake that they currently share in ownership of The Davinci Resort and Casino, she wants the house in Summerlin, and she wants the $10,000,000 that is in the joint savings. According to our records, Mr. Jones has another savings account that he opened last year. In that account is $50,000,000 that he had hidden from Mrs. Jones. She wants that as well. She wants to keep all vehicles that are currently parked at the home in Summerlin. She also wants all stocks and bonds that they have purchased since being married. The estate in Miami, he can have and the home in Flint, MI she has no interest in."

Carter scoffed as if he had just heard a joke.

"This should not be amusing Mr. Jones. Mrs. Jones is very serious about her demands. Considering that there was no prenuptial agreement . . ."

"She's not getting my casino," Carter interrupted coolly, with a calm but serious tone.

"That is my casino," Miamor said. "While your ass was hiding out from a Fed case in Saudi, I was here with Breeze, with Leena, establishing The Davinci."

Carter stood to his feet and Einstein followed his cue. "Let us know when you have a serious offer. Mr. Jones is willing to offer a generous settlement. He has no intention of putting Mrs. Jones out in the streets. He wants to ensure that she is comfortable. But these demands are ludicrous. No judge will grant them," Einstein stated.

"A judge won't have to," Miamor replied. "I've got more than enough dirt on you Carter. It's in your best interest to give me what I want."

"You're being ridiculous," Carter stated. He could see the hurt in her eyes. No matter how hard of a front Miamor put on, Carter knew her. He could feel the disappointment and resentment radiating from her heart. He turned to Einstein. "Take Levie and step out of the room."

Levie objected. "I don't advise my client to speak with you without me."

Carter's eyes turned dark as he turned his attention to Miamor's attorney. "Leave the room," he demanded, his shoulders squared in authority as his baritone banished both men from the room.

He turned toward Miamor when they were alone. It was the first time he had seen her in weeks. She had accepted no phone calls from him and hadn't been home since she had found him cheating. Carter had no idea where she was even staying. "Can we talk?" he asked.

"No," she replied, stubbornly.

"It's not what it looks like. If you let me explain . . ." Carter started.

"I caught a bitch half naked in your bed, it's exactly what it looks like. There's nothing more to say," Miamor spat. Her words were so sharp that they cut Carter to the core. He could hear the contempt lacing her words. She was scorned, dejected, and scarred by all of the promises that he had broken. So many apologies sat on the edge of his tongue, waiting to leap out of his mouth, but he held them back. She was too full of anger to hear anything that he had to say at the moment.

"I want it all," she continued. "Every dollar, every business, every asset."

"You're pushing me Miamor," Carter warned. "I'm trying to be patient with you because I know that I hurt you, but don't take that as weakness ma. You out of everybody know what it is. You know exactly what I'm capable of."

Miamor cut her eyes low in disgust. "Yes I do know Carter, but clearly you have forgotten what I'm capable of. You'll soon find out. There is a price to pay for breaking my heart. I'm going to ruin you nigga."

Miamor stormed out of the conference room, bypassing both Levie and Einstein as she made her exit. Heat pulsed through her as she made her way to her chauffeured vehicle. She was so full of emotion that it felt like she would combust. The history that she shared with Carter made it so hard to let him go. She had made him her everything and now that he had let her down, she was left with nothing but resentment.

She looked at the world through bitter eyes as she slid into the plush interior of the Cadillac truck. The driver closed the door and Miamor leaned her elbow against the windowsill. Rest. Contentment. Peace of mind. She wondered if she would ever feel those things again. Turmoil had taken over her world and a sick knot was always present in her gut. She was sick from grief as she mourned the loss of the greatest love she had ever known. She let her head fall to the side as her chin rested against her balled fist. Tears came to her eyes. *How did I let another woman sneak into his bed?* she pondered, miserably. She tried to think of where she had gone wrong. What had she done to deserve the disloyalty that Carter had shown her? She hadn't even seen the signs or had she seen them and just ignored them? She had trusted Carter and he had burned her. Miamor was lost. She was once a woman who needed no one until Carter had changed that. He had convinced her to trust him, had gotten her dependent on his affection. Now that they were at odds all she felt was pain. Her pain made her want to cause pain and she had her cross hairs focused on the man whom had wronged her. Killing his little jump off wasn't enough. Miamor wanted Carter to pay for making her feel like just another lovesick girl. Taking his empire was the only way to make him feel as small as she did right now. Despite her hate for Carter, she couldn't bury her love. It had been too strong. It would take years for her to get over Carter Jones. He was undoubtedly the great love of her life. Miamor knew that the type of bond that they had shared would never exist again. As her mind drifted down memory lane she looked for someone, something to blame.

She couldn't blame anyone but herself. She had gotten lost in love and had trusted too much. Miamor had broken her number one rule. She had let her guards down.

"Where to boss?" the goon asked.

Before Miamor could respond a tap on her window caused her to look up. Carter stood, calmly with one hand tucked in his designer slacks, impatiently waiting for her to roll down her window. She did and for the first time she allowed him to witness her tears.

The anger was peeled away like the layers of an onion and she reeked of hurt. Her story of heartbreak was written in her eyes.

"Mia," he whispered.

"You ruined me Carter," she sniffled. He opened the car door and leaned into her.

"I don't know what I was thinking ma, and I'll tell you I'm sorry everyday for the rest of my life if I have to. Just come back home Miamor. I don't want this. This ain't us. We've gotten through worse right?" he said, trying to get her to remember their history of overcoming the odds against them. He wasn't pleading. Carter wasn't the begging type but he could feel her slipping away. The way she looked at him . . . the glow in her eye that was strictly reserved for him was fading. He was losing her. Or had he lost her already? He didn't know, but he couldn't see himself letting his pride get in the way of saving his marriage. Miamor was the very best part of him.

"We got through worse because at the end of the day I knew you were mine. It was me and you against the fucked up world. I don't know that anymore. You broke your vow Carter and you pulled the switch that shut everything off for me. I'm not this girl. I should have never been this girl. Stupid in love over a nigga that will never give back the amount of loyalty I give to you. All you do is take Carter. Now I'm taking from you. Apparently I've been too nice. I've got to murder a bitch to make you remember who I am?" she asked.

Carter's face fell. "What are you talking about Miamor? What did you do?" he asked. The evil smirk on her face answered his question. "Where is Yasmine ma?" She slapped him swiftly.

"She's not dead yet," Miamor said with a condescending laugh. "A bullet to the head would have been too kind. I've been hurting for months behind the bullshit that you two pulled so I thought a slow death would be more appropriate."

"Where is she?" Carter asked.

"Don't ask me about your whore. Nigga if you wanted her alive you shouldn't have fucked her. You already knew what my reaction would be. Should have controlled your actions. Her death is on you," Miamor sneered.

"Miamor this isn't one of your Miami hits. You can't . . ."

"You want your whore alive . . . you take your ass out to the desert and dig her up," Miamor said passive aggressively as she thumbed through her phone, blatantly giving Carter no kick it. "I'm sure she's not out of air yet . . . better hurry though."

Carter grit his teeth, feeling as if he could snap Miamor's neck. "Do you know what you've done? Tell me you didn't bury that girl alive?" Miamor shot him a look that showed just how cunningly cruel she was. Carter hit the top of the car in frustration. "Do you know who the fuck her father is going to send our way when he finds out?" Carter exhaled sharply as a weight settled over his shoulder. "I'm talking terrorists Miamor. Fucking assassins. You just signed your death certificate. We have a son! You killed that man's daughter you think he won't take our son," Carter was so livid that he spit as he chastised her. "You should have checked that jealousy at the door and brought your hot headed ass home. You not ready for the type of consequences that Baraka is going to deliver." His tirade only pissed her off more and she pushed him back so that she could shut her door.

"You should have thought about that before you fucked the bitch," Miamor spat. She then stubbornly turned her head as the car rolled away. She couldn't stop herself from looking back at him but when she did, the red dot that illuminated in the center of his chest caused her mouth to drop in horror. Someone had a beam on him and regretfully she knew what was to follow. It all happened in a split second, their eyes met but before she could warn him . . .

BOOM!

"No!!!!!!!!"

The gunshot was so loud that it pierced her ears, causing a slight ring and interrupting the stillness of the day, mixing with the screams that erupted from her soul. Her driver hit the breaks in reaction to the blast. Miamor hopped out of the car and instinct caused her to run full speed to Carter's side. "Oh my God! Somebody help me!" her shrill cries were desperate . . . fear filled. Her love was leaking out of her, betraying her in this moment. She couldn't help but care. She hated him, but the line between love and hate was so vague that she loved him all the same. It was a double-edged sword and as she pressed her hands against his bleeding chest, adding pressure to his wound she wailed. Tears clouded her vision as they ran down her nose and dropped onto Carter's face.

He gripped her wrists as he gasped. "I'm . . . Mia . . . " Tears of excruciation filled his reddened eyes.

"Help me!!!" she screamed. She felt hands pulling her off of him as she struggled to stay near him. "No!! No! I have to be with him! Get the fuck off of me! I need to be with him!" Sirens were heard in the distance and curious bystanders filtered out of the casino. She heard Zyir and Monroe fighting their way through the crowd.

Carter motioned for Zyir as he opened his mouth, attempting to speak. Zyir kneeled by his man. "Don't talk bro, just hold on," Zyir coached. Carter was persistent however and used the little strength he had to pull Zyir.

"Leave . . . town . . . go back . . ." he grimaced as he grit his teeth as blood filled his mouth. "home. Live . . . through . . . this."

Zyir nodded, but Carter seemed to be talking in circles. Live through what? Hadn't they already survived the worst. Carter was speaking as if he knew that today was his day of reckoning; as if this was only the beginning. "Where's the fucking ambulance?!!!" Zyir screamed, fearing the worst.

Pure horror crossed their faces as Monroe sprang to action. "We not waiting on the fucking ambulance. Help me get him in the car!"

Leena rushed out and hurried to Miamor's side, but Breeze paused as she looked at Miamor in doubt. "Did you do this?"

Miamor squinted her eyes in confusion and shook her head in denial. *How could she ask me this? Why would she . . .* "Did you shoot him?!"

The question came out like an accusation, smacking her in the face and suddenly all eyes were on her. Leena placed her hands over her mouth in shock as everyone waited for her to answer. Miamor had no response. She was stunned into silence as she shook uncontrollably. *Did Baraka do this? How did word get back to him so fast?* Miamor had known that there would be repercussions for killing Yasmine. Her rage had prevented her from caring, but now that she was covered in Carter's blood, fear seized her. Zyir helped her from the ground. He didn't know what had gone down, but Miamor was Carter's wife . . . his everything. He knew Carter well and if today was his day to die, Miamor's face would be the last one he would want to see. "Let's go. Figure this shit out later. Carter needs you."

Miamor stood shakily to her feet as she was escorted to his car. She looked up at him with terrified eyes. "Zyir, I fucked up," she whispered with tears in her eyes. "I think I just started another war."

"What did you do?" he asked.

"I killed Yasmine," she replied.

Zyir's eyes widened at the revelation and his jaw clenched as he grit his teeth. He put the car in drive and sped away. Now he knew why Carter had told him to shake town and he knew that his days in Las Vegas were numbered. As soon as he got the chance he and Breeze would kiss sin city good-bye and start their lives over somewhere else. Zyir didn't know how to clean up this mess but he was sure of one thing. There was a storm coming and he didn't know if The Cartel could weather another disaster.

Fly Boogie quickly dismantled the M-24 sniper rifle with speed and placed it in a large duffel. Not wanting to draw attention to himself he strolled casually to his Range, tossing the duffel in the backseat before getting in and driving away.

Fuck that nigga, Fly Boogie thought. *She better off without him anyway.* Fly Boogie had just risked it all for Miamor and she didn't even know it. Carter had crossed her and broken her heart but that wasn't enough. Fly Boogie knew that a man like Carter never lost. Miamor loved him too much and as long as he was breathing she would have taken him back. Fly wasn't standing for it. He wanted to throw his hat in the ring and in order to do that he had to get rid of the competition. He only wished he had a better shot. His nerves had caused him to aim low. One to the head would have put a tag on Carter's toe for sure. Now he would have to wait and see how Carter fared before making his move. Malice hadn't been his intention when he first followed the Cartel. In fact, he had nothing but respect for Carter but five years of being next to Miamor had him fiending to make it forever. She would never admit her feelings for him as long as Carter was breathing. All was fair in love and war. When it came to Miamor he would do whatever to ensure that he won her heart . . . if it meant going against the grain and biting the hand that fed him . . . than so be it.

Chapter 24

"Today just might be the day I die."

—Carter Jones

One Week Later

Beep! Beep! Beep!

The steady pace of the heart monitor was the only cryptic sound that filled the room. Monroe sat silently, head bowed, forehead resting on his steepled fingers as he prayed for a miracle. Gangsters weren't at the top of the blessings list. The life style they led made them undeserving of one, but Monroe prayed all the same. Shit was in disarray. Everyone was on edge. Miamor had sparked a flame that was about to burn their entire empire down. Monroe had goons at Carter's door 24 hours a day. Even when visiting hours ended, a skilled gun waited in the lobby for the clock to spin until they began again. Carter was too vulnerable to go unprotected. With a bullet to the chest, he was lucky to even be alive. He hadn't opened his eyes yet, but after days of being on a ventilator he was finally breathing on his own. That was one step in the right direction. The grim reaper was at Carter's door and there was nothing that anyone could do to save him. Carter had to fight it. "Just open your eyes bro," Monroe stated.

The weight of the world seemed to fall on Monroe's shoulders. Carter's wishes were to send Zyir away and although Zyir had fought it, Monroe sent him away. Baraka had been silent but Monroe knew that enemies unseen were the worst kind. He needed Breeze safe. He didn't want her in the middle of another war and although they needed the manpower, Zyir had to leave. Zyir was the only person on Earth that Monroe was sure loved Breeze fully. Zyir would die before he let anything happen to Breeze. It had been imperative that they leave. Monroe had wanted to lead the Cartel for so long. He had wanted to fill his father's shoes, to be the boss . . . but now that Carter's life hung in the balance it no longer mattered. They were blood brothers; the only two men left to carry on their father's legacy. There was a time when their bond hadn't been so strong but now they were each other's keeper. If Carter's death is what it took for Monroe to step into his father's shoes, than he no longer wanted to. It was family over everything, including ambition. Monroe's phone rang and he knew exactly who it was before he answered. Miamor. She had been calling on the hour for a week to see if Carter had awakened. She too had been sent away. Monroe had sent her to Aries' place in Idaho. No one, including Baraka would look for her there. The last thing he needed was for her to die on his watch. Until Carter awakened Miamor would remain in hiding. No matter how gangster she thought she was, Monroe could see the fear in her eyes. She had crossed a dangerous line, and until Carter woke up, it was Monroe's job to keep her safe.

"Money, how is he?" she asked without saying hello.

"He's the same. Not good, not bad. There is no change in his status," Monroe informed.

"I need to see him," she whispered. He could hear her strife in her tone. "I need to see my son. Maybe if I just come . . . if he knows I'm there . . ."

"It's not safe Miamor. Everyone is ducked off somewhere. C.J. is safe with Leena and my son. She will keep them safe. They have protection. Baraka is going to come for you and when he does, C.J. can't be anywhere near you."

"I know . . . I know," Miamor whispered with regret. "I was upset with Carter, but I didn't do this Money. I never meant for any of this to happen. I was so mad. I wasn't thinking straight."

"I know Miamor. Look, I'll keep you posted. I've got to go. Try to rest and don't get restless. Just stay put," he instructed.

"Hmm."

The sound of Carter's groggy moans were music to Monroe's ears. He looked left to see his brother opening his eyes, slowly as if his lids were weighted down. Monroe raced to the bedside.

"Wake up bro. Come back to this side my G," Monroe coerced as he leaned over him, anxiously. Carter woke up, struggling, fear filled as he attempted to rise. "Nah man, you can't Carter. You got to relax. You've been shot."

Carter laid back, exhausted, weak, and in extreme pain. Monroe rushed out into the hall and grabbed the first doctor that he saw. "He's awake. He's finally awake," he said.

The woman rushed in behind Monroe and immediately went to Carter's aid. "Welcome back Mr. Jones," she said, speaking calmly.

"What happened?" he asked.

"You were shot, a bullet pierced your lung and you lost a lot of blood. I would say that you're lucky, but you had a pretty skilled surgeon on your side," the doctor said with a wink. She had skin the color of coffee beans and her hair was cut short. With majestically dark eyes and a smile as white as pearls, Carter felt like he was staring into the eyes of an angel. She was beautiful, not only because she had saved him, but because she was uniquely crafted. God broke the mold when he made her.

"I believe you," he replied in a low tone. "Can you work that same magic and take some of this pain away?"

He grimaced as he spoke and the way he slurred his words made it obvious that he still wasn't clear headed.

"We had you on a mild sedative to allow your body to heal without much effort. I'll run something stronger through the I.V. and be back to check on you in a few hours. The most important thing for you to do is to rest up. You have a good team of doctors. We'll make sure that you make a full recovery," she assured.

Monroe spoke. "That won't be necessary. I'll need his discharge papers immediately. He will heal at home. I'll hire the best doctors . . . you if I have to."

The woman shook her head and frowned in confusion. "I can not issue discharge papers for him. He is in the best care here. Anything could happen. He is in ICU. Once his healing progresses that may be an option but for now, he's not going anywhere," she responded.

Monroe nodded and waited until she left the room before turning to Carter. "I've got the entire floor guarded. There are two at the door and one in the lobby. Nobody's getting to you bro. You're safe. Zyir and Breeze are back in Flint. Leena and the kids are safe . . ."

"Miamor?" Carter asked.

"She's safe. Off the grid. Baraka will never find her as long as she stays put," Monroe said. "She's hard headed than a mu'fucka though bro. You've got your hands full with that one."

Carter couldn't help but give a lazy chuckle. He grimaced as the laughter sent pain quaking through his entire body. "Tell me about it," he replied.

Monroe picked up his cell. "I'll call her. She'll be glad to hear you're awake," Monroe said. He attempted to dial, then frowned when the call failed. "No service," he said. He went to the landline and picked up the hospital phone. "Damn this mu'fucka dead too." A knock at the door interrupted them as Fly Boogie slowly entered.

"Come in li'l nigga, you look like you've seen a ghost," Monroe stated.

Carter spoke up. "Go make that call G. Tell her to stay put and that I love her. Fly can hold it down until you get back, plus there are two on the door. I'm good."

Fly Boogie eased into the room as Monroe made his exit.

"Glad to see you're up big homie," Fly Boogie stated as he stood at the foot of the bed, staring down at Carter. His heart beat rapidly. He felt see through, as if Carter could sense the snake in him. He knew better however. He had been careful. He had covered his tracks. No one, not even Miamor knew that he was the trigger man behind the gun. His only regret was that he had been unable to get a head shot. One between the eyes would have ensured Miamor's widow status and given Fly Boogie nothing but opportunity to move in on her. He would become her shoulder to cry on and once her mourning was over, he would eventually become her man. He wanted to be Carter. He wanted to stand in his shoes. Little did he know, they were too big to fill.

"Glad to be seen my G," Carter responded. "I want to talk to you."

"About what?" Fly asked, nervously.

"Have a seat next to me. I just woke up. I'm weak. Even speaking too loudly hurts," Carter stated.

Fly Boogie slowly walked to the chair next to the bed and sat.

"Zyir is taking a little vacation and shit is about to get real. I'ma need someone to take his spot . . . someone I can trust. Monroe and I can't hold shit down by ourselves. While we were away you held my family down. You were loyal to Miamor and to the Cartel. I want to pull you closer, put some money in your pocket, show you the game."

"I'm good. I'm eating," Fly Boogie stated.

Carter smirked. "That's mediocre money. You're hood rich. You're on the distribution side of the game Fly. I'm talking corporate. Private jets, hundreds of kilos, all that. We ain't on no corner shit. I'm asking you to stand beside me, not behind me," Carter explained. "But there's a war to get through first. Lines have been crossed and if we're going to come out on top I need killers around me; loyal niggas that I can trust. Can I trust you li'l homie?"

Monroe stepped out of the elevator and walked across the marble hospital floor, his red bottom designer shoes hitting hard against the tile. "Fuck is up with the service in this bitch?" he mumbled to himself as he tried to get his phone to work. He stopped over at the reception desk. "Is there a phone I can use?" he asked.

The nurse shook her head and replied, "The phone lines are down in the entire hospital."

He nodded and turned away, "Of course they are," he mumbled sarcastically. "How hard is it to find a working phone?" It was important for him to get the word out that Carter was now awake. It would keep Miamor in place and stop her from doing anything drastic. He stepped outside the hospital doors and held his phone up trying to catch reception. When his eyes caught sight of the red beam that was traveling through the air and aimed at his chest he panicked. "Oh shit!" he said as he backpedaled, rushing back inside the glass doors of the hospital. He looked outside and his eyes widened in shock. Five SUV's sat in front of the entrance. The windows were blacked out, but when one of them rolled down he recognized them instantly. They were Arab. Baraka's men and they had the entire entrance covered. "Fuck!" he uttered. He rushed to the back entrance and opened the door slightly to find that another Caravan of trucks waited there as well. They were surrounded and although he was strapped, and he had guards at Carter's door, they were outnumbered. He rushed back to Carter's room. They had to get out of there one way or another.

"Can I trust you?" Carter asked again.

"Of course, yeah fam, I got you," Fly Boogie replied. Carter held up his hand and Fly Boogie gave him a gangster's shake, but when Carter looked at his wrist he frowned. Carter tightened his grip, using all of his strength as he pulled Fly Boogie near in hostility. "The fuck is this?"

Fly Boogie's eyes went to the tattoo that adorned his wrist. MIAMOR. It read. He had completely forgotten that it was visible. He snatched his arm back, shaking loose from Carter's vice grip as he stuttered. "That's . . . nothing . . . big . . ."

Before he could get the explanation out of his mouth Monroe rushed in. "We've got a problem. The whole fucking hospital is surrounded by Baraka's men. They got this bitch locked down. I stepped one foot outside and almost got my fucking head blown off. Fly you strapped?"

Grateful for the interruption, Fly Boogie averted Carter's deadly stare and lifted his shirt exposing his pistol. "Always my nigga," he replied.

Carter saw red. He wanted to body Fly Boogie, but he kept his cool and placed the issue at the back of his mind. Right now they had bigger fish to fry. "We've got to get you out of here," Monroe said, directing his attention to Carter. "I couldn't get word to Miamor. My phone ain't working, neither are the hospital lines. Hand me your phone," he said to Fly Boogie. Fly immediately tensed because if Monroe went through his phone he would find dirt on him. Fly Boogie had all types of pictures of Miamor in his phone. Pictures that he had taken of her when nobody was even paying attention. Her number was also in his call log too frequently but if he refused he would arouse further suspicion. He could feel Carter eyeing him. The spotlight was on him, he pulled out his phone and looked at it, quickly switching his screen saver from Miamor's face to default. He erased her contact information as well. "The fuck? Li'l nigga hurry up," Monroe said impatiently. Fly passed it to Monroe, apprehensively. Monroe slid the bar across the screen but before he could even dial one number he saw that the bars were low. "Your signal is blocked too."

"Its Baraka," Carter informed matter of factly. "Every phone in this building is probably useless. That's the oldest trick in the book."

"I'll go out and see if I can find a working line," Fly Boogie stated. Just as he was about to slide out of the room Carter stopped him.

"We gone finish that conversation," he stated, his bark fierce . . . territorial.

Fly Boogie didn't respond, but his eyes widened in reaction. He slipped out of the room and Monroe turned to Carter.

"We're sitting ducks in this bitch," Monroe stated.

"One way or another Baraka is coming through them doors. Miamor put Yasmine in the dirt. I love her bro. She's my rib. She sinned. Somebody has to pay for that. It won't be her though. It won't be my son. It doesn't have to be you either Money. You should have left with Zyir. This is my debt. I'll pay it on behalf of Miamor. Get out of here Money. Today just might be the day I die."

Monroe pulled up a chair and sat beside his brother's bed. He pulled the gun from his waist and put it in his lap and then pulled the gun from his ankle and passed it to Carter. "We're brothers. We live through this together or we go out in a blaze of glory together. Either way I ain't running."

He held out his hand and Carter gripped it while grimacing. "That's real shit. I love you bro," Carter said.

"I love you too man." Monroe replied.

Silence filled the room as they waited for the storm that was waiting outside the hospital doors. There was no resolution.

Death was about to rain down upon them and all they could do was embrace it.

"I don't even know why we're here Mia. Monroe told you to stay hidden. The Arabs are serious. Dis isn't a hood war. Dis shit is international. Dey will . . ."

Miamor cut Aries off. "I don't care Aries! We've gone up against plenty of mu'fuckas. Baraka and his turbans don't scare me. Not enough to stay away from Carter. He's shot. He needs me," she argued as Aries pulled into the parking lot of the hospital.

As soon as she pulled up she noticed the caravan posted at the entrance. She ducked down in her seat. As they drove by she watched a security guard approach one of the tinted vehicles. The window of one of the SUV's rolled down slightly and Miamor watched in horror as a silenced bullet slumped the security guard. Two men climbed out of the back seat and picked up the body, stuffing it into the back of the truck without anyone even noticing. Miamor and Aries' were the only witnesses.

"Its him, Baraka's here," Miamor whispered.

"I won't die for Carter, Miamor. I have a child, you have a child," Aries replied.

"Than let's make sure we live to see another day," Miamor replied sadly. Aries drove past the parking lot and back onto the street as their taillights disappeared into the night. Miamor couldn't go up against a force so deadly without a plan. She would have to think first if she wanted to survive. She only prayed that Baraka didn't get to Carter in the meantime. As much as she wanted to be by his side there would be no getting to his room tonight. Baraka knew her face and the army of Arabs waiting beyond the hospital doors were too dangerous to fight off alone. Anyone going up against them, would lose. *What the hell have I done?* She thought.

Fly Boogie rushed into his apartment in a frenzy but halted as soon as he smelled the pungent aroma of weed wafting from his living room. He came off his hip with his pistol and silently followed the path where the smoke was leading him.

"Put that shit down li'l nigga before I lay you out in this mu'fucka."

Murder sat comfortably in Fly Boogie's Lay-Z-Boy chair while smoking a blunt with one hand and holding a pistol in Fly's direction with the other. "You're a hard one to keep up with Fly. I hired you five years ago to get in with the Cartel. Paid you good money too my nigga. Twenty grand. To infiltrate and murk that nigga Carter. Imagine my surprise when I found out you skipped town. You just disappeared out of Miami. In fact, the entire fucking Cartel disappeared from Miami and came here. Only reason I even knew where to find you is because the news reported Carter Jones' shooting outside a popular Vegas casino."

"It ain't like that Murder. I was just putting in work. It took time to get close. I was going to reach out. I finally hit the nigga Carter but he didn't die. The nigga down bad though. He in ICU and everything. I slipped in to finish the job tonight but some shit popped off. I had to sneak out that bitch in hospital scrubs like I'm a nurse or some shit. Money was there and . . ."

"You keep insulting my intelligence and I'ma pop your melon," Murder said, silencing Fly Boogie. Fly Boogie thought about shooting first but Murder read his mind. "By the time you get your aim right I'll have one off already. I'm the better shot, believe that young."

It was true, Murder had hired Fly. Just like Fly Boogie, Murder had a thing for Miamor. They both had a common goal to get Carter out of the way. At first, Fly Boogie was all about business. He had worked his way in. Miamor trusted him. Carter trusted him. Zyir had vouched for him. Monroe never doubted him. By the time he got down fully with the Cartel he was making way more than the measly twenty grand that Murder had paid. So he moved west and said fuck Murder's hit, but by the time Carter got out of jail Fly Boogie had become completely smitten with Miamor. He wanted her for himself and he was determined to knock Carter off so that he could get close to her. Murder's reemergence was another problem he would have to solve. Now not only was Carter in the way, so was Murder.

"I can still finish the job," Fly Boogie said.

"Thing is why? Why would you shoot Carter five years later?" Murder asked rhetorically. He snapped his fingers as if a bright idea had just hit him. "Unless you're in it for self. I recognize that look in your eye homeboy. That's a murder mama spell li'l nigga. You fell in love with my bitch, that's why you cut me out. Once Carter was dead you was going to move in on her yourself."

"Nah, it ain't like that," Fly Boogie lied.

"It's exactly like that," Murder answered. He hit his blunt and chuckled as the smoke blew from his lips. "That's a baaad bitch. She does something to a nigga," he said. "She almost killed me and I'm still running back to that pussy. She's like a drug."

"Now what? You gone kill me?" Fly Boogie asked. "Might as well quit playing games and get this shit over with." He was fearless. He had heart. Despite the treachery, Murder still liked him.

"Nah, you gon' finish what you started. Murder Carter. Then I'ma get my bitch back you gon' shake this school boy crush you got going and we gon' take over The Cartel and the casino," Murder said. "From what I understand it all belongs to Miamor now anyway. It's her kingdom now and once I get her from under the nigga Carter she will come back to daddy. I'm her beginning. I taught her everything she knows. I'm home. A bitch always comes back home . . ."

To be continued . . .